THE FRENCH GIRL

LEXIE ELLIOTT

CORVUS

First published in the United States in 2018 by Berkley,
an imprint of Penguin Random House, USA.

This edition published in Great Britain in 2018 by Corvus,
an imprint of Atlantic Books Ltd.

Copyright © Lexie Elliott, 2018

The moral right of Lexie Elliott to be identified as the author of this work
has been asserted by her in accordance with the Copyright, Designs and
Patents Act of 1988.

10 9 8 7 6 5 4 3

A CIP catalogue record for this book is available from the British Library.

Paperback ISBN: 978 1 78649 556 3
E-book ISBN: 978 1 78649 555 6

Printed and bound in Great Britain by Clays Ltd, Elcograf S.p.A.

Corvus
An imprint of Atlantic Books Ltd
Ormond House
26–27 Boswell Street
London
WC1N 3JZ

www.corvus-books.co.uk

For Mum and Dad, for everything

And for Matt, Cameron and Zachary,
for whom my heart beats

THE FRENCH GIRL

CHAPTER ONE

ooking back, the most striking thing is that she knew I didn't
like her and she didn't care. That type of self-possession at the
tender age of nineteen—well, it's unnatural. Or French. She was very,
very French.

It's Tom who calls to tell me the news. Perhaps that should have
tipped me off that something was wrong. I can't remember when he
last called me. Which is not to say he isn't in touch: unlike most of
my male friends, he's remarkably good on e-mail. I suppose I thought
he would be calling with glad tidings: an invitation to a party, or a
wedding—Tom's wedding—after all, he's been engaged to Jenna for
what seems like years.

But what he says is: "Kate, do you remember that summer?"
Seven years in Boston hasn't changed his accent a bit: still unmistakably a product of the finest English schooling money can buy. An
image jumps into my mind of him, as I last saw him two summers
ago: his blue eyes standing out against tanned skin with freckles
across his remarkable hooked nose, his rumpled dark hair long

enough to curl. He won't look like that now after a hard New England winter, but the image won't shift.

I know exactly which summer he means: the summer after we finished university, when six of us spent an idyllic week in a French farmhouse. Idyllic, or mostly idyllic, or idyllic in parts . . . It's hard to remember it objectively since Seb and I split up immediately afterward. I opt for a flippant tone. "Isn't it a bit like the sixties? If you can remember it you weren't there."

He ignores my teasing. "The girl next door—"

"Severine." I'm not flippant anymore. And I no longer expect a party invitation. I close my eyes, waiting for what I know must be coming, and a memory floats up unbidden: Severine, slim and lithe in a tiny black bikini, her walnut brown skin impossibly smooth in the sun, one hip cocked with the foot pointing away as if ready to saunter off the moment she lost interest. Severine, who introduced herself, without even a hint of a smile to soften her severe beauty, as "the mademoiselle next door," and who disappeared without a trace after the six of us left for Britain.

"Yes, Severine." Tom pauses, the short silence pressing down the phone line. "They found her. Her body."

I'm silent. Yesterday, if I'd thought about it all, which of course I hadn't, I would have said I didn't know if she would ever be found. With Tom's stark words it suddenly seems entirely fated, as if all possible paths were destined to converge on this discovery. I imagine her bones, clean and white after a decade left undiscovered, the immaculate skull grinning. She would have hated that, the inevitable smile of death; Severine who never smiled.

"Kate? Still there?" Tom asks.

"Sorry, yes. Where did they find her?" Her? Was a corpse still a *her*?

"The well," he says bluntly. "At the farmhouse."

"Poor girl," I sigh. Poor, poor girl. Then: "The well? But that means . . ."

"Yes. She must have gone back. The French police will want to talk to us again."

"Of course." I rub my forehead, then think of the white skull beneath my own warm flesh and drop my hand hastily. The well. I didn't expect that.

"Are you okay?" asks Tom, his deep voice concerned.

"I think so. It's just . . ."

"A shock," he supplies. "I know." He doesn't sound shocked. But I suppose he's had longer to get used to the idea. "Will you tell Lara? I'm not sure I have her number."

"I'll tell her," I say. Lara is my closest friend, another of the six. The police will want to talk to all of us, I suppose, or at least the five of us who are left; Theo at least is beyond the jurisdiction of any police force now. Probably Tom has called Seb and Caro already, or is about to. It would doubtless be polite to ask how they are, but I don't. "Will you have to fly back from Boston?"

"Actually, I'm in London already. I got in this morning."

"Great!" Good news at last. "For how long?"

"For good."

"Wonderful!" But there is something odd about his demeanor, such as can be gleaned over the phone. "Is Jenna with you?" I ask cautiously. I'm beginning to suspect I already know the answer.

"No." I hear him blow out a breath. "It's for the best," he adds awkwardly.

As it happens I agree with him, but it's probably not the time to say so. "Right," I say decisively. "Sounds like you need to turn up on my doorstep one evening very soon with a bottle of wine."

"This might be more of a bottle of whiskey type of conversation."

"You bring whatever alcohol you like and I'll cook the meal. Badly."

He laughs down the phone, a pleasant sound. "It's a deal."

It occurs to me he used to laugh more, all those years ago. But then, we were twenty-one, with no responsibilities or cares, and no one had mysteriously disappeared yet. Probably we all laughed more.

A dead body has been found, but life goes on. For most of us, anyway—perhaps time stops for the nearest and dearest, but then again time probably stopped for them a decade ago when she went missing. For the rest of us, it's back to the same old, same old, which today means a meeting with a potential client. A very hard-hitting potential client: a contract with Haft & Weil could put my fledgling legal headhunter business firmly on the map. I stand in front of the mirror in the bathroom of my short-lease office in Bloomsbury. Smart business trouser suit: check. Tailored silk shirt, clean and ironed: check. Thick dark hair pulled back into a tidy chignon and discreet makeup accentuating my green eyes: check. Altogether a pleasing picture of a professional businesswoman. I smile to check my teeth for poppy seeds from the bagel I had for lunch; the image of Severine's grinning skull immediately jumps into my head. In the mirror my smile drops abruptly.

My assistant, Julie, looks up from her computer as I exit the bathroom. "The cab's here," she says, passing me a folder. "All set?"

"Yes." I check the folder. Everything is there. "Where's Paul?" Paul is my associate and a very, very good headhunter. He's here because he has faith in me and even more faith in the proportion of profits he's due if all goes well. I try to keep a close eye on his diary. Paul won't stick around if the business plan fails to materialize.

Julie is checking on the computer, one hand working the mouse as the other pushes her glasses back up her nose. "He's meeting that Freshfields candidate over on Fleet Street."

"Oh yes." I check the folder again.

"Kate," Julie says, a touch of exasperation in her tone. "It's all there."

I snap the folder shut. "I know. Thank you." I take a deep breath. "Right, see you later."

"Good luck." She has already turned back to the computer, but stops suddenly. "Oh, you had a call that you might want to return when you're in the cab." She looks around for the telephone message pad. "Ah, here we are. Caroline Horridge, please call back. Didn't say what about."

Caro. Calling me. Really? "You're kidding."

Julie looks up, nonplussed. "If I am, the joke has passed me by."

I take the message slip she's holding out. "She went to university with me," I explain, grimacing. "We weren't exactly bosom buddies. The last time I saw her was about five years ago, at someone's party." I look down at the telephone number recorded under the name in Julie's neat hand. "This is a Haft & Weil number," I say, surprised. I've been dialing it enough lately that I know the switchboard number off by heart.

"Maybe she wants to jump ship."

Maybe. There isn't really any other reason for a lawyer to call a legal headhunter. But I can't imagine Caro choosing to ask for my help. I sit in the cab and think of ghosts: of poor dead Severine, her bones folded like an accordion to fit in the narrow well; of poor dead Theo, blown into disparate parts on a battlefield; of Tom-that-was, back when he laughed more; of me-that-was; of Lara; of Caro; and of Seb. Always, always of Seb.

I met Seb in 2000, the summer of my second year at Oxford. Lara and I had been there long enough to stop feeling green and naive and not long enough for responsibility to loom large: no exams all year, or at least none that counted officially, and no requirement to think about jobs until the third year. Our tutors felt it was a good year to bed down the solid groundwork for the following exam year. We thought it was a good year to bed down in actual bed after late nights clubbing.

The favorite summer pastime was ball-crashing. Unthinkable now—to dress up in black tie and sneak into an event without paying, to avail oneself of everything on offer just for a lark. But it was a lark; no one made the connection with stealing that would be my first thought now. Perhaps I've spent too much time thinking about the law now, or not enough back then. Anyway, the point was never the ball itself, those were always more or less the same—perhaps a better band at one, or shorter bar queues at another, but the same basic blueprint every time. No, the point was the breaking in: the thrill of beating the security teams, and getting away with it. The high of that was worth far more than the illicitly obtained alcohol.

The night I met Seb the target was Linacre Ball. Linacre isn't the richest Oxford college, and it isn't the largest; there was no reason to think the ball would be particularly good. The only distinguishing feature was that Linacre is a graduate college: right there lay the challenge. Them against us, graduates against undergraduates, security team against students. Drunken students at that, due to the pre-ball-crashing council-of-war at one of the student houses that lay across the sports field from Linacre, where cheap wine was flowing freely. I remember going to the toilet and tripping on my high heels; I'd have crashed headlong into a wall if it hadn't been for unknown hands catching and righting me. It occurred to me then that we'd better go before we were all too smashed to cross the field, let alone scale the walls surrounding the college.

And then we *were* going, streaming out of the new-build house to congregate on the sports field. The darkness was periodically split by flashing lights from the college some two hundred meters away, the grass fleetingly lit too emerald green to be believable whilst the rugby goalposts threw down shadows that stretched the entire length of the field. Someone was giving orders in a military fashion that set Lara off into a fit of giggles as she stumbled and clutched my forearm. I glanced round and realized in surprise that there must be thirty or forty of us ready to storm the college. Lara and I found ourselves split into a subgroup with barely anyone we knew. It was hard to tell in the dark, but at least two of them were men with definite potential. Lara's smile notched up a few watts as she turned her attention to them.

But there wasn't enough time for her to work her magic—we were off. It was sheer numbers that made the plan work. We went in waves, ten or so at a time in a headlong dash across the field—how did we run in stilettos? I cannot think but I know we managed it. Come to that, how did Lara make it across without ripping her skin-tight dress? Mine ended up hiked high, dangerously close to my crotch. I remember the adrenaline coursing through my veins with the alcohol; the battle cries and the shrieks around me; the fractured picture when the lights flashed of black-tie-clad individuals in full flight. Lara and I huddled at the base of the wall of Linacre College, trying to get our breath through helpless giggles. That was probably why we got in: the security team were too busy dealing with the first bunch that surged the wall. I lost track of Lara as we awkwardly climbed the wall, hopelessly hindered by utterly inappropriate clothing and footwear. As I reached the top a hand stretched down from broad shoulders to help me. I caught a glimpse of gleaming white teeth beneath a remarkably hooked nose, topped by wayward dark hair. I grasped the proffered hand and felt myself yanked unceremoniously upright just as the lights flared, leaving me temporarily blinded, blinking awkwardly on the top of the wall as I tried to thank my helper and regain my footing and eyesight.

"Jump!" someone called below, barely audible above the music. "I'll catch you."

I looked across at the stranger on the wall with me. He nodded, gesturing to the black-tie-clad individual below. As the lights flashed obligingly I looked down into a pair of spectacular blue eyes: Seb. Of course it was Seb.

I jumped. He caught me.

Halfway through the meeting with Mr. Gordon Farrow, senior partner at Haft & Weil, when he rearranges his papers for the umpteenth time and continues to gaze a little to the right of me, I realize I'm losing this piece of business. Shortly after that, whilst trying to explain the relative merits of choosing my firm over more established competitors, I realize I never had a chance in the first place. I'm the stalking horse: a competitor brought in to make sure the firm they really want puts in an honest and fair quote. I wind down mid-sentence and snag an oatmeal cookie instead. It takes Mr. Gordon Farrow a moment or two to notice. For the first time, he looks at me properly.

"Is there something wrong?" he asks.

I hold up a finger as I finish chewing my bite of cookie. He waits patiently, his eyebrows raised inquiringly. "Not really," I say when I've swallowed. "Only I just realized I'm wasting your time and mine, since you've already made up your mind. I appreciate you need a stalking horse, but if that's the case I'd sooner eat your cookies and drink tea than knock myself out trying to pitch for unavailable business."

A gleam of appreciation shows in his eyes. He's nondescript in every respect: mid-height, mid-gray in his hair, neither fat nor thin, not obviously fit but not particularly out of shape for a man in his mid-fifties. He wears well-tailored suits, but nothing flashy or unusual. I've heard the only exceptional thing about him is his intellect, though he's yet to show me much of that. "Do you always speak your mind?" he asks after a moment or two. It doesn't escape me that he hasn't refuted my stalking horse claim.

"Less and less as I grow older," I say, smiling a little. "It's a high-risk strategy. Many of the best things that have happened to me came about because of it, but . . ." I grimace. "Many of the worst things also . . ."

He actually smiles at this. "What would you consider one of the best things to happen to you?"

I answer without hesitation. "Getting into Oxford."

He cocks his head, his eyes gleaming again. "How so?"

"I don't have the typical Oxbridge background. Getting into Oxford really opened up my horizons. I don't mean just in terms of job prospects—it showed me paths and possibilities I could never have believed achievable if I followed a different route."

"My daughter was at Oxford," he says. "I wonder if she would say the same."

"I suppose that might depend on her background. And her personality."

He shrugs with a wry smile. "Caro falls into the category of typical Oxbridge candidate."

I blink. "Not Caro Horridge?" But of course not Caro Horridge; his surname is Farrow—

"Yes," he says, surprised. "You know her?"

"We were at Oxford at the same time."

Suddenly I have the full force of his attention; it's a little unnerving. "And do you think Caro would say getting into Oxford was one of the best things to happen to her?"

Caro would never consider the question; Caro would view entry into Oxford as right and proper, exactly what she was due. "Well," I hedge, "we weren't particularly close."

His lips quirk. "No longer pursuing the high-risk strategy?"

I laugh. "Like I said, less and less as I get older."

The corners of his mouth tug upward, then he glances at his watch. "Well, Miss Channing, I know someone as direct as you will forgive me for cutting to the chase. You *are* the stalking horse. I like your business, I like the pitch book you sent through and your fees are ballpark, but you'd be a hard prospect to sell to committee, as you don't have a proven track record yet. I'm not sure it's worth my while to have that fight."

"What would make it worthwhile? A reduction in fees?"

He purses his lips. "It would help, but even that might not be enough. You just—"

"Don't have the track record," I finish for him.

He nods ruefully. "But I can honestly say it's been a real pleasure." His eyes are smiling; it takes ten years off him. I can't see the slightest resemblance to Caro.

In the cab on the way home I record my post-meeting notes on my pocket Dictaphone for Julie to type up later and then I call Lara and rant for five minutes about how I was an idiot to give up my lucrative job to start my own firm, how aforementioned firm will be bankrupt in six months at this rate, how no one will ever hire me again after such an appalling error of judgment, and so on and so forth . . . Lara has heard it all before. She doesn't even bother arguing back.

"Finished now?" she asks when I finally run out of steam.

"For now. Come round tonight—I'll probably bore you with more of the same, but I promise to at least treat you to a curry and some nice wine first." A giggle with the ever-sunny Lara is exactly what I need.

"Sorry," she says, yawning. "I'm knackered. Can we do tomorrow instead?"

"Knackered . . . What were you up to last night?" I couldn't remember her saying she had a date, but Lara picks up men like the rest of us pick up newspapers. She puts them down in the same way, too. She is and always has been unrelentingly and unashamedly promiscuous, but somehow in her it seems . . . wholesome.

"I met someone in the pub after work. Just a bit of fun."

"Lucky you," I say, unable to keep the envy out of my voice. I'm not sure I've ever just "met someone in the pub." I can't recall anyone ever approaching me cold. Unless Seb counts.

"Ah, Kate." I can hear the smile in her voice. "Like I keep telling you, you need to drop your standards. Then you'd have as much action as you could wish for."

"Maybe." But I don't think that's it. I scrub up well—I'm tall and fairly slim, I've got good hair and I've been told I've got beautiful eyes—but none of that quite has the appeal of a buxom beauty of Swedish descent with an easy smile and a relaxed attitude to sex.

"Your place tomorrow, then?" Lara asks.

"Perfect." I'm about to ring off when I remember I still haven't told her about the body. About Severine. "Wait—Tom called me."

"How is he? Is he back in London?"

"Yes, actually, but that isn't why he called. They found . . ." I swallow. "They found the body. I mean, Severine. They found her in the well at the farmhouse," I finish in a rush.

"Oh God," Lara says bleakly. "That's horrible. Though maybe it will help her parents get closure or something. Do they think it was that boyfriend she was talking about?"

"I suppose so." It's an obvious question, but I hadn't considered how she got into the well. Who put her there. Even now, my mind shies away from it. "I don't know. Tom says the French police want to talk to us all again."

I can almost hear Lara's grimace. "Really?"

"It's probably just procedure; after all, we were the last people to talk with her properly." Before she went into town and was never seen again. "She must have gone back, though, since she was found in the well; I suppose that's new information."

"Still, it must have been that boyfriend, surely. I don't mean to be insensitive, but I really hope it doesn't take up much time. We're soooo busy at work right now." She yawns down the line again. "I suppose that explains why Caro's been trying to get hold of me."

"You too?" That's a surprise: if anything, Caro likes Lara even less than me. "She left me a message; I haven't called back yet. But she must have known Tom would tell us; she can't have been calling about that."

"Only one way to find out." She yawns. "Shotgun: you first," she adds impishly.

"All right," I say reluctantly. "I'll call her." I don't want to talk to Caro any more than Lara does, but I may as well find out what she wants sooner rather than later. If Caro wants something, she won't be deterred.

CHAPTER TWO

S everine hovers.

At first she is no more than a feeling, a presence that rests on my consciousness just out of reach of my field of vision. I put it down to the unwanted memories that have floated to the surface of my mind, stirred up by the discovery of her bones. But that is not enough for Severine. One morning I find those very bones, bleached white and neatly stacked in a pile with the grinning skull atop, resting on my kitchen counter; blinking does not remove them, though I know they're not there. On yet other occasions she manifests in a fleshed-out version of walnut-colored skin, secretive eyes and a superior lack of smile. With her comes an insistent tide of memories, fetid and dank after being buried for so long, that will drag me down into their rotten darkness if I yield to them. I trenchantly refuse to succumb; instead I call Caro.

"Caroline Horridge," she answers crisply, after only one ring. I imagine her sitting at her desk in Haft & Weil, her taut frame wrapped in a business suit, with not a hair or a sheet of paper out of place.

"Hi, Caro, it's Kate." There's a pause. "Kate Channing," I add through gritted teeth. This is a classic Caro strategy, forcing me to identify myself; can she really be expecting a call from another Kate with a strong northern accent?

"Oh, *Kate*," she says, faux-warmly. "God, it's been so long. Thanks for calling back."

"No problem." I can feel my cheeks aching from my fake smile. Someone once told me if you smile on the phone, the caller hears it in your voice; apparently it doesn't matter if the smile is genuine or not. I'm not going to deliberately antagonize the daughter of a man who could hand me a major contract. Any accidental antagonizing can't be helped. "How are you?"

"Good," she says breezily. "Though busy. Which I can't really complain about in this market. You?"

"Same. Good. Busy." Not as busy as I'd like, which is evident when I glance at my computer screen and see my sparse diary for the week, but she doesn't need to know that.

There's a pause. I wait for her to get to the heart of the matter. "I take it Tom's spoken to you?"

"Yes. Not exactly the sunniest of news." My smile has dropped. The skull with yawning darkness for eyes is still waiting for me, just a step beyond conscious thought.

"Do you mean about Jenna or that girl?" I take a sharp breath in—is she really suggesting that murder and a broken engagement are on a par?—but Caro is still talking. "It was always just a matter of time on the girl—surely no one was expecting a different outcome—"

"Severine," I say bluntly. The bones demand to be named. I wish they would make their demands on someone else.

"What?"

"Her name was Severine." Not even a minute into the conversation and already I'm getting testy. I paste on the fake smile again.

"Yes." Caro pauses. "Well, anyway, the reason I called was that I thought it might be nice to have some kind of reunion for Tom. He must be feeling pretty low after the whole Jenna thing—getting the Oxford crowd back together and having a few 'welcome home' drinks might be just the ticket. I'm thinking next Friday, at my flat. We can always go on from there to somewhere on the King's Road if everyone feels up for a big night."

"Um, that's a nice idea," I say faintly. It is. I'm frankly astonished.

"Don't sound so surprised," she says dryly. "After all, I practically grew up with Tom and Seb. I can't wait to have them both back in London."

"Both? Seb too?" The words are out of my mouth before I can clamp down on them.

"Oh, you haven't heard?" I can certainly hear the smile in *her* voice—a thoroughly self-satisfied one. If she was fishing to find out if Seb and I are in touch, she's made her catch. "Seb is coming back. New York doesn't suit Alina, apparently." Alina. His wife of perhaps three years now. "Though he won't be back in time for Friday. We'll just have to do another get-together when he's back."

"Sure. Lovely." I'm absolutely positive I will be busy that evening, whenever it is.

"So you'll come? Next Friday?"

"Let me check." I flick through my electronic diary, though I already know I'm free. Maybe it works like the fake smile. "Um, yes, that should be fine. Thanks."

"Great. Can you do me a favor and tell Lara? I haven't managed to get through to her yet. No doubt you two are still thick as thieves."

"Oh, thicker," I say blandly, then hurry on before she can interpret that as mockery. Which it may be. "I'll tell her."

"Great. I'll e-mail you my address. See you next Friday."

I hang up and gaze blankly for a moment at my computer screen with that under-endowed calendar. It could be that Caro is simply being nice, with no hidden agenda. Lara will think that, when I tell her. But Lara lives in a world where sunshine is always just around the corner: a lovely idea, like Santa Claus and the tooth fairy, but requiring of a certain willing suspension of disbelief to maintain. I was born more suspicious.

Severine hovers.

The day of Caro's drinks party two things happen. Haft & Weil call me—or more specifically, Mr. Gordon Farrow's secretary calls me—and the police call me.

Gordon Farrow's secretary is calling to set up lunch for Tuesday, which makes absolutely no sense unless the firm he really wants have somehow dropped the ball. I spend the day refusing to get excited because it will all come to naught whilst also meticulously planning my sales pitch. It's an exercise in believing two mutually exclusive ideas; it's exhausting.

In comparison the call from the police is much less disturbing, at least in immediate terms. A French detective will be making the short hop across the English Channel next week and would like to interview me; would I be available? I eye the paltry diary again: far too much white space into which I can imagine Severine sauntering, stretching out each slim brown arm to take as her right. Other than Tuesday's lunch and a few other meetings in relation to two small contracts I've landed, I'm available. I'm depressingly, continuously available, and nothing I achieve all day changes that. By the time the end of business hours rolls round, I'm quite partial to the idea of a drink.

Tom, Lara and I have agreed to meet beforehand at a bar near Caro's place. Safety in numbers and all that. I come in from the rain, shaking off my umbrella, and scan the crowded room for Tom. It's easy to spot his tall figure at the bar, ordering; he must have just got there himself as raindrops still glisten like tiny crystals in his dark hair, which is once again too long and starting to curl. He used to look more like Seb, I think. Or perhaps I deliberately dissociate them now.

"Make mine a vodka tonic," I say, slipping into a space next to him.

He turns from the barman, a grin already splitting his face. "Kate!" He pulls me in for a proper hug; none of the nonsense of London double-kisses for Tom. It's something I know yet am always surprised by—he gives really good hugs. I can feel the beaming smile on my own face as he wraps me up. This smile is genuine.

"It is so good to see you," I say into his neck. He smells of a mix of wood and spice.

"You too," he says, pulling back to look at me. His grin hasn't abated yet. The freckles aren't there anymore, and neither is the tan, and I think he may have been hitting the gym a lot lately, but otherwise he's reassuringly the same. "You look really well."

"Ten sixty," interrupts the barman impatiently, plonking the vodka tonic down beside Tom's beer.

"Jesus," mutters Tom, pulling out his wallet. "London prices double every time I come back."

"Then never leave again, for the sake of my bank balance if nothing else." Still smiling, I scoop up my drink. "I'll hunt down a table. Lara's running late, by the way."

It's too crowded to get a table all to ourselves, but I find us two free seats at the corner of the bar, and we do our best to cover almost two years in five minutes, our heads leaned together conspiratorially to combat the noise. Severine can't hold court here, among this warmth and life.

"I'm sorry about Jenna," I offer, after a while. I *am* sorry, even if

I didn't think them well suited. "I didn't really get to know her well when we visited you guys, but she seemed . . ." I grope around for the right adjective. Nothing fits. "Like a girl with her head screwed on," I finish lamely. Jenna's cool gray eyes had missed very little, in my opinion. It had been lovely to see Tom again, and Lara and I had both loved Boston, but I rather thought the tight corners around Jenna's eyes hadn't smoothed out until we were well on our way to the airport.

Tom's lips twist briefly, and he spins his pint glass back and forth in the cradle of his long fingers. "She wasn't on top form when you two came over. She really is a nice girl, it's just . . ." He trails off.

"I know. Lara is a lot to take."

He looks up from his beer, startled. "Lara?"

"Well, she's a difficult proposition for any girlfriend to cope with. Even supposing your boyfriend hasn't slept with her," I add dryly. Does he imagine I didn't notice him and Jenna during that visit, in secluded corridors and corners, standing too close and speaking low and fast to each other? I can see them now, Jenna's right hand making sharp, flat gestures while Tom's ran through his hair in frustration. "Or maybe you didn't tell Jenna about that." Tom and Lara's affair, dalliance, whatever one should call it, happened a long time ago—during that fateful French holiday—and Lara always maintained it was nothing but fun. Tom said the same, though I wondered if there was more to it for him. After Jenna's coolness during our Boston visit, I wondered even more. Wives and girlfriends always know.

"I did tell her actually, and anyway, Lara really wasn't the problem," he says, a touch irritably, then blows out a breath slowly. "It doesn't matter anyway. We just weren't . . . right. I couldn't see us together in fifty years. I realized I couldn't imagine what that would look like. Soon after that, going to the gym got more appealing than going home."

"Fifty years," I say caustically. "I'd settle for knowing what the next six months is going to look like. Or even tonight." I grimace and knock back some more of my drink.

"Don't look like that," Tom says, laughing. "Caro will be on best behavior. The gracious host and so on."

"Mmm," I say noncommittally. "Oh, I wanted to ask you, how come Caro has a different surname than her dad? I know her parents are divorced, but still . . ."

"Well, it was pretty acrimonious." He takes a swallow of his beer and looks to one side, remembering. "From what I recall, Gordon had an affair, and Camilla—Caro's mum—did *not* take it well. Hell hath no fury, et cetera . . . though hers was a very passionless type of fury." He frowns, trying to find the right words. "Like she wasn't so much angry with Gordon for cheating on her as angry with him for disrupting her perfect life. Anyway, Caro took her mum's side. She must have been about thirteen at the time. She officially changed her surname to her mum's maiden name, though to be fair, I imagine her mum put her up to it." His lips twist ruefully. "I always felt sorry for Gordon, to be honest. If I was married to Camilla, I expect I'd've been having an affair a darn sight sooner than Gordon."

"She's difficult?"

"Not exactly difficult." He shrugs, trying to find the right word. "She's *cold*. And nothing is ever good enough for her. Caro's got the same sharp tongue, but at least she can have a laugh." He glances at me, one eyebrow raised, as if waiting for me to make a snide comment, but I don't, partly because what he says is true—Caro can indeed have a laugh; even I have to admit she can be wickedly funny—but also because I didn't know any of this before. It adjusts the picture somewhat. "Well, anyway, it was a tough time for Caro. That's when Seb and I"—he glances at me quickly—"started spending a lot more time with her; I think she just wanted any excuse to get out of the house."

Seb. Tom usually avoids that name with me; tricky since they are not only best friends but also cousins, but nonetheless he tries. I keep my face expressionless. "Is her dad still with whoever he had the affair with?"

Tom shakes his head. "No. Caro refused to see him if he was still seeing her, so he stopped." I absorb that for a moment: the child laying down the law to her father. There's a reason children are not supposed to have that kind of power; I wonder how that felt, for both of them. But Tom is still speaking: "You know, now I wonder if her mum put her up to that, too. My parents seemed to think it was a crying shame, that Gordon and this woman would have been very happy together. But Caro was adamant, so . . ." He shrugs. "That was that."

"Interesting that she works at his firm."

"Yeah, I didn't really know what to make of that when I heard she'd joined Haft & Weil." He is frowning, still trying to puzzle it out. "It's not like she didn't have other offers, either." He finishes his beer with one swallow, then eyes the empty glass. "Time for another? How late is Lara going to be?"

"She should be—ah, here she is." I start waving to catch Lara's attention as she scans the bar from the doorway. Half of the bar is scanning her in return. As she spots us, her open smile breaks out and she heads our way.

"Tom," she says, hugging him warmly. "Look at you! Do you have a job anymore or do you just lift weights?"

He laughs and climbs off his bar stool to offer it to her. "You're one to talk, looking gorgeous as ever."

"I'm at least six pounds overweight. But since it all seems to be residing in my boobs I can't really be bothered to do anything about it," she says complacently, perching her bottom on the proffered bar stool.

"How is it that you've only been in the bar thirty seconds and already we're talking about your boobs?" teases Tom. I'm used to their easy, affectionate flirting, but suddenly I'm more alert to it. The context has changed: Tom is single. I'm not uneasy, exactly, but it would change the dynamic if they were to become a couple. I like things how they are.

"Well then, how about a much more macabre subject: did you guys get a call from the police today?" Lara asks, and immediately Severine reaches through time to tug me back. She sinks with studied elegance into a chair by the farmhouse pool, dressed in a loose black linen shift, and crosses one leg over the other; after the slim brown calf comes a slender foot, complete with shell-pink-painted toes from which a sandal casually dangles. Seb can't take his eyes off that sandal.

I knock back the remains of my vodka tonic and wrench myself into the present. Tom is nodding. "About interviews next week? Yeah, I did."

"Me too. Though I don't know what help we can be a decade on." I add, almost defiantly, "I can hardly remember a thing."

"Me either," says Lara. "I wonder if it will be the same one." She has an odd look on her face.

"Same what?" I ask, confused.

"Same detective. Only they don't call them that in France, do they? Investigator. Officer of judiciary police, or whatever the phrase is."

"I shouldn't think so," says Tom dismissively. "Wasn't he about sixty? He'll have retired."

"You two have finished your drinks," Lara says, in a sudden change of gear. "Can I get us all another?"

I shake my head, grimacing. "Shouldn't we really screw our courage to the sticking place and venture forth?"

"Macbeth? Isn't that a little dramatic?" protests Tom, but he's laughing. "It'll be fine. Especially since you two are going to behave impeccably." He fixes us both with a mock-glare that lingers longer, and with more steel, on me than Lara.

"Such blind optimism," Lara says, fluttering her eyelids in a deliberately over-the-top fashion. "A man after my own heart."

I wonder.

C aro's flat smells of vanilla. Later I track the source to a number of expensive candles dotted around the space, the sort that have three wicks and cost more than a boozy restaurant meal for two. The enticing smell, the cozy lighting and the welcome warmth of the flat after the driving rain outside add up to give a Christmassy feel even though it's March. Caro has a couple of teenage girls with heavy eyeliner answering the door, taking coats and pouring champagne. It's all exceedingly grown-up.

There are perhaps twenty-five people already there when we arrive. At a quick glance I know a few, and there are others I recognize but can't put a name to; all from Oxford days. I spy Caro across the room, wearing a severe black minidress and truly lethal black suede ankle boots, with her dark blond hair scraped back from her face. Skinny, blond, self-assured and possessing of a delicate bone structure that screams English aristocracy: posh totty. I almost drowned in an army of girls just like her at Oxford before I learned how to swim in a big pond. It's important to kick.

"Relax, Kate," says Tom quietly, amused.

I exaggerate taking in a deep breath and letting it out slowly. His blue eyes, similar to Seb's but flecked with gray, are crinkled at the corners at my theatrics.

Caro breaks off a conversation when she spots our entry and crosses to us quickly, zeroing in on Tom with a delighted smile spreading across her face. She's even thinner than I remember, and older, of course—we all are—but for Caro the extra years have gnawed away any softness. Now she appears brittle. I try to imagine the thirteen-year-old girl that she once was, taking refuge in her friendships with Tom and Seb, but I can't form an image in my mind. Still, Tom's words drift around me; they herd me into a corner where I can't help but feel that my dislike of Caro reflects badly on me. Surely I *ought* to like her: she's a strong, smart, ambitious woman who is working very hard in what is still a heavily male-dominated workplace; she's sharp and cleverly funny, and moreover, Tom likes her, which has to count for rather a lot . . . and yet . . . and yet . . . She's *too* sharp. She cuts. Or at least, she used to.

"Tom! The guest of honor!" she is saying, as she kisses him on both cheeks; Tom doesn't try to hug her, I note. Then Caro turns to Lara and myself; Lara gets the double-kiss treatment first. "It's been so long," Caro exclaims to her. "You look . . . just the same." Lara murmurs back something innocuous.

"Hi, Caro." I'm last in line. I dutifully offer my cheeks; the spiked heels on her boots almost raise her up to my height. There's no contact in either kiss.

"Kate," she says, her lips curving in a smile that her eyes don't entirely match. "I hear you met my father."

"Um, yes." I'm a little surprised she would choose to lead with that. "I think we're meeting again next week, actually."

Her eyes narrow a fraction, but she nods emphatically and says, "Excellent. I told him weeks ago that he wouldn't regret giving you a chance."

"Thank you," I say, thrown. "That was . . . kind of you." At least, it would have been kind if it were true. I'm absolutely positive she's lying. Her father would have already known about our acquaintance had she spoken to him.

"It's nothing," she says with a dismissive gesture. "It can't be easy starting up your own business in this economic climate. Now, you all have drinks, yes? Then come join the melee." She links her arm through Tom's and drags him off; I watch her stretch up with a sly smile on her face to deliver something to his ear that elicits a sharp bark of laughter. He's soon ensconced in vigorous hellos complete with enthusiastic back-thumping with three or four men whose faces I vaguely remember, but not their physiques; ten years has done a lot of damage to hairlines and waistlines.

Lara and I sip champagne. We mingle and chat. By and large the faces I don't know are the other halves of people I do. Some more people come in, and the music moves on to a more upbeat tempo. The volume of the chatter and laughter increases. We drink more champagne and do some damage to the trays of nibbles. I take in the flat: a property like this must be hideously expensive in this part of London. I wonder if her father helped her buy it, and if he did, I wonder at the dynamic of refusing his name but taking his financial aid.

Caro joins us. "I'm so sorry I haven't had a chance to chat with you two. But you know what it's like at your own parties—you hardly get time for more than a hello with each person before you're dragged off." She rolls her eyes as if it's a chore, but she's in her element. The gracious host indeed.

"Great turnout," says Lara, raising her glass to Caro.

"It is, isn't it?" She has a satisfied smile on her face as she scans the room. Then she turns back to us. "Sorry to speak of unpleasant things, but I expect you both have meetings with the French investigator next week, too?"

"Yes, Monday," I say.

"It was such a long time ago, I wondered if we should discuss beforehand. Make sure we're all singing from the same song sheet, so to speak."

Lara opens her mouth, most likely to agree because it's the path of least resistance, so I jump in quickly. "What's to discuss? She was alive and well the night before we left, and that's the last we saw of her."

Caro is nodding. "True. Then she went into town." She frowns. "Odd that she came back to her cottage when she told Theo she was going to Paris."

"Did she?" I didn't know that.

"When did she say that?" asked Lara.

"The night before we left, I think. Theo had a long chat with her." I remember that: I see the pair of them now, lying on their backs in the dark of nighttime on sun loungers beside the pool. Severine has a glass of white wine resting on her stomach, and the red glow of a cigarette makes a repeated arc up to her mouth then down to dangle off the armrest. She's still in the black linen shift, but her sandals are now tossed carelessly beside the sun lounger. I don't want to look at Seb in case he's drinking in the sight of her; instead I watch Severine myself. After a time she turns her head to look at me directly; it's too dark and she's too far away to see the expression in her eyes. Not that there was ever anything to see in Severine's eyes.

I shake my head. Caro is still talking: "I just thought, well, maybe we should all compare notes . . . After all, I can barely remember that last night, what with the alcohol." She gives a high, tinkling laugh.

"And the drugs," I say evenly. Her laugh stops, and she cocks her head and meets my eye. Lara is looking from Caro to me and back again. Across the room I can see Tom repeatedly glancing away from his conversation to keep tabs on the three of us; he's easy to spot on account of his height and that bold nose. And his shoulders, now, after all that relationship-avoiding gym work; he must be even bulkier than Seb these days. "It's okay," I say after a moment. "I didn't mention it back then, and I won't now."

Caro nods, a short, quick movement. It's not exactly a thank-you, but close.

"It was a pretty crazy night," says Lara, smiling.

"Yes," laughs Caro, happy to move on. "Didn't you end up skinny-dipping with Tom?"

Lara is grinning. "I seem to remember something like that. Then World War Three broke out and we were trying to calm everyone down whilst naked and dripping wet." She frowns. "I can't remember, what were you guys arguing about anyway?" she says with wide-eyed innocence. I glance at her sharply, then look at Caro. Twin spots of red are burning in her cheeks.

Suddenly Tom appears at my elbow waving an empty bottle of champagne. "Caro, are there any more of these?"

"Oh, crates of them, literally. Let me sort that." She grabs the bottle gratefully and disappears quickly through the crowd.

Tom turns a stern eye on Lara and me. "Didn't I tell you guys to behave?" he says, running a hand through his hair in exasperation.

"You want *us* to behave?" asks Lara archly. "Caro's the one who wants to airbrush our response to the police to make sure there's no mention of drug-taking. You might be happy to forget that she smuggled Class A drugs through customs in Kate's bag, but I don't think I ever will. And nor will Kate." I can't stop a smile spreading across my face: this is so unexpectedly combative of my easygoing best friend, and in that moment I love her fiercely for it. It seems I was wrong: where Caro is concerned, even Lara is naturally suspicious.

"I haven't forgotten," says Tom quietly. "If you remember, I was furious with her. But you don't have to rub her nose in it now. It was a long time ago and she did apologize."

"Not until the next day," I mutter mutinously, temporarily forgetting my previous inclination to a generosity of spirit toward Caro. "And as far as apologies go, it was distinctly underwhelming." Her so-called apology had been accepted as it was offered: with no charm at all, and under clear duress.

"You really want to go into all that again right now?" asks Tom. He is glaring at me with an expression I can't quite interpret. Suddenly the exasperation melts away, and he tilts his head. I'm close enough to see the gray flecks in his eyes. "Come on, Kate, let's not dredge up the past," he says softly.

I breathe out slowly. He's right. I've no desire to let those particular memories out of their box; though they seem to be seeping out regardless. I find a smile and clink my glass against Tom's. "To the present."

"And to Tom," says Lara, clinking her glass against Tom's also. She smiles winningly at him. "Nice to have the voice of reason back." Tom shakes his head and smiles back, then glances round the room. The crowd is thinning out; I glance at my watch and am surprised to see it's past 1 A.M.

"Come on," he says. "Let me escort you two home."

We get a cab together. It makes geographical sense to drop me off first; I hug them both good-bye and climb out, then watch the taxi disappear. In my mind I replay the scene of them intervening with Seb, Caro and myself, in the glory of their birthday suits. Lara's impressive frontage jiggles hypnotically until Theo throws a towel round her, discomfort making his cheeks as red as his hair. When Tom works out what's happened, he rounds on Caro; I've never seen Tom angry, and it's majestic. I'm surprised she can remain upright in the face of such a biting onslaught. Lara is openmouthed in awe, but I'm too full of hurt and acid fury and cheap wine to truly appreciate the display. Mostly hurt, because Seb thinks I'm overreacting. His lack of support is a physical blow; it literally takes my breath and speech away. The shock of it strips away all my defenses and forces me to face the truth: it's over.

At the time amidst the mayhem I barely noticed Severine, but now she has my attention. She sits casually to one side, observing detachedly as she calmly finishes a cigarette, then collects her sandals and walks unhurriedly to her cottage, leaving the chaos behind. I stumble alone to the bedroom Seb and I should be sharing, tears

LEXIE ELLIOTT

streaming down my cheeks. Six months, even two months, previously he would have followed me, but no longer.

Back in the present, I'm also going to bed alone. Seb is presumably in bed somewhere with his wife, give or take a time difference impact. Who knows what Caro's sleeping arrangements are? Theo—well, Theo is dead. Severine, too, though death seems to hold her too loosely as far as I'm concerned. And Tom and Lara are together in a taxi.

CHAPTER THREE

Monday morning. I'm immersed in Excel spreadsheets, surveying the health, or lack thereof, of my company, when Gordon Farrow rings. The pleasantries don't take long, but he *is* pleasant, and genuine. A decent man. Even without Tom's damning account of Caro's mother, if Caro is the average of Gordon and his ex-wife, I have no desire to meet the ex-wife.

"So who's on your list, Kate?" asks Gordon. We've moved on to first-name terms. He means who would I target for the open positions at his firm; I've been prepping for exactly this question, only I'm a little thrown to be answering it on the phone on Monday rather than at lunch on Tuesday. Still, I move smoothly into my "here's-one-I-prepared-earlier" answer, and we bat back and forth on that for a few minutes.

Paul enters the office we share as I'm talking, loosening his silk tie as he sinks into the chair behind his desk. His blond eyebrows, so pale as to be not worth having, rise as he listens to my half of the conversation while drinking his take-out coffee. "Haft & Weil?" he mouths.

I nod, then my attention is fully caught by Gordon's next comment, stated with such deliberate casualness that it's clear this is what he's been waiting to talk about all along. "You haven't mentioned Dominic Burns."

"Not Dominic," I say instantly. It's an instinctive response—I should have prevaricated, I should have given myself time to find out if Gordon is hell-bent on hiring this man, but it's too late for that now. Across the room Paul is choking on his coffee.

"Why not Dominic?" asks Gordon diffidently. "He's a prime candidate, with his experience. And I hear he's looking to move; he wants to head up a meaningful business area with the right support to really make a dent into private equity clients."

"Do you have any plans to retire, Gordon?" I ask. "In the next, say, five years?" Paul's eyes almost pop out. He makes urgent gestures.

"I'm not following you," says Gordon, after a moment.

"Dominic Burns doesn't want a job heading up a business area. He wants *your* job. Managing partner."

"He doesn't have that kind of experience," Gordon objects.

"Not yet. But he's aggressively ambitious, and after a couple of years at Haft & Weil, he'll start to feel he deserves a shot. Which is fine if you're looking for someone to hand the reins to. But if not, he'll go looking for a firm where he can get the opportunity he *really* wants. You'll have him in place for three years tops." Paul is standing now in obvious agitation. His frantic hand-waving may be interpreted as ordering me to stop talking or to immediately slit my throat. I ignore him and continue: "When he jumps ship he'll take all your lovely new clients with him, and probably a host of your up-and-coming juniors, too." I give Paul a one-fingered gesture of my own, which isn't open to any misinterpretation, then spin my chair to face away. I like Gordon. I don't want to see him make the wrong hire. "And you'll be back at square one."

There's silence down the phone line for a long moment, then Gordon says, "You sound like you know him well."

"I do, actually. I worked under him for a while at Clifford Chance."

"Interesting. Well, that's certainly food for thought, Kate."

I put down the phone and spin round to find Paul looming over my desk, almost incoherent with frustration. "What are you doing?" he groans, one hand clutching his head. "The first rule of service industries: give the client what they want. The man wants to hire Dominic Burns, so tell him you'll get him Dominic Burns. It's a no-brainer!"

"It's the wrong hire," I argue. "He needs to know that."

"No! He doesn't! He needs to hire him, and pay us a whacking great check!" I can't deny a whacking great check would be helpful. Paul sees my weakness and presses on. "Kate, we need this, and you've just blown it. Why the hell would you torpedo it? If he's got his mind set on someone, then we get them. It's as simple as that."

"He'll respect us more for giving him honest, open feedback," I fire back, stung by his "blown it" comment. Though of course he may be right. "We don't need this so badly that I'm going to forget how to do a good job."

"If we don't get a big contract soon, you won't be doing any job." He lets out a long breath.

"We're fine." I spin the computer screen to show him what I've been looking at. He perches on the desk and leans in to run his eye down the figures. "See, the small stuff is going to tide us over. We've got time, and we're obviously building a name or Haft & Weil wouldn't even be talking to us."

"The small stuff keeps the lights on and the printer running," he says dismally. "It doesn't, you know, *pay* us. Which I've got to say, I'm quite attached to, as a concept." He runs a hand through his hair. I realize he looks tired. It doesn't sit well on his fair skin. "I don't think I'm going to land the Freshfields guy."

"Ah."

"Ah indeed." He sighs and climbs off the edge of the desk, then turns back to me. "Haft & Weil are going to cancel the lunch, you know."

"They won't." It's only dogged bravura that forces me to disagree with him. Nobody calls for an in-depth strategy session if they intend to keep a lunch date the following day.

"You'll see," Paul says wearily.

That afternoon Gordon Farrow's secretary calls me: not to cancel, but to postpone due to "Mr. Farrow's travel commitments." Paul wisely says nothing.

Monday evening finds me back at my flat unusually early for the appointment with Mr. Modan. Actually *Monsieur* Alain Modan, *Investigateur, OPJ*—whatever that stands for. Basically the French detective. He would have met me at my office if I'd preferred, but I'd rather Julie and Paul not know about this. *Helping the police with their inquiries* could end up sounding like a euphemism for something more sinister after a few Chinese whispers, and who wants to hire a legal recruiter that's in trouble with the law?

"Thank you for seeing me," he says as we settle into my living room.

"It wasn't clear to me I had the option to refuse." I smile to lessen the sting.

He is rummaging through his bag and looks up at my words, his long, intelligent face already pulled into a half-ironic smile. There are deep smile lines framing his mobile mouth, and a slim-fitting dark gray suit hangs on his too-lanky, too-thin frame; somehow the sum of the parts is an unexpectedly attractive man. I can't possibly imagine a British detective in the same mold. "There is always the option, *non?*" he says, his accent unmistakable. "Though I would not think it the wisest choice." The smile flashes again, then he returns to his bag. I watch as he finds his notepad and flicks through the pages.

"Tea? Coffee?" I make the offer once the silence has grown uncomfortably long from my point of view. In truth I want a glass of wine, but not one that comes with Modan's interrogation.

"No, thank you," he says without looking up. Finally he turns his dark eyes on me. "I'm sorry, this is very inconvenient for you, but please, a few questions. You probably answered the same ten years ago, but it's . . . how you say . . . procedure." He spreads his hands wide, palms up, with a Gallic shrug, inviting me to sympathize: *Procedure. What can you do, eh?*

"It was a very long time ago," I say steadily. "I doubt I can add anything. Probably the opposite—I expect I've forgotten so much that I'll confuse things for you."

He shrugs again. "Well, let's see. Yes?"

"Yes. Of course, go ahead." He's here now, in the country and in my living room. Of course he's going to ask his questions. Of course I'll have to answer them. And all the time Severine will be waiting for her chance to appear. I had thought she would fade away after a few days, once I'd got over the shock, but no. Severine has more staying power than I anticipated.

"*Bon*, so you left the farmhouse on Saturday the sixteenth, yes?"

"Yes."

"All six of you?"

"Yes, all six of us." Six on the vacation. Really four plus two, but not the two I'd expected. I'd imagined it would be Seb and me, plus a selection of our friends. It turned out to be Lara and me, plus Seb and his friends.

"You drove back to London?"

I nod. "In my car." We'd planned to use Seb's father's BMW, but there had been some problem, I can't remember what. The others had been extremely rude about my ancient little banger until it turned out it was the only vehicle we could get hold of.

"Ah yes. In your"—he checks his notes—"Vauxhall Nova." He

checks again. "Really?" He looks at me doubtfully. "Six of you? That would be very . . . squished."

"Four of us. Theo and Tom took the train back together; I dropped them at the station that morning, then went back for the others."

"Ah, Theo." He pronounces it the French way: *Tay-o.* "Afghanistan, yes? Very sad." His long face does indeed hold sympathy; whether genuine or not, I can't tell. I expect he's very good at his job.

"Yes. Very sad." It is sad, and senseless and a waste and a whole lot of other things I can't possibly put into words, but even if I could, it wouldn't change the outcome. Theo is dead.

"He was very patriotic?"

"I'm sorry?"

"He loved his country very much? He always wanted to be a soldier, to fight for her?"

I rub my forehead. "No, I don't think . . . We were all quite surprised when he enlisted." Theo hadn't seemed the type. Too nervous, too self-conscious. The army seemed to me like a grown-up version of a boys' boarding school; Theo had hated boarding school. I shake my head abruptly. "I'm sorry, what has this got to do with—"

He puts out a placating palm. The man has an elegant gesture for everything. "Forgive me, forgive me. We must return to the point. What time did you leave the farmhouse?"

I try to remember. I must have dropped Theo and Tom at the train station before nine, I think. The rest of us had planned to be on the road by nine thirty, but Caro wasn't ready. One more reason to be furious with Caro—not that I needed another reason that morning, after the revelations of the previous night. "Erm, perhaps ten thirty?"

He nods and makes a note. "Were you the driver?"

"Yes. I was the only one insured."

"You drove all the way back? You didn't share?" His surprise is clear.

I remember the journey, although I don't want to. The car lacked air-conditioning; I was hot and tired and tight-lipped with hurt and resentment. Caro sat in the back, uncharacteristically pale and quiet; I wondered if she was suffering in the aftermath of the drugs and thought savagely that it would serve her right. Lara was golden and sleek, full of catlike satisfaction after a few days of frolicking with Tom; she slept almost all the way. And Seb . . . I don't want to think about Seb. I swallow. "Like I said, I was the only one insured."

His lips twist and he makes another note. "*Bon*, so, a Vauxhall Nova. Were there any other automobiles at the property?"

"No. We just used my car." My mobile rings: Lara. "Sorry," I say, quickly turning it off. I can call her later; I want to get this over with.

"You're sure? Nothing in the garage?"

"Well, there was an old Jag that belonged to Theo's father, but we never touched it. No one was allowed to drive it." The farmhouse belonged to Theo's parents back then; they sold it later, after Theo died.

He is nodding; he obviously knows about the Jaguar. "Did you see Miss Dupas on the morning of departure?"

"No." I can feel my muscles tensing, as if anticipating an impact.

"The day before, perhaps?"

"Yes." My answers are brief, clipped.

"Was that . . . habitual?" The word choice is odd; perhaps he has translated directly from the French. "Did she pass much time with you during the week?"

I nod again. He assesses me with his dark eyes and sits silently, waiting for more. I sigh: monosyllabic responses are not going to get me through this interview. "Theo's family and hers were on quite friendly terms. Both families had been spending most of the summer down there for years. Severine's parents' place didn't have a pool, but Theo's parents let them use theirs whenever they wanted."

Severine has appeared, swept in on the flow of words. She's facing away from me on the steps of the pool in a black bikini, knee-deep in the cool water, her narrow back perfectly straight. Seb, Lara, Caro and I have just arrived, and Theo, who arrived earlier, is showing us round; the unexpected sight of a girl in the pool draws us all up short. "Severine!" exclaims Theo, bounding toward her. "I didn't expect to see you." She turns her head and regards us all, then climbs out of the pool to treble-kiss him hello, apparently completely unselfconscious despite her scant attire. I find it hard to look away. The narrowness of her hips is a marvel; her belly is flat yet soft, like a child's. Her shoulders and arms shimmer with the sheen of sunscreen. "Theo," she says solemnly, her English heavily accented. "I did not know I would be here, either." She looks at the rest of us, weighing and measuring. "I am Severine," she says. "The mademoiselle next door."

"You saw her every day?" asks Alain Modan. I'm grateful for the question; it dissolves Severine's presence.

"Yes. She would come to the pool, and often she would eat dinner with us."

He nods. "How was she?" I look at him blankly. He snaps his fingers repeatedly, frustrated with himself as he tries to find the right words. "Her . . . emotions, her . . . temperament, how was she?"

"Well, she was . . ." I stop, trying to find the right words myself. "She was a very . . . self-contained girl. If there was anything bothering her I wouldn't have known."

"Was she closer to one than another? Perhaps she spent more time with Theo, since they already knew each other?"

"No, not Theo." He looks up sharply from his notebook at my tone and raises his eyebrows. "I mean, not with anyone specifically," I add quickly.

His eyebrows have not quite descended fully, and his eyes remain on me. I work hard to hold his gaze and I don't think of Seb.

After a moment he gives a minute shrug and looks at his notebook again. "Did she speak about her plans for after she left the Dordogne?"

"Not with me. Though Caro said that she told Theo she was heading back to Paris."

He cocks his head to one side. "Caroline Horridge? She said that?"

I nod. "The other night."

He is making notes again, in his little book. His handwriting is like tiny spiders multiplying across the page. "So. The well. There was—how do you say, workings?—going on?"

"Building works." It's a relief to move on to something less personal. "Theo's parents wanted to rent the place out. They needed a few things done to comply with the safety regulations."

Modan is nodding. "*Oui.* A fence round the pool. And the well filled in."

"Probably." I shrug. "I remember the builders doing the pool fence." Suddenly the significance of what he's saying hits me. "Oh. The well. She . . . God, she must have been in there before they filled the well." The skull appears, but it's no longer gleaming. Sand fills the eye sockets and spills out of the grinning mouth. I find my hand is at my mouth and carefully remove it to descend to my lap. "Is that why you didn't find her? I mean, till now?"

"We didn't find her because we were looking in the wrong place," he says simply. His eyes are fixed on me again. I can't fathom his expression.

"Do you think it was her boyfriend? Ex-boyfriend, I mean?"

"We're looking at all possibilities—"

"Yes, but you must be looking pretty hard at him in particular," I say impatiently, suddenly fed up with the one-sided nature of this interview, even though that's how interviews are meant to be. "There was a history, right? Severine said she'd had to call the police about him before."

"There's no record of that." He's looking at me as if he's waiting for something.

I pause. "No record?" Severine lied. Why would she lie about that?—but I instantly know the answer. To appear more mysterious, more alluring. The kind of woman a man would literally go insane for.

"None," says Alain Modan calmly. "And the ex-boyfriend, he was doing a science project, some very intense work for his thesis. He was in the laboratory every day in June, even weekends, attending to his cultures or some such . . ." His hand waves expressively. "So." He is still watching, waiting for me to catch on to something. I shake my head dumbly. He tries again. "So . . . unless the well was not filled in until July—"

The doorbell buzzes, cutting him off. He cocks his head questioningly at me. I shrug then raise myself up from the sofa to go and answer, and find that I'm stiff. I've been sitting unnaturally still for a very long time now.

I know it's Lara before I open up; I can hear her rustling in her bag for the spare key she keeps. "Lara, the detective is here," I say quickly as I unlatch the door, forestalling her greeting.

She looks past me, alarmed, as if she can see through the hall walls to the living room. "I thought that was tomorrow," she whispers urgently.

"No, today. You may as well come and say hello."

"But I don't . . . I'm not . . . But . . ." I look at her, puzzled, then she takes a deep breath and smooths her dress. "Okay." She comes in, taking a quick glance at herself in the hallway mirror before she follows me into the living room.

Mr. Modan has climbed to his feet and is looking out of the window. He turns as he hears us enter the room, and his face goes oddly still. Before I have a chance to say a few words of polite introduction, Lara speaks up from behind me. "It's you."

I glance at her, not understanding the words or her tone. Her cheeks are flushed, and she's half turned to the door, as if she still might flee. The French investigator could be a statue. I'm not completely sure he's breathing. Then with an effort, he comes alive and shoots the cuffs of his suit before crossing the room to shake her hand. "Yes. Alain Modan."

"Lara Petersson," she says quietly. "But of course you know that."

I look from one to the other. *I wonder if it will be the same one?* She wasn't talking about the lead investigator. "I take it I've been very rude and failed to remember you from the earlier investigation," I say dryly to Alain Modan.

He turns to me with a quick smile and raises a hand as if to say, *No matter.* "It was a long time ago. I was very junior, one of many assisting." He looks back at Lara, then away quickly. Then he collects himself. "Miss Channing, you have a guest. We can continue another time, if I have more questions."

"Oh. Okay. Fine." If I'd known having a guest would roust him, I'd have arranged for an interruption long before this, I think sourly. Except I wouldn't have, really. Better to get these things over and done with.

He turns to Lara. "*À demain*, Miss Petersson." *Until tomorrow.*

"*Oui, à demain*," she says, then follows up with something too quick for me to catch. I forgot Lara's French was rather impressive; she's one of those irritating Scandinavians with umpteen languages to their credit.

When I've closed the door on Monsieur Alain Modan, *investigateur*, I follow Lara to the kitchen and find her already pulling a bottle of white wine from my fridge and studiously avoiding my eye.

"What was that all about?"

She pours two glasses. Very large glasses. She seems to be giving the task more attention than it deserves. "Nothing. What do you mean?"

"Don't give me that. Did you and he . . . ?"

"No!" She looks up, appalled. "Of course not!" I hold her gaze until she breaks and takes a sip of her wine.

I reach out for my own glass and take a sip, still watching her. She's avoiding my eyes again. "Lara," I say warningly.

"Oh, all right!" She folds, like I knew she would, and finally looks up. "Nothing happened, truly. He, um . . ." She takes another sip of wine, then says in a rush, "He wouldn't. He said it wouldn't be proper. Appropriate, I mean. Under the circumstances." She's blushing, more furiously than I've ever seen before.

"Oh my God," I say wonderingly, a smile breaking out slowly on my face. "He's that mythical creature. The one that got away from Lara Petersson."

"He's not . . . It's not . . . Oh, fuck off," she says, screwing up her nose prettily. She takes an unfeasibly long drink from her glass, then looks at me dejectedly. "Only it's still not appropriate, right? Not until he clears us from the investigation. And then he'll be back in France."

"I can't believe you never told me any of this." I'm not hurt; I'm just amazed that I missed this.

She ducks her head apologetically. "Well, like I said, nothing happened. And you and Seb had just split up, and you know what a state that left you in. I didn't want to dump my crap on you . . ."

For once the mention of Seb slides by almost unnoticed; I'm too thrown by this revelation. What else did I miss when I was licking my Seb-inflicted wounds? She takes in another large slug of wine, and I gaze at her in bemusement. Not only did the rejection matter to her then, it clearly still matters now. This is a Lara I haven't seen before.

And then I think, *Poor Tom.*

CHAPTER FOUR

dream of Severine, among others.

She has no right to be in my dreams, but that would never have stopped Severine. I'm back at the farmhouse, of course, and I'm trying to find something, or someone, but what? Who? I stick my head in the rooms, some empty, some not; some of the occupants weren't even part of that fateful vacation, but somehow I'm not surprised to see them. I keep looking. Caro is alone in the kitchen; she's wearing a white bikini top and a red chiffon sarong, and she looks up then laughs at me when I pass through. I realize I'm clad in jeans and a heavy-duty winter jumper, but I know I've nothing else to wear. Severine is smoking in the garden. She tells me something very seriously, but I don't listen; in fact I'm picking up speed, running to the barn. The jumper is uncomfortably hot. I throw open the barn door, then catch my breath when I find Seb there. He's wearing long beach shorts that are slung low on his hips. His hair is lighter than Tom's, almost golden at the tips, and curlier; his muscular bare chest is tanned, and dark, springy hair makes a trail down his abdomen—a fully-fledged man whereas his peers are still leaving boyhood. Just like Caro he looks me up and down with those blue eyes that could be Tom's, then laughs. It's not a kind laugh.

The dream doesn't fade when I wake; it presses on my temples and adds to the throbbing left by one too many glasses of wine with Lara. Getting out of bed—in fact, all of what the day requires—seems a supreme effort, but then I imagine Paul and Julie at the office wondering where I am, and that provides the necessary impetus. By the time Tom calls my mobile that afternoon, the headache has dulled but the effort remains.

"How was it?" he asks. I can hear a very particular hubbub in the background: sharp orders and staccato words in the male register. He's on the trading floor at his bank; Tom trades interest rate derivatives. I'm on Oxford Street myself, en route to meet a prospective client; I expect my own background noise is equally loud.

"How was what? Please tell me you're not rigging the markets while chatting to me."

He laughs. "No, I have people to do that for me now. And for the benefit of the recorded line: that was a *joke*. Anyway, I meant how was the thing with the French detective."

"Pretty awful actually." I look around, then back at the map in my hand. New Bond Street is a big street. It can't have disappeared.

"How so?" he asks cautiously.

"It's . . . well, I don't really want to think about what might have happened to her." I don't really want to think about her at all. I look around again. There's a disappointing lack of street name signs. "Jesus, where is this place?" I mutter. I spy something that might be a sign and march in that direction.

"Lost?" asks Tom, amused. "Where's your legendary sense of direction?"

"Lara drowned it in wine last night. It's her turn with the detective today, actually."

"Yeah, I know, I spoke to her this morning," he says easily. I stop walking. Lara must have given him her number. "It's tomorrow for me. Listen, I have to jump. I've got a dicey option expiry approaching, but I was wondering if you fancy coming down to Hampshire for Sunday lunch. My folks would love to see you."

"Um, sure. I don't think I have anything on. Sounds lovely." Which it does—I've met his parents half a dozen times over the years, though never at their home; his dad is charmingly eccentric and his mum is lovely. "Is Lara coming, too?—oh, she's in Sweden this weekend, I forgot."

"Yeah, she's away." He already knows what her weekend plans are. "I'll drive us down. I'll call you on Saturday to figure out timings." I hear someone calling his name in the background. "Yeah, just coming," he calls back, then to me, "Speak Saturday."

"Saturday." I pocket my phone and look around again. New Bond Street is right there, where it's always been. I still have a headache.

Sunday. Tom turns up at ten thirty in something retro, white and low-slung that he's visibly excited by. Cars mean nothing to me, but Seb would be envious, I think, then I shut down that train of thought.

"Am I supposed to be in awe?" I ask Tom teasingly.

"The salesman promised me the mere sight would make women drop their knickers," he deadpans.

"I would, but it's a bit chilly today and I don't fancy a draft up my skirt." I walk around the car. Even to the uninitiated, it's a very cool car. "How old is it?"

"Considerably older than both of us. It's a Toyota 2000GT; well, mostly. Some of the parts have been replaced, which reduces the value." The sun makes a brief appearance, bouncing off the immaculate white paintwork. "I picked it up this morning." He can't keep the smile off his face as he talks. It's infectious. He reaches out a long arm and opens the passenger door, waggling his eyebrows suggestively. "Can I take you for a ride, Miss Channing?"

I laugh and fold myself into the seat. "I thought you'd never ask."

The seat is uncomfortable and the heating intermittent, but the sun comes out and stays out. That, and the car, and Tom's mood have me giddy for the first half hour, which carries us through the London traffic. When the roads open up and the car settles into a steady thrum through increasingly green countryside, our chatter tails off into comfortable silence.

"Do you want some music?" asks Tom, glancing across at me. His lips are tugging upward at the corners; I wait for the punch line. "Cos if so, you'd better start singing—the radio doesn't work."

"Will you get one fitted?"

He shrugs. "I don't know. It would reduce the value, but I didn't buy this purely as an investment, otherwise I wouldn't even be driving it." His eyes crinkle at the corners. "I've always wanted this car."

"A psychologist would have a field day with that. Given the timing and all."

"They'd probably be right to," he admits, with a sheepish grin. "I'm basically driving the deposit I'd saved for a house with Jenna."

I can't help laughing. He doesn't join in, but he's grinning.

"You've been lucky settling back into London," I comment. "Back in your old flat, back on your old desk at work, except a few rungs up the ladder . . . Did you think about staying in Boston?"

He shakes his head. "Boston is a great city. But I never felt . . . settled there. Maybe it was my fault; I didn't properly commit to staying long-term. Once Jenna and I split up, there was nothing to keep me there." The sun is streaming directly through the windscreen; he finds some sunglasses and puts them on one-handed with remarkable dexterity. "What about you? What made you go out on your own? Starting your own business in this climate can't be easy.

I don't remember you even mentioning the idea when you came out to Boston."

I close my eyes and rest my head back against the seat, feeling the sun soak into my face. "Oh, you know me," I say airily. "I'm basically unemployable."

"Rubbish. You have a first from Oxford and the best CV of anyone we know."

"Slight exaggeration, but anyway, I didn't say I was unhirable. I'm unemployable. As in, unsuitable for employment." My eyes are still closed.

"Ah," he says, understanding. "You mean, much better suited to being the employer."

"Exactly." I open my eyes and turn my head, still resting on the headrest, to look at him. I can't see his eyes through the sunglasses, but I know what they look like. Seb doesn't freckle, though. "I got fed up of being overlooked in favor of inferior lawyers who had the right accent and went to the right school." I grimace. "I may have been vocal about it from time to time."

"How can you spot a balanced northerner?" asks Tom. He goes on before I can answer: "They have a chip on *both* their shoulders."

He's teasing me, but I know he understands, at least in part. Tom's whole upbringing has put him on the outside looking in: looking in on Seb, whose father is some kind of nobility—a marquis or a baron or an earl, I forget exactly what—with the stately home and vast grounds one might expect along with such a title. Tom grew up in a cottage on the estate, gifted by the earl-or-marquis-or-baron to his little sister, Tom's mother, when she married a penniless academic.

"Anyway, one day one of the partners told me I was the best candidate for partner he'd ever come across, but if I couldn't learn to shut my mouth and put up with some crap from time to time, there was no way I'd even make the short list. I'd be turfed out."

"What did you say to that?" Tom asks.

"Not much at the time. I was too furious to say anything at all really. But then I thought about it . . . and he was right. There's no way they could make me partner the way I was; it would be like . . . like putting itching powder on everyone's skin."

"And you didn't want to change?"

"I could have changed . . . well, maybe . . . but not for that firm. Too traditional, too old-school. It got me thinking about how important it is to get the right fit when you hire someone. I mean, they should never have hired me in the first place. I expect they were trying to fill some diversity quota: female, went to a state school . . ."

Tom remains quiet. I close my eyes again and turn my face to the sun. The thrum of the car is soporific. Time becomes elastic; I have no idea how much is passing.

"You never told me much about your meeting with the detective," I hear Tom say.

I open my eyes again reluctantly. I don't want Severine to intrude today. She doesn't belong in the sunshine. "Not much to tell. He just went over the timings of when we left, really."

"Nothing else?" he asks casually.

"No," I say, bemused. I think back to the meeting; it doesn't seem my place to tell him about Lara's fascination with the detective. Though perhaps I should if Tom is going to get hurt . . .

"What?" asks Tom, noticing my hesitation.

"Nothing." I grope around for something to cover with. "Just—well, he said he didn't think it was the boyfriend."

Tom is nodding. "Yeah, Theo's dad told me he's out of the picture."

"Modan was a bit more conditional than that. It seems to hinge on the timing of when the well was filled in, I think." I frown. "But surely they know when that was done."

Tom shakes his head and says carefully, "There's some confusion." He appears to be intent on the road; with his sunglasses on, I can't read his expression at all.

"How come? Can't they check with the builders?" I can see the two builders in my head: both in their thirties, unmistakably brothers, with the same swarthy complexion, dark hair and heavy eyebrows. I remember watching them watch us; I remember the resentment in their eyes and the sense of unease it put in me. I could see us from their perspective: the careless, awful presumptions of privilege. I wanted to say, "But I'm not one of them!" Only I was, at least for that week.

"Haven't tracked them down again yet. But according to the records that the police looked at then, the well was filled in on the Friday." He glances across at me. Oddly I have the same feeling as with the detective: he is watching me, waiting for something. I shake my head dumbly. He elaborates. "Friday, Kate. The day before we left."

"But that's . . . that's impossible." I'm no longer sleepy. "Severine was with us on Friday night."

"I know that. You know that." He shrugs.

I am upright in my seat now, twisted sideways to stare at Tom's profile. He's calmly focusing on the road ahead. "There's CCTV footage of Severine at the bus depot on Saturday morning," I argue heatedly. "And the bus driver remembered her getting on at the stop by the farmhouse. So she obviously wasn't, you know, stuffed in a well at that point." The skull is there, with the dirt and the sand and the insects; I shake my head violently. It doesn't dislodge.

"I know, I know." Tom takes a hand off the wheel and spreads it out, palm up. "I'm just saying, there are inconsistencies. Things like that, they muddy the waters. Which could be rather . . . inconvenient for us, until it's all sorted out."

I'm still staring at him. He turns his head and takes in my expression. "Kate," he says gently. "It's going to be fine. I just wanted to bring you up to speed. It will all be fine."

He smiles in what's meant to be a reassuring manner. But I can't see his eyes behind those sunglasses.

Lunch is a pleasure, or should be a pleasure, but I can't shake a sense of unease. It flows beneath every conversation and fills every silence. Tom's parents don't notice—his mother is glowing to have her son at home again, however temporarily, and his dad's gruff welcome belied the delight in his eyes—but Tom's gaze rests on me frequently. I can't read what his eyes hold, which only adds to my unease. Tom's dad has a heavy hand with the wine; by dessert I'm surreptitiously drinking as much water as possible in mitigation.

"How is your mum, Kate?" asks Tom's mother kindly. "Do you get up north to see her much?"

"She's well, thanks." Tom's mum has her head cocked on one side, listening to me sympathetically. I can see Tom in her. It makes me more open than I might otherwise be; that, or the wine. "She seems happy. She remarried last year. I guess I don't go up now as much as I used to."

"You don't get on with her new husband?"

I shake my head. "No, he's fine." I hear my words and correct them. "He's nice, actually. Dad's been gone a long time." Almost ten years. I got the news only weeks after Seb and I broke up. "It's great to think that she's not on her own anymore. But it's just . . . different, I guess."

Both Tom and his mother are looking at me. I duck my head and take a swallow of wine.

After lunch, Tom's parents won't hear of us helping with the clearing up; instead they shoo us out to walk off our overindulgence on the estate grounds. We climb a small ridge and are suddenly presented with an uninterrupted view across a lawn to the main house. Seb's house. Well, his father's house.

"You would think—" I say, stopping to stare at the enormous white-painted building. It's from the Regency era, I seem to recall. There are columns and wings and more windows than I could reliably count. I start again. "You would think I would've been here." I look at Tom. He isn't meeting my eye. "Don't you think?" I challenge him. "Wouldn't you think that if you went out with someone for a year, you might see where they live when they're not at college?" Tom doesn't answer. I persist. "Wouldn't you think that?"

"I don't think it was intentional," Tom hedges. "He didn't deliberately *not* invite you."

"Maybe." I find a large rock to sit on. I've had too much to drink. I think of Caro, in France. *Of course, you've met Lord Harcourt, haven't you? Such a dear.* Her sharp eyes watching me, birdlike, readying to swoop in on any tidbits I give away. *You haven't? Really?* "Then again, maybe not."

Tom runs a hand through his hair and sighs. "Look, Seb's relationship with his father is—complicated. I'm sure the lack of invitation had nothing to do with you and everything to do with that."

"Maybe," I repeat. I lean down to pick up some earth and watch it dribble through my fingers. "Maybe not."

"It's been ten years, Kate," Tom says. The hard note in his voice snaps my head up to look at him. "When are you going to get over it?"

I look away; I can't speak. We don't do this, Tom and I; we don't bring up this particular elephant in the room. We can be friends provided we skirt round the edges. I must be drunk to have violated that. I don't think he has the same excuse given he's driving.

Suddenly Tom is hunkered down in front of me. "Kate, I'm sorry." He reaches out a hand to turn my face to him. His eyes are unhappy and his mouth is twisted in remorse. "Oh Christ, please don't cry, I didn't mean . . . It's just . . . I'm sorry."

I take a shaky breath, then meet his eyes briefly and attempt a smile. "Me, too. I think I'm what's known as tired and emotional."

"Come on, you." He stands up and pulls me gently to my feet. "Let's get you home." My face feels cold where his hand has been. He threads my arm through his and we walk back to the cottage in companionable silence.

In the car on the way home I can't fight the thrum of the engine and the alcohol in my system: I fall asleep. I wake slowly with a memory or a dream of someone stroking my cheek. Tom is grinning at me affectionately. The day of sunshine has brought out some of his freckles. "Wakey wakey, sleeping beauty," he says. For a moment I'm displaced; the world hasn't yet dropped into position around me. For a moment Tom is just Tom and I'm just Kate, without any past or future. Without any context.

Then everything rushes back.

CHAPTER FIVE

On Monday morning, Gordon Farrow's secretary calls to resurrect our lunch, for two days hence. I would crow over Paul except I've lost all faith. In any case, Paul looks like he can't take another cycle of hope-raising and -dashing. A small contract he was counting on—that we were both counting on—has fallen through. His trenchant defeatism curls around him like a fog; being near him brings a chill. I haven't known him long enough to estimate how long this will last; at this rate I may not keep him long enough to find out. I return again and again to the financial spreadsheet that holds my future in its tiny white cells. The entries don't change.

Even lunch with Lara fails as a tonic. We meet at a café halfway between our offices; uncharacteristically, she's beaten me there. There's a glass of wine in front of her with a lipstick mark on it. I nod my head toward it after we kiss our hellos. "Taking the rest of the day off?" Lara can't function professionally after the merest sniff of alcohol. She has few rules, but no lunchtime drinking is one of them.

She shakes her head. "I'll be there in body if not in mind." She takes a sip of the wine, then puts the glass down. Then picks it up again. "Anyway, shall we order?" She puts the glass back down.

"Sure . . ." We nab the waitress and order our usuals, then I sit back and look at Lara. "Is everything okay?"

"Sure. Of course." She smiles brightly, but it doesn't reach her eyes, and her eyes don't reach mine.

"How was Sweden?"

"Same old. Mum has a new man."

"How is he?"

"Very . . . Swedish," she says wryly. "Bearded. Friendly. Earnest. But kind of sweet." Finally I see her eyes. They're jittering around, as if it hurts to settle her focus. "Anyway, how was your weekend? Did you have fun with Tom?"

"Yeah, it was lovely," I say, out of habit, then wonder if that's accurate. It was lovely on the surface, but I have a sense of something lurking underneath. Or maybe my paranoia over the possibility of Paul jumping ship is bleeding into the rest of my life. I mentally shake myself and look at Lara's eyes again. "Jeez, Lara, did you spend the weekend taking drugs or something?"

"Of course not!" she exclaims, scandalized.

"Then what's with you?"

"Nothing! Except . . . I think I had one too many Red Bulls this morning," she confesses, propping up her temple with the heel of one palm. "You wouldn't believe how my heart has been racing." She gestures at the glass of wine. "Alcohol's a depressant, isn't it? I thought it might counteract the caffeine."

"Honey, alcohol is just fanning the flames." It would be funny except Lara doesn't look like she's having any fun. She looks almost feverish. "Let me put that glass aside—here, have my water instead. Why the caffeine overdose, anyway?"

She takes a long drink of the water and shrugs. "My flight was delayed so I was late to bed and then I couldn't get to sleep for ages." She pauses. I wait; there's more to come. Whatever it is, she's half defensive about it. I'm not sure what the other half of her is feeling. "I bumped into Alain at the airport." Her eyes flit to mine then away.

Alain. Not *Monsieur Modan*, or *the French detective*. "How very coincidental," I say evenly. "Had you told him what flight you were on?"

"No, it was just a chance meeting. He was on his way back from spending the weekend in the south of France." She takes in my expression and puts her hand on my arm, leaning forward entreatingly. "Come on. You have to admit it really *could* be a coincidence."

"It could," I say non-contentiously. But I doubt it. "What did you talk about?"

She blushes. "You know . . ." I don't actually. I shake my head questioningly. "We just *talked*. Nothing happened, really." Really? Now I'm wondering what *did* happen. Her hand is still on my arm, her eyes urgent. I nod, though I still don't understand; the nod is enough to allow the words to flood out of her. "I know we ought not, with the investigation and everything, but it's not like the six of us had anything to do with that. Alain and I . . . well, we just talked about . . . what we might do when this is all over. What we would like to do." Her expression is begging me to understand. I shake my head minutely; I don't. "You know . . . to do to each other . . ."

I stare at her, openmouthed. She's squirming, but her eyes are bright with excitement. It's not the caffeine overdose that's making her feverish; she's the girl with a secret that's just bursting to tell. Jesus. Lara has been talking dirty with the French detective. I rediscover my voice. "All this in, what, the baggage reclaim lounge?"

"Of course not! We, um, we grabbed a drink in the bar."

"Ah." I don't know how to convey the alarm bells that are ringing in my mind. Lara is never this excited over a man, ever; I suspect she won't take it kindly if I steal the wind from her sails, but this . . . I don't know what this is, exactly, but I do know it's not a good idea. I struggle to find a casual tone. "Did he . . . did he ask about Severine?"

She nods. "A bit. Well, not so much Severine, more about that week in general. You know, about all of us, how we met, who was with who, that sort of thing. It wasn't like an interview; it was just idle chat."

"Of course, idle chat. In between the virtual sex, that is."

"Kate!" She giggles. She's actually giddy. "It wasn't like that."

"Uh-huh." Idle chat. About a murder case. I think of Alain Modan. I imagine his active brain working away behind those dark, ironic eyes; scurrying like a rat in a maze to explore all potential avenues. Tom's words float back to me: *There are inconsistencies. Things like that, they muddy the waters.* "Did he tell you they're looking into when the well was filled in?"

She nods. "He mentioned that. I suppose they have to tick every box, but it seems a waste of effort since it was obviously after we left. But they have to do it. Apparently they even have to try and pin down exactly which ferry we were on so they have confirmation of when we left the farmhouse. It's really hard work for him," she says earnestly, then looks up as the waitress arrives with our plates. "Oh, thank you."

I start eating mechanically, my mind full of Monsieur Modan, and Tom's words, and Severine—always Severine, with her walnut skin and secretive eyes, hovering just out of sight. "Why is he even back in the UK?" I ask suddenly.

"What?" Lara looks up from her salad.

"Modan. I thought he interviewed us all. Why is he still here?"

"Oh. Yeah, he said he had a few more questions."

"For who?"

"For whom," she corrects with a glimmer of a smile. Lara prides herself on having better English than any native-born. "Actually, for you, I think." She shrugs. "Probably my fault, I suppose; after all, I did interrupt your session with him."

Another interview. I reach for the wineglass.

"And for Seb, of course," she adds, with an apologetic grimace. "Apparently he'll be back in the country this week." She goes on hesitantly, "Are you . . . Are you okay with that? Seb being back, I mean?"

"I daresay I'll cope." It comes out harsher than intended; Lara flinches. I'm instantly remorseful. "I'm sorry, honey, I don't mean to snap; I'm just having a shitty week." She nods sympathetically, accepting the apology. I feel guilty enough to consider her question more carefully. "I actually don't know what I feel. I suppose I spent so long avoiding thinking about him that I'm not sure *what* I think anymore."

She cocks her head. "So maybe it would be good for you to see him."

"Maybe." I take a swallow of the wine. "But in an ideal world, not in a week where my business is going under and I'm being interviewed in connection with a murder."

She laughs. "Come on, that's a little dramatic. We're just helping the investigation; we're not really *suspects*."

"Well, that depends."

"What do you mean?"

"That depends on when the well was filled in. Or at least, when the police think the well was filled in."

She stares at me. Her eyes have finally found their focus. "You really think—but he hasn't said anything . . ." She trails off, then visibly shakes herself. "But of course the well was sealed after we left. The builders will say that."

"Of course," I agree easily. "When the police find them."

"When they find them," she echoes. She is silent for a moment, then cocks her head and looks at me piercingly. "You think I'm being played."

"I don't know," I admit reluctantly, but honestly. I remember the sudden stillness in Modan's face when he saw Lara again. "I think— I think that he would very much like to do whatever he told you he'd like to do to you . . ." Now I'm the one blushing. "But whatever you said about the six of us—he can't 'unhear' it. You weren't being interviewed, but he'll use it, if it helps him." She looks at me thoughtfully but doesn't say anything. I don't know if she's upset, and if so, with me or Modan. "I'm just saying . . . be careful, honey." I reach out and touch her arm. "I don't want you to get hurt."

Finally she catches my hand in hers and smiles. "I know. I'll be careful." She changes the subject deliberately, and as we talk, I see that half of her focus is elsewhere: reliving aural sex in a transport hub, perhaps, or dreaming up meetings yet to come; in any case, half her mind is threaded through with *Alain, Alain, Alain.*

I suspect Lara's definition of *careful* won't match mine.

W ednesday dawns bright and sunny, but blustery, with a bite in the wind. It's the kind of day that could go either way. Fitting.

I'm early to the restaurant; the staff haven't quite finished preparing our table. I deposit myself on an uncomfortably low sofa in the entrance area, flicking through a newspaper that was laid out for just this purpose. The economy is not improving, small businesses are going under at an alarming rate. I turn that page quickly.

"Kate?" I look up, my automatic welcome smile pasted on, only this isn't Gordon. It's not even a male voice.

"Caro," I say with unconcealed surprise. I scramble to my feet inelegantly from the low seat. She's wearing an impeccable dark skirt suit that looks ultra-fashionable and ultra-expensive, and beautiful kitten heels. Her hair is scraped back into a perfect chignon. It's alarming how closely she fits the image I had of her in work attire. We double-kiss, our cheeks barely grazing. "What a surprise. Are you eating here today?" For a confused moment I wonder if Gordon has asked her to join us.

"No, I was just stalking you," she says breezily, then grins impishly at my expression. "Relax. I was just passing—this place is a stone's throw from our office." This is true; it's why Gordon's a fan of the restaurant. "I spotted you through the window. How are you?"

"Um, good, thanks. You?" I'm still thrown. She spotted me, and she actually *chose* to come in and talk to me?

She flaps a hand. "Good, busy—you know, same old, same old." She pauses. "How did it go with the detective?"

"Fine," I say, shrugging. "Though we got interrupted so I'm meeting him again this week."

"What a bore for you," she says, rolling her eyes theatrically. "What sort of things was he asking?"

"Much the same as he asked everyone, I suppose. When we left, how we got home, that sort of thing. You?"

She nods quickly. Too quickly. "Yes, that sort of thing. Lots on everyone's timings that last morning. And about the builders and the well and when the girl was planning to leave." Her head is cocked on one side, watching and waiting. I wonder exactly which of her words she's expecting a reaction to.

"Severine," I say quietly. "Her name was Severine." The skull grins knowingly at me.

"God, you do have a bee in your bonnet about that." Caro sounds amused, but somehow I don't think she is. "Did he show you the CCTV footage?"

I shake my head. "No, what footage? Do you mean Severine at the bus station?"

She nods. "It's a joke," she says, throwing up a hand expressively. "You can barely tell it's a person. Technology has moved a looooong way in the last decade, believe me. Thank God the bus driver remembered her getting on his bus, or things might be rather more uncomfortable for us all right now." She laughs a high, tinkling laugh, much less genuine than her earlier sly grin. I think of breaking glass.

"Caro," says a mild voice behind her. Gordon has arrived.

"Dad," she says, turning to him. This time the smile she pulls on is overly bright. "Don't worry, I'm not stealing your lunch date." He rubs her arm awkwardly in lieu of a kiss; perhaps they never kiss during the working day. I suppose it would be a little disconcerting for others around the office.

"Hello, Gordon," I say, smiling. We shake hands and tell each other it's a pleasure and so on. Which it actually is, at least for me.

Caro explains to her father: "I just popped in to tell Kate that we have a date for Seb's return." I feel a quick burst of triumph that I knew this already. She turns to me. "He'll be back this week, so we'll have to have another get-together of the old gang. Maybe a restaurant this time. What do you think?"

I'm on my best behavior given Gordon's presence. "Good idea." Then I look for something intelligent to add. "Less people, which might be better for Alina. Less overwhelming."

"Oh, I wouldn't worry about that," Caro says, unconcerned. It's not clear whether she means that Alina, whom I've never met, is not easily overwhelmed, or whether Caro simply doesn't care whether she's overwhelmed or not. "I just thought it'd be a nice change since we just did the drinks party thing for Tom." She glances at her watch and grimaces. "Oops, back to the grindstone. I have a conference call in five, which may well last till five—no rest for the wicked." She rolls her eyes again. "Enjoy your lunch."

I look at Gordon as he watches her clip smartly out of the restaurant; perhaps I'm expecting to see love or pride or benevolent affection. Instead he seems . . . what? I can't decipher his face, though he watches for longer than feels comfortable. Then he feels my eyes upon him and turns with eyebrows raised. "Well, shall we?"

We order and eat and talk business, but general business, not the specific business I'm chasing. Other firms and their hiring practices, the restructuring taking place in the legal industry, the mergers that are being rumored: these are the things we discuss. I wait for Gordon to broach the subject, but our main courses swoop down, and then dessert, and then coffee, and still we're circling around.

Gordon reaches for the sugar and drops a cube into his cup, paying the task more attention than it deserves. Now, I think. Now we will come to the matter at hand.

"So," he says. He's too precise for such a casual opening; it comes out strained. "I understand from Caro that you, too, have been dragged into this awful French investigation. It must be rather unpleasant for you."

I blink, completely thrown. Why is he bringing this up? "Well, I . . . Of course I'm happy to help the investigation, but rest assured, it would have no impact on my company's ability to perform under the contract, if we were to be engaged—"

"Oh no," he interrupts me, startled. "I didn't mean—I didn't think that for a second."

I look at him uncertainly. He seems a little embarrassed.

"Caro seems rather shaken by the whole thing," he says diffidently. "I just meant to . . . well, to ask how *you* are. That's all."

"Oh." I watch him stirring his already-stirred coffee, then realize I ought to say something more. "Well, that's very kind of you." Before I can add something appropriately inane, like *I'm fine, though it's certainly unsettling*, before I can reassert my professionalism without seeming callous in comparison to the "rather shaken" Caro (really?), Severine's skull begins to laugh mockingly at me, sand streaming from one eye socket. I hastily grab my coffee cup and take a sip.

"On to business, then," says Gordon. He seems as keen to move on from this little interlude as I am.

I agree quickly. "Yes, on to business." Business I can do. Business is what I need.

I take the tube back from lunch. The stark white spreadsheet cells have been telling me that cabs are not advisable at present. In any case, I like the anonymity of London's crowded public transport system; it gives me space to think. All these people thrown into a confined space, yet nobody feels a need to talk. Or to ask questions.

Gordon has been asking me many questions; it's exhausting. When I get back to the office, Paul will ask what Gordon asked me. Alain Modan has been asking me different questions, and apparently he's going to keep asking. Caro has been asking me what Modan has been asking. Now I come to think of it, even Tom has been probing me about what Modan is asking.

Severine doesn't ask questions. Those dark, unreflective eyes made their judgment a decade ago.

CHAPTER SIX

'm staring at the spreadsheet again. The once-clinical black numbers have developed their own presence; they cross the divide between my eyes and the computer screen and beat malevolently into my brain. Two small alterations were all that was required for the verdict to go from "solvent, for now" to "completely underwater": a change in tax law that means a hefty payment cannot be deferred, and my landlord demanding an increase in rent, which he's entitled to do at this point in the lease, though the size of the increase he's asking for is outrageous. I can fight him on it, I *will* fight him on it—or at least, I *want* to fight him on it, but that will cost money the business doesn't have. He probably suspects this and is trying to squeeze me out. With more detachment I might admire his Machiavellian streak, but right now admiration is not high on my list of feelings. Ditto detachment.

I drop my head into my hands to escape the spreadsheet's toxic radiation. I could move the business location somewhere cheaper—my living room, say, or perhaps somewhere more extreme, like Croydon or Thailand—but not whilst keeping Paul, and without headhunters, is there really any life in a headhunting firm? It was a key part of my business plan that I not be a one-woman shop: numbers inspire confidence. Though not the ones in this spreadsheet.

"You okay, Kate?" asks Julie, as she comes in from the outer office.

I lift my head quickly and paste on a smile for her. She has her glasses in one hand and is pinching the bridge of her nose with the other. I wonder why she doesn't wear contact lenses, but not enough to ask. "Fine," I say brightly, probably too brightly. "Just a headache from too much screen time."

"I'm popping out for a sandwich. Want me to grab you anything?"

"No, thanks, I'll get something later and give my legs a stretch."

"Okay." She glances across at Paul's empty desk, frowns briefly, then turns to go.

"Julie, what's Paul's schedule today?" I ask casually.

She turns back. "I'm not sure," she says awkwardly. "I thought he'd be here now."

"Mmmm." I tap my teeth with a pen, then realize she's still there, unsure of whether to leave or not. "No worries." I adopt a reassuringly cheerful tone. There's an emptiness in my stomach; it's growing and hardening. "I'll give him a call. Go on and get your lunch."

"All right."

All right. All right. No, nothing much is *all right*, but I have to go on as if it is. I sigh and lift the phone to vehemently threaten my landlord with legal action I can't afford.

Alain Modan. Monsieur Modan. French detective, *Investigateur*, *OPJ*—and whisperer of naughty things in the perfect ear of my best friend, Lara. Alain Modan is sitting on a sofa opposite me once again, though this time we're in a comfortable corner of Starbucks rather than my living room.

I have little patience today. I can feel it inside me; there's a recklessness bubbling up around the malignant tumor of worry about my business, a recklessness that's pushing me to want to cut through bullshit, to tell and hear it straight, to face the worst and know what I'm up against *right now*. Alain Modan is probably the last person I should be talking to in this mental condition, but I am here and so is he; we have our coffees and we've covered the pleasantries—with no mention of Lara—so now we begin.

"*Alors*," says Modan, placing a manila folder on the table and flipping through his pad. He's removed the jacket of his suit; underneath is a slim-fitting pale blue shirt. I wonder if the skin under that shirt has the same soft grain as that on his face; I wonder if there is a tangle of chest hair under that spotless cotton. Perhaps it's his French flair that makes me consider these things, or perhaps I'm trying to see through Lara's eyes. Perhaps both.

Modan's eyes have moved from his pad to my face. I force myself to focus. "I should bring you up to speed, *non*?" He sounds pleased with himself for the figure of speech.

I glance at the folder. In films, folders like this one—this size, this shape, this color—always hold photos, gruesome murder scenes frozen in an instant of time. Bodies at awkward angles; blood pooled beneath caved heads; open, staring eyes: death immortalized forever. I don't want to see inside this folder. "Go ahead," I say shortly.

"You are in a hurry?" he asks, his mouth quirking.

"Not especially, but I do have a business to run." I almost laugh as I hear the words from my mouth, though it's not in the least bit funny.

He nods. "Of course. Well, we have found one of the builders, Monsieur Casteau. He has gone through his paperwork, which states that the well was filled in on the Friday. The day before you left."

"Bullshit."

He looks at me. "Excuse me?"

"Bull. Shit," I say clearly. "You have six"—I shake my head abruptly: *Theo*. Not six, not ever again six—"no, five people who can attest to that. The builders did the pool fence while we were there, but I don't remember them anywhere near the well. The paperwork is wrong and the builder is lying." The recklessness is spilling over; I struggle to stamp it down.

Modan is not fazed by my combativeness. "It was a long time ago," he allows. "And Monsieur Casteau thinks it was his brother who actually did the work on the well; he can't remember doing it himself."

"And what does the brother say?"

"We haven't been able to speak with him yet. He's on"—he stretches for the word—"ah, *miel*, ah, honey . . . moon. Honeymoon, *oui*?" I nod. "Trekking. In the Himalayas." He makes a movement with his mouth that shows that yomping through the Himalayas is not his idea of a post-wedding treat.

The folder lies there still, untouched. "Regardless. You have five people who say the well wasn't filled in. Why are you spending time on this?"

One eyebrow raises a little. "It's our job to be thorough."

I press on. "What about the bus driver? He remembers Severine, right?"

He looks at me, his long face displaying nothing except his habitual watchfulness. "The bus driver remembers that a young girl climbed on near the farmhouse and traveled to the station. He described her as wearing dark sunglasses and having her hair tied in a red scarf."

I see Severine, smoking a cigarette at the end of the garden whilst speaking rapidly on the phone. It's morning; there's still a freshness in the air that the sun will beat into submission within an hour or so. Severine's dressed in her uncompromising black bikini, a red chiffon scarf tied turban-like on her head; her back is to me, and I can see the delicate wings of her shoulder blades moving under her skin as she gestures with her cigarette hand. It's a look that's reminiscent of the 1950s, of glamorous movie stars in oversize sunglasses lounging on the French Riviera. At that moment I wish she was gone with an intensity I don't understand; more than that, I wish she had never been. But today, to Modan I murmur, "Yes. Severine."

He shrugs, a curiously nonsymmetrical movement that suggests his limbs are moved by a puppet-master. It should be awkward, but not so on Modan. "Perhaps."

I look at him sharply. "Perhaps?"

He shrugs again, right shoulder then left. "Perhaps."

"And the CCTV from the bus depot?"

He reaches for the folder and holds it out to me. "*Regardez-vous*. Please, look."

I force myself to breathe as I take the folder from him and slowly open it. Inside there is indeed a photo: a grainy image, not so much black-and-white as shades of gray. In among what must be the bus depot forecourt, I can make out a figure that is most likely a slender girl, perhaps with her hair tied under a scarf or perhaps wearing some kind of cap. She appears to be standing by a large bag. I look up at Modan, dismayed. "This is it?"

He raises a couple of fingers briefly, somehow conveying *we really tried* and *c'est la vie* in one small movement. "That is the best picture we could get."

I look back again at the photo. Caro may have exaggerated a little—it's definitely a person—but her point is still valid: this counts for nothing. I keep looking, as if it's a digital image that needs time to resolve, but the fuzzy edges refuse to settle into a clear picture. All the while my mind loops over the same cycle: the well, the bus driver, the CCTV image. The well, the bus driver, the CCTV image.

One of these things is not like the other . . . the well, the bus driver, the CCTV image . . . one of these things . . .

I thrust the folder back at Modan. "Why are you still here?" I ask him abruptly.

"I have a few more questions—"

"Yes, but why are you still *here*? As in, in this country?" I interrupt impatiently. "I know you have to be thorough. You've *been* thorough, you've spoken to us all, so what's keeping you here? You have five people who saw her alive on Friday night, you have a bus driver who had someone exactly like her climbing on his bus on Saturday, you have a picture of that same girl at the depot with a bag; it all points pretty clearly to her being alive and well after we left." The recklessness has its head and won't be quieted. "But you're still here, and I can't figure it out, unless you're looking for an excuse to spend more time jeopardizing your career by ambushing Lara in airports"—he looks away quickly and rakes a hand through his hair, then fixes wary eyes upon me, but I won't be derailed—"or unless you actually don't believe us. Is that it? Do you actually believe that all five of us are lying? Are we in fact suspects?" I stop abruptly. The recklessness is spent.

Modan looks at me for a moment, his face expressionless. I have no doubt he is busy working out how best to handle me. Then his face softens. "Miss Channing," he says gently. "This is difficult. It is always difficult, murder is . . . *alors*, murder is not a nice thing. No one wants to think about it too hard; it's upsetting, it's intrusive, it is frustrating, it is inconvenient. But to find whoever did this, we have to investigate, we *have* to ask questions." He makes one of his elegant hand gestures, spreading his hand wide with the palm up, almost as if inviting me to place my own in it, while his lips move in a sympathetic smile. "So . . . *s'il vous plaît* . . . may I continue?"

I hold his gaze for a moment. I can't read what is going on behind those dark, watchful eyes, but I know he's better at this than me.

Better at this than almost everyone, I would think. I'm suddenly exhausted. "Go on," I say wearily. "Ask your questions."

Afterward I know I should go back to the office, but I can't face the possibility of an empty chair opposite me, or staring again at that spreadsheet. Instead I wander aimlessly. A short walk takes me into the throngs on Regent Street. The gaggles of foreign tourists are easy to identify, with their cameras and white socks pulled up and sensible shoes, but what is everyone else doing on a shopping street in the middle of the day? Are they students? Or do they work nights? Do they work at all?

I wonder what I will do when I finally call time on my company. I won't be able to go back to practicing law: I'm not sure I'd be able to convince any firm that I really wanted to—mainly because I don't. I suppose I could work for another legal recruitment firm, but my credibility will be damaged by a failed solo venture; it might take quite a while to land any position, let alone one I really want. And the truth is that the one I want is the one that's slipping away from me right now.

I walk into French Connection then walk back out again. It's too busy, and anyway, I don't really have the will or the patience to look at clothes or try anything on. I start walking again and see my reflection moving from one window display to the next, a wraith in a dark trouser suit slipping unnoticed past the mannequins in their forward-thinking summer attire. I could just . . . leave, I think. Get on a plane, find myself somewhere hot and dusty where living costs a pittance. Slough off my skin and take a waitressing job, or tend bar—take any job, unfettered by the pride and expectations that are built up by an Oxbridge education; built up until they wall you in.

My mobile phone rings; number withheld. I hesitate, unwilling to be wrenched back into the real world, but the phone continues to chirp aggressively. I sigh and hit the answer button. "Kate Channing."

"Hey, it's Tom. How are you?"

"Halfway to South America."

There's half a beat of silence. "Really?" he asks uncertainly.

"No, not really. Just wishful thinking. Bad day."

"Well, in that case I'm taking the spot on the plane next to you. Bad day here too." He does in fact sound exhausted. "Want to grab a drink later and commiserate?"

I hesitate. "I'll be dreadful company," I warn.

"Yeah, me too," he says grimly. "We might as well get smashed together rather than poisoning the mood of anyone else."

"Jesus." This is a far cry from the easy, steadfast Tom I'm used to. "What happened to you today?"

"Can't talk here," he says laconically.

He can't talk in the office. Intuition strikes me: all those articles about the poor economy and downsizing in the major banks . . . Surely his firm wouldn't have been so stupid as to agree to relocate him from Boston to London just to fire him? Except I know banks can be exactly that stupid, and more so. "You still have a job, right?" I ask urgently.

"I do. Others . . . not so much."

"Jesus." The atmosphere must be awful on the trading floor. "Well, my company is well and truly fucked so I'm just the girl for a truly depressing night on the town. Seven at the same pub we met at before?"

"Done." He pauses. "Is it really fucked?"

"Yes," I say baldly. "Only a miracle will suffice at this point."

I hear a sigh down the phone. "I'm really sorry, Kate." His words are heartfelt; I feel a rush of warmth toward him.

"I know. I am, too. About your situation, I mean." About my own, too.

"Well, at least one of us still has a paycheck," he says with dark humor. "Which means I'm buying tonight. I can keep you fed and watered for one night, at least."

"No argument from me. See you at seven."

I disconnect then look up to see my ghostly self hovering in front of a swimwear montage, a smile still in place from the phone call that fades as I watch. The promise of a new life, a different life, still lies tantalizingly in reach. But I have things to do before I meet Tom at seven.

I head back to my office.

I don't look at the spreadsheet and I don't look at Paul's empty chair. Instead I deal with e-mail and bash on determinedly with the calls I have to make. It's not so much a fighting spirit as a grim fatalism that drives me on: the few contracts we do have, we need to deliver on—on time and in style. Nobody should be able to say Channing Associates failed through a lack of professionalism.

"I've got Gordon from Haft & Weil on the phone for you," calls Julie.

For a moment I consider telling her to take a message. I've been expecting a call from him, to tell me he's awarding the contract to a rival firm. I could do without the final nail in the coffin . . . but why delay the inevitable? "Put him through, please."

The phone in front of me buzzes after a moment. I find a smile to drape on my lips. "Good afternoon, Gordon. How are you?"

"Very well, thank you. Is this a good time?"

"Absolutely. Fire away." *Fire away*. Not that he can really fire me since he's never actually hired me, but still, the inadvertent gallows humor amuses me. I will tell Tom that later, I think. I can already see his eyes crinkling above that unmistakable nose.

"I want to tell you that OpCom met last night." OpCom is the operating committee of Haft & Weil. Whatever recommendation of recruitment firm Gordon made would have had to be ratified by them, but really as a rubber-stamping exercise. "We've decided to award the contract to Channing Associates." He pauses, but I'm literally speechless. "Subject to agreeing final documentation, of course."

I sit bolt upright and find my voice. "Well. Thank you." I work hard to sound professional, as if contracts from firms like Haft & Weil drop in my lap every day, but inside the tumor of worry has begun to fizz, dissolving like Alka-Seltzer in water. *Yes! Yes! Yes!* "That's wonderful news. I'm . . . well, I'm delighted to hear that, as I'm sure you can imagine. Delighted, and not a little surprised."

"We felt it was time for some new blood." I can hear the smile in his voice; he likes it when I'm direct. "And I think you and I will deal well together."

"I do, too," I say sincerely. "I'm looking forward to working with you."

"On that note, I've had a contract drawn up. It's fairly standard and has the terms we discussed previously. Shall I send it across now?"

"Perfect." I pause, then add, "Though I should mention that we'll require the retainer fee to be paid quarterly in advance." If he agrees, Channing Associates is definitely solvent. If not, we have some creative accounting to do to get through the three months until the fee comes in. I find I'm holding my breath.

"I can't see a problem with that. Just amend the draft."

Yes! The fizzing has spread to my limbs now; my legs are literally jiggling with suppressed excitement. "I'll do that, and we'll get it back to you as soon as possible. We're keen to start making progress for you."

"Excellent. Speak again soon."

"Absolutely. And thank you again. This is fantastic news."

I put the phone down and put both palms to my flushed cheeks for a moment, feeling my cheeks bunch in a wondering smile. I look across at the empty desk. "Julie!"

"What?" she calls from the outer room.

"We got it!" I spin in my chair exultantly.

"Got what?"

"The contract!" I'm on my feet now, on my way to her room, but she's moving, too; we meet in the doorway. "Haft & Weil. We got it!" I realize I'm actually bouncing.

"That's fantastic!" Impulsively she grabs my hands and begins jumping with me. From the look of relief on her face, I wonder if I should have been paranoid about keeping her as well as Paul.

The external door opens, and Paul comes in, cursing at his disposable cup, which is dripping latte everywhere. He looks askance at Julie and me, still bouncing, our smiles as wide as our mouths can stretch. "What?" He dumps the leaking cup on Julie's desk and looks from me to Julie and back again, nonplussed. "What?"

"We got it!" I croon. "We got it, we got it, we got it!"

"Haft & Weil?" he asks urgently. "Really?"

I nod, beaming at him. "Awesome!" he roars. "Haft & fucking Weil! Fucking awesome!" Then he's slinging an arm round each of our shoulders and all three of us are jumping together and grinning inanely, and I think: *I should remember times like this, remember perfectly. I should bottle them somehow. You don't know how many of these moments you might have in your life.*

CHAPTER SEVEN

By the time I reach the pub a few minutes after seven, I am drunk. Mostly drunk on excitement and drunk on relief, but the champagne Paul nipped out to buy and cracked open in the office has played its part, too. Paul, Julie and I sat on the floor and ate posh crisps whilst drinking the bubbly from mugs. Paul was still shaking his head and saying at regular intervals, "Haft & fucking Weil!" with a broad smile and looking at me with something akin to renewed respect; and Julie was flushed and decidedly unsteady when she eventually left to catch her train. I thought, if we succeed, we will be telling this story in years to come: the anecdote of how Channing Associates celebrated their first big win.

But here and now I'm mildly tipsy, standing just inside the door of the pub once again scanning for Tom. This time I spot him at a table; he's been here long enough to be a third of the way through a pint, with what looks like a vodka tonic waiting for me on the table. His attention is on his phone, and he's had a haircut. For a moment it throws me off balance: he looks sharper, older—*other*. But then he looks up and catches sight of me; he gets up to deliver his trademark hug, his face breaking into a welcoming grin, and I see he still has freckles on his nose—he's Tom again.

"You look . . . suspiciously happy," he says, releasing me and cocking his head in confusion.

I nod and slip into the chair opposite him. My smile needs very little encouragement this evening, already it's spreading across my face. "That miracle I needed. It happened. We just landed a major contract." I adopt a contrite expression. "I'm really sorry for not being miserable."

"Don't be ridiculous, that's fantastic!" He waves away my apology, looking genuinely delighted for me. "I'd much rather toast your success than drown my sorrows. Who did you land?"

"Haft & Weil," I say proudly, taking the vodka tonic he slides across the table to me. "With a big enough retainer to tide us over for a little while. But I'm quietly confident we'll nail the performance fee, and this big a contract is great publicity, I wouldn't be surprised if we get a lot more interest after this—"

"Breathe," he teases affectionately.

"I know, I know; only . . . I really thought we were fucked." The last few days catch at me: the ever-present dread, the seemingly inevitable failure looming over me. I take a deep breath and try to rid myself of the memory, but an echo of it lingers.

"I know," Tom says soberly. "I could hear it in your voice on the phone."

"One contract does not a business make, but still . . ."

"You have to celebrate the wins," Tom says, almost fiercely. "They're important. Regardless of . . . well, regardless." He looks away, almost as if he's embarrassed by his own vehemence.

I take a sip of the vodka tonic. "Well, cheers. And thanks for this. Anyway, tell me about your dreadful day. How many did they let go?"

"Hundreds," he says tiredly. "About fifteen percent all told, apparently. A massacre. The thing is, I'm head of the desk now, so . . ."

"Oh God." My hand is at my mouth. No wonder he's had such an awful day. "You had to do some of the firing."

He nods bleakly. "Four guys. Well, three guys and a girl, actually. I barely knew them—Jesus, I'm fresh off the plane; I've barely had a chance to get to know anyone. At least I didn't have to decide who; the list was already fixed." He takes a swallow from his pint then stares gloomily at it for a moment, slumped in his chair with the pint at the end of his outstretched arms. "I knew there was some kind of restructuring afoot when I moved back here, but I wasn't expecting this. I only heard the details two days ago."

"Do you think it made it easier that you didn't know them? Who you were, well, firing, I mean." I wince a little on the key word.

He shrugs. "I don't know. On the one hand, yes—it's not like I know if they have families to support or anything. On the other hand . . . *shouldn't* it be personal? I mean, you work all hours for a firm—granted you expect to be paid for it, but it's an emotional thing, too; you work hard for your colleagues, you have a laugh with them, you have the odd drink with them . . . Don't you deserve to have someone who actually knows you shake your hand and say—God, I don't know what. *Thank you? It's been a pleasure? You're really good, this is not the end for you . . .*" He shakes his head and stares across the table at his pint again. "Something. I don't know."

"Oh, Tom." There is nothing I can think of to say to that. I take a drink and am surprised to see my glass is almost empty. We sit in brooding silence for a moment. Around us the pub is getting busier and louder.

"You know, there's a good chance at least one of them was really crap," I say eventually, with mock seriousness. "Or had bad breath."

The corner of his mouth tweaks upward a little. "One of the

blokes was quite sweaty," he concedes. "Unpleasantly so. And the girl dressed like she was still a student. Not jeans or anything, but ridiculous floaty skirts that were too short for a trading floor, of all places. And no tights."

"There you go. Definitely best not to be personal, then."

He nods, a ghost of a smile in place, then pulls himself a little more upright. "You know, I used to think that we'd get wherever we got in life because of hard work, because we deserved it," he muses, elbows on the table. "Don't get me wrong: the hard work definitely counts. It's just that luck seems to play a much bigger part than I ever figured."

I think of Theo, of Severine. Luck, or lack thereof. It's an uncomfortable thought. Blaming luck means it could have been any of us: *there but for the grace of God* . . .

He visibly shakes himself. "Anyway, another?"

"Let me get them."

"Nope. You haven't got the money in the door yet; this is still on me." He flashes a quick grin. "When you float Channing Associates for millions, you can pay me back. With interest."

I grin back, then watch him head toward the bar. As the bartender works his order, he checks his phone again, or perhaps it's his work BlackBerry, and for a second the otherness is there again: Tom, but not Tom. Or a different Tom from the one I used to know.

The evening wears on, and we move to a pizza place nearby, where Lara joins us, she and I facing Tom across the table meant for four. We are celebrating, but not; we are commiserating, but not—it was a delicate balance in the pub, but Tom and I were managing it; now Lara's presence is thoroughly destroying the equilibrium. Tom has become more taciturn, Lara is twitchy, and I'm too watchful, though not sober enough to interpret anything I see. And all the while Severine sits at the table too, coolly offhand as if utterly unin-terested, although I suspect she's taking in every nuance with those black eyes.

"At least we're done with Modan," Tom says, out of the blue, unless I missed the segue—or perhaps I'm not the only one who cannot ignore Severine. Lara is peeling the label from a bottle of San Pellegrino. For a moment her hands still, then she takes up the task again.

"You *are* done with him, right?" Tom persists, looking at me.

I don't look at Lara. "I think so."

"Did he interview Seb?" Lara asks; now it's her turn to avoid looking sideways. She sounds brittle and self-conscious; I wonder if she already knows the answer.

Tom looks at me carefully, if a little blearily. "Yep, today," he says mildly.

Lara is looking at me warily too. "It's okay," I say testily. "You're allowed to mention Seb's name around me. I'm not going to freak out." They're still looking at me. "Seriously, guys," I say in exas-peration. "It was a long time ago. And we'll be living in the same city, so . . ." I shrug, unwilling to complete the sentence. So . . . what? *So . . . we're bound to run into each other? So . . . we'll have to be civil? So . . . we've both moved on?* Severine turns her black eyes on mine, and for once the expression within them is entirely clear: scorn. It jolts me.

"In that case, how *is* Seb?" Lara asks Tom.

"Traitorous cow," I say, tongue in cheek. Tom gives a short bark of laughter, then frowns a little and peers at the red wine in his glass, as if uncertain what it might be. *Beer before wine, makes you feel fine . . .*

"I don't know, actually," he admits. "I saw him the other night, but only briefly, and Alina was with him and we couldn't really talk." He frowns again, slumping down even farther in his chair. "There's something . . . You know, he's not in great shape. Physically, I mean, which is unlike him; you know how he likes to work out. I don't know . . ."

I see Seb, what used to be my favorite image of Seb, wearing jeans but his chest still bare—the classic Levi's model look. His beauty is heartbreaking; it's too much, he's too vital, it's impossible to look at him without an awareness that it cannot last. An awareness of mortality.

Tom is still musing. "Caro's seen him, too, a couple of times I think. I should ask her what she thinks."

Caro has seen him a couple of times. Severine looks at me deliberately, a secretive smirk lurking near her mouth. I search for something to say to keep up my end of the conversation. "So you haven't managed to show off your car to him yet." Tom smiles and shakes his head. "He'll be envious."

"I don't know why," says Lara, still busy with the bottle. "It's not like he would ever have bought it himself. He wouldn't be that original." I look at Tom and see my own surprise registering on his face. Lara lifts her head on our silence. "What? He's not. He likes to follow the trend, not set it."

"That's not entirely fair," begins Tom, then stops.

I'm still gazing at Lara. She's right, it's entirely fair, but I would never have seen it that way myself. Lara is a very smart girl, academically speaking, but she's not usually overly given to psychological analysis. "When did you get so insightful?" I murmur.

She ducks her head and turns her attention to shredding a napkin. Alarm bells ring in my mind, and I feel the reverberations in my stomach. "Have you been talking about us again?" I ask urgently.

She turns her head and gives me an accusatory look; I wince internally as I belatedly remember our audience. It's too late now: Tom sits up a little, aware he's missed something.

"What?" he says, when neither of us speak or break our shared eye contact.

After a beat or two she concedes, rolling her eyes. "Go on then," she says, turning back to her napkin.

I turn to Tom. There is no easy way to say this, but I try to find one. "Lara has become . . . friendly . . . with our favorite French detective."

He's already sitting still, but on hearing my words it seems as if even the blood in his veins has stopped moving. After a moment he says, "I see," his face blank and his voice emotionless.

"No, you don't see," says Lara, suddenly close to tears. "Nothing is happening, nothing will happen, until this bloody investigation is cleared up, and now that's going to take even longer—" She stops abruptly, then balls up the napkin and pushes it away from her, not looking at either of us.

"Why is it going to take even longer?" I ask uneasily. She doesn't answer. "Lara, why?" I demand more urgently.

She shakes her head, but she's still Lara, she's still the sunshine girl and she can't keep a secret, either from us or from Modan. "Because they managed to speak with the brother," she says miserably. "The builder brother, I mean. He said he filled in the well on the Saturday. The day we left."

"But—" I'm abruptly cut off by the appearance of the waitress with our long overdue pizzas. I look at Tom in consternation as she busies herself laying them in front of us. His face is still blank, shuttered tight, presumably against revealing his feelings about Lara and Modan. Still, it crosses my mind that he doesn't seem surprised about the well; that he hasn't seemed surprised about anything, right from when he first called me.

"But—" I say again. This time I'm stopped by an infinitesimal shake of Tom's head. He cuts his eyes deliberately to Lara, whose head is down as she recovers her composure, the high spots in her cheeks gradually fading. Then he looks back, and the tiny headshake comes again. The message is clear: *not in front of Lara.*

Lara lifts her head, and her China blue eyes are full of anxiety. "I shouldn't have told you that," she frets, her gaze jumping from me to Tom and back again. "Please don't tell anyone I told you that."

"Lara, it's *us*," I reassure soothingly. "Of course we won't tell." Tom nods in agreement, while I wonder, who would we tell? And why would Modan mind?

"Okay," she says, only slightly mollified. "It's just that, well, he was so disappointed not to be able to rule us all out. We were planning to meet up in Paris next weekend, and now . . ." She looks down at her pizza, tears hovering.

In a moment of alcohol-fueled clarity I see what Lara feels like she's lost. Not just a weekend away, with all the anticipation and intoxication of clothes-tearing-off sex with someone new. Lara sees it as possibly the first weekend of the rest of her life. I can't remember if I felt like that with Seb. The clothes-tearing-off phase I remember. But nobody gets married at university these days, or anytime soon after. I always thought we were playing a long game. In France I realized he'd stopped playing altogether.

"In that case, you'll just have to spend the weekend with us instead," I say, putting my hand on hers. "I foresee two days of epic frivolity. Shopping on the King's Road. Maybe some romcom watching in there, too. Certainly a *lot* of decadent eating out and *absolutely* too much white wine." I'm rewarded by a heartfelt, if tearful, smile from Lara.

"I can cope with the romcom, but can I skip the shopping?" asks Tom dryly.

"Nope," says Lara, gamely trying to recover her equilibrium. "You look like an American. You definitely need to update your wardrobe if you want to be a passably metrosexual male in London."

"Do I *want* to be a metrosexual male? What exactly *is* a metrosexual male?"

I eat my pizza and watch them bat back and forth, the same as they've always done. Except I don't know if it's the same. They were like this before that week in France, and they were like this when they were sleeping together—but surely there must have been differences, some nuances I missed. And now, Tom has realized that Lara is in love, or at least infatuated, with someone other than himself. How can they behave just the same? Perhaps it's a pattern, a learned behavior that one drops into by rote. Perhaps I'll learn something similar with Seb and we'll skate lightly over the surface together whenever we meet in London. How very British. *Everything's fine, just don't mention the war . . .*

As we're finishing up, Lara slips off to the bathroom. Tom watches her go, his face unreadable. I dither on whether to attack the situation head-on. He's never spoken to me directly about her—in the same way that he and I don't discuss Seb—but maybe in this instance I should extend an invitation.

"Are you okay?"

He doesn't answer—he doesn't even acknowledge the question—but as soon as she's out of earshot he leans forward and speaks urgently in a low tone. "Listen, you can't tell Lara anything. You can't talk to her about the case at all. Everything you say is going straight back to Modan."

His urgency pulls me forward, too, mirroring his position. "I know that—of course I know that. But really, what can I say that makes any difference? None of us have anything to hide." Except Caro with the drugs . . . Severine looks at me again. She is whole, but her mocking eyes are as dark as the sockets would be in her bleached white skull.

He makes a sharp cutting gesture with one hand. "It's not about that anymore. The police will be looking to see if any of us could have had a motive."

"We never met her before; well, none of us except Theo. What kind of motive can they possibly come up with?" If Lara comes out of the bathroom and we have our heads together we will look horribly conspiratorial. I sit back in my chair.

"Some subset of the usual, I expect. Jealous rage. Spurned lover." He's watching me closely.

"Spurned lover? But there wasn't any . . ." I stare at him, at the freckles on that unbowed and unbent nose, and feel my world spinning around. There are many things he could be intending with his words. I don't know where to start to unpack his meaning.

I don't get a chance to even try, because suddenly Tom starts talking. ". . . and in the States your vacation entitlement is such an insult. I'm looking forward to some decent looong holidays now I'm back." I stare at him in bemusement. He looks over my shoulder. "Ah, Lara, we were just talking holidays. Any plans?"

"Kate probably told you we were thinking about a safari . . ."

I stare at Tom as Lara reseats herself and chatters on. He glances at me, but there's nothing to read in his face. It was so smoothly done; I would never have guessed he was capable of such casual duplicity—once again, he is *other*. Tom, but not Tom. I wonder, is everyone not who I thought? Maybe nobody ever *really* knows anyone.

And then I wonder: in that case, does anyone know me?

CHAPTER EIGHT

I call Tom the next morning.

It's not the first thing I do when I wake up, and I didn't wake early. In fact, it's barely still morning when I finally allow myself to pick up the phone.

"Kate," he says after a couple of rings. His voice is sleepy, and deeper, more gravelly than usual.

"Sorry, did I wake you?" I'm not the least bit sorry. At this time of day I feel well within my rights to wake anyone.

"No, I've already been to the gym." Maybe the alcohol is responsible for the gravel in his voice then. I hear him yawn. "I figured you'd call. Want to come over? I'll throw something together for lunch."

It's both a relief not to have to ask to see him and embarrassing to have him find me so predictable. "Done." I glance at my watch and perform the mental maths. "I can be there around half twelve if that works for you?"

"Perfect, see you then."

The tube is full of the weekend crush. Tourists and families and self-consciously cool teens, all in pairs or groups, as if nobody travels alone on a Saturday or Sunday. I turn my head to stare out of the window. This part of the tube runs through a series of tunnels and open-air sections; I see overgrown leafy embankments interspersed with the bleached-out reflection of the carriage. Neither gives away much about London. I'm thinking of Tom's words, as I have done repeatedly since I woke up, as I must have done somewhere in my subconscious all night. *Jealous rage. Spurned lover.* I won't allow myself to think beyond that; I have my imagination on a tight rein. Just those words are permitted: *jealous rage, spurned lover,* then an abrupt stop to all thought. Severine should be here now, gloating, that smirk hovering millimeters from her mouth, but for once she's conspicuous by her absence.

Jealous rage. Spurned lover. It doesn't matter. It shouldn't matter. But here I am, in a grab-handbag, brush-hair, that-will-do kind of hurry, on my way to Tom's flat—which Tom entirely anticipated. It's surprising how little surprises Tom.

Tom's flat is in a quiet, wealthy street lined with Regency town houses, all high ceilings and sash windows and expensive heating bills. I press the bell for the top floor, and after a moment there is an obnoxious buzz and the front door releases. The communal hallway is on a dignified slide into genteel shabbiness, the once thick carpets now worn in the center from years of use. I climb the creaking stairs to find Tom's front door ajar; I can see a two-inch-wide slice of his hallway, with a newspaper dumped casually on a side table. I can't quite remember the last time I was here; actually, I can't remember being here more than three or four times, and always with a crowd, for a party or some such. Rapping on the door solo, I feel an unexpected twinge of nerves.

"In the kitchen," calls Tom's deep tone; he has expelled some of the gravel now. I close the front door behind me then aim for Tom's voice and find myself spilling into an open-plan room, with the kitchen at one end, a living room type space at the other, and a large glass dining table separating the two. At the living space end, floor-to-ceiling windows open out onto a small terrace. Tom is at the stove in the kitchen, working on something in a frying pan.

"I don't remember this," I say, making my way over to him. I may have only been in this flat a handful of times, but I've never been in *this* room.

He pulls me in for a one-armed hug, the other hand occupied with the frying pan, which contains the world's largest Spanish omelet. "I remodeled before I went to Boston. Just in time for a tenant to enjoy it instead of me. Do you like?" he asks casually, but I can see he cares about my answer.

"It's great," I say truthfully. It's modern without being sharp; it still feels warm and livable. Unlike Caro's place. Unlike Caro. "You've done it really well." I gesture toward the hob. "Can I help?" It's not the question I want to ask, but I don't know how to get there from discussions of renovations in a sun-drenched kitchen.

"Nope, nearly done, just grab a pew," he says, gesturing to the bar stools on the other side of the counter. "I take it omelet is okay?"

"Perfect. Thanks." I clamber aboard a stool and watch the back of him cook, given the layout of the kitchen. He can't be long out of the shower; his hair is still wet. He's wearing jeans and a casual shirt with the sleeves rolled up. For no reason at all I see Seb alongside him—Seb as he was, the Adonis, the man among the boys; I don't know the Seb of now. *Jealous rage. Spurned lover.* Tom, a man now, too, glances over his shoulder with a quick smile. I instinctively look away quickly, as if caught staring.

"Done," he says, efficiently cutting the omelet in two and delivering it to waiting plates. "Voilà."

"*Merci bien.*" I pause. I force myself to ask something conversational. "Do you like cooking?"

He settles himself on the bar stool next to me. "Not particularly, but I like eating fresh food, so . . ." He shrugs his shoulders.

The omelet is good, very good. We munch away, or at least Tom does; my appetite is letting me down. I've eaten with Tom any number of times, though never at his kitchen counter by his own hand. But still, there should be companionable silence; there always has been for Tom and me. Not today. Something is different—*we* are different. I glance over in his direction. He looks tired, the crinkles round his eyes more pronounced. Perhaps he is paler; his freckles seem to stand out more.

"So . . ." he says, between bites. "Lara and Modan? Is that for real?"

I grimace. "Well, she certainly seems smitten," I say apologetically. I wonder if that question has itched away at him all night.

"Yeah, that much was obvious." There's no emotion in his voice. He takes a bite and chews thoughtfully, staring unseeingly across the kitchen. "It's not ideal."

Not ideal. It's an oddly phlegmatic turn of phrase for heartbreak. "I guess. On any number of fronts." I put down my fork, unable to eat and unable to wait, and twist on the bar stool to face his profile. "What did you mean last night?"

He turns to look at me, his head cocked to one side analytically. Then he lays his cutlery down, too, but he's actually finished, the enormous omelet polished off in a handful of bites. He knows exactly what I'm referring to, and to his credit he doesn't try to dissemble. "Severine was an attractive girl," he says carefully. I nod and wonder where she is. Surely she wouldn't want to miss out on this conversation. "Modan seems to find it hard to believe that none of us were sleeping with her. He's playing a 'what if' game right now. What if . . . well, what if Tom was sleeping with Severine? But that's unlikely because everyone knows I hooked up with Lara that week, and Modan clearly thinks Lara is more than enough for one man to cope with." His tone is heavy with irony. He pauses for a moment; I can't tell if he's remembering the past or looking to the future, but regardless, it seems the view is bleak. "But what if Seb was sleeping with Severine? Well, that would certainly make things interesting . . ."

He stops, holding my gaze. The question that we both know I'm going to ask hangs in the air between us, solid enough to reach out and touch.

"I want to know," I say quietly.

Tom looks away and runs a hand through his hair, then fixes me in his gaze again. "Do you really care?" There's an edge to his voice. "After all this time? Ten years have passed since that week in France—ten years and a bloody marriage ceremony."

"I care about whether I was made a fool of." I sound bitter. I feel bitter. And impatient. "I care about whether all my friends knew what was going on under my nose but didn't tell me."

"So it's all about pride."

"Yes. No. I don't know—look, was he fucking her or not?"

"Yes," he says simply.

I open my mouth to say something, but nothing comes to mind. I close it again. *Pride*, I think. Tom is right on that score: my pride is well and truly hurt. Severine has finally made her entrance: she's watching me from across the kitchen and my fingers curl in an urge to drag my nails down those perfectly smooth cheeks, an urge so strong that I almost recoil from myself: the poor girl is dead; no one can possibly feel envious of her ever again. She watches me, and I fancy she knows what I'm thinking: she looks coolly to the side, as if utterly uninterested in my opinion. Tom is watching me, too, his brow furrowed in concern. I start to slide down from the bar stool.

"No," says Tom assertively, bringing me up short by grabbing my arm. "You don't get to disappear now. You wanted to know, so you have to listen to it *all* instead of building up all sorts of crazy scenarios in your head." His eyes are fiercely intent. "Kate, this is not some conspiracy theory; nobody has been whispering behind your back. It was a onetime thing, on the last night only. Hardly anyone knows about it. Seb doesn't even know that *I* know about it."

I process that for a moment, fighting my urge to flee. The last night. "After the fight, then." He nods. His grip loosens on my upper arm; instead he rubs his hand reassuringly up and down from my shoulder to my elbow. The last night, after the fight. "You said hardly anyone. Who else?"

"I don't know for sure," he says uneasily. "But maybe . . . Caro."

"Caro. Of course. It would have to be Caro." Of all people it would have to be her. I bet she has loved having that piece of knowledge secreted away, ready to be deployed at just the right moment for maximum personal advantage. I can just imagine how superior it has made her feel. I find my hands have clawed; I force myself to breathe out slowly and relax them. "How *do* you know about it then?"

"I saw them," he admits. "I don't know for sure, but I think Caro did, too; or at least, she put two and two together." I can see him gauging my reaction, trying to work out if each additional detail makes things better or worse, but nevertheless he's unflinching in his delivery. He releases my arm and runs his hand through his hair again instead. He looks as if, on balance, he'd much rather not have seen . . . What did he see exactly? I steel myself for the malevolent march of that thought eating away at me, the rot spreading at a steady rate until I can see nothing without an overlay of Seb and Severine in various different tangles of limbs, artfully backlit Hollywood-style—but a thoroughly unexpected dose of pragmatism hits me. The last night of the holiday, that famously eventful Friday night? Logistically, it couldn't have happened until after the fight, at which point Seb was already so drunk that, at some point when I have some perspective, I may be impressed that he managed to cheat on me at all. I'm fairly certain there was no cinematic glow involved that night. But . . .

"How do you know it wasn't happening all week, and you just didn't see it the other times?"

"Come on," he says, one eyebrow quirking upward. "We're talking about Seb. Subtlety and subterfuge have never been his strongest suits." I don't react. He sighs then looks at me searchingly, all humor gone. "Did you never wonder? Not even when the two of you broke up?" I shake my head, but we both know I'm lying. "Why did you think you broke up?"

"Christ, Tom. Can anyone ever answer that succinctly? Why did you and Jenna break up?" I counter.

He doesn't miss a beat and he doesn't break eye contact. "Because I didn't love her. Not the way I want to love whoever I'm going to spend the rest of my life with."

His starkly brutal honesty leaves me speechless, caught in the grip of his ferociously intent eyes. Like Seb's but not; now all I can see are the differences, not the similarities. I'm still groping around for a response when suddenly his phone starts to ring and dance across the counter. He glances at it long enough to register the caller ID, then picks it up and grimaces apologetically. "Sorry, I've got to take this; it's work. Don't go away."

I slide off the stool and wander into the living area of the open-plan space. Why did I think Seb and I broke up? I glance back at Tom. He's roaming the kitchen as he listens, his tall frame telegraphing alertness and focus. I turn back to the living room, inspecting the few framed photos resting on a shelf. There's one of him with his parents and his younger sister on his graduation day. His dad has clapped his hand firmly on Tom's shoulder and is beaming proudly. A wave of longing for my own father crashes over me, taking my breath away with its sudden onslaught. I turn quickly to the next photo: Seb and Tom at perhaps fifteen years old, beside a sailing boat with a gentleman that can only be Seb's father. The whippet-thin figure of Tom is a step back and half turned, as if he was about to get into the boat when the photo was taken; Seb's father's hand is on his shoulder, tugging him into the photo. Seb is square to the camera on his father's other side, smiling broadly. It's not a version of Seb I ever knew; he was more complete when I met him. More of a polished product. I look at that photo for a long time and think about all the different versions of Seb, including the one that cheated on me. The bitterness is an all-encompassing sea of bile, roiling around in my stomach and threatening to race up my throat to choke me.

Why *did* I think Seb and I broke up?

I'm so very, very tired of caring.

Tom has moved from receiving mode into delivery mode on his telephone call. "No, I don't actually," I hear him say authoritatively. "The basis risk on this structure is significant. Someone has to take it, and if it's going to be us then we have to charge for it. But the real problem is that this is the wrong structure for what they really want to do. We should get in front of them with a presentation and educate them." I find I'm watching him as he talks. He's still moving around the kitchen, his right hand accentuating his points. For a moment I find myself assessing him as I would any candidate that crossed the path of Channing Associates. It dawns on me that he's a fixer, a problem-solver; entirely in keeping with his degree in engineering, but somehow I've never paid attention to this side of him. He feels my eyes upon him and looks across, mouthing what could be "two minutes" whilst holding up two fingers. I nod and make a show of turning unconcernedly to another photo, and find myself looking back at me.

I'm not the only one in the photo, of course; there's Tom next to me and Lara on his other side. We're all sitting on the side of the pool in France, our feet dangling in the water. Lara is almost spilling out of her bikini and looks how she always looks: as if she's just climbed out of bed after hours of languorous sex, but would be more than willing to tumble back in for another round. Tom is Tom, at least the Tom I know the best: relaxed, laid-back, secure in his own skin but quietly observant. I'm the Kate I like the least, awkwardly folding my arms across my stomach at the glimpse of a camera, a half-hearted smile hung on my face. It's not surprising; there was no heart in any of my smiles by the end of that week.

Suddenly I realize Tom is behind me, looking over my shoulder at the photo. I hadn't noticed him finish the call. "Cracking legs you have on display there," he says mischievously.

I smile, touched; it's gentlemanly of him to comment on me rather than the bombshell that is Lara. I gesture toward the sailing photo. "Did you sail a lot growing up?" It's the only non-contentious thing I can think of to say.

He shrugs. "Uncle Edwin was really into it. He taught Seb and me." He looks at the photo a moment longer. "Did you know he paid all my school fees before I got the scholarship?"

Uncle Edwin. Lord Harcourt. I shake my head. "I didn't." I think about that for a moment: the younger sister and her penniless academic husband living off the generosity of the lord in the grand house. "I guess that must have created a certain dynamic."

He glances down at me. "No, it was—" he starts to say, as if parroting the party line, then he stops. "Actually, yeah," he admits. "My folks never said anything, but I could see how relieved they were when I won the scholarship." He looks back at the photo. "But it was a bit awkward with Seb, since he just missed out."

"But you two never seemed competitive with each other," I say, confused.

He shrugs. "Seb likes to win." Before I can try to puzzle that out, he shakes himself and turns away from the photos. "Anyway, where were we?"

"Nowhere I want to go back to."

His lips twist apologetically. "I'm sorry I didn't tell you before."

"Don't be ridiculous; Seb is your family." I can't blame Tom in the slightest for keeping Seb's secrets. I can blame Seb for having them, though. I can and I do.

"Yes, but . . . Well, anyway. You wanted to know." He cocks his head and assesses me, lips pursed. "How do you feel now you do?"

I turn away, scrubbing my face with my hands. "God, I don't know. It's hard to find perspective." Does Tom think I'm taking this well, or badly? Should I be more upset or less upset? Exactly how upset am I? What is the proportionate response when discovering decade-old infidelity?

"Kate," he says, a little too loudly, as if he's said my name more than once. Maybe he has. I turn back toward him, eyebrows raised inquiringly. "They're going to try and pin this on one of us," he says quietly. "Theo's dad says there's been a lot of publicity on this case in France; the police are getting hauled over the coals in the press for not finding the body at the time. There's a lot of pressure on them to get a result."

"But it *wasn't* one of us." I sound like a child, railing against the injustice of life: *it's not fair!* But life isn't fair, he will say. I know that. After irrevocably losing Seb and my dad in close succession, albeit in different ways, I couldn't fail to recognize that life lacks a sense of fair play.

Tom doesn't even bother to argue the point; he's already moved on. "I think you need to get a lawyer."

"A lawyer." I stare at him. "You're serious." He nods grimly. "Do *you* have one?"

"Nope. But my other half wasn't sleeping with a girl who subsequently turned up folded origami-style at the bottom of a well."

I can see her bleached skull grinning maniacally from the pinnacle of a pile of clean white bones. My breath catches. "Well, when you put it like that—"

"Modan, the French police—they *will* put it like that."

"But they don't know he and she . . . Ah."

Tom is nodding. "Yes. Caro. I don't know for sure that she knows, and I don't know if she would say anything, but . . ."

He spreads his fingers, palm up. I know he intends to convey uncertainty—*she might, she might not*—but I know the truth of it: *she will.* Unless there's some personal benefit to her that I haven't yet divined, without a doubt Caro will say something. If she hasn't already . . . I stare at him, my mind skittering on many levels. "They need hard evidence to prosecute, right? It can't be purely circumstantial?"

He shrugs. "I'm not exactly an expert in the French criminal judiciary system."

"Me neither." Which, at present, seems a wholly unsatisfactory gap in my legal education. Eventually I say again, "So, a lawyer. You're serious."

"Yes." There isn't a shadow of doubt in his eyes.

"I . . . Okay then." I'm still staring at him, my mind whirring.

"And stop talking to Lara about the case," he presses.

"Yes. Okay." He's still looking at me as if waiting for more, so I say it again. "Okay."

He nods and lets out a breath. "Okay."

I take a cab home. I can't face the bustle and thrust of the tube; I'm too brittle. I may fracture if jostled. The cabdriver tries to start up a conversation but trails off into silence when I fail to offer a single response. Lara's name lights up the screen on my mobile as we drive, the shrill ringtone demanding a response. I look at the phone in my hand, and all I can see are spider's threads leading from it. Lara to Alain Modan. Lara to Tom. Tom to Seb, his own cousin. Tom and Seb to Caro, their friend from childhood. Tom and Seb to Theo, their friend from university. Theo to Severine. Severine to Seb. Tug on any one thread and the reverberations will be felt by all.

The phone falls silent. I don't call her back.

CHAPTER NINE

B y Monday Severine has found an additional medium through which to make her presence felt: print. The case is making enough waves in France to be worthy of several column inches in the European news section of the *Telegraph*. There's a political angle I don't fully comprehend, not being an expert on French politics over the last ten years; another unsatisfactory gap in my knowledge base. They have a picture of Severine—of course they do; she is nothing if not photogenic, especially in a bikini as in the chosen photo. She lounges unsmiling in black and white on a sunbed, looking at the camera with no trace of concern about being framed on all sides by the words that attempt to capture her life and death and the chaos left by both.

Channing Associates is in the press, too. Paul comes into the office, a perfect storm of tailored suit, energy and enthusiasm, waving a copy of *Legal Week*. He pulls up his calendar as I take the paper off him to read it. It's a good article. Apparently despite being newly established, "Channing Associates, headed up by Kate Channing, is comprised of experienced hands who are fleet of foot" and are "the team to watch."

"I reckon I can lobby Cadfields again on the back of this publicity," Paul is saying. "They kind of left the door open. I'll try them, and then there's Wintersons, and I heard about an in-house general counsel role at BP from a mate at . . ." He babbles away. The Haft & Weil win has given him renewed vigor beyond all expectation; I wonder if he's further up the bipolar curve than most.

I put *Legal Week* down on my desk, next to Severine. One article where I'm mentioned by name; one where I'm simply one of the "English holidaymakers staying in the neighboring farmhouse" at the time, who are "helping the police with their inquiries." It's not an even match. Severine continues to gaze from her sun lounger, and I can think of nothing else.

I need a lawyer. Which ought to be funny given I'm a legal headhunter, except that it's not funny at all. Because I need a lawyer.

M odan again.

He's waiting for me when I emerge from Pret, clutching my coffee and my lunch in a bag. I stop short in the doorway when I spot him lounging against a lamppost. "*Bonjour*," he greets me, inclining his head.

I sigh and start walking. "*Bonjour*. I'm afraid I don't have any time for you today." *And I don't have a lawyer yet.*

He falls in beside me and shrugs. "Surely a few minutes."

"Not really, I'm afraid."

"Perhaps I talk and you listen. While you are eating your lunch, *non*?"

I'm walking back to my office, but it occurs to me that he will very likely follow me all the way there. I definitely do not want Paul and Julie exposed to the charming Alain Modan and the no-doubt innocent-sounding questions that he would produce. I stop walking and look at him. He cocks his head and smiles his most beguiling smile, the deep lines in his long face curving to frame his mouth.

"I'll listen. That's it." I take a detour toward a nearby courtyard with a bench that will be in the sun, if there's any sun; it's warm enough today to justify eating outside. The bench is empty; I navigate to it carefully given that cobblestones, a cup of coffee and kitten heels are a difficult mix, but I make it there unscathed and sit at one end, with my coffee placed precariously on the arm of the bench. Modan sits also, at the far end, spreading his arms along the back of the bench. The sun makes an unexpected appearance, and he tips his head back to enjoy it, eyes closed. Today he's wearing a pale pink shirt under his suit, with a silver gray tie; very Eurotrash, but it works for him. I wonder if he looks at my clothes in abject horror: this dress is probably two years old. At least I'm wearing designer shoes.

"*Alors,*" he says, pulling himself upright into business mode. I'm unpackaging my chicken wrap and pay him no heed. "So, I talk. As promised. We have the answer on when the well was filled in." He looks at me expectantly. I remember that I'm not supposed to know this and raise my eyebrows obligingly over my mouthful of wrap. "Saturday the sixteenth."

Having a mouthful is useful; it gives me time to think. About what to say, how to say it; about whether to say anything at all. "You said Friday before. Now you say Saturday," I comment mildly when I'm done chewing. "What makes you so sure you've got it right this time?"

He inclines his head: a silent *touché*. "The papers say Friday, but Monsieur Casteau—the younger one—tells me it was Saturday. He remembers that his girlfriend arrived in town unexpectedly, so they went off to . . ." He spreads his hands eloquently. "He came back on Saturday to finish the job." He looks at me again as if waiting for a comment, but when he sees I have another mouthful he goes on, with a wry twist to his lips. "He wrote down Friday on the paperwork because of the contract: there was a bonus if the work was finished on time. On Friday. You see?"

I do see why Modan believes Monsieur Casteau the younger; even I believe this, and I'm hearing it secondhand. "Does Theo's dad plan to sue him for return of the bonus?" I ask, tongue in cheek.

Modan's lips quirk. "I don't believe he considers it a high priority." He gives this last word the French pronunciation: *priorité*.

I take another mouthful and chew thoughtfully. Saturday. The day we left. Modan tips his head back to enjoy another brief appearance of the sun.

I try to nudge the conversation forward when I have finally swallowed. "What time on Saturday?"

He's been waiting for this; for him this is all a game that he's very, very good at. He tips his head forward again and blinks a few times while his eyes adjust. "He doesn't remember exactly, but he thinks perhaps lunchtime."

Lunchtime. Severine would have had plenty of time to return from the bus depot and then . . . what? Get herself killed by person or persons unknown and stuffed in a well? My breath catches: it's not a game; I don't want to play. I put down my suddenly very unappetizing chicken wrap. "I presume you've considered Monsieur Casteau," I say in a rush. "Younger or elder."

"*Bien sûr*. Of course." He purses his lips and moves his head this way and that as if trying to look at something from different angles. "They do not seem to . . . fit."

"And neither do the rest of us." I can't hide my frustration. He gives an equivocal one-shoulder shrug. I stand up to dump my leftovers in a nearby bin, annoyed with myself as well as Modan. I have no lawyer. I shouldn't be here. I pick up my handbag and my as-yet untouched coffee.

Modan watches me gather myself together without getting up,

his long arms still laid across the back of the bench, the very picture of relaxed elegance. "Stranger danger," he muses. "That is what you say, *n'est-ce pas*? That is what you teach *les enfants* at school? For murder, it is most of the time . . . *bof*, most of the time it is rubbish. Most of the time the murderer is in the home, or the street, or the place of work. Someone nearby. Someone known."

"Thanks for that," I say sweetly. "On that cheery note, I must get back to work to spend the rest of the day in fear of my colleagues and neighbors."

"Ha!" He seems genuinely amused by this; his long face is split by his smile. "Have a good afternoon."

But I don't have a good afternoon. I have a busy afternoon, even a productive afternoon; I have an afternoon that in the ordinary course of events would be a perfectly fine afternoon, but not in this world, not after these events. Not with the shadow of Modan looming over me and the ghost of Severine flitting through my office at will.

Caro calls; I get Julie to take a message. She'll be calling about either Seb's welcome dinner or to pump me for information—likely both; and I have no energy for either.

I meet Lara for a drink after work: investigation or no investigation, I can't avoid my closest friend. I can't remember ever deliberately keeping something from Lara. *Seb cheated on me with Severine.* The words beat around inside me, looking for an exit, but I force them down. Denied escape, they become a solid ever-present weight that sits in my stomach.

But Lara doesn't notice anything amiss—she's too busy keeping her own secrets. She doesn't ask me if I've seen Modan; she doesn't ask me anything about the case. She's trying far too hard to avoid the subject. I wonder whether she's seen him, or talked to him on the phone. I wonder whether they have put into action those desires whispered in an airport bar. The weight in my stomach grows heavier as we talk of all the things we usually talk of, which no longer matter at all.

"Oh, Caro called me," she says suddenly, wrinkling her pretty nose in distaste. "She's got that dinner she's been planning for Seb arranged for Thursday." She cocks her head and looks at me pleadingly. "Will you come? Please?"

Will I? I hadn't intended to go, but now I think about it. "I suppose so." I'm bound to run into Seb sooner or later; I may as well get it over with.

"Yay! It will be no fun without you, and Caro kind of forced me to say yes. She'll probably put the full-court press on you, too, at some point. You know," she muses, "much as I hate to admit it, it is nice of her to have arranged it all. I bet Seb will be really touched." She takes a sip from her wine, then asks hesitantly, in an almost word-perfect repeat of Tom's question on Saturday: "Do you still care? After all this time?"

I look at our half-drunk wineglasses, Lara's with a distinct lipstick smudge on one side, mine with only the merest suggestion of a lip print. In my darkly introspective mood even that seems highly symbolic, a deliberate motif designed to illustrate that I move through life leaving barely a trace to show I was ever there. "I don't know," I reply at last. I think of Tom's follow-up—*why did you think you broke up?*—and I see Seb's eyes when he told me it was over; I see the way they slid away from mine. I thought that underneath it all he felt guilty, for a myriad of reasons but one particular being he was ashamed that for all his assertions that background didn't matter, in the end he had to acknowledge that he wanted someone from his world, someone who fit. Now I have a different thesis about the source of that guilt, though not one I can share with Lara. "It's hard to say. I haven't actually seen him since—well, since he dumped me, actually."

Lara's eyes widen. "Really? Not once? How can that be?"

I shrug. "I guess I didn't want to see him at first, and then Dad got ill so I was up in Yorkshire for a bit." It was cancer. Pancreatic cancer. I pause, remembering the phone call from Mum, the hopelessness in her voice as she forced herself to utter the dreaded C-word, followed by the mad dash to get the very next train home. I cried silently for almost the entire three-hour journey, sitting alone in a quiet seat facing a luggage rack. By the time I got to the hospital I was ash white and out of tears. "Anyway, by the time I came back his bank had sent him off to Singapore or somewhere like that."

"Hong Kong, I think. Tom and Caro went to visit." She takes another sip of her wine, laying down another mark of her presence with an overlapping lipstick print. "Makes it kind of hard to find *closure* if you've never actually seen him since." She uses her hands to hang an ironic set of quotation marks around "closure" and gives the word an American twang.

"Closure," I repeat, mimicking her twang. "Closure." I take a long swallow from my glass, then try the word again in my own accent, rolling it around my mouth. "Closure." I shake my head. "Nope. Word has absolutely no meaning."

She giggles. "I think you're too British for the concept of closure."

"Or too northern. We don't grin and bear it; we just bear it and don't bother with the grin."

"We Scandies don't bear it at all; we just off ourselves."

We smile at each other, enjoying the connection and the levity, and the weight in my stomach lifts a little. *It will be all right*, I think. *When all this is over, everything will be all right again.*

The feeling lasts until I climb into a cab home to find Severine already in occupation. The sight of her is like a slap in the face, or a brutal thump back down to earth: it shocks the sense back into me. *All right*: what an appallingly trite sentiment. It won't be *all right*, at least not for everyone; how could I have temporarily forgotten I've long stopped believing in guaranteed happy endings? There was a time with Seb where what I felt for him, what I thought he felt for me, was like a rising tide, buoying me up over all obstacles. The inevitable crash when the tide abruptly receded was shattering, all the more so because I should have known better, because I *did* know better. Oxford was an education in more ways than one: I learned that like sticks with like. Bright, outspoken girls from underprivileged backgrounds might be fun to hang out with, but they don't ultimately make the inner sanctum of the Sebs of this world. Somehow, even knowing that, even in the face of all evidence to the contrary, I allowed myself to be fooled into believing our relationship would be different, that things would be *all right*.

I won't be a fool again; I won't allow it. I need a damn lawyer.

"Eight o'clock tonight," says Caro emphatically down the phone on Thursday afternoon. Julie rang her earlier in the week to confirm my attendance, but it's clear Caro isn't taking any chances. "I know this is, well . . . difficult for you, but I won't accept any last-minute excuses; after all, Borderello's is hell to get a table at." Her tone is carefully constructed to sound like a lighthearted tease mixed with sympathy, but Caro is not that kind of girl: she doesn't gossip and sympathize and commiserate. She pokes and prods under the cover of witty repartee.

"Of course I'll be there," I say calmly. "I'm looking forward to it." For a moment I entertain the fantasy of turning up with an adoring Adonis on my arm—who? where would he come from at such late notice?—but I'll have to settle for Lara and Tom. Perhaps the Adonis trick would be too obvious anyway.

"It'll be great to have the old gang back together," she says brightly. "Like old times." *Old times.* The thought makes me shudder. Caro's *old times* must be very different from mine. I try to strip the irony from any potential response, but she's already forging on: "That's all I seem to be talking about these days, what with the investigation and everything. Modan can't seem to stop with the questions, can he? Have you seen him, too?"

"Not really. He dropped by on Monday, but I was too busy to have more than five minutes for him."

"I made the mistake of freeing up half an hour for him. I don't know what for, really—all he wanted to talk about was who was sleeping with who, and whether anyone was sleeping with Severine."

"Well, I certainly wasn't," I say flippantly. "Girls have never been my thing. What about you?"

She gives what may be a genuine laugh. "No, me neither. I'm boringly bourgeois that way. But seriously, I suppose it changes things a bit if someone *was* sleeping with her."

"How so?" I ask, making my voice as uninterested as possible. Does she really know about Seb and Severine? Is she trying to find out if I know? *Does she know that I know that she knows that . . .*

"Motive, I suppose—crime of passion or some such thing. God, I sound like *CSI*." She laughs it off. "It's all a bit grubby, really, having a stranger like Modan poring eagerly through all our tangled love lives." She switches gear audibly. "Anyway, tonight. Eight o'clock. Borderello's."

"See you there."

I put down the phone, her words turning over in my head: *our tangled love lives*. I was with Seb. Lara was with Tom. Other than Seb's infidelity, where lies the tangle? Come to that, Caro wasn't with anyone: why would she say "our" love lives? I start to run the payroll software that I use to manage Julie's and Paul's salaries, but I'm too distracted to make sense of the process. Abruptly I shut down the program and grab my phone.

"Kate, hello." Tom sounds harried.

"Bad time?" I glance at the clock: it's ten to three. "Oh shit, sorry, it's almost expiry time." Foreign exchange options usually expire at three.

"Yup. Can I call you back after?"

"Sure."

He pauses. "You okay?"

"Yes, fine. It's nothing. Call me back later." My voice sounds too bright, too forced.

"Okay."

I put down my mobile and stare at it for a moment, then I shake myself and open the payroll software again with grim determination. It's sufficiently alien that to make any progress I have to concentrate to the exclusion of anything else; it's curiously calming. When my mobile finally rings I'm startled.

"Kate?" It's Tom. The real world floods back in and temporarily robs me of breath. "Kate? Can you hear me?" he asks.

"Yes, sorry. I'm here."

"Everything okay?"

"Yes . . . actually, no. Was Seb sleeping with anyone else?"

"What?" He's genuinely taken aback. "Where's this coming from?"

"It's just something Caro said. I wondered . . ." I feel a cold sweat on my torso. It's excruciatingly embarrassing to have to ask this. It's embarrassing to even have to wonder it. In time I will feel anger at Seb for putting me in this position, but all I feel at the moment is shame.

"Hold on a moment, this sounds like something I shouldn't be broadcasting over the trading floor. Let me get to my office." There's a pause and some muffled noises, then he comes back on the line. "Fire away."

"It's just . . . I'm probably getting the wrong end of the stick, but I wondered if Caro was sleeping with Seb." I add as an afterthought, "Or you, actually." Theo I don't consider a real possibility.

"Me sleeping with Seb?" He sounds genuinely bewildered.

I can't help but laugh. "No, with Caro, you idiot."

"Hand on my heart, I can promise you I have never slept with either Seb or Caro. Nor do I have any wish to." Humor warms his deep voice.

"And Seb? Seb with Caro, to be precise."

His pause is significant. "I don't think so," he says finally. There's no trace of the humor now. "I think . . . well, Caro has always had a thing for him. You must know that."

I suppose he's right; I've always known that. "And?"

"And nothing. I think that's all it's ever been, an unrequited thing. He kind of knew it, but I don't think he ever went there. He never felt the same, and it would have been a disaster given how close all our families are if he were to screw her over." Of course, it was fine to screw *me* over, with my unconnected, unimportant family . . . "At least, that's my take," he says at last, but I get the sense he's still mulling something over.

"Would he have told you, do you think? I know you're close, but he didn't tell you about Severine . . ."

"True." I hear him take a breath in then blow it out. "I don't know," he admits reluctantly. "Before you came along, then I'd have said yes, for sure, he would have told me anything. But after . . . I don't know." I want to ask what changed, but there's no way to do it without sounding like I'm looking for some validation, some sign I was important in Seb's life, and I refuse to be so pitiful in front of Tom. "Where are you going with this?"

"I don't know. I just suddenly feel like . . . God, I don't know. I don't know what the hell was going on that week. Modan is asking questions, and I'm not even sure I can answer *anything*, because nothing is how I thought it was, and . . . and . . ." I'm suddenly aware I'm close to tears.

"Hey, whoa there," Tom says softly down the line. "It's okay."

"No, it's *not*."

He's silent for a moment. "No, it's not, is it? Look, why don't we meet before dinner tonight? Have a drink and talk all this through. I can get to Knightsbridge for around six. Okay?"

I take a deep, shuddering breath. "Yes. Okay. Thanks. Sorry about all this."

"You have nothing to be sorry for. Oh—did you get a lawyer?"

"I'm meeting one tomorrow."

"Good." He sounds genuinely relieved. "See you at six."

I put down the phone and rest my eye sockets in the heels of my hands for a moment. When I lift my head again I find Severine watching me. For once there's no trace of hostility beneath her smooth exterior; she's simply watching me.

"Haven't you anywhere better to be?" I ask her. It's the first time I've actually spoken to her; unsurprisingly she doesn't answer, so I do it for her. "No, I don't suppose you do, under the circumstances."

Julie comes to the doorway, pushing her glasses back up her nose. "Did you need something?"

I shake my head, smiling brightly. "No, sorry, just talking to myself."

She's already moving back to her seat. "First sign of madness, you know," she says over her shoulder. The thought had crossed my mind.

CHAPTER TEN

The evening starts badly.

I'm at the pub a few minutes after six and predictably find Tom—reliable, steady Tom—already there; but so, too, is Lara. From Tom's ruefully apologetic expression I divine he had no choice. I pull myself together to kiss Lara hello. "What a pleasant surprise!"

"I was sure you'd want to meet beforehand, but I couldn't raise you on your mobile this afternoon, so I called Tom," she says breezily.

"Really? My phone must be playing up again. I didn't see that you'd called." Lying is becoming easier with practice, but the guilt remains the same. I turn to hug Tom hello; his breath strokes my ear carrying a murmur of, "Sorry." He's been home to change after work; he's dressed in jeans and a shirt, and smells of newly applied aftershave. I'm still in work clothes, but it's a deliberate choice: I have a fancy that the combination of this dress with these stiletto heels shows off my legs to their best advantage. Absent the Adonis arm candy, it's really the best I can do.

"Here, Tom got you a drink." Lara passes over a vodka tonic.

"Thanks. Love your dress." It occurs to me that I'm overcompensating, though she does look fabulous. She's wearing a stunning bodycon dress the color of autumn leaves, with heels at least an inch higher than her usual choice for work. Most of the bar watches as she settles herself in a chair and crosses her endless legs.

"Well, I thought I'd make an effort," she says casually, but there are spots of color in her cheeks. The effort is not for me or Tom, or even Caro or Seb, I'm sure. I'd lay odds she has post-dinner plans with the indefatigable Monsieur Modan.

"What about me? How do I look?" Tom asks, mock-preening. He's compensating too.

Lara bats her eyelashes at him. "Devastatingly handsome as ever."

"Very metrosexual," I add slyly; he turns to me, appreciative laughter glinting in those blue gray eyes. They are resolutely Tom's eyes now. I wonder if this evening will shake that.

We drink and we talk and it's excruciating. Lara is too bright, too excitable, drinking too quickly. It's impossible to fathom what's going on under the surface, and given the secrets each of us are keeping, there's no way for me to ask. Subterfuge doesn't sit well with her, though. She ricochets through topics, always realizing each pitfall too late; she can't talk about her love life, she can't talk about the case, she can't talk about how she's spending her free time—almost nothing is safe for her. I'm so awkwardly aware this is not the private chat Tom and I had planned that I'm working too hard to keep the conversation Lara-friendly and save her from verbal suicide. On the surface Tom is his usual relaxed self, complete with mildly flirtatious banter with Lara, but I can see he's uncharacteristically tense, and oddly fatalistic, as if waiting for an ax to drop rather than killing time before a homecoming dinner for his cousin and closest friend. Perhaps he, too, can see that the light within Lara is shining for someone other than her current audience. I wonder how much that pierces him.

It's hard enough to battle on with this charade whilst sober; I shouldn't have another vodka tonic. But I do. And another.

Finally, Lara glances at her watch. "Shouldn't we make tracks before we incur the wrath of Caro?"

I nod and reach for my handbag, partly relieved to be released, but I expect what's coming will be worse. Tom knocks back the remainder of his pint and deposits the glass on the table with an audible thump. "Out of the frying pan into the fire," he murmurs darkly. I look across at him in surprise—what does he have to be worried about now?—but he's looking toward the exit. The skin round his eyes is tight with anxiety.

The restaurant is a short walk away. Lara walks in the middle and links an arm through one of Tom's arms and one of mine, as if to prevent us from escaping. There's no time for even a deep breath before she has hustled me through the door into what seems more akin to a theater dressing room than a restaurant. I busy myself leaving my coat and bag with the cloakroom attendant, both reluctant to look round and reluctant to be seen looking round. Tom hovers near me as I pass my things over, tension visible in his jaw.

"Are you okay?" I ask him quietly, bemused.

"What? Me? Of course." He brushes it off. "I'm just worried about you."

I shake my head minutely as I take the ticket from the attendant. "No need."

"If only," I think I hear him say; I look at him sharply, but I can't follow up because Caro is descending upon us. I have to manufacture a smile to endure whatever thorny welcome she will greet me with, but she's too caught up in her favorite role of hostess to deliver anything of consequence. Then there's no longer an excuse, I'm being swept inexorably toward a long table that can only be our reservation; and there is Seb.

He's standing by the table, his hand on the back of a chair that's occupied by a slender blond woman sitting sideways. He looks up on hearing the bustle of our approach, a grin spreading across his face. He is Seb. It's a shock, somehow. He is still so very much Seb.

Lara—bless her, a thousand times bless her—steams in ahead of me, an unstoppable force of bosom and smile and hair, all outstretched arms and double-kisses. "Seb!" she says in a suitably delighted tone. "So good to see you! And this must be Alina . . ." Alina stands to greet Lara. She's tall—taller than I—with the fine-boned features that somehow speak of years of Pony Club and expensive schooling; her accent when she replies to Lara only confirms that. She is everything I expected she would be. Tom is following in Lara's wake: he and Seb are grinning above a manly handshake that becomes a one-armed hug, then almost descends into a boyish rough-and-tumble in their pleasure at seeing each other. But now Tom is switching his attention to Alina: it's my turn.

Seb is waiting, smiling at me, an arm ready to steady me for the double-kiss treatment. "Kate," he says quietly, warmly, as I draw close. "It's been too long."

It hits me that there's a familiarity in the feel of that cheek, of the arm I lay my hand on as we kiss. I don't know if I expected that, after all these years. "How are you?" I ask as I draw back. It's the polite thing to say under the circumstances. It's possible I'm interested in the answer, but I've resolved not to dissolve into self-analysis this evening. Tonight I have to simply make it through.

"Good, great." He spreads his hands. His hair is shorter than before, and there are little flecks of gray above his ears. He's wearing jeans and a casual shirt, like almost every other male here, though both may be more expensive than the average. "Great to be back." He runs an appreciative eye over me. "You look well. I hear you're doing well, too, running your own company—" Someone claps a hand on his shoulder with an accompanying bellow, and he turns away, but not without catching my gaze with his extraordinary eyes and mouthing over his shoulder, "Later."

There's an intimacy in that look, in the way he delivers the word—as if he were being dragged away from me. I look after him for a moment. I have no idea what to make of the entire encounter.

I blink and collect myself, turning aside to find Tom watching me, despite ostensibly being in a conversation with Alina and Lara. His face is tight. I cock my head questioningly, and his expression clears deliberately; he lifts his eyebrows—*are you all right?* I nod and even manage a reassuring smile, then step over to join the three of them. Tom's eyes are Tom's eyes, I think. And Seb's . . . well, they are Seb's. They are how they always were.

Shortly we sit. Caro has mustered eighteen of us: we're a raucous party of fractured conversations and sudden hoots of laughter from different directions; though more often from Seb's area than anywhere else. Tom and Lara have made pains to sit on either side of me; we bracket the end of the table. I have prime viewing position. Caro, flushed and buoyant with the success of the evening, has seated herself next to the guest of honor at the middle of the long table; Alina is opposite. Four bottles of wine are dispatched before the exasperated waiter manages to get a dinner order from us all.

"Okay?" Lara asks under her breath. I nod briefly. "He looks good," she laments on my behalf.

"He always did," I mutter back. If I was hoping to find him a far cry from his former glory, that certainly isn't the case. I look across at Seb, trying to see what caused Tom to suggest he wasn't in good shape. It's true he's bulkier than before, but it all appears solid; he's hardly run to fat. He's still, objectively speaking, the most attractive man in the room, but the heartbreaking, breath-stealing vitality of youth has gone; his beauty no longer burns. I watch him pour himself and Caro another glass of wine, his shirtsleeve rolled back to reveal a tanned forearm. Caro is reveling in Seb's attention; it softens her edges, makes her almost girlish. I don't remember her being this obvious a decade ago, or perhaps I chose not to see it. *Wives and girlfriends always know* . . . I glance at Alina and find her eyeing the two expressionlessly whilst not drinking her wine. Very deliberately not drinking her wine: the glass is raised to her lips, but nothing passes. Someone says something to her on her right; she turns to them, an attentive smile quickly in place. I watch as she gesticulates to make some point, then casually lifts her wineglass and pretends to drink.

I pick up my own wineglass and join the conversation around me. We eat, we drink, we laugh, we talk. The food is unmemorable, but the wine is good; Tom refills our wineglasses whenever they run dry. I'm actually having fun, though it feels desperate, reckless, like dancing while the *Titanic* sinks. I sneak glances at Seb and Caro and Alina. Lara and Tom sneak glances at me. Seb is performing the same function as Tom in the middle of the table, but twice as frequently, and he never misses his own glass: Seb is drinking hard while his wife isn't drinking at all.

"A toast," calls Caro, standing up as she taps a glass ineffectually with a spoon. The table quiets down, all except a large chap at the end who is still talking to his neighbor; I can't quite remember either of their names, but the faces are familiar. Caro raises her voice: "Do shut up, George. Tilly has heard all your jokes three times already." That raises chuckles from around the table. She glances down at Seb, smiling. "A toast. Raise your glasses to welcome back . . . Seb, and Alina!" There's the merest pause after she says Seb's name, just enough for anyone so inclined to interpret the mention of Alina as an afterthought; I am so inclined. If that's Alina's interpretation, there's nothing to show it: she smiles graciously, playing her role of guest of honor perfectly.

Seb climbs to his feet. His cheeks are heavily flushed now. "Thank you all from both of us; we're thrilled to be back. And thanks for coming tonight, and to Caro for arranging everything." He smiles and clinks his glass against hers; Caro inclines her head in acknowledgment, the fizzing joy inside almost bursting through her eyes. "It's great to be able to catch up with so many of you again all at once. The thing Alina and I have been most looking forward to about coming back is—"

"The beer!" shouts some wag.

"The sense of humor!" shouts another.

"The dentistry," murmurs Tom in my ear. I giggle. Lara glances across at us. The merest frown crosses her face before she turns back; I wonder if I was too loud.

Seb laughs. "Wonderful as those are, they're not what I was about to say. What we've most been looking forward to is being close to our friends. And on that note . . ." His expression turns somber. "I'd like to propose a toast to one who can never be here with us again." The table is quiet now. "To Theo."

"To Theo," we all murmur before we drink. I glance at Tom; his face is starkly bleak; one could photograph him and name it *A Study in Grief*. As I watch he deliberately locks eyes with Seb and gives a small nod—*well done*—and Seb nods back, the merest movement. Theo was Tom's friend first and foremost, I remember. They were in the same college, they both read engineering, they even shared a set of rooms in second year; if there is such a thing as the keeper of the grief, Tom has the right of that title in this group. I want to say something to him, but I've no idea what.

The conversation warms and expands again, slowly regaining volume after the moment of solemnity. More wine is called for. I eat chocolate profiteroles that I don't really like because by now I'm drunk and I'll eat practically anything. People are switching places or hunkering down between two chairs to catch up with those they haven't been seated near. I see Alina rise from the table. Seb is chatting, leaning over someone seated in a chair near hers; he pulls her in for a kiss as she passes, drunkenly tactile, but she keeps it brief, barely breaking her stride. He gazes after her receding back for a moment, before his attention is drawn back into his conversation. I look away, wondering how much one can divine about any relationship from observing a single moment, and am shocked to find Severine's white skull on the table in front of me, atop a pile of sand and sticks and assorted debris. The image is so sharp, so sudden, so vicious that for a second I feel like I'm falling through space.

I push my chair sharply away from the table and head for the toilets, ignoring Tom's concerned call—*Kate?*—reeling from both the wine and Severine's malevolent appearance. I bang inelegantly through the doors. The toilet cubicle, thankfully, is mine and mine alone; no intrusions from the dead here. I close the lid and sit hunched with my forehead propped up by the heels of my hands. I'm angry with Severine, and I have that right—why shouldn't I be angry with the girl who, in life, slept with my boyfriend right under my nose, and then has the temerity to haunt me in death? Why me? Why not Seb? That would be much more fitting, I think maliciously. And if not Seb, why not Caro? Yes, Caro—what a pity hauntings can't be directed. Perhaps I should ask Severine if she takes requests . . . Still, why me? Not that I would wish it on them, but why not Lara or Tom? I remember Tom's stark, grief-ridden face, staring unseeingly down the table. Not Tom, not ever Tom; that would be beyond unfair.

With a sigh I collect myself and exit the cubicle more elegantly than I entered it, only to stop short when I find Alina at a sink, dabbing a paper towel to her mouth. She instantly scrunches up the paper towel when she sees me and makes a show of tidying up her eyeliner instead. The eyeliner is already perfect, but the eyes it frames look tired.

"Hi," I say into the mirror as I step up to wash my hands. She gives a small smile in return. "Are you having a good evening?"

"Lovely," she says unenthusiastically. "Though it's hard to keep track of names." She looks at me expectantly.

"Kate. Kate Channing." There's not the slightest bit of recognition in her face. "I was at Oxford with Seb." Still nothing. I make a gesture. "And Tom and Lara and Caro, among others." It's laughable. Apparently I wasn't even important enough in Seb's life for him to mention me to his wife.

"Kate. Got it. Forgive me, I'm so useless with names. And since Seb and I met in New York, I haven't really had a chance to meet any of his friends from back home. Except the ones who came to the wedding, and that was ages ago."

"I'm sure there are easier ways than this evening's trial by fire," I say wryly as I dry my hands on a paper towel.

"Well, Caro was very insistent." She leans forward to inspect her eyeliner again, and then adds, as if realizing her words could be interpreted as a tad ungrateful, "And of course, it's very kind of her to take the trouble."

"Mmmm," I say, unable to keep the irony out of my voice. Alina shoots me a quick look in the mirror, and for a moment her composure slips. She looks exhausted and utterly fed up.

"Are you pregnant?" I blurt out before I can stop myself. My hand flies to my mouth in horror, as if I can catch the words and pop them back in.

Her eyes jump immediately to mine, betraying the truth, then she quickly schools her face to give a surprised laugh. "No, of course—"

"God, I'm sorry, I'm . . ." I stop and shake my head, genuinely appalled at myself. "It's none of my business." We both look at each other—properly, not in the mirror this time. "Sorry," I say again, truly contrite. I shrug my shoulders and offer the only lame excuse I have. "Tom's been doing *too* good a job of topping up my wine."

"It's okay," she says slowly after a moment. There's no role-playing now; she makes no bones of the fact that she's carefully assessing me. I wonder what she sees. She shrugs. "Since you've asked I may as well admit it: yes, I'm pregnant. Nine weeks. It's been quite a journey." The smile that steals across her face is half fearful and half excited and only lasts a heartbeat. "Please keep it to yourself. Though Seb is smashed enough tonight to tell the whole world anyway," she adds, not without a note of frustration. It crosses my mind that tonight at least, I wouldn't wish to be in her shoes, but I push that aside. The ban on self-analysis is still in force. She tosses the scrunched-up paper towel into a waste bin, no longer hiding it. "There's nothing 'morning' about my sickness."

"Well, I guess . . . congratulations." I smile awkwardly. "And I hope the sickness passes soon."

She looks at me for a moment then nods thoughtfully. "Thank you." We head back into the restaurant together. I think wryly to myself of the kiss I observed. The additional information of Alina's sickness puts a very different spin on it: the nauseous wife surreptitiously hurrying to the bathroom. I follow Alina's long, narrow form that betrays no hint of a tiny life inside and wonder how Caro will take the news.

Back at the table the waiter is moving round with a handheld machine taking card payments and someone is suggesting a move to a nearby club, but on a Thursday night the idea has no traction; we all have to work tomorrow, and none of us are twenty-one anymore. Lara has already rescued our coats from the cloakroom; she's holding mine ready for me by the exit. I look round for Tom and instead spy Caro and Seb, half hidden behind an enormous fern. They are close, too close. Caro has one hand on Seb's arm and is speaking to him urgently; his head is bent to hear her. As I watch, Seb scans the room quickly, as if checking they haven't been seen, then focuses on Caro again. I turn away. I wish I hadn't seen them. I wish I didn't have to feel achingly sorry for Alina and furiously disappointed with Seb. Despite everything, I had expected better of him.

Tom has returned from the gents, and as a group we're now tumbling out into the night. Alina and Seb are doing their rounds of good-byes while various people try to figure out who best should share the taxis they're trying to hail. I turn to Lara. "Shall we share a cab?"

"Actually, you and Tom can share. I'm . . . ah . . . going in a different direction," she says clumsily, not meeting my eye.

"Lara." By now I am fed up of this charade and too drunk to hide it. "I know where you're going and you know I know." Her lips thin mutinously as she bristles. It's so out of character I almost laugh: Modan is drawing out new depths in our Lara. I grab her arm. "No, look, I'm not . . . I'm just saying, be careful, okay?" She looks at me warily. "I worry about you. Look after yourself. That's all."

A smile breaks over her face, and she pulls me in for a hug. "You, too, honey," she says quietly. Her breasts crush against me as we hug; I smell her perfume and some kind of floral scent in her hair. I wonder how that would feel to me if I was Alain Modan. Then she climbs into the cab Tom has hailed for her and disappears off.

I feel a hand on my shoulder and swing round to find Seb beside me. "Sorry," he says ruefully, charmingly. "We didn't get a chance to talk after all."

"I'm sure there will be other occasions." I don't want to speak to him at all tonight, and maybe not ever, after witnessing his tête-à-tête with Caro.

"Oh, definitely." He pulls me a little to the side and suddenly looks awkward. "Listen, Kate, all this stuff with Severine being found . . . I just wanted to say, well, some stuff might come out that . . . doesn't reflect well on me." I gaze at him nonplussed. He grimaces. "I mean, some stuff about me and Severine." It dawns on me that he's confessing to his infidelity, right here, outside a restaurant, when we've both had too much to drink. I'm temporarily speechless. He's still speaking, however. "I just . . . didn't want you to hear from someone else and be hurt by that. It was just the once; it didn't mean anything . . . We were all so drunk that night—"

Wordless, bitter rage broils inside me. I make a sharp gesture with my hand, cutting him off. "I don't want to talk about it." He blinks, taken aback by my vehemence. I look around for Tom.

"Well, it was a long time ago. It's just, with that policeman and everything, everything is coming into the open. Best to be honest in this situation, I think. I mean, you can't really lie to the law. And you and I both know I came to our room that night and passed out, so whatever happened to Severine was nothing to do with me."

I swing back to stare at him. I worried about Caro telling Modan about Severine and Seb; it didn't occur to me that Seb would own up himself. He's running a hand through his hair and has on his best contrite expression, like a little boy caught with his hand in the cookie jar. I desperately want to tell him to *fuck off*, but it turns out Tom is right: this is all about pride. I would be yelling an endless stream of invective at Seb right now if it weren't for the fact it would draw everyone's attention. I can't bear the thought of them all talking about me afterward. *Poor Kate. All these years and she still hasn't got over Seb. She hasn't really had a serious boyfriend since, you know* . . . I look for Tom, desperately hoping he has a cab ready to whisk me away; he's waving at one that has its light on, but it's not quite close enough for immediate salvation. I stare fixedly at it, willing it closer.

"Kate?" says Seb uncertainly.

The cab finally draws up. "Say good night to Alina for me," I bite out, not looking at Seb. As I turn toward the cab, I realize Caro is watching us. Or rather, watching me. Watching my reaction.

"Okay?" asks Tom as he helps me into the cab. I glance back

through the window of the cab. Seb and Caro are sharing a look, and suddenly I feel the ground shift under me. What if Caro and Seb aren't having an affair after all? What if the secret they're keeping is something else entirely? "Kate?" Tom says again. "Are you okay?"

The cab starts to pull away. Wild laughter bubbles up inside me. I'm still drunk, I realize. Of course I am. Seb's confession and the night air may have been sobering, but given the amount of wine I've sunk, physically I can't be anything other than smashed right now. Tom looks at me across the wide seat of the cab. The laughter evaporates just as quickly as it came. "No," I say truthfully. "I'm not okay."

"Yeah," he says softly. He looks down, his expression hidden in the shadows of the cab. "I didn't think so."

CHAPTER ELEVEN

I wake slowly with the dawning realization that I'm horribly hung-over and this is not my bed: the covers don't feel right, the light from the window is coming from the wrong place, and I'm wearing my bra, which I never sleep in . . . I turn over cautiously to check whether I'm the sole occupant. The bedroom door is slightly ajar, and through it I can see the back of someone very familiar in a kitchen I recognize, drinking a cup of something.

Tom. I'm at Tom's.

Images of last night surface in a haphazard, fractured fashion, with no suggestion of how one led to another: the dinner; the cab ride afterward; drunkenly climbing the stairs to Tom's flat; making coffee; kissing.

Kissing. Dear God, kissing. Kissing Tom.

The memory takes hold, and I'm there now, in the secretive gloom of the corridor that leads to his bedroom, the length of him pressing me against the wall—solid, warm, strong. One hand buries into my hair while the other cups my breast; I arch into him. When

I kiss his neck I both hear and feel the rough groan in his throat that sends a reckless thrill running through me.

Reckless. Reckless indeed. But—if there was no Seb (how unthinkable, no Seb! Only not so unthinkable now, after seeing him again—as he is, not how I'd imagined him to be—and after kissing Tom . . .), and no Lara or Severine or Alain Modan . . . I wrap up the memory and put it away, a dark, delicious, thrilling secret to unfold slowly and savor much later. But for now . . . I can't recall what happened next. I look across at the other side of the bed again; it doesn't appear to have been slept in at all. In the kitchen Tom's wearing jeans, but no shirt—the same jeans as last night, I think. The tan of the back of his neck contrasts with his paler, freckled shoulders. There is tension in those broad muscled shoulders. Even from here I can sense it thickening the atmosphere. I feel my sense of uneasiness growing. What happened after the corridor? I have a horrendous growing suspicion I may have passed out on him. God, how embarrassing. Perhaps dented male pride is responsible for his palpable tension . . .

What to do now? I debate internally for a moment before I sit up awkwardly, trying to keep the duvet tucked across my chest, and aim for a sheepish smile. "Morning," I call.

He puts his cup down with a decided thud and turns round. "Tea?" he says unsmiling.

I smother a yawn. "Yes, please. I feel like shit."

"You deserve to," he says shortly, then moves out of my line of sight to make the tea, leaving me blinking in surprise. Tom is not just tense; he's furious. With me.

I have no idea what's going on, but I definitely want to face it wearing more clothing than this. I look around the room for my dress and find it tossed over a chair, beside my shoes, bag and coat. I have just enough time to scramble into the dress; I'm sitting on the edge of the bed nearest the door, running my fingers through my no doubt ragged hair when he returns, a mug cradled in his hands. He has long, strong fingers: I remember the feel of them buried in my hair, the sureness of his touch. Suddenly I realize he's been holding out the mug for a few seconds now; I take it quickly. "Thank you."

"You're welcome," he says shortly, leaning against the doorframe and avoiding my eyes. The breadth of his shoulders nearly fills the open space.

"Funny, I don't feel very welcome." I look at him, willing him to catch my eye with a rueful smile and turn back into the Tom I know. But he's someone different now; the kissing last night did that. I can't look at him like yesterday or the day before or ten years ago. He has a tangle of dark hair across the planes of his chest, spreading down across his abdomen to disappear in the waistband of his jeans. He didn't have that a decade ago, nor the muscle bulk; he's not the same as he was. The corridor secret threatens to burst forth from where I've buried it: I want to touch him and I want to cry at the same time. I look away quickly and take a sip from my tea.

He still hasn't said anything—not *Of course you're welcome*, or *I'm sorry you feel that way*. A defiant anger suddenly sparks within me. I carefully place the cup of tea on the bedside table. "Want to tell me exactly what I'm in the doghouse for, or am I expected to guess?"

That whips his gaze round. "I thought we were friends."

"We are," I say, surprised.

"*Good* friends," he says impatiently, batting away my response as if I'm deliberately missing the point. "I thought our friendship was important to you. I thought you rated it more highly than to behave like that."

"Like what exactly?" My voice is rising and I'm standing now. "We were drunk—"

"*You* were drunk—"

"And you were stone cold sober, were you?" I stare him down; after a moment he jerks his head and looks away, conceding the point.

"We kissed. You may have to fill me in on a few of the details given the aforementioned drunkenness, but it's hardly the scandal of the century."

"Oh, so it's nothing, is it? We'll just carry on as normal, nothing's changed?" he shoots back, snapping his gaze back onto me. "I thought—Jesus, I actually thought our friendship was something you would take pains to protect, and instead you practically throw yourself at me." A hot wave of humiliation courses through me. Did I really throw myself at him? How embarrassing, how—God, how immature, how *teenage*. Though from what scant memories I have, he didn't exactly seem unwilling . . . But Tom is still speaking. "I get that it's difficult for you to see Seb—"

"It's not—"

"Don't give me that. I saw your face when he kissed Alina. His *wife*, Kate, and Christ, it's been ten years! He kissed his wife and you had to leave the fucking room—"

"That's not . . ." I start, but he's still in full flood, and in any case, what can I say? *Actually, I realized last night that I'm over Seb. I left the room because Severine's skull appeared on the table. Yes, I see her regularly. I would ask her who killed her except she never speaks.*

"—you were near as dammit physically ill at the sight. So don't tell me you don't care about Seb. Only next time you're looking for a pick-me-up shag to make you feel better, have the decency to try someone other than me."

He stops, breathing hard, his blue eyes boring into me. In that moment I see myself as he sees me and it's at such odds to how I imagined that I'm temporarily cut off from speech. The hurt is staggering.

"Oh," I hear myself say eventually. There's nothing else I can say. It doesn't matter that I'm not in love with Seb; it doesn't matter that the corridor memory is something precious to me. All that matters is what Tom thinks, and now that I know his opinion I can't look at him. I turn and gather up my shoes, bag and coat from the chair in the corner and push past him without resistance into the corridor—the corridor. Can I really have this memory of the intimate darkness, the sweetness, the desire, while Tom holds something entirely different inside him? Is this really Tom? I turn as if to check before I leave; he's still standing by the bedroom door, but I can't see his face in the shadow. I don't know who this is.

The hurt hasn't ebbed, nor the excruciating humiliation, but my sense of injustice is fanning those embers of anger. "So," I say slowly, deliberately. I hear my voice, but it doesn't sound like me; it's too high and clipped. "In your eyes I'm a desperate, lonely old spinster looking for anybody or anything to take my mind off Seb." He makes a movement with his hand, but I go on. "Well, there were two of us there last night. What's your excuse?"

"Kate—" he says, moving toward me, but I don't wait for his answer. In truth it has just occurred to me: ironically the accusation he's thrown at me is more appropriate for him. I was a substitute for Lara. I pull the door closed sharply behind me and go down the tattered steps to the front door of the block of flats, only pausing at the bottom to put on my shoes. I had tights on last night, I think inconsequentially; they must still be in Tom's flat. Did he undress me and put me to bed, the pathetic old basket case who couldn't hold her drink? I see a cab as soon as I spill out of the lobby onto the street, and it stops for me.

"Where to, love?" asks the driver.

Where to, indeed? I look at my watch. My head is pounding from the hangover, and I feel greasy and gritty, but I don't have time to go home for a shower before I'm due to meet my lawyer. I give him the address of my office instead. I half expect Severine to join me in the cab, but I spend the journey alone, gritting my teeth and focusing solely on staying above the riptide of hurt that beats up inexorably at my throat and threatens to drag me down.

I make it into the bathroom at my office before I give in to that current, sitting on the loo seat in the cramped WC sobbing soundlessly into my hands. It's an indulgence, I know, but I'm temporarily unable to restrain myself. It's hard to even pinpoint why I'm crying, other than through battered pride. But that dark, thrilling corridor encounter . . . I never thought of Tom that way; he was Lara's, or Lara was Tom's, or something—and anyway, there was always the intangible presence of Seb between us. But it turns out I haven't been in love with Seb for a very long time, if I ever was at all; I'm starting to wonder if the Seb of my memories ever existed. Nobody seems to be who I thought they were. Tom's words echo in my head. *Next time you're looking for a pick-me-up shag* . . . Nobody is who I thought they were, and that apparently includes me.

There's a rap on the door. "Kate?" I hear Julie's muffled voice. "You probably ought to leave for your next appointment soon."

"Um, thanks. Be right out." I blow my nose on toilet roll and wipe my eyes then survey the damage in the mirror. The combination of a hangover and a crying fit clearly doesn't suit my skin, and splashing cold water on my face turns out to be an ineffectual remedy. *Grin and bear it*, I tell myself, forcing my mouth into a smile. Then I see Severine's grinning skull supcrimposed on my own reflection and it's all I can do not to vomit.

When I emerge some minutes later Julie's eyes sweep over me, her face anxious, but she has the good sense not to comment. Thankfully Paul is not there, and for once I couldn't care less whether that's a good or a bad sign. It's only on the route to my lawyer's office that it occurs to me all this emotional drama has distracted me from the fact that last night I was wondering whether Seb and Caro had something to do with the death of a young girl in France ten years ago.

"Well," remarks my lawyer from behind her desk, looking at me over the top of her reading glasses. I'm not quite sure why she's wearing them; it's not as if she has anything in front of her to read right now. Instead she's been in listening mode, a small frown appearing from time to time on her narrow forehead, occasionally a nod of her neat, dark head as she takes in my disjointed account. I'm trying to get the measure of her, Mrs. Streeter—or was it Ms., or Miss?—but it's hard in the small, hot room with my head pounding so fiercely. She reminds me of a magpie, dark and bright and quick, though she must be almost fifty; there are gray streaks in that black close-cropped hair. "Well," she says again, more thoughtfully, pursing her lips, which are incongruously painted with uneven layers of a greasy lipstick that's far too pink for her. I want to pick up a tissue and wipe it off her. She hasn't offered me a cup of tea, which I'm irrationally resentful over. I'm sure her fees are going to bankrupt me, so surely a tea bag and a splash of milk isn't too much to ask?

She leans back in her chair and adjusts her reading glasses. This will be the pronouncement, I think; this is where I find out exactly how much of a mess I'm in. "You're a lawyer, yes?" she says abruptly.

"Yes. Well, no, not anymore. I run a legal recruitment company."

She waves a hand. "But you have the training. You know, for example, that we have an adversarial system here in Britain: the police and prosecution gather evidence likely to convict, and the defense gathers evidence likely to acquit, and then it's all hashed out in open court. Given your training, you likely know an awful lot more detail than that. In practice, in high-profile criminal cases, what tends to happen is that the police very quickly establish a theory and work to find evidence to support that. Anything they turn up that doesn't quite fit the working theory is not exactly overlooked, but it certainly gets less attention." She grimaces, her mouth a slash of uneasy pink. "It's imperfect. All systems are imperfect. But we have habeas corpus, and presumed innocence until proof of guilt, and the court framework in which the trial takes place is very open." She fixes her dark, bright eyes upon me, and I realize I'm expected to respond in some way.

"Um. Yes."

She nods briskly. "The French system is very different. It's based on civil law, rather than common law, which as you know means there is no concept of precedent . . . but I digress. The important point vis-à-vis your situation is that it is not an adversarial system. All criminal cases—at least, all criminal cases of a serious nature such as this—are investigated by a, well, the technical term is *juge d'instruction*, which translates roughly as *examining magistrate*, I suppose. This magistrate is independent of the government and the prosecution service, but nonetheless works closely with the police. It's their job to analyze all the evidence and opine in a report as to whether the case should go to trial." She pauses and looks at me closely again. This time I'm quick to nod. "The important point here is that, generally speaking, weak cases don't even get to trial; they're thrown out by the investigating magistrate before that. The corollary is that the conviction rate is very high, and whilst there's the concept of innocent until proven guilty, in practice . . ." She shrugs her shoulders and executes that queasy pink grimace again. "There's a high presumption of guilt if the case gets as far as trial."

My mind is racing ahead. "But what of the checks and balances on the magistrate?"

She shakes her head almost apologetically. "Next to none. It's one of the major complaints against the system; effectively a huge number of cases are tried in secret by a single person rather than in open court subject to a jury of peers. On the whole the magistrates are very good, but as a principle . . . I should probably add there's no concept of habeas corpus, either, though in most circumstances a *juge d'instruction* would need another magistrate to sign off before a person can be held. Oh, and while trials are generally very quick, the preceding investigations can be very long."

"How long?"

"Two years is not unusual."

It may be the hangover, but I don't think so: suddenly I feel sick again. The idea of this hanging over us all for years doesn't bear thinking about: Modan appearing at intervals with his oh-so-elegant suits and his sly questions, inducing Lara to a permanent state of self-absorbed giddiness, Caro needling and prodding and pecking away at any exposed quarter, Tom—no, not Tom, I can't think about Tom—and Severine . . . It occurs to me that I've been relying on Severine disappearing once this has all gone away. I wonder if she sees it quite the same way.

"Are you all right?"

I realize I'm rubbing my forehead with notable force. I drop my hand and attempt to look at her, but another wave of nausea hits me and I have to look down and grit my teeth. The office floor is carpeted with faded blue tiles, which provide nothing to focus on; I try the edge of her desk instead. There's a scratch in the dark varnished wood that shows the cheap sawdust-like MDF underneath.

"Perhaps a cup of tea?" She doesn't wait for my answer; she leans forward and presses a button on her telephone to issue the tea-making instruction to a disembodied voice. Disembodied: a voice without a body. But Severine is the other way round: a body without a voice. Dear God, two more years of Severine . . .

"Are you all right?" she asks again.

"Sorry. It's just a little hot in here," I say unconvincingly. The nausea is passing.

"Of course," she says smoothly. "Ah, here's the tea."

I take my cup gratefully, and also a couple of biscuits, which I nibble at cautiously at first, but then devour rapidly as I realize I'm starving. She takes her own cup, adds milk and stirs in economical movements, then sits back with the cup resting on her leg, the saucer abandoned on the desk. I focus on my own life-giving tea.

"What do you think happened?" she asks, in a musing tone.

I look up inquiringly, my mouth full of another biscuit.

"You've told me the bare facts of what happened," she explains. "All of which I could have got from the French papers, to be frank—of course I've been following it; it's exactly my area and quite a high-profile case over there. But what do *you* think happened?"

I take a sip of tea to wash down the biscuit before answering her. "I don't know. It was so long ago . . . Now I'm not even sure I can trust my memories." Or my interpretation of those memories.

"Understandable. But you were questioned quite soon after; that usually helps the details to stick, so to speak."

I shrug.

"So, all caveats notwithstanding, what do you think happened?"

"Well, at first I thought—well, I thought it was nothing to do with us. Her ex-boyfriend, maybe, or just something totally random, some sick psycho or something . . ."

"And now?" She tips her head to one side.

"I don't know. No, really, I don't. I suppose since Modan told me it wasn't the ex-boyfriend I've been thinking about whether it *could* have been one of us. Just hypothetically."

"And?"

"I suppose . . . not Lara, obviously; it's just not within her. And not Tom."

"Why not Tom?"

"Well, he was with Lara all night. And even if he hadn't been . . ."

"Let me guess: it's not within him; he just couldn't." It's not said unkindly; she's almost smiling, but I know she's deliberately holding up a mirror to show me the flaws in my thinking. "That's what you were going to say, correct?"

"Something like that," I concede weakly, but it's not true actually. Tom could, if it was necessary. He has that steel within him, the ability to get things done. I see his stony face from this morning . . . But if Tom had done it, he'd have done it *right*. He wouldn't have allowed a body to be found ten years later. "Anyway, like I said, he was with Lara all night. From what I gather, they didn't do a lot of sleeping," I add wryly. I think of Lara and Tom entwined, and my mind immediately skitters away from the image.

She inclines her head, conceding the point. "Which leaves Caroline, Theo and Sebastian. And you, but you were in bed, later joined by Sebastian, after his assignation with Severine."

I wonder if I would have flinched even a day ago to hear her say that so baldly. Now it's simply a fact. "Yes. Only I didn't know about the assignation at the time."

"What time did he join you?"

"I'm not sure. About 3 A.M. I think." At least, I think that I think that. It was so long ago . . . Suddenly I'm back in that bedroom in France, groggily opening my eyes to see the glowing red digits of the clock radio showing 6 A.M. in the foreground, and in the background Seb stepping out of his boxer shorts after a trip to the bathroom. Without moving my head that's the extent of my vision: a sideways image of a clock and Seb, from waist to knee. He's close enough that I can see the first rays of the morning sun, undeterred by the ineffectual curtains, turning the hair on his legs into golden glowing wires. I can't face dealing with him, so I close my eyes tightly and pretend he hasn't woken me.

Seb's words of last night (was it only last night?) float back to me: *And you and I both know I came to our room that night and passed out, so whatever happened to Severine was nothing to do with me.* And I think again of Caro's and Seb's heads, conspiratorially close; of Caro watching Seb as he spoke to me last night. Do I think he came to bed at 3 A.M. because he told me that at some point?

"And you say Caro and Theo were together till they went to bed."

"Yes. So I understand." How do I know that? Certainly there's no Theo to ask.

"Was Sebastian the last person to see Severine alive then?"

"No, the bus driver. And the CCTV." The bus driver. Of course.

I forgot that last night. It doesn't matter what time Seb came to bed; it doesn't matter whether Caro and Theo were together: Severine was alive enough on Saturday morning to take a bus. Something inside me unwinds a little.

"True. If it was indeed Severine." She frowns for a moment. "Though the chances of another young girl matching that description getting on in that location . . . Mmmm." She ponders silently for a moment, leaning back and tapping her teeth with a fingernail. I wonder if she will later find that dreadful pink lipstick all over her fingers. She straightens up. "Right. Plan of action. No talking to Monsieur Modan without me present."

"Okay. What else?"

She shakes her head, smiling. "That's it for now. All we can do is wait."

I stare at her, nonplussed. "Wait?" I'm paying painful amounts per hour, and all she can come up with is *keep quiet* and *wait*?

She nods. "Yes, wait. Believe me, Modan is not here on a whim. He has information he's not yet revealed. Perhaps from the autopsy, or something else . . . At any rate, there's something he's not telling you. Because otherwise, there is literally no evidence to tie any of the six of you to this crime, and it's quite a stretch to find a motive, too, despite best efforts to paint you as the jilted lover. So if the *juge d'instruction* still has Modan digging around over here, you can be sure there's something up his sleeve. So . . . we wait."

Jesus. "I'm not good at waiting."

"No," she says contemplatively, as she pushes back her chair to stand up and extend her hand. "I wouldn't think you are."

I'm not quite sure how to take that.

CHAPTER TWELVE

All day Severine hovers.

I've decided it's a sign of tiredness, or distraction: like an illness, she can creep in much more easily when my defenses are low. Not that she creeps. She strolls, she saunters, she claims territory as her own with a single languid glance; everything about Severine is on Severine's terms. Except her death, of course.

I'm back in my office after the appointment with my lawyer, and despite my hangover, despite Severine, despite the—what? drama, row, contretemps?—with Tom, I'm getting rather a lot done. The trick is bloody single-mindedness, a strong personal trait of mine. Do not pick up the phone and call Lara; do not pay attention to the slim, secretive-eyed dead girl who perches casually on the edge of my desk, swinging one walnut brown ankle; do not descend into introspection and speculation; do not pass go, do not collect £200.

Gordon calls early afternoon. We now have a weekly catch-up call in the diary for each Friday afternoon, though I've been forewarned he will frequently have to reschedule, or skip it altogether: Mr. Farrow is a busy man. I presume he's calling to reschedule, but instead he says, in his mild manner, "Why don't you drop by the office instead of having a call today?"

"Sure, let me just check my schedule." I have a couple of calls in my diary before then, but I should still be able to get across town in time. "That's fine, I can come over. Everything okay?"

"Fine, fine. Just thought it's been a while since we had a face-to-face catch-up. I'm a little quieter today, so it seemed best to take advantage."

"No problem. See you at 3:30." I hang up, thinking that I should take Paul with me, to broaden the relationship and so forth, but I know I won't. Gordon enjoys meeting *me* (and vice versa); he will find Paul too slick, too accommodating.

I wonder if I will be bringing Severine with me.

Either Severine finds business meetings uninteresting, or I am sufficiently focused to keep her at bay, but whatever the reason, I'm flying solo when I meet with Gordon. We run through an update on the candidates he has seen: what he thinks of them, what they think of the opportunity, what other firms appear to be thinking of them . . . Recruitment at this level—partner, soon to be partner, which is what we're concentrating on first—is a strategic game. The next step is the associates, but a good number will simply follow the partners they've worked with most closely.

"If we get those two, it will be quite a coup," says Gordon thoughtfully, tapping the sheet of names that lies on the table in front of us, flanked by our empty coffee cups. We're in one of the meeting rooms on the top floor of the Haft & Weil building, with a glorious view over the city. I can see the gleaming curve of St. Paul's dome, with glimpses of the flashing silver ribbon that is the Thames popping up unexpectedly between buildings. From this height, London has a stately gravitas in its lofty architecture, standing indomitable and proud in the sunshine. It would be easy to forget the hustle and grime one encounters close-up.

"We'll get them," I say confidently, wrenching my gaze back to the paper.

"Well, I suppose the size of the guarantee we're offering is hard to ignore."

I shake my head. "It's not about the guarantee." Gordon glances at me, a question in his eyes. "That's necessary, obviously, but what I mean is, it's not about the money for those two. It's about what the money means. They feel undervalued, underappreciated where they are, and they hate the lack of collegiality. The guarantee just proves to them that you value them. If you manage them properly once you get them across, make them feel safe but also give them opportunities to feel like they're making a difference, then I think they'll do very well for you."

Gordon's sharp eyes are assessing me. "You have strong views on management styles, I take it."

I shrug. "In my job, you need to have an instinct for who would fit where. No point putting a diffident technical specialist into an aggressive American setup, for example."

"You need to be a good judge of people." He's toying with his empty coffee cup, as if turning something over in his mind.

"I like to think I am. In a professional context." My mind skitters to that week in France, to Seb, to Tom, to Lara, Theo, Caro, Severine, and the spider's web that entangles and binds us all. With everything I know now, I can only think that my judgment was disastrously clouded back then. Possibly—probably, even?—it still is. "In a professional context," I repeat. He's still turning the coffee cup this way and that. "Why, is there something troubling you?"

He glances up, surprised. "No, I . . . No. Well." He looks away again, as if reluctant to look at me, to acknowledge we're having this conversation. "Caro is on the slate this year."

135

LEXIE ELLIOTT

The slate: the list of prospective candidates for partnership. It's pretty much an up-or-out culture: those who don't make the cut are expected to leave the firm. I do a rapid calculation of how long Caro has been a qualified lawyer, and the timing is about right; I'd expect her to be on the slate around now. "And how does it look?" I ask, although I know the answer, or we wouldn't be talking about it.

He puffs out a breath. "Between you and me . . . dicey. Speaking plainly, it's good that she's female; we need more women in corporate. Not that we're supposed to kowtow to the statistics, but . . ." He grimaces, and I nod. We both know the score on gender balance in the workplace. "And anyway, she's very good, and a tough negotiator, no question about it, and the clients that love her *really* love her, but there's a perception that she's . . . well . . ." He's searching for a way to say it that doesn't make him feel disloyal. "I suppose . . . not a team player." He looks at me directly. "If you were placing Caro, where would you put her?"

I consider hedging my bets, coming up with a carefully worded non-answer, but then I remember this is Gordon: he likes to hear it straight. I can only hope that extends to opinions about his daughter. I take a deep breath and muster an even tone. "Haft & Weil wouldn't be my first choice for her. I would think she would be more suited to an aggressive American outfit. Eat what you kill and so forth."

He nods absentmindedly, looking out over the expanse of the city skyline; thankfully he can't see my relief that he isn't offended by my bluntness. "I wouldn't disagree with you. But since she's trying to make it in this firm . . ." He trails off.

I look for something helpful to suggest, though no doubt whatever I can think of he will already have considered. "Perhaps she needs to get involved in some management initiatives during the coming year. Show that she can be a more rounded candidate."

"Perhaps." He purses his lips thoughtfully, then sighs, still gazing at the skyline, though I'm not sure he sees it. "We're making up less partners each year, you know? I don't know how we expect to keep all the associates working at this intensity when the prize is getting harder and harder to grab. Used to be that if you did a good job for long enough and kept your nose clean . . ." He collects himself and turns back to me. "Good idea on the management side; I suppose that type of involvement might give her an edge." He nods to himself, as if making a mental note to speak with her about it. "Though you can't cut corners . . ." He trails off again, his gaze sliding back down to his empty coffee cup.

You can't cut corners. Only, Caro would. Caro would cut a swath down the middle and everyone else be damned if that was the most convenient route for herself. I suddenly realize he knows the problem is more far-reaching than just *not a team player.* Deep down he doesn't think she'll make partner, and he doesn't think she ought to, either, though he's trying hard to convince himself otherwise. For a moment I ache for him, this clever, thoughtful, kind man who wants the Caro he lost when she was thirteen, and is bewildered every day by the woman she's become.

It's barely 4 p.m., but I go straight home after the meeting with Gordon; I'm exhausted. All I want to do is sink into a hot bath. Though perhaps taking a moment to relax will be like removing my head from the sand: reality will rush in and I will have to face it all— Tom, Severine, Modan, the whole shebang. I dither for a moment then run the bath, dumping in industrial quantities of an expensive bath foam Lara bought me. If reality is going to rush in anyway, I may as well face it whilst lounging up to my ears in soapsuds.

Lara calls just as I'm settling into the bath with an inadvertent sigh of pleasure. "Have you got plans?" she asks. She sounds uncharacteristically drained. "Or do you fancy a quiet night in? Takeout in front of a chick flick or something?"

"Done," I say, thinking warmly of all the chick flick nights we've had in the past, gossiping over the local takeout and drinking rather more wine than is warranted by a quiet night in. Only that was before, when Lara was just Lara, with no subterfuge, and I was just Kate (albeit *desperate, lonely old spinster* Kate), and Severine was a strange mystery from a summer long, long ago. I want everything back how it was so badly that my eyes are pricking with tears. I shake my head impatiently, and the mountains of soapsuds rise and fall gently. "I'm already home and I can't bear the thought of moving again—do you mind coming to me?"

"Not a problem. Your take-out place is better anyway."

"You sound done in. What time did you get home last night?" There's a pause. "Ah. You didn't make it home."

"Well . . . no. What about you, were you late?"

I could lie, now I've become so very good at that; I could obfuscate, I could dodge the question, but it's just so bloody exhausting. "I didn't make it home either."

"Really? But who . . ." I can practically hear her brain whirring. *"Tom?"* The surprise is genuine. She has no right to mind, but still I wonder if she does.

"Yes. But it's not like that. Not really . . ."

"What does *not really* mean?" Is she a little forced, or am I over-analyzing?

"It means I'll tell you later. Not that there's anything much to tell. What time do you think you'll be here?"

"Around six, I think, if not sooner. My brain is good for nothing today; there's hardly any point in me sitting here."

"Well, I'll be here, so whenever."

I put down the phone and lean my head back against the rim of the bathtub. Severine, dressed in the black shift, has perched her neat behind casually on the edge of the tub, her slender limbs stretched out ahead of her, crossed at the ankle. She turns to look at me expressionlessly with those dark, all-knowing eyes. It's the contrast that catches attention, I muse: the eyes that have seen far more than fits a face so smooth and unlined. I think of the crow's-feet developing round the corners of my eyes, of the single gray hair I found (and immediately plucked out) last week.

"I'm thirty-one," I say aloud. Severine is still looking at me. "I suppose you'll be—what was it?—nineteen forever." She looks away, disinterested, presenting me with her profile. Her nose has a small bump in it, but if anything it works for her; it makes her face stronger. "Why are you here anyway?" She looks at me again. There's no intensity, just a cool appraisal, then her gaze slides off, as if I'm simply not interesting enough to retain it. It's more than a little galling. I reach for the shampoo and lather up my hair, then try again, irritation creeping into my voice now. "Since you're here, do you mind telling me who killed you?"

She's smoking a cigarette now, one leg crossed over the other and her sandal dangling off her narrow foot again, in the way that hypnotized Seb all those years ago; she glances at me, one eyebrow raised. It's as strong an expression of amusement as I've ever seen on her face.

"Yeah, okay, I didn't really think it would be that easy," I mutter. Then I sink under the still-hot water to wash out the shampoo, and when I surface she has gone.

"So," says Lara expressively, as soon as she has a glass of wine in her hand. *So.* A single word, two letters—how can it be loaded with such meaning? "Spill." She looks tired, so tired that it seems an effort to hold herself together this evening; even her facial features are rumpled at the edges.

I look at the glass in my own hand: it's beautiful, long and elegant and fragile; a gift, though I don't remember who from. If I applied pressure, it would crack instantly. I have some sympathy. I wonder how resilient Lara is feeling. "You spill," I say tightly. I don't mean to be combative, but . . . I sort of do.

She takes a sip and tries to smile, but it doesn't come off, and I instantly feel guilty. "Are you okay?" I ask quietly.

She shrugs. "Sort of. Maybe." Again, the effortful smile, through tears that can't be far away. "You?"

I shrug. "Pretty much the same." Though in my case there are no tears hovering, I won't allow myself to wallow again. I take a sip of the wine. It will go to my head quickly tonight if I'm not careful. "Come on. Let's order the curry and watch the film. We can do all the spilling later."

And so I spend the evening with Lara. It's a nice evening; an evening that harks back to happier times. We watch a romcom, we eat too much curry, we drink too much wine. It's comforting, this old habit of ours; the only thing that has changed over the years is the quality of the wine. Severine stays away, which isn't really a surprise; I'm well aware she's a figment of my (frankly, fevered) imagination, and my imagination cannot possibly conjure an image of Severine watching anything containing Reese Witherspoon. I see her more as an art house kind of girl.

But in truth more has changed than our wine budget. When the film has finished we can't avoid the dual elephants in the room. "So," she says again, turning to face me and arranging herself cross-legged on the sofa we're sharing. She's borrowed from my wardrobe a pair of slouchy pajama bottoms and a hoodie; on me, they're definitely hide-at-home clothing, but on Lara they're transformed by her blondness, her bustiness, her sheer wholesome sexiness: she could be an advert for Abercrombie & Fitch. No wonder Tom continues to hold a torch for her. It never bothered me before, but now I find I'm analyzing: score 1 for Lara for instant sex appeal; score 1 for Kate for her quick intelligence; score 1 for Lara . . . I am appalled at myself—has one single drunken kiss with Tom really dragged me down to this level?—but still I can't completely stifle the ugly green-eyed monster lurking within me.

"So," I counter. "How are things with the dear detective?"

"Ah." She looks down and traces a circle on the sofa with her finger. "It's . . . complicated."

It seems she's ready to talk. I rearrange myself on the sofa to mirror her position. "Where is he tonight?"

"He went back to France."

My heart leaps. "For good?"

"No, he's coming back on Monday; it's just for some family thing. A christening, I think. Not because of the case." She's still making the circles. "Not that he'd tell me if it was because of the case; he won't talk about it with me since . . ."

"Since?" A blush is crossing her cheeks, and suddenly I know exactly what she means. I wonder how she will phrase it.

"Since we . . . ah . . . crossed that line." Bravo, neatly put. I can't bring myself to ask any of the usual gossipy questions, and she doesn't seem to expect me to: she glances up at my face, both embarrassed and rueful, and adds, "So, sorry, but no insider information here."

"A man of principle," I say, only half ironic.

"He is!" She's leaning forward, her whole body imploring me to listen, to understand. "I mean, I know how it looks—he's screwing one of the witnesses in his case—but we're keeping it totally separate; he won't discuss it *at all* with me, not a word, and anyway, it's not like *I'm* under suspicion."

"No, but I am."

She pauses, then nods dejectedly. "Yes, I think you are. It doesn't make any sense to me, given she was alive on Saturday morning, but you are. And Seb and Caro and Theo."

"But me more than most. On account of Seb's complete lack of self-restraint." Tom would be annoyed with me for talking with Lara about this. A streak of rebellion surfaces: Tom is stratospherically annoyed with me anyway, so what the hell.

She shakes her head. "I don't . . ." Then her blue eyes widen as she twigs. It's a gratifying confirmation that Modan really isn't talking to her about the case, though I hadn't planned it as a test. "Seb and Severine? Really? I would never have guessed that . . . I mean, I knew he found her attractive; all the guys love a bit of that French ooh-la-la, *soooo* predictable . . ." She rolls her eyes. I can't help a private smile at Lara of all people, who plays the Swedish blond bombshell angle to maximum effect, being so dismissive of Severine's application of her own cultural advantages. Lara is still absorbing. "Wow. What a complete fuckwit Seb is. Was. Still is, I should think." She shakes her head again. "When did you find out?"

"Just recently. I had started to wonder, and then Seb—apropos of absolutely nothing—admitted it to me last night. Only because he's already told Modan, and he didn't want me to hear it through that avenue."

Lara is frowning. "But—how? They must have been very discreet. We were pretty much on top of one another in the farmhouse."

"Apparently it was just the last night."

"Oh. I suppose it was a pretty crazy night all round." She shakes her head, still digesting. "I can't believe I missed that. God, what else did I miss?"

She means it as a rhetorical question, but it's actually *the* question, the all-important nub of the matter. "Yeah, I've been wondering that myself," I say quietly.

"You don't mean—but she was alive on the Saturday morning," Lara says impatiently. "She got on the damn bus."

I nod. "Agreed, she did, in which case what happened to her has nothing to do with any of us. Or she didn't; it was just a coincidence that someone fitting her description got on at that stop—"

"Hell of a coincidence. How many girls even exist in the world who are that height, and build, and who wear a red chiffon scarf over their hair?"

"True, but just a coincidence, in which case . . ." I spread my hands and shrug. "It seems your Modan is rather taken with the latter possibility."

"He's not my Modan," she protests, though without any conviction.

"Really? He does seem to be yours. Head to toe, heart and all."

"I would think so, except . . . he won't talk about what's going to happen after all this is over and he goes back to France." She looks at me, her eyes over-bright. "I know he had a long-distance relationship before, and he hated it . . . It's crazy, I can see it's crazy, we hardly know each other, but . . ." She lifts her hands helplessly, and suddenly I sense her desperate fear: she knows she has already jumped off the precipice. "And he won't even talk about it. He just says *we'll figure it out*. How are we supposed to do that if he won't talk about it?"

"Maybe he needs to concentrate on one thing at a time. Maybe he just wants to get the case over so you two can stop skulking around." I can't believe I'm defending the man who seems intent on painting me as a murderer. But I've seen how Modan looks at her. It's unmissable, it's cinematic—as if he's a reformed alcoholic and she's the very drink he's been craving for years: that man has no intention of letting her go. "Maybe he's worried about how *you* will feel when he puts your best friend in prison," I add sourly.

"But she got on the fucking bus!" She smacks her hand into the sofa in frustration.

"I know, I know. But that aside . . . if *you* were constructing the case, who would you have as your prime suspect?"

She pauses, considering. "Not Tom, or me, for obvious reasons—and don't think you're off the hook on Tom, I'm coming back to that—and I know it wasn't you; you didn't even know about the affair till just now, so what possible motive would you have?"

"Not a rock-solid basis for excluding me," I tease.

"Oh, hush. If I'm going to have to think about this, let's not waste time on definite no-no's. Theo: no motive. He knew her forever, and apparently they'd always gotten on well. I'm sure he fancied her, but let's be honest: even if he tried it on and got a knock-back, I can't quite imagine Theo summoning up a murderous rage."

"Fair point." I see Theo, his cheeks flooding pink at the slightest jibe, his back covered in thick factor-50 to protect the milk-pale skin that is the curse of the true redhead. I cannot imagine Theo, with all his good intentions and awkwardness, having the courage to make a pass at Severine. Come to think of it, I don't remember Theo ever making a pass at anyone.

"Is it totally un-PC to say I was really surprised about the way he died?" Lara asks hesitantly. "I didn't know he had it in him."

"Totally un-PC. But yeah, me neither." Theo died by throwing himself on a live grenade, thereby saving four of his colleagues. I can only imagine it was an instinctive reaction. At the funeral, Tom said that Theo's parents were unimaginably proud, astonished and despairing in equal measures.

"Yeah . . ." She shakes herself after a moment. "But anyway. That leaves Caro and Seb." She frowns. "I can't see why Caro would . . . or Seb . . . but he *was* with her . . ." I'm quiet, reluctant to influence her thinking. This *is* a test, in a way, and I'm almost holding my breath. If Lara alights on the same theory that has been slowly building in my subconscious, I can't dismiss it as another product of my demonstrably overactive brain. "So, Seb was with her, but why would he kill her? I mean, he wouldn't, not on purpose"—*here it comes*—". . . God, not intentionally, but what if something happened by accident?" Her eyes widen. "You know, Kate, it could all have been just a tragic accident. Something went horribly wrong, and rather than face up to it all he stuffed her body in the well. I mean, he's strong enough."

Bingo. We look at each other, wide-eyed.

"Last night Seb seemed very keen to stress that he came back to the room and passed out," I say quietly.

"And did he?" she asks.

"I'm not sure. I pretty much passed out myself. He woke me up going to the bathroom at something like six in the morning, so sometime before then I suppose." The clock, Seb stepping out of his boxer shorts, those glowing golden hairs . . . the clock, Seb . . .

"So he could have come in anytime before that."

"I suppose . . ." Only it has just occurred to me that in my memory Seb is on my side of the bed. The side with the chair, where he'd got into the habit of tossing his clothes when he undressed. And he's stepping out of boxer shorts. In the entire time we'd been in France, he'd always grabbed a towel from the hook behind the door and wrapped it round him to go to the communal bathroom—or on occasion run the gauntlet naked. He'd never ever bothered to fish around for a pair of boxer shorts. "Or maybe . . . maybe that was him coming to bed for the first time. I don't know . . ." What do I really remember and what is a reconstruction? I can't trust in anything anymore.

"How *do* you accidentally kill someone?"

I shrug. "Unlucky blow to the head, perhaps? She could have tripped and smacked her head on something. I suppose the autopsy would show that."

"And how long do you suppose you need to accidentally kill a girl and dump her body?" Lara asks, with deliberate drollery.

"Well, in my vast experience of accidental homicide . . ." I reply, equally drolly. I have definitely had too much wine if I'm being this flippant about the girl that haunts me. "Jesus, I don't know. I suppose he must have spent some time screwing her first, though God knows how long that would have taken in his drunken state."

"And then surely there must have been a period of panic, deciding what to do . . ." She trails off. "But, you know, this is all just a thought exercise. It's not even hypothetical; after all, she got on the bus. Right?"

Her eyes catch mine and hold, and I recognize the uncertainty in them; it matches the tight knot in my belly. She wants me to reassure her. I wanted her to reassure me, and look where that landed me.

"Right," I say quietly.

CHAPTER THIRTEEN

I suggest Lara stays the night, half expecting to hear, *No thanks, I'd rather wake up in my own bed*, but she accepts gratefully. I try to remember the last time she did that; we used to stay with each other a lot in the years just after leaving university, a subconscious attempt to re-create the messy hubbub of student housing, where nobody need ever be alone. It occurs to me that now I am almost always alone: long periods of isolation broken by short human interactions that don't leave me feeling any less solitary. It's probably not good for me—at least, it's probably not good for me that I don't mind. In any case, I think with dark humor, now I have Severine for company.

I have a spare bedroom, but Lara crawls into bed with me like days of old, and turns on her side, resting her head on her bent arm. In the warm glow of the bedside light I can see her eyeliner is smudged and her eyelids are heavy with the wine; she looks blowsy and sloppy and decadently sexy. Modan wakes up to this, I think. Does the effect ever wear off? One day will he look at her and move on without lingering, his brain ticking over his to-do list for the day?

Or will he always stop for a moment, arrested by the sight, and perhaps touch the back of his hand to her cheek? And Tom, does he remember what she looked like in his bed all those years ago? Does he yearn to see her there now? I cut off that train of thought quickly and turn on my back to look at the ceiling instead. There were times at Oxford, and in the years after, when I had stabs of jealousy toward Lara: for her effortless magnetism, her easygoing take-it-or-leave-it flirting, for how her very presence dimmed mine in the eyes of the male population. Then I would reason those feelings away; I would console myself that I appealed to the more discerning gentleman . . . I thought I had grown up, cast off my insecurities, but here we are a decade on: it's so *demeaning* to realize that actually nothing has changed.

"Tom," says Lara uncannily if sleepily, pulling my gaze back to her. "Come on, time to tell all."

I rub a hand over my face, not trusting my voice for a moment, then recover and say, "Not much to tell."

"You're pretty upset for not much to tell."

"I was drunk—well, we both were. We were sharing a cab, and I went up to his flat for a cup of tea—no, really, just tea!" I protest on Lara's raised eyebrow. "Then somehow, I don't know, we were kissing and then . . . God, I think I passed out." I pull the pillow over my face. "It's beyond humiliating," I say, lifting it enough to let the words out. "And then this morning Tom was livid with me—he thinks I abused our friendship—and he was . . . mean. And it upset me." I shrug and put the pillow down, concentrating on the ceiling. "It's fine that he doesn't want to . . . doesn't want anything between us"—*no it's not, no it's not, it doesn't feel fine at all*—"but he was pretty nasty." It doesn't feel fine to be confessing my humiliation at not being wanted to the girl he really wants, either. I wonder if she's pleased that she hasn't been usurped, and then I'm promptly ashamed of myself.

"Tom nasty?" Lara's eyebrows are raised in astonishment, the hairs glowing golden in the light.

"Believe me, he's very good at it when he tries. Very efficient." Of course he is. Tom is the man who does what needs to be done, no matter what.

"I know, but . . . nasty to *you*? What did he say?"

"It doesn't matter—no, really, it doesn't." I shake my head at her. "I don't want to drag you into anything." I look at the ceiling again. Does it need repainting? Or is it just that the lamp is casting uneven shadows? I wonder where Severine is sleeping—does she even sleep? She's only in my head, so I suppose she must sleep when I do, except that I can't imagine that at all. I can imagine her still, even imagine her with her eyes closed, but there's a readiness there, like a panther in repose. At the slightest movement or sound she would unhurriedly raise her eyelids and survey the surrounds with her dark, secretive eyes. The thought is oddly comforting, like having a guard dog on the premises. Severine, my protector. I almost laugh out loud.

"Did you want it to turn into anything?" Lara asks carefully after a moment. I turn my head to look at her, but this time she's the one inspecting the ceiling. There are mascara flakes on her eyelashes; I will find smudges on my bed linen in the morning that are hell to get out. "You always just seemed like . . . mates. What about Seb?"

It crosses my mind that Seb never looked to Lara first. Right from our very first meeting he honed in on me. In retrospect I wonder if that was part of the attraction. "Seb and I broke up a decade ago." She turns her head to look at me with unashamed skepticism, and I can hardly blame her for it. If I didn't know myself that I was over Seb, how could I expect anyone else to? "Seb now . . . he isn't the same as the Seb I knew back then. Or thought I knew . . ." I'm not sure Seb was ever who I thought he was. "Maybe if I'd seen him in the intervening years I'd have been over him long ago." Or maybe not; maybe it's the stark contrast of now versus then that allows me to see things more clearly.

"Closure," she says thoughtfully. Then again, with a tired smile and an American accent: "*Clo-sure.*" A large yawn arrives, which she covers delicately, somehow putting me in mind of a cat, and then I think of her again on that car journey back from France, golden and sated, the cat that got the cream. I close my eyes tightly, but the image remains. "But Tom," she is saying. "Did you really want something more?"

Is she being more or less tenacious than I expect? Is she schooling her expression or is this a natural reaction? I can't stop the second-guessing. "God, I don't know. I never thought of him like that, and then suddenly . . ." Was it so sudden? I think of coming to the surface in his car after the journey back from lunch with his folks: *wakey wakey, sleeping beauty*, of that instant before the world rushed back in. Perhaps that fleeting moment lingered in my head, setting off ripples . . . I shrug, somehow disturbed by that thought. "I don't know." Her yawn is catching; I'm yawning myself now.

"Mmm," she says, her eyelids drifting closed.

I reach out and flick off the bedside light. How is it that I can feel her warmth stealing across the inches between us, sense the rise and fall of her chest as she breathes evenly: the physical connection plus the intangible webs that link us—how is it that all of this binds us, yet we're still alone inside our heads?

On Monday Julie has a message for me when I get back to my office after a meeting: *Call Caroline Horridge*, followed by a Haft & Weil number. There's no message from Tom, not that he would call my office number, and not that I expect him to call at all. I answer a few e-mails first, but the yellow Post-it with Julie's curly script sits on my desk and glares at me unrelentingly until I recognize I'm prevaricating. I grit my teeth, pick up the phone and dial, ignoring Severine, who is lounging against the wall inspecting her fingernails.

Caro answers exactly as she always does, stating her name in crisp tones after a single ring. "Hi, Caro, it's Kate Channing here," I say breezily, determined to cut off any of her game-playing tactics. "You left a message at my office."

Nonetheless, she leaves a beat or two, as if, even after hearing my full name and exactly why I'm calling, she's still struggling to place me. "Ah, yes, Kate," she says warmly, when she finally does speak. "Apologies, I've just been immersed in some difficult drafting. Back to the real world, though: I was calling to talk with you about the recruitment progress."

I have no idea what she's talking about. "In relation to . . . ?"

"Haft & Weil, of course. Our recruitment plans. I'm sure by now Gordon has told you that he's handing over the reins of that project to me."

"Um . . ." My fake smile slides right off my face.

"He hasn't? Oh, I am sorry"—*no, she's not*—"I didn't mean to jump the gun"—*yes, she did*—"I was sure he'd spoken to you." *She knows he hasn't.* "Well, he has, so you and I are going to be working together on it from now on." She pauses expectantly.

"Interesting," I say. It is, actually, on a number of levels, but of course she expects something more than that. I recover the fake smile and plaster it on. "Well, welcome aboard." I'm sure Gordon would have wanted to tell me himself; I wonder how he will react when he realizes he's been leapfrogged.

"Thanks. I was hoping you might have some time tomorrow to drop by my office and bring me up to speed. Does that work for you?"

"Absolutely." I glance at my electronic calendar, these days gratifyingly checkered with meetings and calls, my smile doggedly in place. "I can do 11 A.M. or anytime after 3:30 P.M. tomorrow."

"Let's do 11 A.M. and then we can grab a bite to eat afterward. Sound good?"

"Perfect," I manage. "See you then."

Paul comes in just as I'm putting the phone down. "Kate!" he exclaims. He's definitely on an uptick these days. "Glad I caught you. We should discuss the Cavanagh account, and I really think I'm close to getting Struthers to bite, and—"

"Slow down," I say, laughing. "I'm not going anywhere. At least take your coat off first."

Severine glances at him with disdain, and suddenly I wonder: if Severine is a creation of my mind, are her reactions my own deeply hidden feelings? I observe Paul as he struggles out of his smart spring raincoat, trying to see him afresh. You could mock him if you wanted to, with his sharp city clothes, his urbane manner and his unflinching ambition. But I've seen him gray faced and crumpled with exhaustion on a Friday evening, having worked a seventy-five-hour week; I've drunk champagne out of mugs on the floor of this very office with him. I have no wish to mock him. I'm willing to concede that Severine—this Severine—is my creation, but she's not me.

"What?" says Paul, looking up to find my eyes on him as he pulls his chair across to my desk.

I clear my face. "Nothing, nothing. Just . . . just thinking we've been gratifyingly lucky of late."

"It's not luck," he says seriously, his vanishingly pale eyebrows drawing earnestly over his eyes. "It's hard work."

He really, truly believes it. Did I believe that once? Did I think that good things came to those who earned them? "Well," I say equivocally, unwilling to burst his bubble, "it's both."

M odan, Alain Modan, *Investigateur, OPJ* and lover of Lara . . . a man of many talents. Later that day I start to realize that one of them is the ability to toss everybody else off balance with an elegantly judged metaphorical tap-tackle; I should think he has put effort into that talent over the years, carefully honing it to cause maximum consternation with minimum effort. He starts this particular campaign with the simplest of requests: a meeting.

"All of us, mind," says Lara again, through the mobile that's clamped between my ear and shoulder to leave my hands free to pack up my briefcase for a meeting. Either she's exceptionally tired or she has just been speaking to her family in Sweden: there's a slight lilt to her voice that only ever comes out in specific circumstances. "He says he'd rather not repeat everything five times."

"Mmmm."

"You don't believe that's the reason," Lara says. It's a statement, not a question.

"No." I would have expected Modan to prefer five separate interviews, which would provide five separate opportunities for analyzing reactions—why the change of tack? I pause as I flick through the documents I'm adding to the bag. "And neither do you, I suspect."

"No." She lets out a long sigh that sweeps through the city and delivers her frustration into my ear. "It's . . ."

"Infuriating?" I give up on choosing which documents I need and just drop them all in.

"No. Well, it is, but mostly it's just . . . unsettling. He's lying, I know he's lying, he knows I know he's lying—I think he even *wants* me to know he's lying, like that makes it less awful or something . . . How the hell are we supposed to base a relationship on this?"

"You're not," I say sweetly, snapping the briefcase shut. "That's why policemen aren't supposed to fraternize with witnesses."

"Oh, fuck off," she says, half laughing.

"I shall. I've got to run to a meeting." I switch the mobile into my hand. "Listen, Lara—this will pass; it won't be like this forever for you guys. You just need to . . . ride it out, as best you can."

"I know." This time the long sigh curls around me, heavy and brooding. The sunshine girl is fast losing her sun. If this thing runs for another two years . . . It doesn't bear thinking about. "Well, I'll see you there. Tonight at six thirty."

"Got it. And everyone is coming?" I ask this as casually as I can, but of course Lara isn't fooled.

"Yes. Though now I don't know who you're most worried about seeing, Seb or Tom."

"Caro, actually," I say dryly. "Always Caro."

t's 6:30 P.M., and we are meeting at the enormous 1960s glass and concrete monstrosity that is New Scotland Yard, the home of the Met Police. I didn't pay much attention to that when Lara gave me the details over the phone, but now, standing outside by the familiar triangular sign that I must have seen in thousands of TV news items, I feel the knot in my stomach tighten. Modan is not just the tricky Frenchman who's screwing my best friend. He's a man with the weight of the law behind him—both the law of his own country and of mine. Recognizing that this intimidation is intentional doesn't make it any less effective. I look around in the vain hope that perhaps Lara might be arriving at just this moment and we can brave it all together, but no. I am on my own. I square my shoulders and push through the door.

The inside is sparse and clean and hard-edged, but I'm not really in the frame of mind to take much note. The solid-faced uniformed officer behind the reception desk is expecting me; within minutes I'm led into a conference room with a pine-effect conference table and twelve chairs—surely six too many—clustered around it, though none of those chairs are currently occupied.

"You're the first," says the officer, pointing out the obvious. His tone is cheerful, but his face doesn't change. Perhaps that's what a career in the police does to you—though Modan seems to have retained the faculty of facial expression. "I'm sure Detective Modan will be along shortly. There's a coffee machine just down the hallway on the right if you're so inclined." Then I'm alone with the functional furniture. I drop my handbag onto one chair and look around. The gray London street beyond the window is slightly distorted; I wonder if the glass is bulletproof. It's certainly soundproof; I can't hear the traffic at all. From the hallway I can hear the muffled buzz and chatter of life continuing, but in here both I and the oversize room seem to be holding our breath, as if suspended before the roller coaster drops.

Then I hear Tom's distinctive rumble and Lara's giggle; I feel a sudden lurch as the roller coaster picks up speed again, and then they spill into the room with Seb on their heels. I put all my focus on Lara, absurdly self-conscious as I hug her in greeting, but I can't hide in our hello forever; I have to release her and turn to Tom and Seb. Both of them step forward at the same time, but then Tom gestures awkwardly and steps back, leaving the field for Seb.

"Hello, Seb," I say neutrally. Behind him I can see Caro enter the room, her blond hair pulled back into a severe chignon.

"Kate," says Seb warmly, though perhaps I detect a touch of apprehension lurking in his eyes. "Good to see you, though of course I'd rather we were in a pub or something." He leans in to kiss me on each cheek. I stay still throughout, imagining my cheeks are marble, and all the while I'm looking at Tom, who in turn is looking at Seb and me with a shuttered expression. When his eyes catch mine he immediately glances away. And Caro watches us all.

"Hello, Tom," I say quietly, crossing to him.

"Hi, Kate," he says, not quite meeting my eye. Then he leans in and kisses me on both cheeks, Tom who never kisses, Tom who always hugs. Yet again my cheeks are marble, this time not in silent protest but because it's all I can do to hold myself in one piece. I can feel I'm beginning to tear apart, and I don't know how to sew myself back together.

"Tom—" I start when he steps back, but Seb is talking over me.

"Christ, I need a coffee," he's saying. "Shall I grab you one, Tom?"

"I'll come with you," Tom says quickly, with what sounds suspiciously like relief. I watch the two of them leave together, and for a moment I see them as a stranger might: two men similar enough around the eyes and in frame as to be brothers, though very different in coloring. Seb always seemed older, and he seems older still, but that's no longer a compliment. A decade ago he was a man among boys, but now he is a man hurtling more quickly toward middle age than the rest of us; in the light of day there's a slackness to him that becomes more noticeable next to Tom's clean bulk.

Caro is speaking to Lara and me whilst simultaneously fishing something out of her slimline soft leather briefcase. "God, I thought I'd never get here on time. I was leading a negotiation for a major client; I couldn't really just up and leave." I feel my jaw clench. Not just a client, a *major* client. Not just in a negotiation, but *leading* it. It's petty and mean and plain exhausting to be so attuned to the slightest word or expression, but I just can't stop myself. Perhaps it's just not within me to gift Caro with the benefit of the doubt. "Anyway," she says, finally looking up, BlackBerry in hand. "How are you two?"

"Fine," says Lara brightly. "Just—oh, here's Alain."

I turn to see him pause at the doorway, an elegant gray suit encasing his long limbs, accentuated today by a powder blue tie. His eyes scan the room and stop on Lara momentarily—just long enough for something to pass between them that I could almost reach out and touch—then resume their survey. Finally he steps forward. "Ladies," he says, a smile lurking at the edge of his mouth. "And gentlemen," he adds as Tom and Seb return with their coffees; they each deposit their cardboard cups on the table to shake his hand. I notice that he didn't shake hands with Caro, Lara or me. "Welcome to the glamour that is New Scotland Yard," he says with an ironic lift of his eyebrows.

"Are police stations in France similar?" asks Lara.

He considers this seriously. "Ah, *oui*, in many ways. Though"— he looks at the flimsy cups on the table and wrinkles his nose in distaste—"the coffee is better." This is greeted with great hilarity: we are all too tense, too desperate in our efforts to project good-humored ease. "And the food is better. And the decor, and the furniture . . . so, ah, maybe no, nothing like the same." He smiles, acknowledging the laughter his words have elicited, deep lines bracketing his mouth. I haven't seen him in this kind of environment before, where he has an audience and it's his show. I can see that he and Lara are birds of a feather; they wear their skin with such effortless charm.

He glances round as if performing a head count. "*Alors*, we are complete. Please, sit."

So we sit, Modan at the head of the table, Lara and I on one side and Tom, Seb and Caro (and her BlackBerry) on the other. It's a split that's reminiscent of the divisions during that fateful week in France; it doesn't feel accidental. Caro is the last to choose a chair: I see her evaluating the options. The artificial light reveals shadows under her eyes that even her careful application of concealer has failed to hide, and there's a gray tinge to her skin: exactly what I'd expect for a lawyer in the run-up to partnership. As she settles into the seat next to Seb I try to step outside of myself, to see her as I might if she was a prospective candidate to be placed through my firm, but I can't do it. My dislike of her is too pervasive.

I disliked Severine, too, but that was in life. I'm growing accustomed to her in death. I can't imagine that she would miss this, and sure enough, there are only five chairs too many: Severine has settled herself in one at the far end of the table. Her face doesn't betray any interest—of course it doesn't, this is Severine—but there's a stillness within her that gives her away.

"We are complete," says Modan again, when everyone is settled. I see Tom glance around the group, and a brief flash of despair crosses his face before he schools it back into submission. Perhaps there are only four chairs too many. I don't expect Severine has the monopoly on haunting. "*Alors*, thank you, all of you, for coming." He looks around the table slowly, his long face grave. Opposite me, Tom and Seb have both pushed their chairs back from the table and have their long legs stretched out. I wonder if they teach it in public school, this ability to take ownership of a room by an elegant display of casual relaxation. For whose benefit is the display in Tom's case? Mine or Modan's? "I wanted to tell you all together that we now have the results of the autopsy on Mademoiselle Severine." I glance across the table and see Seb look up sharply, his hand tightening on the coffee cup. By contrast Tom continues to look as if Modan is merely discussing the weather, and not terribly interesting weather at that. "The conclusion is that she died by what you here call foul play." I wait for him to continue, but he simply looks around the room again, overlooking no one.

"You didn't get us all here just for that," I say abruptly. I'm tired— at least I'm tired of the showmanship—and I'm upset and I'm not censoring myself quickly enough. Lara puts a hand on my arm, but it fails to halt me. "Seriously, she ended up concertinaed at the bottom of a well. How could it not be foul play?"

Modan frowns. "Concertinaed. What is this?"

Lara reels off something in rapid-fire French.

Modan's expression clears. "Ah, I understand." He tries out the new word. "Concertinaed. Yes, indeed, a fair point, though of course we always have to rule out suicide or *accident*." He pronounces the last word in the French fashion, but I'm still caught on the incongruity of *suicide*. I stamp down on the highly inappropriate urge to laugh:

had he seriously considered the possibility she stuffed her own self in the well? I glance down the table, and Severine's dark eyes gleam as they meet mine: quite apart from the logistical difficulties of that particular theory, we both know she's not the suicidal type.

"But you are right; there is more." Modan continues, unaware of the weight of Severine's dark eyes upon him. Across the table, Caro has her head cocked, her body leaning forward and BlackBerry forgotten, a textbook example of a person listening intently: because she is, or because that's what she wants to portray? Tom and Seb are still sprawled out, but the tension in Seb is obvious; he doesn't have Caro's inherent artifice. "After this length of time, unless the body is somehow preserved, the autopsy can have, ah, nil result. Inconclusive, yes? In this case, we have a body that spent ten years in a warm, mainly dry, environment, which is the most efficient environment for leaving just the bones." Beside me Lara shudders, the most minute of movements, but nonetheless Modan picks up on it. I wonder if he would have had it been Caro or myself doing the shuddering. "I apologize, this is not a pleasant topic, but it is necessary. So, as I was saying, there are just bones." He spread his hands. "Broken bones."

"Broken?" asks Lara. "From what?"

"We cannot tell if the breaks are pre- or postmortem." He shrugs, his fingers flexing out briefly in a synchronized movement. "They would fit very well with a car crash, a . . ."—he searches for a word for a moment, then snaps his fingers—"a hit-and-run." Across the table I see Tom's gaze sharpen and jump sharply to Modan. In less than a blink that honed focus is gone, and once again he's the only-casually-interested observer he has been all along. Tom is surprised by something. It's the first time I've detected surprise in him since Severine was found.

"Or," continues Modan, "they could have occurred when the body was put in the well. Concertinaed, as Kate says." He inclines his head in my direction. There's no smile lurking around his mouth—that would be in terribly poor taste—but I know it's inside him.

"So you're saying," says Caro, her expression clinically professional, "that you have no evidence of cause of death? In which case shouldn't you pack up and go home?"

Lara's hand tightens on my arm. Modan doesn't look at her. "Regrettably, *non*." He adds a theatrical sigh. "You are correct, we do not have cause of death, but we do have her bones. The human body is amazing." He shakes his head a little, half smiling. "Truly amazing. Even after death it still finds ways to speak to us." *Tell me about it*, I think with dark humor. Severine's bones are far too communicative as far as I'm concerned, though I imagine they are communicating with Modan through a somewhat different method. "We have her bones, and what they tell us is that Severine was not at the bus depot on the Saturday morning."

"What?" says Lara, confused. "But the CCTV . . ."

Modan is shaking his head. "Not her. *Non*. Similar height, similar build, similar, ah, thing with the scarf"—he twirls a hand expressively above his head—"but not her. The proportions are wrong. I cannot translate the technical details, but there is something with the length of one bone in relation to another one . . . along with photographs . . . Ah, the experts, they are absolutely certain. *Absolument*. It is not Severine on the CCTV."

And so. It was one of us.

His words plow into me with the weight of a wrecking ball. Somewhere inside, I've been expecting this, dreading this. It was one of us. Like the discovery of her body in the well, it suddenly seems inevitable, unavoidable, obvious. One of the five of us—six, including Theo—killed Severine. For all one could construct a theory to say otherwise, I now believe it with a sickening certainty that is absolute, as if I've always believed it.

I look around the table and see varying degrees of shock on the faces. Lara is still stuck on what he actually said; the full implication hasn't hit her yet. I hear her mutter, "Hell of a coincidence." Tom is very, very still, but behind those hooded eyes I imagine the activity is frenetic. Caro says, "Really? You're sure?" to which Modan nods, and then she steeples her hands and props her chin on them, frowning thoughtfully. And Seb looks . . . tired. Gray. Defeated. He looks like he's been dreading this, too.

"*Alors*," says Modan, not quite spelling it out, "the five of you were the last to see Mademoiselle Severine alive."

"And Theo, of course," interjects Caro casually. Tom stiffens at this and casts her a dark, thoughtful look, and I know why: the games have begun, if they hadn't already . . . We're now in a macabre version of pass the parcel; when the music stops nobody wants to be left holding *this* prize. It would be incredibly convenient for all if Theo, the only person whose life can't be wrecked, were to shoulder the blame. But as I look at Tom, I can't imagine he will allow that without a fight. I look around the table again. It's impossible not to think, as each face passes under my gaze, *Was it you? Could you have done it?* And, most disturbing of all, *How far will you go to blame someone else?* When I get to Severine she returns my gaze coolly, then slides down her chair and tips her head back, closing her eyes: sunbathing. Severine and Lara, I think bleakly: the only people I believe are innocent, and one of those is the victim and, moreover, dead.

Modan inclines his head to Caro in agreement. "*Oui*, of course, and Theo, too. I'm afraid I will need to conduct more interviews, but as we're all here first I thought we might try to properly establish the timeline that night. It's a little . . ."—his expressive hands dance—"unclear at the moment."

Seb starts to say something, but Tom leans forward suddenly, giving up all pretense of disinterest, and speaks over him. "Should we have lawyers present?"

His words hang in a silence that is only broken by Lara's sharp intake of breath; she has finally caught on. I look at Tom speculatively for a moment. I spoke with my own lawyer only hours before this meeting, and her instructions had been very explicit: *if you must go at all, just observe, listen, and whatever you do, don't answer a damn question without me present.* I wonder if Tom has taken legal advice, too. Modan stretches out his long arms and tweaks at one of his cuffs before answering. "If you wish you can certainly have a lawyer present, though you are not under arrest. Of course." He spreads his palms. "This is just, ah, fact-finding, *non?* And of course you all want to be helpful, cooperative. Waiting for lawyers . . ."—he rolls his eyes expressively—"well, it is rather a waste of time." I can't help admiring his performance even as the intent chills me.

"Still," says Tom robustly. "Obviously, I can't speak for everyone, but I think I'd rather take legal advice at this point." In phrasing it like that—*I can't speak for everyone*—he *is* somehow speaking for us, as if he's created a group mentality by the mere suggestion that there could be one. He stands, pushing his chair back abruptly with the action. "And if we're not under arrest, then of course we're free to go at any point, correct?"

And just like that, he has wrested the power from Modan and the meeting is over.

CHAPTER FOURTEEN

We loiter outside the police station, a reluctant group—unwilling to depart, but equally unwilling to engage in conversation.

Lara breaks the silence. "It's real now, isn't it?" she says, almost as if she's talking to herself. "We can't pretend this isn't serious anymore. I can't . . ." She trails off.

Seb speaks into the void she's created. "Anyone know a good lawyer?" He aims for a joking tone and directs the question toward Caro and me, but he looks anything but playful. It seems to me I can see straight through to the skeleton beneath his surface; the muscle and skin and tissue are just window dressing draped on the bones of him. He might unravel at any moment.

"Criminal law's not really my area," I reply. I try to inject some humor myself: "Though if you're looking for a good corporate lawyer I'm absolutely the person to talk to." Nobody bothers to honor my effort with even a smile.

Caro is already back on her BlackBerry. She speaks without looking up. "I'm sure my dad will be able to come up with someone. Or your dad," she adds as an afterthought.

Seb grimaces. "Yeah, really looking forward to *that* conversation." Tom glances across with a sympathetic twist of his mouth. Seb's father's influence has clearly not waned over the years.

Caro's head lifts at that. "Come on, Seb, don't let Modan rattle you. I mean, he has nothing. Nothing! No physical evidence at all and just a load of conjecture." She looks round the group impatiently. "None of us have anything to worry about. This is all going to go away."

"Or linger on forever," says Lara darkly. She glances back at the entrance to the building for the third or fourth time, and I realize she's expecting Modan to follow her out.

"What do you mean?" asks Seb uneasily.

She shrugs. "The best outcome is that they find who did it and put them away. Then it's all neatly wrapped up. Otherwise . . ." She shrugs again. "It's never really over. Even if they consign it to the cold case pile, it could still come alive again. New evidence, new political pressure to take another look."

Her words cause another blanket of silence to fall heavily on the group. She's probably quoting Modan, I think uneasily. How many cases has he worked on that end up like that, never resolved but never entirely forgotten, either?

"Well, I have to get back to the office," says Caro abruptly. "Can I drop anyone at Westminster tube on the way past?" It's presented as a general offer, but she's looking directly at Seb when she says it.

"Sounds good," he says after a pause.

"Best head that way to get a cab," Tom says, pointing. "I'll call you later, Seb, okay?"

Normally we would all accompany our good-byes with some kind of physical display, but today Seb simply lifts a tired hand in salute, and Caro takes his other arm, calling over her shoulder, "See you all soon—in fact, see you tomorrow, Kate."

Oh joy. "See you then," I say sweetly.

Tom watches them go, a frown between his eyebrows. Is he worried about Seb's behavior, or Caro's? And for whose welfare is he concerned, his own or someone else's? A movement in my peripheral vision pulls my head round, and I see Modan making his way across to Lara, who has moved a couple of paces away from Tom and me. Her gaze is fixed on Modan, but her expression is unexpectedly conflicted.

"I'll call you later, Lara," I offer, presuming she will leave with him.

She glances at me swiftly, shaking her head. "No, wait for me. Please, wait."

"I . . . Okay." I'm slightly nonplussed. Tom takes my arm and pulls me aside so we are partially hidden by a tree, his eyes fixed on the pair. "What—" I start to say, but he shushes me. I realize I am as close to Tom as I was in the corridor that night, close enough to smell his aftershave. It makes me absurdly self-conscious; I turn my head quickly and focus on Modan and Lara. The detective must have seen us on his route to Lara, but the tree cover does give the illusion that they have some privacy, and in truth I can only pick out the odd syllable from what they are saying. Lara is doing the bulk of the talking, in a low, earnest tone, spots of color visible in her cheeks. She's trying not to cry, I realize. Something she says cuts at Modan: he flinches and interrupts urgently, reaching a long arm out to her, but she shakes her head resolutely and takes a step back. It finally dawns on me what I'm watching, and I instantly feel grubby, but it's impossible to look away. Modan tries to make his point again, frustration clear in every line of his long frame, but Lara is resolute. She must be resolute to hold firm in the face of the heartrending misery that slowly steals over Modan's face. I don't look at Tom. If he were to display any pleasure at all at this outcome I might actually punch him.

Then Lara is walking toward us in short, quick steps, the color still high in her cheeks. Her eyes are remarkably dry. "Oh, honey."

I step out from the tree as I speak and move to hug her, but she gives a quick shake of her head and I realize she will fall apart if I do. "Come back to mine. Let's find a cab."

She nods. Tom reaches out a hand and touches her cheek briefly. "I'm sorry," he says, with what seems like genuine empathy. He looks like he has more to add, but he checks himself; her face crumples briefly at that, but she catches herself. I link an arm through hers just as Tom spots a taxi and hails it for us. Lara climbs in first. I glance down the street and see that Modan is still standing there, his long face indescribably bleak. I look away hurriedly and move to follow Lara, but Tom stops me, gesturing me toward the front of the cab, out of earshot of Lara.

"We need to talk," he says, decisively, looking me straight in the eye for possibly the first time today.

"I know." I feel relieved almost to tears to have him make the first move. "I mean, I can't right now, what with Lara, but I am so sorry—"

He cuts me off with a sharp, flat chop of one hand. "Not about that." My face freezes, and something flickers in his eyes. "I don't mean . . . Look, I know we do, but not now. I meant we need to talk about the case. Severine."

"Right. God forbid I should put our friendship higher up the priority list. Only—that's strange, isn't it? Because according to you I don't care a jot." I know I'm lashing out, I know it's destructive, but I'm hurt. I'm hurt and he did the hurting and I can't just put it aside.

"Kate," he says, running an exasperated hand through his hair. "Don't think I don't appreciate the biting sarcasm, but we just don't have time for it. This—the car—it changes everything. It—"

"Not now, Tom. I'm going home to take care of Lara." I turn away and start climbing into the taxi.

"Tomorrow then," he insists through the open door.

"Whatever." I pull the door sharply shut and give the driver my address.

"I had to do it." The words spill out of Lara as soon as we are under way. "It was fine when it wasn't real, when none of us were really under suspicion. But it's not a game anymore, is it? Success for him is finding enough evidence to arrest one of us. Me—well, probably not me, but maybe you. Or Tom, or Seb or Caro . . . I can't spend time with him wondering if something I say, something completely inconsequential to me, might make all the difference to him . . . I can't be part of that. I can't . . . I can't . . ." Her blue eyes are swimming now, her breaths are shuddering gasps and the tears are starting to stream down her cheeks. I pull her into a hug, not the easiest thing in a moving cab, and she sobs into my neck in painful, body-racking gulps.

"Oh, honey," I say helplessly, past the lump in my own throat. "I'm so proud of you." It's true. Having seen firsthand exactly how giddy and reckless Modan makes her, I'm in awe of the strength she has just displayed. I wonder if I would be able to do the same, but I can't quite put myself in her shoes. Was I ever as swept away by Seb as she is by Modan? The memories are there to suggest it, but they don't re-create the feeling within me. I say again, "I'm so proud of you. You chose to protect your friends from him." After a moment, I add blackly, "Though on balance I'm starting to think that maybe he can have them all except you."

"You don't. Mean. That." Her gasped words are muffled by my now-damp collar.

"No, I suppose not," I concede with a sigh. "Except maybe—"

"Caro," she finishes for me, and for a moment we are both laughing as well as crying and I think perhaps she's going to be all right after all.

I call my lawyer first thing the next morning, though it's mid-morning before she gets back to me. Thankfully Paul is out of the office so I am free to talk uninhibitedly; she listens intently to my account of the meeting and asks a couple of pertinent questions before she gives her verdict. "He's got more up his sleeve," she says in her usual decisive manner. "That the girl on the CCTV isn't Severine—well, it was never a given that it was; that's not a game-changer. So he has more. He wouldn't still be here without it. Do you think any of the others will speak to him without a lawyer?"

"I don't know." I think about it. Not Lara, I don't think; not anymore. And not Seb. Probably not Caro, either, unless she's playing some angle that I can't foresee. Tom? I don't know about Tom. "Probably not, but I don't know for sure."

"Mmm." I imagine her tapping her teeth with her fingernail, hopefully whilst wearing a less garish lipstick. A soft taupe, perhaps. "Obviously what I said before still stands: you mustn't allow yourself to be questioned without me present, but the trick is to appear co-operative. Antagonizing the police is never a good strategy."

"*Appear* cooperative?" I stress the first word with an ironic twist.

She laughs. "Well, yes, appear. If you actually happen to *be* co-operative, too, that's fine, but not actually necessary." She pauses, and I sense the shift of gear; the moment for humor has passed. "Have you thought any more about what happened on that Friday night? If there was some piece of information, however small, that you hadn't mentioned before, you could come forward with it—with me present, I hasten to add—which would go a long way to demonstrating co-operation."

"Or demonstrating a desire to shift blame."

"I wouldn't worry about that. Believe me, right now the lawyers for all of your little band will be advising their clients to shift the blame." She waits to allow her words their full impact. "So," she finally continues, "is there anything you can think of, anything at all, that you haven't mentioned?"

I'm silent. There's so much I haven't mentioned, both from that night and since. The smuggled cocaine and subsequent blazing row,

Caro and Seb's recent conspiratorial assignations, Tom's continual absence of surprise (apart from during last night's meeting), Modan and Lara's relationship . . . "I'll need to spend some time thinking about that," I say at last.

"You do that." Her voice has hardened; there's a warning note in it: I haven't fooled her at all. "I can't help you if I don't have all the facts. I don't want you bringing up things at the eleventh hour when you're already under arrest."

I'm temporarily unable to breathe. "Arrest," I croak when I finally find my voice. "Is that likely?"

"Well, not off the current known facts, but as we've already discussed, Modan must have something more up his sleeve. He isn't here for nothing."

"Right." I rub my forehead. "Right."

"I think we should meet again and go over everything once more." Her voice has softened a little. "My assistant will call you to set something up. In the meantime, promise me you'll rack your brains about that evening."

"I will. I promise." One would think I would have dwelled on little else since yesterday, but last night Lara's emotional state had required a certain amount of dedicated focus. And if I'm honest, I've always shied away from memories of that week. But now . . . now the stakes are growing day by day, it seems. I should approach this as I would a problem with my company, I think; I should set aside time to apply dedicated thought. I look at my online calendar for today and decisively block out 5 P.M. to 6 P.M. I can't think of what to put in the subject box, so I mark it private so that Julie can't see the content and leave the subject blank, which in retrospect strikes me as highly ironic—marking an appointment private to hide the fact it says nothing at all. Then I wonder who else is speaking to their lawyer and setting aside thinking time, and it doesn't seem at all funny anymore.

By happy coincidence, Gordon is hurrying through the Haft & Weil lobby just as I swing in through the revolving doors, a small frown and his short, quick steps betraying the time pressure he's under. Nevertheless, he stops when he sees me, and the frown clears. "Kate," he says, shaking my hand. "I've been meaning to call you." He takes my arm and draws me aside, out of the way of the revolving door traffic. "I'm so sorry I didn't get the opportunity to explain to you in person the change of spearhead at our end. That was . . ." He pauses, and for a moment I see the legendary Farrow steel in his eyes. "Well, that was badly done." I'm absurdly pleased that he's annoyed with Caro—for once not because it's Caro, but because he understands the lack of respect implied by that episode. He lowers his voice and continues. "The idea of putting her in charge actually came from your suggestion of finding her some management initiatives to get involved with, so thank you for that. Though I have to say I'm going to miss our little meetings." He smiles a little ruefully.

"Me too," I say honestly. "It's been a real pleasure." His eyes crinkle at the edges, then he glances at his watch. "But you're on your way to something." I am anxious not to impose. "Don't let me keep you."

"I'm sorry, I do hate to say hi and bye . . . Actually, what are you doing for lunch today?"

"Caro invited me to have a bite with her after our meeting."

He brightens. "Excellent, I'll gate-crash." I laugh. "And if she cancels lunch on you—which is rather likely; she's under the cosh on something big right now, and I can't imagine she's getting much sleep, let alone time to eat properly—then you won't be left in the lurch. Perfect," he says, with a satisfied air. "See you then." He turns away, tossing a smile over his shoulder, and I think that I can't see a single atom of him that resembles Caro.

And neither can I see an ounce of Gordon in Caro when she joins me in the meeting room—basement this time, no spectacular view; in fact no view at all—after a wait that's only been long enough for me to pour a cup of coffee from the attendant silver flask. She does indeed look tired, even more so than at last night's meeting: the shadows under her eyes have deepened, and she's even paler, though that might actually be the effect of the rather stark, though very sharp, black trouser suit she's wearing. We greet each other with air kisses and then I say, "I saw your dad in the lobby. He's planning to gate-crash our lunch."

She shakes her head, rolling her eyes. "Shameless man. Though since I'm waiting on a call from New York, which will of course come just as we're sitting down to eat, I might be best leaving the two of you to it." She pulls out a seat, snags a biscuit and takes a bite of it in what seems like one continuous movement. Caro is running purely on adrenaline, I realize.

"He did say you're rather snowed under at the moment."

She nods vehemently as she finishes her mouthful. "A rather full-on hostile bid. I haven't been home to my flat since I saw you yesterday." She raises her eyebrows ruefully. "You remember how it is during the crazy times. If you get home at all, it's never before midnight, and on the odd occasion that you do, there's a stack of laundry to get through and bills to pay and you have no inclination to do either."

It's an odd sensation to be feeling sorry for Caro. I don't enjoy it. But I do remember exactly what she describes. Before I left the practice of law, I did everything that is expected of a lowly associate, and what is expected is to give your all—all your time, all your energy, all your social life; all is consumed by the beast that is the modern top-tier corporate law firm. I remember the late nights in a deserted office, when even the air con had stopped working and the air grew still and heavy and hot. I remember strip lighting and the faint glow from the few computer screens still on, and eyes so tired and scratchy that I could barely read my monitor. The adrenaline rushes occurred in the day, fueled by the enthusiasm of the other team members, but the real hard graft usually happened at night, alone or perhaps with one colleague, with no more camaraderie on tap to spur you on. Mostly I remember the sense of disjointment, of being outside of everything—outside of the firm, where I could never quite belong; outside of my circle of friends whose social life didn't halt but went on happily without me; outside of my very own life. I left the practice of law for reasons that had nothing to do with the working hours, and in starting up Channing Associates I've been no stranger to long days that bleed into nights, and weeks that spread a stain into weekends, but I wonder how I would cope with 110-hour weeks now.

"I suppose the period before partnership is even more brutal," I respond neutrally. Typically candidates continue to work at the same breakneck pace, but with the added stress of continual scrutiny of every single decision they take, every strategy they suggest.

Her face tightens a fraction. I suspect Caro is aware her campaign is not going perfectly. But she simply says, "Yes," then busies herself selecting another biscuit. I remember that, too: the diabolic diet that comes from having lost all sense of normal body rhythm, leaving you lurching from one sugar fix to another. After a moment she adds, "At any rate, I think I'm going to be stuck here all week and all weekend too."

"Did you have plans?"

"I was going to visit my mum, but . . ." She shrugs ruefully.

"Do you see her much?" I ask, genuinely curious.

She shakes her head, a small, economical movement. "I always think I should go down more." She grimaces, but not without humor. "Right up to the point when I'm there, and then I rather think the opposite."

That pulls a chuckle from me. "You don't get along?"

She shrugs again. "It's a well-trodden path. Things start well, but sooner or later the criticisms will come out. She didn't want me to become a lawyer, you see, but I always wanted to follow Dad into the law. She can't see the point of me working so hard when surely I could marry money, or live off Dad's . . ." She trails off and grimaces again, but the humor is gone; she seems suddenly defenseless, and for the first time ever I can imagine the thirteen-year-old girl that she once was, trying to navigate through the trials of teenage life with a mother she can never please who is using her as a tool against the father she longs to emulate. I think of my own mother, a geriatric nurse, gently proud but benignly uncomprehending both of the job that I do and why I would want to do it, given the stress and long hours—it was always my father who understood. For the first time ever I want to reach out to Caro, but I have no idea how.

"Anyway," she says briskly, breaking the moment, "I certainly could have done without having to sprint across to New Scotland Yard last night." She eyes me across the table as she takes a neat bite, her small, sharp teeth gleaming white. Perhaps she's had them bleached. She's the Caro I expect once again, but that moment has shaken me. I can still feel the reverberations. Perhaps beneath the brittle painted surface of Caro, there are other versions, stacked like Russian dolls, years upon years of them, right back to the vulnerable girl that she must have been at the time of the divorce, and beyond— all of them inside her. Perhaps I should take more care with the shell. "What did you make of all of that yesterday?"

I grimace, looking for a noncommittal answer. "I'm not sure I understand why Modan hasn't given up and gone home. It doesn't seem like there's anything to support any one of us as a suspect over anyone else who happened to be in the vicinity."

She nods vigorously as she finishes her mouthful. "Totally. Completely agree." She adds, almost as an afterthought, "Which makes it weird that he keeps asking me about Theo."

"Really?"

"God, yes, like a dog with a bone. And what can I say? I mean, we were together until we went up to our beds, and then . . ." She waves a hand airily. It's not a gesture that suits her; it's too vague, and Caro is never vague. "Well, then I was asleep, and who can vouch for anyone when they're asleep?"

"Well, that applies to us all," I say tightly. "There must have been a couple of hours when everyone was asleep and no one is accounted for." Except for Lara and Tom, entwined in coital bliss . . .

"Absolutely. Of course. Which makes it odd that he's focusing on Theo particularly." She shrugs. "Though—distasteful as it is to say, if it *had* to be one of us . . ." I stare at her, not so much appalled as bewildered—does she not know Tom at all? Surely she realizes he would fight ceaselessly to prevent any besmirching of Theo's name. She shrugs again. "Well, onward and upward: why don't you give me an overview of where we stand with the candidates?"

So I do, and we discuss. The process is extremely developed by now; there's not a lot she can add. Her questions are professional and intelligent, though she is clearly far more focused on immediate benefits to the firm from prospective new hires rather than their career development within the company, which is not quite the message Gordon would be sending candidates—I will have to be careful she doesn't ruin the groundwork we've laid. I make a couple of careful allusions to it that are obviously less subtle than intended: after the second one she stops and laughs. "Kate," she says through a smile that holds genuine amusement. "Don't worry, I know how to stay on message. I won't scare the horses."

"I know, of course not; it's just that collegiality and long-term career opportunities are the main reason a couple of these candidates are considering this place."

"I get it. Don't worry." She puts down her pen and yawns, half-heartedly covering her mouth. The adrenaline has been slowly leaching out of her during our meeting, and the yawns are coming closer together. "Oh," she says suddenly, brightening a little. "I meant to tell you, you may get a call from a chap called Hugh Brompton at Stockleys." Stockleys is an enormously successful mid-tier UK firm with a footprint just about everywhere; it doesn't compete with Haft & Weil, as it wouldn't generally get the cutting-edge, high-profile deals, but there's an awful lot of work around that isn't cutting-edge or high profile. "We use them quite a bit when we need to outsource some of the drudge work—much cheaper for the client than Haft & Weil personnel." She's watching me carefully as she speaks, her head slightly cocked and her tired eyes gleaming birdlike. "Anyway, they're looking to beef up certain areas, and I told Hugh about you and suggested they give you a call. It's a big job, from what he says, and the contract is basically yours—as far as he's concerned, if you're good enough for Haft & Weil, you're good enough for him."

I'm temporarily floored, then I say, "Thank you," because of course I can't say anything else, but inside I'm scrabbling around to figure out the angle, because of course there's an angle, and if I don't know what it is then I'm exactly where she wants me. Or at least, that's how it would be for the Caro I thought I knew, but perhaps this Caro is something different . . . I adopt a smile that's at least half genuine. "That's kind of you, very much appreciated."

"Well, we're in business together, and business partners help each other out." Her eyes gleam, and she has a self-satisfied smile as she adds slyly, "I told you I could stay on message."

I laugh, both out of surprise and because her wicked little dig is genuinely funny, and for a moment I see her as she may well be, or perhaps I see her as Seb and Tom see her—a clever, sharply witty, fearless woman. I can't tell if what she's presenting now is only part of the picture or if the picture has changed: it leaves me uneasily off-kilter.

Her mobile goes off, and she takes the call with a quick apology, firing out a series of short responses and checking her watch while she paces the room. "Sorry," she says with a grimace when she hangs up. "That call from New York is going to happen in ten minutes. I'm afraid you and Gordon will be on your own for lunch."

"No problem." We exit the windowless room into an equally windowless passageway. "You know," I say conversationally, "I always wondered why you joined your father's law firm. You could have gone to any number of competitors, I'm sure."

"Oh, sure," she says offhand as we climb a sweeping glass-and-metal staircase to the main lobby, where I find myself blinking, somehow surprised at the daylight. But it's lunchtime; of course there is daylight. "But Haft & Weil was really the best opportunity for me. You can't do better than best in class, after all."

"Bravo," I say, raising my eyebrows with a half smile. "Once again, admirably on message."

She lays a hand on my upper arm and laughs, a genuine laugh, and it softens her; her sharp edges become impish rather than cutting. "I told you I could." She looks over my shoulder still smiling, then exclaims, "Right on time! Here's Gordon. You know, I probably see more of him now than I did growing up, what with the divorce and boarding school and all." She smiles a hello over my shoulder at him and then shakes my hand, quick and firm, cordially professional. "I'll leave you in his capable hands; you two have a lovely lunch."

"We will," Gordon says, smiling at her, then he turns and ushers me through the lobby. "Looks like you two are getting on famously," he remarks, and it suddenly crosses my mind that perhaps Caro knew he was there and staged that little tableau—the laugh, the little touch—and then I realize how loathsomely paranoid I've become and I hate myself for it.

CHAPTER FIFTEEN

The designated thinking hour arrives and departs without a single moment spent in contemplation, because Hugh Brompton does indeed call, and the job in question is dynamite, the kind of contract that really establishes a new firm—but of course they want our strategies and suggestions at a meeting tomorrow afternoon. So Paul and I work late, eating take-out sushi at our desks and mainly ignoring our mobiles. Actually, mainly ignoring Paul's mobile: judging from the number of times it rings, he either has a very active social life or an extremely jealous girlfriend. In contrast, mine rings only twice: the first call is Lara, and I take it to quickly check how she's holding up; the second is from Tom.

"Do you need to take that?" asks Paul, and I realize I'm staring at the mobile screen as it rings.

"No," I say brightly as I reach over to hit the reject button. "I can deal with it later." A moment later the phone beeps with a voice mail alert; I deliberately ignore it and turn back to Paul. "Where were we? Oh yes—do you think we're promising too much with this timeline?"

It's one in the morning before I climb into a cab and settle in the back, glancing at my phone out of habit. A tiny red alert reminds me I have a voice mail. I play the message, and Tom's deep baritone greets me. "Hi, Kate, it's Tom." A pause. "We really do need to talk about the case. Are you able to come round after you finish work? I'll be home, so just give me a call whenever . . ." He sounds uneasy, awkward even. "I . . . Well, give me a call."

It hardly credits belief that a single drunken kiss can reduce years of friendship to dodged calls and stilted voice mails. I stare out of the cab window in a state of torpid exhaustion and watch London slide by, lit patchily by garish neon signs and streetlamps that deliver a stark, pale light without color or warmth. After a moment I pick up my phone again and type out a text message.

Been working late, big pitch tomorrow afternoon. I can drop
by after work tomorrow. Kx.

I read it over again before sending. *Kx* is my habitual sign-off with Tom, but now every character is fraught with meaning and open to misinterpretation. I remove the *x*.

The presentation to Stockleys goes well: Paul is a good presenter, suave and relaxed, and he thinks well on his feet; his style is a good complement to my own direct approach. Caro was right: the contract was ours to lose, and by the time we are shaking hands and saying good-bye I know we haven't done that. Paul hails a cab, and we jump in and animatedly dissect the meeting on the trip back to the office.

"One thing I meant to ask you," Paul says as he waits on the pavement for me to pay the cabbie. There's an odd note in his voice that makes me glance over at him. His almost-translucent eyebrows are drawn together in a frown.

"What?" I turn back to the cabdriver to collect my change.

"Well, Mark Jeffers—"

"The Clifford Chance associate?"

"That's the one. Well, he asked me if I was in line for a promotion." I look at him blankly, not understanding. If he's angling for more money, this is an odd approach. The cabdriver has pulled away, leaving the two of us together on the street by our office, but neither of us moves toward the doorway. "When you get arrested."

"What the fuck?" My mind is racing. How in the world did Mark Jeffers get hold of this? And how many other people has he spread this gossip to? This sort of rumor could cut off a fledgling company at the knees: even more than most companies, a recruitment firm's only asset is its people and their reputation.

He smiles in a thin line. "Actually, that's exactly what I said. But he said he had it on good authority that you're under investigation for a murder, of all things. In France or something. I told him he needs to get better sources." He looks at me uneasily. "If there was anything to it you'd have told me about it. Right?"

I take a deep breath. This will need careful handling. "I am not under investigation," I say robustly. "A girl went missing from the next-door farmhouse when a group of us were in France on holiday ten years ago. Her body turned up recently—"

"Turned up?"

"Was found." I see her again, the bones in a crumpled pile, ghostly white in the dim underground light. "In a well, actually," I admit, the words somehow slipping out.

"Jesus, Kate, and you're just telling me this now?" He's building up a head of righteous anger. I need to stomp on that quickly.

"Come on, Paul, it's nothing." I make a show of impatience,

stamping on the guilt that rises as I ostensibly belittle Severine's death. I carry on defiantly. "Since the six of us were the last people to see her alive, obviously the police want to talk to us again, but that's all it is. I can assure you I'm not about to be arrested." I throw all my powers of persuasion into the eye contact we're sharing and hope to high heaven that every word I've said is true.

"You should have told me. The last thing we need is any kind of stain on our name. You know how people think: no smoke without fire."

"Rubbish. We have a contract from Haft & Weil and now one with Stockleys; that's what clients will focus on, and those kinds of firms don't employ headhunters under investigation for murder. This is just industry gossip that will be forgotten the minute some senior partner gets caught shagging his secretary." *Perhaps* . . .

He's almost mollified; his anger has switched into sulkiness. "If it's nothing, then why didn't you mention it?" Does he have a point? We're partners in a business together; we see each other every working day—would it have been normal to have mentioned this to him? I suppose so, especially if there was any chance of it impacting the business. Except I never thought that there was . . . Once again I wonder how the hell Mark Jeffers got hold of this. None of our names have ever been in the papers, except Theo's parents as owners of the farmhouse.

"Because . . ." I take another deep breath, and this time I tell him the absolute truth. "Because I don't like talking about it. She was a family friend of the guy we were staying with; we practically spent all week with her, and then she . . ." I trail off. "I'm sorry. I should have told you." Though it simply didn't cross my mind to discuss it with anyone. I wonder how many people Lara has spoken to about it, or Seb or Tom or Caro.

"Oh." Paul is chastened; the personal impact didn't quite occur to him. "No, *I'm* sorry. That must have been awful." He touches my arm awkwardly, and I find a weak smile for him, appreciative of the gesture. I know I'm too comfortable being a solitary creature, but for the first time I realize that in an office of three, where we work long hours, that means I'm forcing solitude on Paul, too, who is definitely not naturally suited to it. I should make more of an effort to be social with him and Julie.

"Come on," I say, turning for our office. "Let's go find Stockleys some candidates." I look for Severine as we enter the office, almost unable to believe that she wouldn't have wanted to eavesdrop on that little scene with Paul, but she's not lounging at my desk as I'm expecting. I was hoping to see her, I realize, to . . . what? To apologize? To tell her that I'm sorry, but I'm fighting to keep Paul's morale intact and that's more important than hurting the feelings of the ghost who haunts me?

Still, she was murdered. It's not nothing. That's what bothers me more than anything—that whoever did it might get away with it, and that would make it seem as if it doesn't matter, as if Severine never mattered, because if our world continues without a hitch then we might as well be condoning it, and we don't. I don't. It's not nothing.

Back at my desk, the first thing I do is reschedule the thinking time.

Tom's flat. I loiter outside and try not to think about the last time I was here. I'm waiting for Lara: at the last minute I chickened out and called in the cavalry. And in truth Lara should be here, too; she's already shown her colors by overthrowing Modan, and Tom has made it perfectly clear he only wants to talk about the case. Though I haven't failed to notice the desperate, clichéd irony of my support system being exactly the person Tom wants instead of me, which is why I need the support in the first place . . .

Lara appears from the direction of the tube station in a powder blue dress, her blond locks lit luminous red gold by the evening sun that bleeds red ribbons of cloud across the horizon. Severine is beside her, walking barefoot with a loose feline grace in the familiar black shift dress, her hair wrapped in the red chiffon scarf. Her sandals are dangling from one finger. I walk down to meet them, marveling at the tableau they present with the setting sun behind them. Lara and Severine, one light, one dark. Are these two really all I can trust in the world?

"How are you, honey?" I ask as I hug her. It's not a pleasantry; I pull back to search her face as she casts around for an answer.

"Okay," she says, with a slight rueful twist to her lips. She looks a touch pale, and she's wearing less makeup than usual, but her cornflower eyes are clear with no telltale red rims. "Not great, but . . . okay."

We head back toward Tom's flat, chatting about this and that. She's Lara, but a dimmed version; I can't feel her usual vibrancy, and the lack of it makes me ache for her. At the bottom of the steps, I can delay no longer, and I stop her for a moment. "One thing I've been meaning to ask . . ."

"What?" she prompts as I hesitate.

"That night in the farmhouse . . . with Tom . . . was there ever a time you were apart? And . . . well, did you sleep?"

She assesses me shrewdly, her eyes narrowing. "You're trying to figure out if it could have been Tom."

"I'm just looking at every angle," I say stiffly. I honored the thinking hour this time, and this question is one of the consequences.

"What about me then?" she challenges. There's a wild light in her eye that I don't recognize. "If you're willing to accuse Tom, why not me?"

"Of course it wasn't you."

"Why not?" The light flares into anger. "Why does nobody consider me? *Pretty, vacuous Lara—she's not even capable of a murder. Best not trouble her pretty little head with all of that.*"

I look at her in astonishment. I know this is tied up with Modan somehow, but I'm not quite sure how to navigate it. "Well . . . okay, then, tell me: did you murder Severine?"

"Of course not," she says, the anger suddenly leaving her. "I couldn't possibly do such a thing."

The absurdity strikes us both at the same time, and we start to giggle. When the last bubbles of laughter have died out, I say quietly, "It's not a bad thing, Lara. You're full of light, you think the best of everyone, we all see it, it draws us in. But nobody thinks you're vacuous." She inclines her head a little ruefully, not entirely accepting my words. "Did Modan say something to you? Are you still talking to him?" I ask cautiously.

"I doubt it after our last conversation," she says frankly. "He thinks I'm going to go off and screw half the men in London—the half I haven't already screwed, that is." She shakes her head in frustration. "When he asked before about past boyfriends, I was honest—more fool me. I didn't expect to have it thrown back in my face. And aren't the French supposed to be more liberal than the British on that sort of thing?"

"I'm sure French men are just as susceptible to jealousy as British men." Poor Modan. He must be incredibly cut up to lash out like that: he doesn't strike me as a man who usually makes such appalling missteps. "Are you? Going to screw half of London, I mean? Only maybe someone should warn the poor creatures, give them time to prepare . . ."

"Stop it," she says, laughing again. "That was then." She sobers and puts a hand on my arm, earnestness shining out of her. "I'm different now."

"I know," I say gently, though a shameful part of me wonders how long she will be different for. But I realize I'm being unfair:

surely we're all different now, from how we were in a French farm-house a decade ago. Perhaps it just took a little longer for the impact to hit Lara.

A slight frown crosses her face. "You don't believe me."

"I do," I reassure her quickly. "Of course I do. I was just . . . I was just contrasting with that week in France . . ." She cocks her head questioningly. I try to find the right words. "I mean, we're all different now. Even Caro, maybe . . . Everyone is different, or—gone. Or maybe I'm seeing different sides of everyone . . ." When I try to think about what might have happened to Severine, it's like trying to solve a puzzle based on the picture on the box, but the pieces have evolved—or maybe the picture on the box was never the right picture in the first place. Lara still has her head cocked to one side, the quiz-zical look still in place. I shake my head. "Never mind. Come on, we should go up."

We link arms and turn toward the entrance to Tom's block of flats. Lara buzzes to announce us. I hear Tom's voice through the intercom, made tinny and weak. If he's surprised at Lara's presence it doesn't show, other than perhaps through a slight pause before he speaks that could instead have been a result of the technology.

"I never answered your question, though," Lara says as we start to climb the threadbare stairs. "We weren't apart that I was aware of, except to go to the loo, but we did sleep. I don't know how long for—maybe just a couple of hours?"

Tom has left the door of his flat ajar; we push through, and despite my now numerous visits, it still surprises me to see this oasis of light and modern style after the genteel shabbiness of the common areas. Following noise, we find him hunting down some wineglasses in the kitchen. "I presume a glass of wine wouldn't go amiss, ladies?" he says with a grin, raising the bottle of white in his hand. He's had time to change after work; he's wearing jeans and a blue T-shirt that picks up the color in his eyes.

"Now that's what I call a welcome." Lara smiles flirtatiously as she kisses him hello. I glance away and thus am completely unprepared when he wraps his arms around me in his bear hug of old. The T-shirt is of the softest cotton, and he smells of the same aftershave from that dark, delicious corridor; for a moment the ache is blinding. When I pull myself together enough to return the hug I think I hear the stroke of his warm breath deliver *Sorry* into my ear. When he releases me I stare after him, trying to search his eyes, but he busies himself hunting down a corkscrew and then Lara pulls out a bar stool for me and I'm left wondering what just happened as I settle beside her on one side of the kitchen counter.

Tom is facing us, the dark granite kitchen counter between us. "So, what news?" he asks, uncorking the bottle. He's meeting my eyes from time to time, but I'm failing to divine anything from his expression. The bar stool is an uncomfortable height: I can't rest my elbows on the counter, and my feet don't reach the floor, yet there's no strut for them to rest on. I feel perched and precarious.

I shrug, leaving Lara to fill the gap. "Not much," she says lightly. "I've turned celibate, and Kate is trying to figure out whether you could have killed Severine."

She's being flippant, of course she's being flippant, but Tom pauses in the act of pouring, his eyes leaping to mine. "And?" he asks after a beat, placing the bottle carefully down and maintaining the eye contact. It's clear he's completely disregarding the celibacy comment; whether that will irk Lara or not I don't know or care, because I currently feel like killing her for putting me in this position. I can feel her shifting uneasily beside me as it dawns on her that her comment is actually being taken seriously. "Do you think I'm capable of it?" Tom asks in a measured tone.

It feels like a challenge, though over what I'm not sure. Still, I rise to it. "Yes," I say simply.

"Kate!" I hear Lara exclaim, but I'm still locked in a gaze with

Tom. There's nothing I can read in his eyes. Then he inclines his head a little and returns to pouring the wine.

"I'm not saying he did," I explain in an aside to Lara, though my eyes keep darting back to Tom, looking for something, anything, that tells me what he's thinking. I try to hook one ankle round the leg of the stool, searching for some balance. I need an anchor. "I'm just saying he's capable of it. Under the right circumstances." I take a sip of the wine that Tom has pushed toward me. "Probably all of us are under the right circumstances."

"Not all, I don't think," says Tom thoughtfully. He has a beer instead; he takes a long pull of it. "Well, maybe everyone is capable of an accidental murder," he concedes. "But the cover-up—that's the crucial bit. Not everyone would have the self-possession to do that rather than calling the emergency services."

You would, I think immediately; then I realize he's watching me and have the uncomfortable feeling he can read my mind as he smiles thinly and raises his beer in a mock toast.

"Well," says Lara after a pause. "We've certainly bypassed the small talk this evening." She picks up her own wine and takes a long draft.

"Have either of you eaten?" asks Tom abruptly. "I've already warmed the oven; shall I shove some pizzas in or something?"

The process of deliberating over the food options dispels the atmosphere; for a few moments this might be simply a social evening. But once the oven door has been swung shut, Tom takes another swig of his beer and I see him change gear.

"Right," he says decisively, looking at Lara and me in turn. "I think it's cards on the table time now. What do you guys think happened that night?"

"My cards *are* on the table," Lara complains. "They've *always* been on the table. I never thought it was one of us." She spreads her hands wide in exasperation, almost knocking over her glass. "Oops, sorry, I already had a glass or two after work with some colleagues . . . Anyway, so . . . unless you, Tom, managed to kill Severine, get rid of her body, clean yourself up and get back into bed with me in the space of a little more than an hour, maybe two, then I have absolutely no information."

I'm taken aback by the casual way in which she can mention being in bed with Tom—*with Tom*—in public, to Tom himself, without an iota of a blush. I glance at him quickly, but he doesn't appear fazed in the slightest. "I'm good," he says with dark humor, "but not that good."

I try to stamp down my swelling sense of injustice—that Lara, who casually slept with him then tossed him aside, gets entirely forgiven, yet I am held out to dry for a mere kiss—but there's a thread of irritation that leaks through into my words. "But you're presuming the same person did it all," I declare bluntly. "It's possible more than one person was involved. Maybe an accidental killing by one, then one or two more involved in the cover-up . . ." This discussion is so abstract, so passionless, that it's hard to remember the girl it relates to. I glance around for her, but she's not in attendance. I feel an extra prickle of irritation: what kind of ghost wouldn't be interested in discussions on their own death? Though I suppose it's not as if she doesn't know the punch line . . .

Tom nods. Somehow I feel an unexpected sense of approval from him. "Sounds like you have a theory."

"No, I just . . ." I shift awkwardly on the very awkward stool. I don't have a theory. I have a collection of disquieting observations that add up to a maelstrom of unease, but nothing that could be called a theory.

Lara shifts herself so she's half lolling on the counter and cocks her head in sympathetic listening mode. "It's just us, Kate."

"Come on, Kate," says Tom. He's standing with his hands on the granite surface, leaning toward me. With his height the body language sends a curious message of encouragement mixed with intimidation. "You have to trust someone."

I look across at him, meeting those familiar blue eyes that are Tom's not Seb's, above that unmistakable nose, and I am suddenly so blindingly angry with him that for a moment I can't speak. I used to trust him, I even *want* to trust him, so why won't he let me? He knows something, I know it, and by now he must realize I know it given Lara's comment, yet he won't let me in, and now I wonder if he's Tom, if he ever was the Tom I thought I knew, and if I got that wrong, what else have I been mistaken on? A cold fear is twisting my insides, and a raw anger spears through my throat at Tom—*Tom*—for putting it there. "Really?" I say bitingly, when I recover my voice. "*I* have to trust someone? That's rich. Who do *you* trust, Tom? The only damn things that I'm sure of in this whole macabre debacle are that Seb and Caro are hiding something, and you know a hell of a lot more than you're letting on, yet somehow it's *my* life that's getting trampled on. So if we're talking about *trust*, how about we start with you, Tom?" Tom's eyes are widened in surprise at my attack; I catch a glimpse of Lara staring at me, completely nonplussed, and it halts me: I bite off the vitriolic torrent that's just gaining momentum. If I let it free, I may never stop. I grab my wineglass and focus on it determinedly in the suffocating silence that follows my words while the remaining anger subsides along with my breathing, leaving me in acute danger of bursting into tears. The immediate urge to apologize for my un-British outburst is offset by a streak of rebellion fueled by the remaining anger that claims this was merely a fraction of what he deserves. Of what is inside me right now, of what this world deserves.

It's Lara who breaks the silence, which has grown so thick, so heavy that I'm almost amazed anything can penetrate it. "I shouldn't have come," she says quickly, slithering down from the stool. "I really think you two need to talk and—"

"No, stay. Please. Stay." I put out a hand to keep her there, still focusing on the wineglass. "I'm sorry." I take a deep breath and look up at her. She's half turned to go, uncertainty and concern in her eyes. I'm resolutely not looking at Tom, but I know he's watching us; watching me, mostly. I can feel it on my skin: through my skin, even, like a pressure on my bones. "It's not—that—anyway. It's . . ."

"What?" she asks.

"My life—my business—really is getting trampled. There are rumors in the market that I'm about to be arrested for murder," I say miserably. "Mark Jeffers, this associate candidate at—well, never mind where he's at—anyway, he told Paul. And if he told Paul of all people how do I know he's not telling the whole world?"

Lara sits down again, accompanied by a sharp intake of breath. We all know this isn't the sole reason for my abysmal lack of composure, or even the main reason for it, but they're both kind enough to tacitly redirect their attention. Tom finally speaks his first words since my outburst. "How did Paul react? Do you think he will jump ship?"

I feel my mouth twist sourly. How typical of Tom to be able to set aside my diatribe and focus. It forces me to respond with a civility I still don't feel. "I don't know. I don't think so, not yet anyway. We've got two very prestigious contracts . . . but if the rumors escalate and we lose one of those, then yes, he's Paul, he'd jump ship." I shrug. "He was upset I hadn't told him about it." I take a sip of the wine then look at both of them curiously. "Have you guys told anyone about all of this?"

Tom shakes his head. "It's hardly something I want to bring up on the trading floor. I can just imagine the fun they'd have . . ." He grimaces, no doubt imagining the taunts that would inevitably haunt him for the rest of his career. As a mob crowd, traders are not known for their sensitivity. "And I don't want to worry my folks. I'm not sure Seb has mentioned it to his parents, either, unless it's to get a recommendation of a lawyer from his dad."

"I spoke to a couple of girls at work," says Lara, "but never any details. I certainly didn't mention your name, if that's what you're—"

I shake my head. "God, no. I was just curious." Curious as to whether my reluctance to talk about it is another sign of too much solitude, or actually perfectly normal.

Tom is still analyzing. His eyes are fixed on the falling darkness outside the kitchen window as he scratches his head thoughtfully. The clouds are now inky smudges against a marginally paler sky. "And this chap, Mark Jenners—"

"Jeffers."

"Mark Jeffers told Paul you were about to be arrested?"

"So I understand."

Tom is frowning. "Just you." I shrug. "Maybe it's nothing but Chinese whispers, but it seems a bit odd. You couldn't put it together from just the newspaper articles, I don't think. Our names have never been mentioned."

I nod. "That's what I thought."

Lara's cheeks are flushed and her eyelids a little droopy. The glass or two that she had earlier, plus the large one Tom poured for her, are taking their toll. "Big mouth for a lawyer," she comments, finishing in a catlike yawn that she neatly smothers. "Aren't they supposed to be discreet? And aren't you supposed to butter up your headhunting firm, not spread scurrilous rumors about them? I can't imagine this has you and Paul dying to find him a good placement."

It's another of Lara's unexpectedly perceptive moments, though she hasn't followed through to the implications. Tom's gaze and mine jump to lock together, and for a moment it's like the darkened corridor never happened, like I've never ever doubted him, and I can see exactly what he's thinking. "But who?" I say to him.

"I don't know." Tom shakes his head, then frowns again. "I can't see who could possibly benefit."

"Who what?" asks Lara, thoroughly lost.

"Who put him up to it," I explain. "You're right, it's extremely odd behavior. So either he's an irredeemable gossip, or someone put him up to it." I think for a bit. "I can take a look in his file and ask Paul about him. If he's known to be the town crier then maybe it's just incredibly bad luck that he's got hold of this."

Tom turns his attention to the oven. The last few moments have stripped away some of my distrust, or perhaps my growing exhaustion has done that—suspicion is so damn *tiring*. Things would be so much simpler if Tom was on my side. I'm almost sure he is; I'm almost sure Tom is Tom and all the rest of it is just noise. It's certainly what I want to believe. "That night . . . with Severine," I start hesitantly. Tom looks up in the act of removing the pizzas, with a lightness in his eyes that warms me: he recognizes the olive branch. "At first I thought—well, I thought she went to the bus depot the next morning, so I thought it was nothing to do with all of us. Then afterward, when Modan said it wasn't her, then I started thinking. And the thing is, I don't know what time Seb came to bed. I was pretty upset, and pretty drunk, to be honest; I think I just passed out, so I really don't know. But then Seb was really insistent that he was there all night . . ." Lara and Tom are both watching me, letting the words run out of me. "And he and Caro are acting so strangely, so . . . *complicit*, I actually wondered if they were shagging, but I think actually—I think it's all to do with this. With Severine." I take a deep breath, looking at Tom. If I say this it becomes possible. If I say this, I can never take it back. "So I guess I've been wondering if Seb killed her—by accident—and if Caro helped cover it up."

I hear Lara mutter, "*Jesus,*" and in my peripheral vision she reaches for the wine bottle, but I'm focused on Tom. He nods calmly. Thoughtfully. He's not surprised, and by now I'm not surprised about that.

"Caro," he says. He's speaking dispassionately, simultaneously carving up the slightly burned pizzas with a circular cutter, as if we're discussing interest rates or car insurance. "Not me for the cover-up?"

In the moment I am unable to think of anything to say but the truth. "It could have been you. But like you said, I don't think you would have had enough time to manage it without Lara suspecting something. And . . ."

"What?" His cutting of the pizza continues unhurried, and his question is casual, but his eyes on me are anything but.

I shrug again. "I guess I think that if it had been you, it would have been a better cover-up."

"Thank you, I think," he says dryly, but the tension has left him, and a smile lurks round his mouth.

"Was it such a bad cover-up?" asks Lara. "It took ten years for the body to be found."

Severine has perched her bottom on the granite surface beside the sink. She crosses her legs and supports her upper body with her arms braced behind her. She doesn't shock me with her sudden appearances anymore. I wonder if I would miss her if she were to go wherever ghosts go when they're done haunting.

"If it was a random stranger, then it's a poorly executed cover-up that just got lucky," says Tom. "You'd have to expect the well to be searched sometime early on, and a stranger wouldn't know it was due to be filled in soon. But we knew that. Even so, even with it being filled in, you'd have to think it would be searched sooner rather than later."

"What would you have done?" I ask curiously.

"Taken your car keys and dumped her somewhere far away," he says promptly, so promptly that I know he's thought about this before.

"Modan asked about cars . . ." I trail off. There's a tendril of something in my brain that I can't quite catch. Severine has a cigarette in her hand now. She blows out smoke in a slow, languid breath, her eyes fixed on me, as dark and unreflective as always.

"We're really considering this, then?" says Lara to no one in particular. "That it could have been Seb? One of us?" There's nothing to say to that. She reaches for a slice of pizza, then pauses with it partway to her mouth to remark, "If Caro was involved, it would have to be for Seb. I can't imagine her doing that for anyone else." She thinks for a moment more, then gestures with the pizza. "Caro and Seb. God, I hope he's not that stupid."

"He's pretty stupid at times, but even so . . ." Tom grimaces, but then shakes his head. They're both sneaking wary glances at me. The instinct not to talk about Seb in front of me has become so ingrained over the years that they're struggling to shake it. Tom shakes his head again. "I'm sure he's not. He must know it would mean too much to her."

"Has everybody always known that?" I ask hesitantly. "I don't think I did back then—did I miss it? I knew she didn't like me going out with Seb, but I thought she just didn't like *me*."

"She didn't like you," Tom says, not without humor, at the same time as Lara says, "She still doesn't like you."

A smile curls my lips despite myself. "No, really, guys, don't beat around the bush on my account." Tom grins and Lara giggles. "I knew she didn't like me, but I didn't think it was me so much as what I represent—or what I don't represent. I didn't go to the right school, I didn't spend my summers in Pony Club and winters in Verbier, I don't have the right accent."

"Val d'Isère," says Tom. I roll my eyes. How is it that we're now back at this easy ebb and flow? Surely there has to be a reckoning at some point? "But I take your point: she's a snob. Of course she wouldn't like you. But especially not since you were dating Seb."

"You're right, though; she's more obvious now," Lara observes.

I munch on the pizza and let this marinate. The trick is to take in the new without polluting the old, and I don't think I've got the hang of it: it's too easy to project what I know now on what I remember from then. I remember Seb; I remember the faint disbelief I carried around inside me that Seb—silver-spooned, silver-tongued, golden-hued Seb—that he was with me. Part of me *expected* all girls to want him. And Seb . . . well, Seb expected it, too; he took it as his right, and any suggestion that he encouraged it was instantly labeled "jealousy." I decided early on that I would not allow him to brand me with that, but that required a lot of hard work and, in retrospect, willful ignorance. Perhaps it's no wonder I dismissed Caro's long-held unrequited love too lightly.

I finish my slice before I break the companionable silence. "Anyway, we've strayed from the point. Tom, what do you think happened? You've always known more than us."

He doesn't dispute it. "I was actually trying not to drag you guys into it."

"We're pretty firmly mired in it all now."

"Speak for yourself," yawns Lara. "I'm sure I'm off the hook."

I give her arm a gentle poke. "So much for solidarity. Well, I'm pretty firmly mired in it all, at least."

He doesn't dispute that, either.

"You saw something," Lara prompts.

He nods. "I did. I . . ." A loud buzz interrupts him. He cocks his head and turns toward his door. "Probably a mistake. A drunk or something." The buzzer sounds again, in three short blasts then a long hold. "A highly obnoxious drunk." He crosses the kitchen quickly and exits to the hall. We hear him speaking tersely to the intercom by his front door. "Hello?"

"It's me," comes an unmistakable voice, unexpectedly loud through the speaker. Lara's guilt-filled eyes fly to mine, which no doubt display the same. *Speak of the devil* . . . "Let me up. I'm the glad bearer of tidings—the bearer of glad tidings. Or something . . ."

"Come on up then." Tom sounds resigned. He reappears in the doorway of the kitchen. "Seb," he says unnecessarily.

Lara makes a face. "Definitely an obnoxious drunk, then. Though who am I to talk, after all this wine." She slides down the stool and turns for her bag and coat. "I'm going to have to leave you to it."

"I'll come with you." But I'm still perched on the stool, anchored by the same one ankle.

"Stay," Tom says quickly. "I'll get rid of him."

I raise an eyebrow. "Charming. Whatever happened to blood being thicker than water?"

"Doesn't apply when the blood is thinned by alcohol. He'll probably have to slope home to Alina soon anyway."

Lara is not too sleepy to have missed this exchange: I see her eyes dart back and forth between us as she pulls her coat on, but her face is carefully expressionless. "Call me tomorrow," she says to me neutrally. "You can fill me in on the outcome of the rest of this Nancy Drew session."

And so I stay.

CHAPTER SIXTEEN

S eb is drunk.

Not just a little squiffy, or even moderately tipsy, but un-equivocally drunk. The sort of drunk that can only be achieved by dedicated effort—a long, brutally determined session—or by a staggering lack of tolerance. But I'm beginning to suspect that Seb's tolerance has been well bolstered over the last decade.

"Jesus," says Tom, as Seb stumbles in through the kitchen door that Lara has just slipped out of, catching hold of the frame to steady himself. He's in a dark suit, the tail of his tie dangling from his trouser pocket, and there are stains on his white shirt, but it's his face that really arrests attention. His eyes are glazed and patterned with red veins like cracks; he's flushed, heavy jowled and loose lipped. The tan that sits on his skin is too insubstantial to hide the damage of his night's work. "Look at the state of you. Where have you been?"

"The King's Head by the office. Leaving drinks. They're firing half the bloody floor; there's been leaving drinks for weeks . . . Then a bloody good wine bar in Knightsbridge. Then, God, I don't know."

He peers across the room, as if struggling to see through darkness despite the kitchen being well lit, swaying slightly despite the support of the doorframe. "Kate, too? You know I just saw Lara on the way up the stairs." His speech is slurred: he has particular trouble with *Lara*; it could be *Lalla* or *Lulla*.

"Hi, Seb." I make no move to climb off the stool. He is not something I want to kiss hello.

"Come and have a glass of water," Tom says, running the tap in the sink. He eyes the difficult stools. "On second thought, maybe we should move to the sofa."

"Not water," says Seb, shaking his head, but he lets Tom shepherd him through the open-plan room in the direction of the living room area. I take the water glass off Tom in return for a muttered thanks and then follow the pair of them. "Need something stronger. Wet the baby's head. Alina's pregnant. Going to be a dad. Fuck." He sounds astonished, as if he can't quite understand how he got to this point.

"Congratulations! Didn't know—woah, there!—you had it in you." I can hear the exasperation under Tom's words as he tries to stop Seb ricocheting off the walls, knocking awry the photographic prints Tom has hung there.

I pause by the dining table that separates the kitchen space from the living room area and compose myself. Seb has collapsed onto one sofa, legs sprawled out, shoulders hunched over well below the line of the sofa back. Severine sits in the opposite corner of the same sofa, her feet curled up under her, eyeing Seb with unmistakable distaste. Tom switches on a couple of table lamps, then sits in the armchair.

"Congratulations, Seb," I say, holding out the water. He doesn't take it—I'm sure he can barely see it—so I put it on the coffee table. I can't bring myself to sit on Severine—or near Seb for that matter, so I settle on the footstool. "How is Alina feeling?"

"Oh, fine, fine. She's always fine."

I think of Alina with the crumpled paper towel in the bathroom of the restaurant. No, Alina is not always fine.

"How far along is she?" asks Tom.

"Ten weeks. Not supposed to say yet, but . . ." He shrugs. I can barely discern the movement, his head is sunk so deeply into his chest. "Fuck. A baby." A phone starts to ring from the depths of his suit jacket. He clumsily pulls it out, peers at the screen then leans forward to deposit it on the table without answering. He passes a hand over his face, then collapses back into the sofa again. Just when I think he's passed out, he turns to me with an unexpectedly shrewd look. "What are you doing here anyway? Have I interrupted something?" He starts to laugh as if the idea is hilarious. "Sloppy seconds, huh, Tom?"

In that instant I detest him with a force that's blinding. I actually want to physically hurt him. It scares me.

"You just saw Lara, Seb," Tom reminds him evenly, but his jaw is clenched. He's not looking at me. It feels deliberate. "You think I'm screwing them both?" *Screwing*. To screw, a verb. I screw, we screw, they screwed, screw you . . . it can never sound anything but cheap, sordid. Is that how he thinks of the corridor kiss?

"Ha-ha," Seb snorts. "Don't tell me it never crossed your mind. Certainly crossed mine once or twice." In another world, in other circumstances, this would be harmless fun. The kind of flirting men do with attractive female friends that elicits a naughty giggle and a warm glow. But we're not in that world. There's a hard edge to Seb's words, a nastiness. Was he always like this when he'd had a few? I recall Lara's words: *Definitely an obnoxious drunk, then*. I can't specifically recall it, but it doesn't quite surprise me, either.

I stand up abruptly. "I think I'll head home after all. The company's better there." Severine eyes me from the sofa, as close to a smirk on her face as I have ever seen. At least I've conjured up a figment of imagination that appreciates my sly digs.

"No, don't," says Seb. He struggles himself a little more upright and lunges out with an arm to try and stop me. "I'm sorry. Don't take it like that. Was just having fun. Don't have to take everything so seriously! Sorry, sorry . . ." His mumbles trail off, but he continues to look at me beseechingly, somehow both aggrieved and hangdog, a little boy mostly pretending to be ashamed of himself. This I remember. Seb is a master at apologies that somehow make you feel like the fault is more than likely your own.

The phone starts to ring again; he drops my arm. "Alina?" asks Tom, but from my vantage point of standing I can see on the screen that it's not Alina calling.

"It's Caro," I inform them, but I think Seb knows that. He's made no move to answer. I can see he's missed eight calls; I wonder how many are from Caro. The phone subsides into sulky silence.

"Would never have met you if it wasn't for Tom," Seb rambles, as if there's been no interruption. He seems to have found a philosophical bent. "That's why we went to that party, you know, when we crashed Linacre Ball. Tom wanted to see some girl . . ." He trails off, smirking at Tom. I catch a glimpse of Tom's face, set with tension. I don't understand the undercurrent.

"Who?" I prompt, when Seb doesn't go on. I've never heard this story before.

"Yes, who was that girl? I don't think you ever told me," says Seb with faux-innocence, but in his inebriated state, subtlety is beyond him. Seb, I deduce, knows exactly who it was.

"Who knows? It was a long time ago," Tom says tightly, but he's interrupted by Seb's mobile ringing once more.

"It's Caro again," I say neutrally.

"I know," he mutters. His head is sunk on his chest again. "Fuck." This time it's more of a moan.

"Why is Caro calling you so much?" Tom asks, as if it's only of the mildest interest to him.

"I'm not sleeping with her if that's what you think." He's both belligerent and defensive. His fabled charm has most definitely fled him this evening.

"I never said—"

"Yeah, well, you implied it. Of course I'm not sleeping with her; I'm not completely stupid. Never have in all these years." His head lolls again. "Barely even kissed her," he mutters. He rubs a hand down his face, then lunges drunkenly for my arm again, and catches it, pulling me down awkwardly so I'm half hunched over. "I fucked up, Kate," he mumbles urgently, looking straight in my eyes. "Should never have given up on us. Everything was okay, wasn't it? We were good, weren't we? But then I fucked up. And now . . . oh, fuck . . ." I start to feel a sense of foreboding building in my stomach. Seb releases my arm abruptly, and I lose my balance, grabbing at the coffee table to steady myself. When I look back at Seb he has his arm raised, shielding his eyes with his forearm. I glance at Tom questioningly. He shakes his head, nonplussed.

"Seb, what's wrong?" I ask hesitantly. "What is it?"

"Leaving drinks." His lips fumble around the words, thick and rubbery. "*My* leaving drinks."

"But you just came across from New York. Surely they wouldn't fire you when—"

"Not fired. Resigned. *Not* fired. My boss was—kind—enough to give me the option." His arm is still over his eyes.

"What did you do?" Tom asks, brutally direct.

"What I always do. I fucked up." He lifts his arm away; it's hard to tell in the dim lighting, but I think his eyes are wet. "Not like you, eh, Tom? You always hit the mark. *Tom is doing so well at school. Tom's won a scholarship, didn't you hear? Tom's really racing up the career ladder; you know he's head of FX trading now? Why can't you be more like your cousin?*"

My breath catches in shock. I can't imagine Seb would ever betray such bitterness were it not for the amount he's drunk, and I can't imagine he would want me to see this. I feel instantly grimy, like I'm peeping in on a private scene. Tom's face is impassive. I wonder if he's heard this before or simply guessed at the simmering resentment. "What did you do?" Tom repeats, remarkably undeterred.

Seb rubs a hand over his face, and all the fight seems to leave him. "I was drunk," he says hoarsely. "At work. All this stuff with that fucking French girl, and Alina and the baby, and then Caro in my ear—it just . . . got too much." He presses the heels of his hands into his eye sockets and leaves them there. "Fuck!" he says with explosive savagery.

When Tom shakes his head, I can see exasperation warring with pity upon his face. "Oh, Seb," he says softly.

That fucking French girl. A literal statement in this case, since he was the one fucking her. But one look at Seb's distress robs me of my ironic amusement; there's nothing to laugh at here. "I'm sorry," I say inadequately. I look at Tom. "You should call Alina and let her know he's here; she's probably worried sick."

He nods and picks up Seb's mobile to scroll through the directory for Alina's number, stepping toward the corridor to make the call. I wonder if he's also checking how many times Caro has rung; I would be.

Seb is falling asleep, I think. I suppose he will have to stay here, and therefore Tom and I are unlikely to have our tête-à-tête tonight after all. I should go; in fact, I'm eager to go—watching someone unravel is far from comfortable, and Severine has already ditched the scene. I make a move toward the corridor, but suddenly Seb lunges for my arm once more: not asleep after all. He pulls me into that awkward crouch again, but this time I'm forewarned; I brace myself on the arm of the sofa. "It wasn't me," he says urgently, pleadingly, his bloodshot eyes seeking mine out directly. "You have to know that. It wasn't me—I would have remembered if it was me, wouldn't I? It couldn't have been me. I came to bed; it couldn't have been me."

"I . . ." I'm helpless for words. Hypothetically discussing Seb as a suspect for murder in Tom's kitchen over pizza is a far cry from facing down the mess that is the man himself. Tom's footsteps sound behind me, and I turn, relieved at the interruption, but I see Tom halt abruptly at the sight of us, his face frozen. I'm suddenly horribly aware of how close Seb's face is to mine.

I start to disengage my arm just as Seb blurts, "I think I'm going to vom—" He releases me and lurches upward as I scatter backward; Tom starts back into action, practically hauling him by the collar toward the bathroom. Moments later I hear the unmistakable sound of Seb's stomach evacuating itself.

I climb back onto my feet and go in search of my coat and my handbag, both of which are still in the kitchen. The dirty pizza plates are still on the counter; if I were a truly wonderful guest I would wash them up, but given it's now past midnight I am definitely no-where near wonderful—the most I have the energy for is to stack them in the sink, since on inspection the dishwasher is full. My mind is flitting from Seb's desperate, pleading eyes to Tom's shuttered face, and back again . . . It's hardly the most important question, but I keep wondering who the girl was, the girl that Tom dragged Seb to the party for. Once upon a time I would have landed upon one name only, but I'm starting to think there's a second option.

I pick up my coat and exit the kitchen to find Tom hovering in the corridor, lit only by the yellow slash of light coming from the bottom of the bathroom door, and the dim light spilling in from the kitchen and living room.

"You got hold of Alina?" I ask, to cover my awkwardness. Tom and I, alone again in this same corridor—how could it not be awkward?

"Yeah. He's going to stay here for tonight." He's leaning his back against the wall; I can barely see the white of his teeth as he yawns. "She knew about him losing his job. She brought it up; I was wondering whether Seb would have told her or not."

"How did she sound?" I put my bag down and begin to pull on my coat.

"I don't know. Frustrated mostly, I think."

Another deep retch comes from the bathroom. My eyes are adjusting to the light; I can just make out a grimace of part distaste and part sympathy on Tom's face. "Christ. He's going to feel like death tomorrow."

"Who was the girl, Tom?"

He knows what I mean; he doesn't try to dissemble. He simply shakes his head tiredly. "It doesn't matter."

It does, though. "Was it Lara?" We're speaking quietly. The darkness winds its way around us, enveloping us, comforting us. It's a blanket under which words can be uttered that would never be broached in the light of day.

"What? No, it wasn't Lara." I know he's looking at me; I can feel the weight of his gaze, though I can only discern his eyes from a slight gleam. I have the sense his head is cocked, but perhaps I'm projecting his mannerisms upon this dark canvas. "Why would you think that? That was just a holiday fling. It didn't mean anything to either of us."

Not Lara. Not only not Lara, but seemingly never Lara. I file that away for future analysis. "So who was the girl?" I ask again, doggedly intent.

He doesn't speak for a moment. He's so still I could believe he has fallen asleep standing. Eventually his words come, barely more than a whisper. "You know who it was."

Yes. I do know. There's an inevitability about it, a permanence, even though I recognize that I didn't know at all. I swallow. "Now I do," I whisper. "I didn't before." Things I've been scared to acknowledge I've wanted and hoped for are gathering together inside me, a pressure that's building, straining, until I'm afraid to move lest I burst open.

His hand reaches out, and I feel the back of his fingers trail gently down my cheek. I find I'm holding my breath. "I'm sorry I was such an unforgivable shit. It's just . . . there was a moment there, the other night, when I thought I was getting everything I'd always wanted. And then—reality set in." His fingers drop, he turns his head away and suddenly my stomach clenches into a hard knot. I know beyond a shadow of doubt that I will have to close myself off again, stamp down on all those things so eager to burst out. "And I was so fucked off—at myself, mostly—for allowing it, for putting myself in that position. Because I knew better, really. You can say whatever you choose to say, pretend whatever you think you should feel, but I see it in you, tonight like every other night. It's always been Seb for you, hasn't it? You never even saw me. And I'll always know that."

He has it all wrong, just like I've had it all wrong about so many things. "No, no," I protest urgently, my voice rising, "that's not fair, that's not right—"

But he barely notices my interruption; he's still talking, in a low, oddly persuasive rumble. "When this—when Modan—is done, I'm going to move back to Boston—"

A sudden crash comes from the bathroom. It sounds as if Seb has pulled something over: quite possibly the radiator judging from the metallic reverberation. Tom is already moving in that direction. "Shit. Sorry, Kate, you'd better go," he throws over his shoulder, then he's pulling the bathroom door open. I catch a glimpse of his face in the yellow light that leaps out to paint him, harsh lines etched round his mouth. "Shit!" he says again. Then he disappears inside and the door shuts abruptly. I'm left alone in the passageway.

For a moment I stand there, completely at a loss. Surely I can help with whatever disaster is now unfolding—but then I realize:

that's not the point. He doesn't want me here, and this is a convenient way to politely get rid of me. I consider that for a moment more, then take a shuddering breath, pick up my bag and quietly leave the flat.

In the taxi on the way home I replay the night of Linacre Ball, when I first met Seb, and when, of course, I also first met Tom. I think about Tom dragging Seb along to the party, with quiet plans of speaking to a girl—me, as it turns out. I wonder where he had come across me before. I don't suppose I'll ever find out. I wonder how different things would have been if I'd turned back for the man-boy with the marvelously hooked nose after jumping off the wall, but I have to stop that train of thought before I come apart a piece at a time. Then from nowhere Tom's words from an afternoon not so very long ago in his flat float back to me: *Seb likes to win*—and I put that together with Seb's sly look—*Yes, who was that girl? I don't think you ever told me*—and I'm flooded with such savage fury that I want to scream with it.

I know I'm an unholy mess. I wish beyond all reason that my dad was still alive. But he's not here, and I am, in a taxi driving through the deserted streets of London. So I go home to an empty flat—truly empty, as Severine is nowhere to be seen—and crawl into bed with all my clothes on, craving the oblivion of sleep.

When I was growing up my mother often used to say that things look better after a good night's sleep. I've always been my father's child, and he was never so blindly optimistic. In the morning, I'm still under suspicion of murder and my love life still has not improved. And I remember that I still haven't found out what Tom saw all those years ago at the farmhouse.

The office provides little respite. A potential client—big job, looking to flesh out their whole litigation team, but we're in stiff competition with two other recruitment firms—asks me diffidently about any "events in the private lives of the key personnel of Channing Associates that could be potentially reputation damaging" were they to enter into a contract with us; I know immediately that the rumors aren't confined to Mark Jeffers.

"Ah," I say with what I hope is a knowing laugh. "You're actually asking about the completely ridiculous rumor that I'm about to be sent down for murder."

"Well, I . . ." I can practically hear the squirming down the line.

"To tell you the truth, it's all horribly sad. A girl disappeared in the neighboring farmhouse to where I was staying on holiday in France ten years ago, and her body has just been found. Naturally the police have spoken to all of us who were staying there, and naturally we're all keen to do anything at all we can to help." I pause and add meaningfully, "As I'm sure you would be, if you were in my shoes."

"Yes. Yes, of course. We just have to be very careful. As a firm we pride ourselves on our unimpeachable reputation . . ."

It's hard not to zone out. No matter what I have said or can say now, we've lost this one. It was a tight race anyway, and rightly or wrongly, this just gives a reason for them to pick another horse. They won't say that, of course. I'm mildly curious to see what excuse they will come up with. My money is on them labeling us "a comparatively new firm that has yet to be sufficiently proven."

Paul comes in, his face grim, just as I'm putting down the phone.

"I know," I say to forestall him, moving around my desk to rest my backside on it. "I just had chapter and verse on reputation from Strichmans."

His mouth is in a thin line almost as pale as his eyebrows. "What did you say?"

"The truth, as it happens, but we've lost it anyway."

"They said that?"

I shake my head. "No, but they will."

He pulls out his chair and flops into it, dispirited. "This isn't going away, Kate."

"It will." But even I can hear that I lack conviction.

"Can't they arrest someone already?"

"I'd be fine with that. So long as it isn't me."

He almost bursts up out of his chair. "What the fuck, Kate? You said—"

"*Joke*, Paul. Just a joke."

"You can't joke about this stuff," he says stiffly, but at least he subsides back into his seat. "It's *serious*, Kate."

"I know. We just lost Strichmans. Though we may never have got that one anyway."

"So what are you going to do?"

The *you* in his question rings out like a bell, loud and clear, reverberating in my brain. Paul is dissociating himself, preparing for the worst. "We're going to do our jobs, and we're going to do them very well." I'm careful not to put stress on the plural pronoun.

"Sure," he says with no vigor. He leans forward in his chair, elbows on his knees and hands hanging in between, staring at the floor.

"Paul." I speak sharply, pulling myself upright. He doesn't look up. "Paul!" This gets his attention. "Don't build this up to be something it's not. We're quite some distance from finished. I hired you because I knew you'd get out there and hustle. So get out there. Hustle. Otherwise you're absolutely no good to me."

He stares back at me for a moment. I refuse to break eye contact. I have the advantage of height since I'm standing; it puts me in mind of wolf pack behavior, fighting to be alpha male. Then I see a small gleam in his pale eyes. "Pep talk over?" he asks dryly. "Or do you want to give me another kick up the arse?"

My lips twitch. "That's it for now." Then a thought crosses my mind. "Oh, pass me the Mark Jeffers file, would you?"

"I haven't loaded it all onto the network yet. Why, do you have something suitable?"

"We'll see," I say evasively.

"I should have it up there by the end of today. Unless you're in a hurry?"

"No rush," I tell him breezily, and circle my desk to sit back at my station, but Severine has planted herself in my chair. I should sit down anyway, I know I should, but I find myself saying to Paul, "I'm running out for coffee. Want anything?"

"No, thanks." He doesn't look up from his screen. "I'm trying to cut back. Though that's kind of like holding back the tide in this job."

It's true. We move from meeting to meeting, mirroring our candidates and clients: if they want a drink, we drink; if they want to eat, we eat. We are a service industry, and the service we provide is confidence. Through the medium of hot beverages and sustenance, every meeting has to whisper, *We're like you, we understand your problems, your needs, we feel your pain and we can solve it.* But how can the clients be confident I can solve their problems when they think I can't solve my own?

My phone rings before I've crossed the road: Lara. "Hi, hon—"

"Can you meet for a coffee? Right now?" There's a note of blind panic threaded through her blunt question; it dredges up the unease always waiting inside me, curled quietly in the depths of my stomach. Lara is not melodramatic, or given to wild fits of runaway imagination; those things take too much energy, and Lara would freely admit she's a little too lazy for that.

"What's up?"

"I just had a late lunch with Alain; I'll tell you in person. Can you meet?"

I glance at my watch, running through the afternoon's schedule in my head. "Yes. I'll jump in a cab toward you. Usual place in ten minutes?"

"Yes." In the uncharacteristic terseness of her reply I can hear her native accent begging for release. I start looking for a cab immediately.

Once ensconced in a black taxi, the unease becomes corporeal, taking on the body of twisting snakes that are no longer confined to my stomach: now they're swaying upward, encircling my lungs, slithering through my throat, threatening to choke me of words and breath. The thunk of the automatic door locks when the cab speeds up makes me jump, heart racing, adrenaline prickling through my skin. Severine appears beside me in the cab, scrutinizing me expressionlessly in her take-it-or-leave-it manner, but I deem her presence a gesture of solidarity; whether it's intended that way, I'll never know, but I may as well take whatever comfort I can get from this creation of my own mind.

The driver is unwilling to cross the traffic flow, so I leap out of the taxi on the other side of the road to the café and spot Lara immediately, already sitting at a table by the window with two tall mugs in front of her. Even through the logo-emblazoned window I can see her face is pinched, but she manages an approximation of a smile and a sketch of a wave when she sees me crossing the road. She gets up to hug me as I enter, and I feel the tension clinging to her frame.

"What's up?" I ask, as soon as we're both seated. She's wearing a dress I haven't seen before, a fitted sheath with a pattern like a snowstorm in the dark. I wonder if the lunch was planned, if she wore the dress especially for Modan. She looks stunning as ever, but older, somehow. Not in her face, which is exactly the same, but in less tangible ways: her carriage, her demeanor, her very self.

"I had lunch with Alain. He wanted to apologize. He was hurt, lashing out. He still wants . . . well, you know." I do, or I can imagine; I can extrapolate from what I know so far. And if I know anything about Alain Modan, it's that he won't give up on Lara. "But I keep telling him, not until this—the investigation—is all done. I told him that again today, and he said that I shouldn't have to wait too long, things were coming to an end. Only he looked very grim about it. I asked if he meant he was dropping the case, and he shook his head and asked if you have a lawyer yet."

"*What?*" The café fades away instantly; all I have in my focus is the beautiful, desperately worried face of Lara.

She nods, a fast bob. "Yes. He asked if you have a lawyer. I said I didn't know—I didn't want to give anything away—and he said you really ought to get one."

"Jesus." I am staring at her in abject disbelief. This can't be happening. "But—"

"Wait, there's more. He had a file on the table, one of those yellow cardboard things. It had *her* name on it, and yours, I could see it. He tapped it and then said he was off to the bathroom, just leaving it there with me." She spreads her hands wide. "It was like he was *inviting* me to look at it."

"Did you?" *Please say you did.*

She nods again—*yes!*—even faster, guilt written on her face. "I know I shouldn't have, but I couldn't shake the feeling that he meant me to . . . I just had a quick look." I'm nodding, wordlessly urging her on. "There was a report on the top. I didn't have time to read it all, I could only skim, but basically—oh, Kate, basically the whole thing was about how he thinks you killed her." The words are tumbling out of her; she can't keep up with them, and her accent is slipping. "Motive, opportunity, the whole nine yards. He reckons Seb passed out in the barn with Severine. You found him there and were enraged; you hit her with something—there was something about an old garden rake still having her blood on it; I didn't know that, did you? Apparently nobody ever washes garden rakes . . . Anyway, they're testing it for other DNA and fingerprints. So you hit her with the rake then dumped her body; you knew the well was being filled in—"

She stops abruptly, and we stare at each other. I can barely think. I can barely breathe. *A garden rake.* Slowly the rest of the café returns: the hum of conversation, the sound of the coffee machine, the disturbance of the air when the door is opened. *A garden rake with blood still on it after ten years* . . . I feel clammy and ill; the hand that reaches out to pick up my mug of coffee is trembling, but my brain is starting to function again.

"And you think he wanted you to look?"

"Yes. He tapped the file." She spreads her hands wide again, her eyes pleading for absolution. "He *tapped* it."

"Don't feel bad. He meant you to look," I say decisively. "We're talking about Modan; he doesn't just accidentally"—I sketch quotation marks around the adverb—"leave a sensitive file in plain view of someone with a vested interest in it." Which begs the question as to why he chose to do just that. Focusing on the strategy is making me feel better. *Don't think about being arrested. Don't think about being arrested.*

"He's using me," she says with sudden fierceness. She's almost vibrating with the intensity of her emotions. "He shouldn't be doing that. He shouldn't be putting me in this position."

"I know. I don't think he would if he had another option." But so much hinges on whether that is really true. If he really cares about Lara, he would only use her as part of a last-ditch attempt to try and help her friend: ergo, I'm in real, undeniable trouble. But if Lara is merely a passing fling, then he might well use her if his investigation is stalling, to try and flush out more information. Here I am questioning that which only moments ago was an incontrovertible truth—wasn't I only just thinking that he would never give up on Lara? *He loves her, he loves her not, he loves her, he loves her not* . . . I find myself examining the woman sitting opposite me again, as if I can read the truth of Modan's feelings for her in the tilt of her nose, the curve of her lips, the sweep of her cheek. *A garden rake*. How does one accidentally kill someone with a garden rake? *Don't think about being arrested*.

"Either way he thinks I know more than I'm telling," I say aloud. What if it wasn't an accident? I see a long wooden handle whistling through the air, landing squarely on Severine's temple. *A garden rake*.

"Either way?" Lara wrinkles her nose, puzzled.

"Nothing," I say quickly. Clearly Lara hasn't considered the possibility that she is being used for ill rather than good. She at least is convinced of his affections. Does that signify? I wonder what Tom will make of it all; there's no question in my mind that I will tell him. Tom may not want a relationship with me, but presumably I can trust a man who was once in love with me to be on my side. Will Tom trust in Modan's feelings for Lara? It suddenly strikes me that I've been wrong before where Lara is concerned; wrong for years, in fact.

"Lara, when—" Something slams into the window right beside us with a loud thud. We both jump, knocking the table; our coffees slop everywhere. I feel the instant prickle of adrenaline sweeping over me again.

"Jesus, what was that?" gasps Lara, her face utterly drained of color.

The window is intact. I'm standing up, craning my neck with my head pressed against the window to look through it, past the coffee shop slogan stuck on the glass to the pavement below. "A bird," I say. "A pigeon." The dirty, gray-feathered body is lying in a heap on the paving. "It's stunned itself."

"Jesus," says Lara again.

I straighten and glance around the coffee shop. The barista continues to serve, conversations are continuing among the paired clientele, mobile phones continue to be inspected by those sitting alone. Nobody else seems to have noticed. I look out of the window; passersby hurry on, unheeding. Severine is among them, in her black shift, blood trickling from her right temple. It doesn't seem to be affecting either her balance or her self-possession.

"That was weird." I grab some napkins and start to mop up our spilled coffee. "There must have been a reflection in the window; it must have thought it was flying into sky."

"That used to happen at school in Sweden sometimes."

I settle down again and return to my almost cold coffee. "Lara, why did you and Tom never give things a proper go?"

She looks up from her coffee, startled. "After France, you mean?"

"Yes." I'm suddenly very self-conscious. Should I be holding eye contact, or not? What impression am I giving about how vested I am in this answer? "I always thought he wanted to but you didn't."

"Oh." She's blushing a little. It underlines how pale she's been this afternoon. "Actually . . . it was more the other way round. To be honest, I would have been up for it—at the time, I mean, not now—but he was definitely not into anything more."

"Oh." I consider that. "Why did I think it was the other way round?"

"I don't know." But she really is too honest to leave it like that. "Except maybe . . . perhaps I gave you that impression. I felt a bit, well, rejected, I suppose. You weren't really around at the time; right after France you and Seb were splitting up and your dad died and then you were up north for ages, and in quite a state even when you got back . . . I think you made the assumption and I never really corrected it, out of pride I guess." I can see the guilty embarrassment squirming inside her; I can see the Lara of years ago, hardly unable to comprehend the concept of a man who doesn't want to climb back in the sack with her. "It hasn't messed things up for you and Tom, has it?" she asks, suddenly anxious.

"I don't think there is a me and Tom." Just like there was never a Lara and Tom. I got that wrong, for all those years, along with just about everything else. Am I wrong about how Modan feels about Lara? Am I being played? "Would you mind if there was?"

"No." She says it hesitantly, like she's testing her answer. "It feels a bit strange, but . . ." She shrugs with a hint of a rueful smile. "I'd have no right to mind, even if I did."

An interesting response. An honest one, I think. I sigh. "Well, it's a moot point anyway. Since I'm apparently going to jail." A French jail, to boot. I wonder, in an abstract way, if that is any better or worse than a British jail. And then it strikes me that it's no longer an abstract consideration.

"It's not funny, Kate," Lara says tersely.

"I'm not laughing." I feel clammy and ill again; I am definitely not laughing. We're many, many steps away from jail, I remind my-self. *Don't think about being arrested.* I lean toward the glass and peer out of the window again, down toward the pavement. The gray-feathered heap has gone.

"You have to speak to Alain. You have to give him something, cooperate. You have to tell him—"

"What? What can I tell him? I don't know anything to tell him."

"Yes, you do. You can tell him about Caro. You can tell him about the drugs."

My eyes leap to Lara's, and she gazes back at me, clear-eyed and unflinching. I look across the divide between us, the corridor of air, and it's like staring down a tunnel through the years, back to where it all began, back to France and Severine. How far we've come, to get to this point, the point where you throw friends under buses. Except Caro is not really a friend, exactly—but I'm splitting hairs. I start to form, then discard, any number of responses.

"What are you going to do?" presses Lara.

A garden rake. "I'm going to call my lawyer."

CHAPTER SEVENTEEN

I leave the café, already dialing my lawyer, but she's busy and unable to take my call. Of course she's busy; she's a professional at the top of her game, high in demand, which is exactly the sort of lawyer one would want to have—only I want her sitting in her office, staring at her telephone and twiddling her thumbs, doing nothing of note except eagerly awaiting my call. I have half a mind to jump in a taxi to her premises, but I resist the urge and instead choose to walk back to my office.

The fresh air fails to do me good. My mind is racing, unable to break free from a spiral track that leads inexorably to a dark pit of all the things I'm not yet ready to face. Surely there must be a way out, a bargain to be made with a God I don't believe in . . . How can this be happening to *me*?

"Jesus," says Paul. He doesn't look up as I enter the office. "Did they have to get the coffee beans from South America?"

It takes me a minute to process the words and divine his meaning, then I glance at my watch. I've been gone over an hour and a half.

But surely not . . . the taxi there, plus the time spent with Lara, plus the walk back: it doesn't quite seem to add up. But my internal clock and the reckoning of my watch cannot arrive at a mutually agreeable answer. I have the sensation that time is rushing past me, rushing through me, like I'm no more substantial than a ghost and there's nothing I can do to stem the tide. "I forgot I had a call with Gordon." It's hard enough to invent an excuse, let alone give it some expression. "I took it at the coffee shop."

Paul looks up from his computer screen at that. "Not a problem there, is there?" he asks anxiously. "I thought Caroline Horridge was the liaison now."

"No problem. Gordon just likes to keep his finger in the pie." The words make sense, but they mean nothing to me. Perhaps in a while Paul and the business and all those small concerns that add up to mean *life* will catch at me with little hooks and lines, pulling me back into phase with the world, but for now I feel like nothing exists except the looming dread of a French jail. Shock, I realize. I must be in shock.

"Well, I've loaded the Jeffers file now if you want to take a look."

"Thanks."

"Oh, I nearly forgot. Someone called for you when Julie was out at lunch, wanting to know when you'd be back, but wouldn't leave a message. A woman, posh sounding."

"Well, that certainly narrows it down." I've refound irony: I must be anchored back in the real world now. Except—I glance quickly around—Severine is not here . . . but no, I've got that wrong; Severine is not real, Severine is not normal . . . My head is pounding. I sit down quickly.

"Are you all right?" I hear Paul ask distantly.

"Fine," I say quickly. "Though I don't think my lunch entirely agreed with me." I'm getting to be quite the liar. Tom would be proud, except why would he? After this is over, Tom is washing his hands of me. But this may never be over, not for me . . . Where the hell is my damn lawyer? I grab the mouse, determined to focus on something else, and the blank monitor springs to life.

After some time—how long? Five minutes? Twenty-five?—my vision clears and the pounding in my head recedes. Sometime after that I realize it must look odd for me to be staring at a screen, and for lack of anything better to do, I look up the Jeffers file, which is exactly where it should be and perfectly up to date: Paul is nothing if not thorough. I skim through, noting his current role, and the familiar process begins to soothe me: strengths, weaknesses, where would he fit? Stockleys? Haft & Weil? But no, not there because . . . I stop suddenly, as a flush of adrenaline prickles over my skin. Definitely not Haft & Weil, because Mark Jeffers has already worked there, started his career there in fact. In none other than Caro's group.

I don't believe in coincidences.

I'm still trying to work out the implications of that when Julie taps and enters briskly, her generous mouth unusually strained. "Sorry, Kate, I have an Alina"—she checks the Post-it in her hand—"Harcourt here for you." Harcourt—but that's Seb's surname, it doesn't fit with anyone else—and then I twig. But what on earth is Seb's wife doing here? Julie is still speaking, her eyes anxious behind the tortoiseshell-rimmed glasses. "I did say you have quite a busy schedule . . ."

Do I? I check the diary, conscious it should have been the first thing I did when I got back in the office, and it's true, I have a few calls coming up. It's hard to reason through how I should respond to this sudden intrusion, to what would constitute a normal response when I feel so far from normal. I suppose I could legitimately send Alina away; it's what I would prefer to do, but I can't help wondering what has driven her here in the first place. I wouldn't imagine she's someone given to impulsive social calls with no warning; she's far too well-mannered for that. "It's okay, Julie, she's the wife of a friend."

Reluctantly leaving my desk to greet my unexpected guest, I find her looking out of the window in the outer room, a sleek gray wool coat buttoned almost to her neck, the belt highlighting her as-yet slim waist. Above the collar her long dark blond hair is coiled into a smooth roll. She turns her head as I emerge from my office, and I see her quickly rearrange her features into a smile. Her makeup is impeccable. She must have taken a great deal of care over it.

"Alina!" I say, finding a smile from somewhere. I kiss her on both cheeks after a slight hesitation that I hope is imperceptible. That's the point of etiquette, I think—to provide a framework of actions to cling to even when your world is falling apart. I need to rely on that. "This is a surprise. How are you?"

She doesn't answer the question. "I'm so sorry for turning up unannounced." She glances around; a quick frown crosses her face before she smooths it away.

"You're not a lawyer, are you?" I ask, conscious of Julie hovering behind me.

"Oh no. Lord, no. I capital-raise for private equity." Alina glances round again. The practicalities seem to be catching up to her. Perhaps she hadn't been expecting me to share an office.

"A social call then," I say. Alina's eyes fly to my face; they're hazel, almost yellow. "Come on, then, let's nip out for coffee where we can chat freely." Whatever she has to say, I'm quite sure I don't want Paul or Julie to hear it.

Alina nods swiftly. "Perfect," she says, relief evident even in her clipped tones. "I *am* sorry to disturb you, but as I was passing, it seemed silly not to drop in." She's a smart girl; she's caught on.

I ask Julie to reschedule my calls and then grab my coat, which seems very shabby next to Alina's sleek number, and Alina and I head across the road to the nearest coffee shop. I have to stretch my mind to think of what one might ordinarily say in this situation. *Follow the rules, stick to the etiquette*: the ordinary steps of life will pull me through. "How are you feeling?" I ask. "Are you still struggling with morning sickness?"

"That," she says without looking at me, her mouth a thin tight line, "is the least of my worries." Then she relents, perhaps realizing how combative she sounded. "But yes, I'm still struggling. God knows what this poor thing is surviving on; I can hardly keep anything down."

We're at the door of the café now. I sit Alina down at a table and queue to buy her a cup of tea and some plain biscuits, ignoring her protestations that she should be the one paying. When I return to the table she has peeled off the tailored coat to reveal a white silk blouse and a neat pencil skirt. The effect is simple, understated: elegantly attractive but not sexy. It entirely suits her. She reaches for the biscuits immediately. "Thank you."

"You're welcome." I study her as she peels open the packet, trying to fit her into Seb, like a two-piece jigsaw puzzle.

She looks up as if she feels my eyes on her, picking over her hair, her clothes, the way she holds herself. "You must be wondering what on earth I'm doing here," she says, without a trace of a smile, when she has finished a biscuit. Her delicately prominent collarbones spread like open wings from the two raised nubs at the base of her throat; her wrists are slender, leading to long, slim fingers. It seems like her very bones have been carefully crafted to fit the image she wishes to portray: refined, elegant, unmistakably upper class.

"Yes," I say. I glance at my mobile phone, which I have placed faceup on the table. My lawyer hasn't rung.

"You used to date my husband."

I blink. "Yes."

"Is that a problem?" Her eyes are an unusual hazel color and fixed unswervingly on my face.

I almost laugh; for a moment I'm tempted to paraphrase her own words: *that's the least of my problems.* Instead I say evenly, "Not for me."

She eyes me carefully without speaking for a moment, then reaches for another biscuit. "Good," she says, with some satisfaction, as if I've confirmed something important to her. "I didn't know anything about your history with Seb until the other day," she remarks. "Caro told me." There's an unmistakable twist of her lips on Caro's name. "Actually, I'd rather assumed you were with Tom."

I don't want to hear his name yet I'm also greedy for something, anything, that relates to Tom and me, to an *us* that has never been; I have to stop myself from asking why she assumed that. Instead I say mildly, "I wouldn't think you're here to ask me that, though."

"No." She puts down the biscuit without having taken a bite. Once again I'm caught in her hazel gaze. She ticks all the boxes I had always imagined Seb's wife would have to tick, but still she is not what I expected . . . She's more reserved, more intelligent, more herself. I wonder if Seb has gotten rather more than he bargained for. "I rather think Caro is trying to steal my husband," she says without preamble or apology. "He's in quite a bad place at the moment: his job, the drinking . . . I know you were at Tom's last night so I hardly need to bring you up to speed on that." Only two red spots high on those perfectly sculpted cheekbones reveal the humiliation I know she must feel on discussing her husband's failings with a near-stranger. "The thing is, it's Caro who is getting him so worked up about it all. Ever since they reopened the investigation on that girl, she's been on the phone nonstop, trying to get her little tendrils into him—" She stops abruptly, cutting off the passion that was threatening to spill into her words.

I stare at her. This is so far from what I was expecting—not that I knew what I was expecting, but this isn't it—that I have to mentally shake myself into responding. "They're not having an affair," I say at last. Perhaps it's a good thing this is such a strange conversation: I can be forgiven for being a little slow on social cues. It wouldn't be appropriate to say what I'm thinking: *I'm about to be arrested for a*

murder that in all probability was your husband's fault, so please excuse me
if I can't get worked up about the state of your marriage.

"I didn't think they were—not yet, at least. Though I'd be interested to know what makes you say that." One part of me notes that
the control she has of her emotions is terrifyingly impressive.

"Caro kept ringing last night. He wouldn't pick up. Tom asked
why she kept calling, and Seb told him he wasn't sleeping with her,
if that's what he was thinking. He said he never had." I remember
the words escaping his mouth in the dim living room, and more
besides. *Barely even kissed her.* So he did kiss her, at least once then. I
wonder when. Probably sometime when they were teenagers. Not
that it matters. Not that any of it matters. But she's here, and so am
I, and there are motions I should go through. I shrug. "So if you
believe in the old saying *in vino veritas* . . ."

"I do, actually," she says thoughtfully. Perhaps I detect a slight
relaxation within her, but equally I could be imagining it. She looks
at the biscuit carefully for a moment, as if considering if it's worth
the risk, but it remains on the table in front of her. She looks at me
again. "Thank you."

"You're welcome." I'm still puzzled as to what she's here for.

"Tom said you and Caro don't really get on."

Tom. "Well, we certainly didn't in the past, but that was a long
time ago."

"I thought perhaps you would be a good person to speak to."

"My enemy's enemy is my friend?" But I see Caro again, admit-
ting to her own mother's disapproval, and I feel that moment of
warmth between us. Caro is not an enemy. Nor a friend, either. I'm
not sure I know the correct word in the English language to describe
what she is to me. Though if she really is to blame for the Mark Jeffers situation, I'm sure I'll find one.

"Exactly." Alina smiles briefly, a genuine smile, not one out of
politeness. On another day, I know it would feel like a gift: I don't

believe Alina offers a genuine smile terribly often. "I don't really know what happened in France: Seb doesn't like to talk about it. He says he doesn't want me to worry about anything with the baby coming." She frowns. "But whatever happened, I think it's somehow giving Caro some, I don't know, *leverage* over him. And quite frankly I find that rather more irritating than the investigation. I mean, it's not as if Seb would really have killed a random girl, is it? He should have nothing to worry about. But she has him all worked up; he's talking to her and not to me, and I need to find a way to put a stop to it."

I look at her blankly. Surely as Seb's wife, she must know more than this? But there is no artifice in her face, simply frustration and a hefty dislike of Caro—Seb really hasn't filled her in. It's probably not my place to do it, either, but in spite of my preoccupation, my distance, I do have some empathy for her. She shouldn't be left in the dark. "Alina," I say carefully. "You do know that Seb slept with Severine, don't you? The girl who died? That he was the last person to see her alive?"

Her eyes fly to my face. "That's not . . . I don't . . ." She starts to shake her head and then stops, considering, a frown corrugating her ordinarily smooth forehead. "But I thought he was going out with you then," she says, confused.

"He was," I say wryly.

"Oh." Expressions flit quickly over her face before it settles on a look of resignation. "I rather think I'd better hear about all of this from you."

So I tell her the bare facts, bereft of any speculation, though I leave out the garden rake since that's information I'm not supposed to possess. She listens carefully, those yellow brown eyes taking account of me throughout. At the end she blows out a breath and mutters fiercely, "*Damn* you, Seb." Her words catch me and throw me years back, to a time when I would have been the one with such exasperation in my voice.

"I'm sorry," I admit truthfully.

She doesn't answer; she has finally picked up the biscuit and is working her way through it. "Well, it wouldn't have been Seb," she says definitively, when the biscuit is gone. "I mean, why on earth would he want to kill her? The police can't possibly suspect him."

"They might think it was an accident."

She waves it away. "But you know what he's like when he's drunk—he passes out; he can't hold his own body weight, let alone carry someone to a well."

"Someone else might have done that bit."

"Who?" she says, disbelieving. "Tom? Caro?" I see the precise moment the penny drops. The color leaches out of her face, and her mouth works wordlessly before she clamps her lips together. I don't say anything. There's nothing to say.

"Leverage," she finally says, almost hisses, though more to herself than to me. "That fucking bitch." She looks across at me again. "Is this what the police think happened?"

No. Luckily for your husband, the police think it was me. This is what I, Kate Channing, think happened. "I don't know."

"This can't be happening," she mutters, again to herself. Then, louder, looking at me fiercely this time: "This can't be allowed to happen."

At that moment my mobile rings out; I grab it as if it's a lifeline. "My lawyer. Sorry, I've got to take this." I duck outside the café before she can answer.

"Interesting," says Ms., Miss or Mrs. Streeter, when I've downloaded Lara's discoveries. "Not enough, though, even if the rake shows up your DNA, or anyone else's. Still simply circumstantial."

"Circumstantial enough to make it to trial?" I left my coat at the table with Alina. I wrap my free arm around myself, shivering a little. I can feel my ribs beneath my thin wrap dress. They feel worryingly insubstantial. I am too breakable for what life is throwing at me.

She's silent for a worryingly long pause. "Ordinarily no," she says at last. "But with the political pressure on this one, it's hard to say. Have you thought any more about cooperation?"

"Yes." Cooperation. A deceptive word. It sounds so collegiate, warm and friendly, yet in truth it's slyly partisan, with its own agenda. Cooperation with the police means betrayal of someone: but who? Seb? Caro? Both? I never thought I was someone who would stoop to this, yet here I am.

"And?"

I close my eyes and speak in a rush. "Caro had cocaine. She smuggled it into France in my suitcase; I knew nothing about it. That's what the arguments were about on the last night—I found out she'd done that. I honestly didn't think it had any bearing, so I never wanted to bring it up." I open my eyes. I never mentioned the drugs all those years ago, and I haven't mentioned them up to now, but in the space of a few short seconds all that counts for nothing: it's done. I wonder what Tom will think of me for it, and then I have to screw my eyes tightly shut again to block out the opprobrium I imagine in his face.

"Did you take any drugs that night?" Her voice is clipped, tightly professional.

"No."

"At any point during the holiday?"

"No. It's really not my thing; ask anybody."

"Believe me, the police will. Have you ever taken any drugs?" she continues, unrelenting.

"What, ever in my life?"

"Ever. As in, at any point whatsoever."

"I smoked pot once or twice at uni, but it just sent me to sleep; plus I don't like smoking."

"Once or twice? Be specific."

"Twice then. Certainly not three times."

"Okay." She has finally relaxed a little; I can hear the tension easing out of her voice. "Okay. That's good. I can definitely work with that. Anything else?"

"Well . . ." *I don't know what time Seb came to bed.* Through the café window I can see a side view of the abandoned Alina, sitting where I left her at the table. One hand is resting on her crossed legs, her thumb beating out an unsteady high-speed tattoo. *I don't know what time Seb came to bed.* The words are there, fully formed in my head, waiting to be sent forth into the world.

"Yes?"

I look at Alina again. She has stilled her thumb with her other hand, but her ankle is jittering now. "Sorry, uh, something just distracted me here. No, nothing else."

"Okay then, I'll set up a meeting with the detective and get back to you. This is good, Kate; it's helpful."

"Great." The word sounds thin.

"Oh, and Kate?"

"Yes?"

"If you have anything more to offer, now's the time. Think hard." Then she disconnects.

The cold overrides my reluctance to return to Alina, pushing me back into the café. Alina looks up as I enter. "Sorry about that," I say as I drop into the seat opposite her.

"You have a lawyer." It's almost an accusation.

"Yes."

"Does Seb have a lawyer?" Her manner is definitely more hostile. I'm the messenger, I realize: she'd really quite like to shoot me. And Seb, too, I expect, for putting her in this position, of being the last to know.

"I don't know. But if he doesn't, he should get one."

"He didn't do it," she says tightly. "I know him. *You* know him. You know he didn't have anything to do with it." I can't bring myself to say anything. Her eyes widen. "Oh my God," she says, genuinely stunned. "You actually think it was him."

"Look, I don't know what happened," I protest weakly, but she's not mollified.

"How *could* you? You went out with him, you *know* him."

I can see the shock turning to bitter fury inside her, and I find myself mentally cheering her loyalty even as I cringe in the face of it. "I just . . . Look, I don't think your Seb is the same as the Seb I went out with. We've all changed a lot since then."

"Still," she insists fiercely, her eyes boring into mine, "he wouldn't have done *that*." She waits imperiously for me to respond, and there is nothing else I can do: I nod. She nods her head sharply, acknowledging her win without any joy, then continues. "I bet Caro's trying to make him think he was involved somehow, responsible even. She's probably pretending she's covering up for him. To make him rely on *her*. That's the leverage she has. I bet she's been doing it for years, actually—he's always been on the booze more after she's been around." I cock my head: Alina may be onto something. It would be just like Caro to milk every advantage out of the situation: a confused, guilt-ridden Seb who owes an enormous debt to Caro is surely much more likely to succumb to her wiles . . . Alina happens to think the debt is manufactured rather than real, but either way, I can see a twisted Caro logic at work. I can just imagine her, late at night, sending poison-laden whispers down the phone line to slither into Seb's ear and take residence, curled inside his desperately worried mind. At least, it would be just like the Caro I thought I knew, but now I wonder; now there's the possibility of an alternative interpretation in my mind. Maybe Caro phones Seb because she can't help herself, because she's hopelessly in love with him. It would be just like Seb to carelessly lead her on, to be the one delivering to her ear sweet nothings carried on whispers that really are nothing at all, except a vehicle for the ego boost he needs . . . Perhaps he drinks after she's been around out of guilt. Then I think again of Mark Jeffers, and I'm back to Caro as poison-whisperer.

"And anyway," says Alina in a sudden change of pace, "surely there's an obvious alternative suspect."

I wait dumbly. Does she mean me? Surely she wouldn't suggest that in front of me, though to be fair I have just been casting aspersions about her husband . . .

"Theo."

I shake my head. "Nobody thinks it was Theo."

"Why not? Did he have an alibi?"

"No—well, I mean, yes, he was with Caro, I think, but I suppose that he went to bed at some point—"

"He's dead," she interrupts bluntly. "Which is obviously quite horrible for him and his parents and everyone who loved him, but all of you are still alive, with lives ahead of you to live. Surely if the blame is to fall on any of you, you might as well make it fall on him."

The brazen suggestion takes my breath away. "What you're suggesting . . ." I trail off. I should finish with *is immoral*, or *is illegal*, or *is an obstruction of justice*; but somehow I can't bring myself to spell it out. Theo as prime suspect. Alina thinks she's simply getting rid of the Caro problem, but it would get me off the hook too, of course. A wave of longing sweeps over me, a longing to be free of the weight that presses down on me, beating me a little smaller, a little weaker every day; to be free of the broiling sea of fear that sits in my stomach and threatens on occasion to erupt from my throat and overwhelm me.

"Yes," Alina says, her steady gaze fixed on my face despite the blush that betrays her emotions. "I know what I'm suggesting." I look at the cold fire within the yellow brown eyes, and I don't doubt her. Seb is so very lucky to have her, grimly fighting in his corner despite no doubt being utterly furious with him. But this particular sally seems too well considered to have just come to her whilst I've been braving both the cold and my lawyer's interrogation outside. "Is this what you wanted to speak to me about?"

She considers denying it but evidently plumps for the truth. "Yes." She shrugs, a glorious sweep upward of the tips of the outspread wings of her collarbones. She should have been a ballet dancer. She has the frame for it, and something else, too, something in her every gesture, each leading seamlessly into the next, that makes it seem like she's moving through a larger choreographed whole. "It doesn't really matter whether I'm right about what Caro's leverage is; if all of this goes away, then so does she."

And you think you'll get your husband back. "Tom will never go for it," I say at last. And now I've skipped over the morality, too: I'm focused on whether her plan can actually be executed. I wonder when I lost faith in the legal system, French or otherwise. Or perhaps it's not a lack of trust in the legal system that's to blame. Perhaps it's just that I know all too well that life isn't always fair; therefore, how can you expect the law to be? I shiver. *Don't think about being arrested.*

"He won't?" She raises her eyebrows. "Not even for Seb?"

"I don't . . ." I realize I don't know. Even yesterday I would have said that Tom would do anything for Seb, but now? The bitterness in Seb's voice last night, the tightness of Tom's face when Seb revealed he'd known all along that Tom was angling for me . . . I don't know who Tom would choose, Theo or Seb. "I don't know."

"And you?" She watches me closely, those slender wrists sweeping up to clasp together by her chin, a picture of poise. Once again I'm in awe of her control, all the more because I have an inkling of what's beneath it.

What would it take to push Modan down this road? I imagine him strolling along the dusty lane by the farmhouse, sunshine beating down on the shoulders of his immaculate suit as he ambles and constructs an argument in his mind for Theo as murderer. Perhaps that could indeed come to pass if he were the recipient of a few well-chosen comments, a few hints . . . Lies. Lies, all. Lies and a betrayal of Theo. Would that betrayal really be any worse than revealing Caro's cocaine use? I could claim that was only what she deserved given I'm sure she's spreading rumors about me through Mark Jeffers, but the truth is that as soon as I felt cornered I barely hesitated; I'd have done it without the Jeffers info. Again, I wonder what Tom will say about that.

"Kate?" prompts Alina.

"I'll think about it." At the least, I have given her a genuine response. I will probably think about little else.

CHAPTER EIGHTEEN

'm saved from having to bring Tom up to speed; it appears Lara has done that for me. He calls me that evening and sounds almost desperate. "Jesus, Kate. The garden rake. I've just been looking up the French for it—*râteau*! I thought she said *bateau*. It was *râteau*."

"What? Who said? What do you mean?" I'm on my mobile in my living room; I quickly hunt for the remote to kill the sound of the television program that I'd been hoping would hold my interest sufficiently to calm the vicious storm of my thoughts. As the characters turn abruptly silent it occurs to me I have no idea what I've been watching.

"I saw Severine. I saw her go into the barn with Seb, but I saw her again after they . . . you know. She was coming past the pool, and she had blood on her face; not much, just a bit, nothing to cause alarm." I'm not sure I have ever heard Tom—steady, reliable Tom—talk in such a stream of consciousness. "I asked her if she was all right; I didn't really get the gist of it at the time. She didn't have the right English word; she kept saying *bateau*. At least I thought it was *bateau*, but it must have been *râteau*." I see a brief image of Severine in the darkened barn, her slim foot stepping on the fanned-out prongs of the garden rake, the other end flipping up to smack her in the face Abbott and Costello style; it ought to be funny, but it's not. "I just thought she wasn't making a lot of sense—there wasn't a boat around for miles, but then we'd all had a lot to drink, so I put it down to that at the time. And she waved me away fairly forcibly and headed off, so I thought she was rather sensibly putting herself to bed."

"Why didn't you tell the police? Then, or now, even?"

He sighs down the phone. "I thought I was protecting Seb. I mean, I see a girl with blood on her face, who subsequently disappears. In retrospect I started to wonder if she wasn't drunk; maybe she was severely concussed—I mean, she was babbling about boats! Except she wasn't . . . Fuck! But given she was coming from the barn, with Seb, I didn't want to implicate him in any way, so I just . . ."

"Kept silent," I finish for him. I sink back on my sofa, the phone pressed against my ear.

"Yes. Yes." He seems to have run out of steam; he takes a deep breath, then blows it out down the phone. It's an intimate sound. I can imagine his breath stroking my cheek. "But at least they won't find any of your DNA on the rake."

"True." I'm silent again, remembering the police taking our DNA samples years ago—in order to easily rule us out, we were told. I didn't demur at all; I simply opened wide for two large cotton swabs. I wonder if I would be more reluctant now in the same circumstances. "But isn't there a saying? The absence of proof is not proof of absence . . . Something like that, anyway."

"Fuck, I'll never be able to forgive myself if I've made it worse for you," he mutters, half to himself.

I don't know yet if he has or hasn't; I'm still trying to work it all through. The police have a murder weapon that isn't really a murder weapon—it's an inciting item in slapstick comedy. "So what did you think happened to her?" I ask at last. "I mean, what did you think at the time?"

"I thought her head wound must have been much more serious than I realized, one of those freak accident things; that she collapsed and died from it." As he speaks I see it happening: Severine in her black shift, sandals hanging loosely from a single finger of one hand. She's passing the pool, barely visible in the darkness, lit only by the shimmering reflection of the moonlight off the water. She takes a step and stumbles, her other hand going to her bloody temple, and then she crumples without a sound. But no, that isn't what happened, because Severine is here with me, lounging in my armchair. Only that's not right, either, because Severine is dead, except not how Tom is describing . . . I find I'm rubbing fiercely at my forehead; my head is throbbing. I've lost the thread of what Tom is saying, but he's still speaking: "I thought Seb found her and panicked, wanted to hide the body, but he'd have been in no fit state to do anything on his own. So someone helped him, Caro or Theo, I thought. Or both. I thought they'd driven somewhere and dumped her."

"In my car?" I sit up, somehow personally affronted, despite the fact that I know this never happened. I almost know this never happened. I can't keep track tonight.

"No, not yours. You were asleep; I didn't believe anyone would have had the guts to go raking through your bags for your keys with you right there in the bed. I thought they used the Jag." I blink. The Jag. It was Theo's dad's pride and joy; it had been impressed upon us all never to go near it. In my mind the Jag was a museum display piece; it hadn't even occurred to me that it could actually be driven. "As far as I know the police never checked the Jag over because they thought she went to the bus depot; I always wondered if they would have found her DNA in it. And then when she was found in the well, I figured the same logic applied, just without the Jag."

"Wait—so you never thought that was Severine at the bus depot?"

"No. All the time we were there, do you remember her ever emerging before eleven?"

I think about this, remembering Severine coming out to the pool in her black bikini, a chic canvas bag filled with the paraphernalia required for serious sunbathing, whilst also watching the Severine in my living room settle into a more comfortable position. "True. Sometimes not till lunchtime."

"Exactly. And with a hangover and a sore head? I doubt we'd have seen her till mid-afternoon."

I missed that point. I should have thought of it, but I missed it in my eagerness to believe Severine was at the bus depot, that her death had nothing to do with any of us. "What do you think happened now?"

"I've been thinking about that," he says slowly. "Modan said her bones were damaged. Consistent with a hit-and-run—"

"The Jag!" I exclaim.

"Yes, that's what I thought. Theo's dad told me the police have been over every inch of the Jag for evidence; he told me he'd looked up how long it takes DNA to degrade, and apparently it depends on the conditions: takes millions of years in ideal conditions like ice, but not very long in heat or sunlight. The Jag has always been kept under cover in a garage, though, so I expect that means any DNA will be usable. I imagine right now Modan has some lab running tests on any DNA recovered. He'll be testing against all of us, I bet."

"It would have to be Caro, Theo or Seb," I say slowly.

"Yes. I don't know which one, or even if we're on the right track." He sounds strained. "It doesn't make any sense. You'd have to be gunning the accelerator to hit someone hard enough to kill them, so then it's hardly an accident anymore." Now I see Severine, in the same black shift, the sandals still swinging from a single finger, except now she's caught in headlights, turning in surprise, raising a futile arm to block her face . . . "Which means the police will probably think you have the most obvious motive."

Jealous rage. Spurned lover. We know so much more now, yet nothing has moved on. I'm still the prime suspect. The movie plays out in my head: Severine tossed up in the air like a rag doll, smashing down on the Jaguar's windscreen, shattering it in a starburst. I look at the Severine in my armchair. She hasn't reacted; her eyes are closed, and her head is tipped back against the cushion, as if she's sunbathing in the dim light of the table lamp and the flickering television. Maybe she is, in her reality. "Wouldn't there have been some damage to the car, though?"

"You'd think so. Though sometimes in a crash the bumper looks perfect and all the damage is behind that. I don't know. Seb was hammered; I suppose he could have fallen asleep at the wheel and hit her, but he's just not that into cars. I can't imagine him climbing in it in the first place."

"Theo?" I think again of Alina's plan. I don't want to tell Tom about that.

He takes a moment to answer. When he finally speaks up there's a reluctance infused in every word. "I don't see it. But I didn't expect him to sign up for the army, either." He sighs again. "And Caro doesn't make sense, either. Nobody does."

"Except me." I sink back on my sofa again. "Always me," I mutter.

"Oh, Kate." It's more of a sigh than a sentence. Then, gently: "Are you okay? I'm getting worried about you."

"No."

"I—"

"Alina wants us all to blame Theo." I've cut him off with the first thing I can think of, before he can say anything else nice. If he does I'll cry, and once I start that I won't stop.

"*What?*"

I explain about her ambush of me.

"Jesus," he says when I've finished. "But she's right," he adds thoughtfully. "It would be the perfect solution. Not to save Seb, though, to save you."

I'm struck again by his pragmatism. "Could you even . . . Could you actually do that?" I ask hesitantly.

"If it came to that, as a last resort?" He thinks about it seriously. "Yes. I could. I could do it for you."

I close my eyes, close to tears, touched beyond words that he would choose me over Theo. "When this is over . . . if this is ever over . . ."

"What?"

"I don't want you to go back to Boston," I whisper.

He's quiet. He knows what I'm saying. He's quiet for a second that becomes a minute, a year, a lifetime.

"Say something," I whisper to him. I turn my face to hide it in the sofa cushions.

"You chose Seb." He's whispering, too. "I'll always know you chose Seb."

"Because I didn't know. You didn't even *try*; you just stepped aside for Seb. You can't hold it against me when you didn't even try." Another second, another minute—I can't bear for the silence to lengthen any further. "Don't say anything now. Just think about it. I'm going to be in a French jail anyway—"

"It won't come to that," he interrupts fiercely, but I ignore him.

"— so it's probably a moot point, but . . . please just think about it."

"I . . ." He trails off. "All right, I'll think about it."

"Night, Tom."

"Night, Kate."

In the morning I almost don't go to work. I've slept abysmally—God knows when I last slept well, which I know is a sign of mental stress, but in this case I think it's rather eclipsed by the fact that I'm regularly seeing a ghost—but at 9 A.M. I'm still in bed, not sleeping, not moving, not doing anything except existing, and I can't even see the point of that. It's a call from Caro that rouses me from my apathy. Pride, it turns out, is a powerful motivator.

"Julie said you weren't in yet, best to try your mobile," says Caro breezily. "Having a lie-in, are you? I hope I didn't wake you."

I can sense her sly glee at the idea, and I can't bear to allow her the pleasure. "Actually no, I've just finished a breakfast meeting with a client," I lie, remarkably glibly. "Julie must have overlooked it in the office diary."

"Oh. Right." She sounds temporarily put out—*yes!*—but she rallies. "Well, I really need to meet with you. How's your diary today?"

I grab my BlackBerry from the bedside table and flick through. "Today is not great, actually." It's true; it would be a pretty busy day even without the lawyer-and-Modan meeting that looms, darkly implacable and immovable, in the middle of the afternoon. "Monday would be better."

"It really needs to be today," she insists. "What about the end of the day?"

I can see I'm not going to be able to put her off. "Well, yes, I suppose I should be able to manage six thirty," I say reluctantly. "Is there a problem? Have you had second thoughts on anyone we're negotiating with?"

"No, no, it's not that at all. Actually, it's more a case of some professional advice. You know, with the partnership process . . ."

That almost floors me. Caro would like to ask my advice: really? Yet again she has me wrong-footed. "Sure, happy to do whatever I can. I know you're up against tough opposition." I've done some digging, and from what I understand, Darren Lucas is fighting for the same partnership spot. He's a small, wiry man with a shock of dark hair, a nose to rival Tom's, and a good line in self-deprecating wit. Clients love him, colleagues adore him and he's a very savvy lawyer. Even when

I try to take my own personal bias out of the equation, I can't see how Caro can win this one, unless the firm bows to gender pressure.

"Darren? Oh, don't worry about him," she says dismissively. I blink. Surely Caro is not so naive as to underestimate Darren? "No, I'll explain it all later. See you at my offices at six thirty."

I put down my phone and look around my bedroom. The digital clock reads 9:11. If I'm quick with my shower, I can be in the office before the ten o'clock call that's in my diary. It's touch-and-go; I almost pull the covers over my head, but the thought of Caro (old or new?) gloating at my slide into depression pushes me out of bed and into the bathroom. *Follow routines, stick to etiquette*, I tell myself. It's all that I can think to do.

In the warm streaming water of the shower it takes me a minute to remember what I'm supposed to do. *Shampoo hair. Rinse. Condition hair. Rinse. Apply body wash. Rinse.* Another routine, something else to cling to. I pick up my razor, but I don't have the slightest inclination to apply it to any part of me, no matter how fuzzy my legs or underarms might be. Shaving is a hopeful act. I think of Tom on the phone: *All right, I'll think about it.* I put the razor back down, unused. It doesn't seem as if shaving is called for.

As I dry myself off, I see Severine in the mirror, leaning against the bathroom wall behind me, but when I turn round she isn't there. I wonder again why Caro doesn't see Darren as a threat. I'm missing something. Now there are two things I don't understand where Caro is concerned: this, and what she has to gain by spreading gossip about me, if indeed she is the culprit. It makes me uneasy, or even more uneasy.

I can't remember when I was last at ease.

I don't have long to wait to find out why Caro doesn't think Darren is a threat. It's the first thing Paul says to me, beating even a traditional *good morning*. "Darren Lucas is under investigation at Shaft & Vile for *fraud*. Can you believe it?"

My eyes fly to his face, which is filled both with shock and excited importance at being the first to deliver news. "Actually, no," I say thoughtfully, mulling it over as I unbutton my coat. "I can't. There must be some mistake. What type of fraud?"

"Fiddling his expenses." He shakes his head, disbelief tracking across his face. "I can't believe it either."

"His expenses? Jesus. What could he get out of that? A couple of thousand a year, maybe?" *Caro*, I think. *Caro.* Then I check myself: would she really? If it is her, she's playing a very dangerous game. But if it's not her, it's a hell of a coincidence. I consider for a moment approaching . . . who? Gordon? Caro's father is hardly going to take kindly to the suggestion that he investigate whether his daughter is framing her rival.

"A couple of thousand, absolute max," Paul is saying. "Not even that, I would think. And he's in line for a pay rise of a few hundred thousand if he makes partner. Why on earth would he jeopardize that? He's just not that *stupid*. But"—he frowns—"if it was a simple mistake surely they would have cleared it up straightaway. This'll scratch him off the slate. For this year at least."

One year is all Caro needs. "He's being stitched up," I say flatly.

Paul looks at me sharply. "That's quite a statement."

I shrug and avoid his eyes by pulling out my chair and switching on my monitor. "I'm just saying it looks that way to me."

He continues to look at me, something odd in his eyes. "Did you go to the gym or something?" he asks abruptly. "Your hair is wet."

I put a hand to my head. He's right. Did I forget to dry it after my shower? My glance at the window reveals bright sunshine outside, so it didn't rain on me on the way to work. It occurs to me that I can't actually remember getting to work. "My hair dryer is broken," I improvise.

"Oh," he says, but I can feel he's still watching me.

"What?" I say, looking up from my screen.

"Nothing." He gives an odd shrug. "It's just . . . Julie's a bit worried about you. She said you hadn't been acting yourself." He pauses, then his words trip out over themselves. "I just wondered if everything is okay. With the murder investigation, I mean."

"Oh. Well, that's all fine. Nothing to worry about. I'm just . . . feeling a bit run-down, is all. I think I'm getting a virus or something." My words don't seem to be enough to convince him; something else seems to be required. I try a smile, and it does the trick. He looks relieved.

"Oh. Okay. Well, don't give it to me; I've got a wedding to go to at the weekend."

His words ring in my head as I pull up the files for my ten o'clock. *She said you hadn't been acting yourself.* Acting. Is that all we humans ever really do? Act, and play, and present an approximation of something that becomes ourselves?

I touch my wet hair self-consciously, frowning. If acting is what's required, it seems that at present I need to pull out a better performance.

Modan again.

I sit in a chair in front of the now-familiar chipped desk and watch him apply his easy, dangerous charm to my lawyer, whilst I grit my teeth semi-consciously. If this was all over, could I come to like this man, this man who wants to be my best friend's other half? I wonder. I respect him, I admire him even, but perhaps I will never be able to hold a conversation with him without the sense that he's quietly analyzing, observing, filing information away for a rainy day. Though it's unlikely to be a big problem for me given that my future social life contains a lifetime of inmates.

I shudder. Even my own black humor is failing to amuse me today.

"Miss Channing?" From the attention both Modan and my lawyer are giving me, it may not be the first time Modan has spoken my name. He's looking at me quizzically, and I almost think I detect sympathy in his chocolate brown eyes, but I can't imagine why that should be. How can he do his job if he feels sympathy for those he believes to be guilty? For some reason this puts me in mind of Caro, and my own ambivalence toward her: feeling sorry for her, almost liking her at times, yet so often barely able to stand her . . . I think again of the Russian dolls. "Shall we begin?"

And so we do. Ms. Streeter, wearing a different lipstick in an equally garish color but thankfully much less greasy in application, does some wonderful verbal gymnastics, laying the groundwork; Modan is, I think, genuinely appreciative of her professional skill. At the end of her monologue, one might be forgiven for pushing for instant canonization of one Kate Channing, on account of her selfless and unstinting cooperation. Except that we all know I'm about to sell someone down the river. And then it's my turn, to do just that.

I know I can't match Ms. Streeter for linguistic virtuosity, but it turns out I don't need to. She shepherds me gently in the right direction each time: a sentence pushing me here, a comment tugging me there, the words flowing from her mouth to jostle against me, encircling me as if they alone can keep me safe. Modan, for his part, is unexpectedly kind. I'm completely lost as to the subtext of this meeting. When I baldly declare Caro's cocaine smuggling, Modan pauses for the merest second, then continues fluently. He doesn't dispute that Caro put the drugs in my bag; he simply asks about my own cocaine use, as my lawyer warned he would. I say I don't, repeat that I never have; I tell him he can ask anyone, they will all say the same, and he nods briefly. I don't know if that means he agrees with me or that he will indeed ask around; perhaps both. He asks about other drug use: I confess the marijuana dabbles, but he's clearly not the least bit interested in that. Caro's cocaine habits come under discussion, but I don't have much to say. I don't know how much she used back then, and I don't know how much she uses now, though I rather suspect she does still use from time to time. But I have nothing to base that on, and I tell Modan so. We talk about the others at the farmhouse, whether any of them used drugs—but if they have I've never seen or heard of it. Would any of them have shared the cocaine with Caro that night? I think about it. I can't say for sure, but it seems unlikely to me. Alcohol was the drug of choice for the rest of us. I think of Seb, unable to take his eyes off that slim brown ankle. Not just alcohol. Sex is a drug, too.

The discussion moves abruptly to the long drive back. I must have been tired, Modan suggests, perhaps even hungover—surely the drive home was shared. I shake my head, tell him no: I repeat that I was the only one insured, and besides, I wasn't that tired—probably out of all of us I'd gone to bed the earliest. And I don't remember being very hungover on that drive back; I suppose I must have stopped drinking when we all started arguing. I remember the gulf between Seb and me in the front of the car, so much wider than the gap between our two seats. I remember Caro and Lara sleeping in the back. I remember being furious at Caro for making us leave late. I remember that fury dissipating as I drove, leaving me utterly, desolately miserable. But I don't tell Modan all of that. I just explain why I wasn't tired and why I wasn't hungover.

Not a single one of the questions are specifically about Theo. He hovers peripherally; I mention him obliquely from time to time, but Modan never pays him any attention. Even if I wanted to throw some red-haired Theo-shaped red herrings into the mix, I can't see how I could achieve it with any degree of subtlety.

When Modan's stock of questions appears to dwindle to nothing, I look across at Ms. Streeter. Her neat, cropped head gives me a little nod, which I interpret to mean I've done well. I'm surprised to see we have been here for over an hour and a half, but not surprised to feel exhausted. Ten minutes of Modan's questions does that, let alone ninety minutes.

"*Bien*," says Modan. He closes his notebook and stands, adjusting the cuffs of his suit. "*Merci*. Most helpful, Miss Channing." He turns his charming smile on me, and it *is* charming. I want to laugh at myself. How is it that he can pose the danger he does, and yet I am not immune to his appeal? "That is all. For now."

For now. I look at Ms. Streeter, but she's already charging into battle. "My client has been nothing but thoroughly cooperative from the start of this process."

"Your client forgot to mention Class A drugs on several occasions." Modan is smiling, but his eyes are steely.

"Understandable given there's no relevance to the murder investigation and she was anxious not to get a friend into trouble. It's certainly not a case of obstruction of justice. Your continued interest in my client without any evidence to link her to the murder is bordering on harassment. It's disrupting her business and putting enormous stress on her, and I'll be extremely happy to explain that in detail to a judge. So I suggest you either charge her with something or leave her be."

Stress. I blink at the stark reference and open my mouth to protest but then shut it again silently. In truth I'm a good bit further down the line than *stressed*, and perhaps this is not the time to display a stiff upper lip. I glance round quickly for Severine and find her loitering near the doorway, drawing lazily from a cigarette. The smoke curls upward, partially obscuring a no smoking sign stuck to the wall. I know she stood there deliberately, and I fold my lips to stifle a grin.

Modan is not in the least bit fazed by Ms. Streeter's attack.

"Noted," he says, deep lines bracketing his smiling mouth. He turns to me, and the smile drops, though the lines remain. I feel him assess me, though again, I see a kindness in his eyes that confuses me. "I truly do hope you are not too . . ."—he clicks his tongue briefly in frustration, searching for the word—"*agitated* by the situation. You have been most helpful."

I look at Ms. Streeter again, completely nonplussed. She smiles back encouragingly, with a slight air of satisfaction, as if this is all a game and it has played out exactly as she expected. Modan, too, seems satisfied. I'm the only one in the room who doesn't have the script. Well, Severine, too, but she doesn't care. She doesn't need to care about anything now. Not for the first time I wonder why she cares to hover around me.

I don't go back to my office afterward. I should—of course I should; there is plenty to do—but I can't focus. I can't even care that Caro will win today. I call Julie and tell her I'm feeling unwell, which I most definitely am, and that she should cancel my appointments and calls, and then I head for the tube. Severine joins me; she's been sticking very closely to me today. I can't imagine that's a good sign vis-à-vis my mental state, but there's something comforting about her presence, so I'm certainly not going to complain. I think carefully about my route home, determined to be conscious of it; on the packed train, I look around at the individuals with the trappings and cares of their lives on display in their clothing, their bags, their faces buried in newspapers and Kindles and phones. *That one with the* Financial Times *must be a banker*, I think, *and perhaps that one an accountant*, but it's nothing but a label. I cannot imagine their lives. I cannot think of anything but the wreckage of my own.

I wish Tom was with me. It's not a physical wish—though a strong arm wrapped round me certainly wouldn't go amiss right now. No, I wish Tom was with me metaphorically: I wish I could reach inside myself and know as an absolute truth that Tom is always there for me, that Tom is mine. But Tom is going back to Boston—I'd have heard from him by now if he'd changed his mind about that—and I'm sitting alone on a tube.

Of course, I'm not completely alone. There's Severine.

My flat feels cold when I get inside, but the thermostat needle points exactly where it normally does, and I realize it's me that feels cold. Perhaps I really am getting a virus. I should have a bath and go to bed, but I know I won't sleep well. Still, I can't think of anything else to do, so I start to run the hot tap into the tub, then drift into the kitchen to make a cup of tea. It takes me a moment to notice an odd buzzing noise above the sound of the kettle boiling, and even longer to identify it as someone at the front door. I open the door cautiously. The burly chap who lives in the flat across the hallway—Ben, I think he is—is at the door, looking mildly impatient.

"These came for you," he says, pushing a tall flower box into my arms. "Sorry, got to dash."

"Oh," I say blankly. "Thank you," I call after him, but he's already taking the stairs two at a time, and simply raises a hand in acknowledgment without turning around. I close the door and put the box on the table, ripping open the top in a quest to find a card. It's nestling inconspicuously among the heads of white lilies interspersed with some pretty green foliage, my name written on the envelope in curly, unmistakably feminine handwriting, presumably by a woman in the flower shop. For a moment I don't dare open the envelope. There is only one person I want these to be from; until I open the card there is still that possibility.

Act like yourself, I admonish myself. *You don't believe in putting things off.*

So I slide a finger under the lip of the envelope and rip it open to pull out a small square card with the flower shop's logo on one side. On the other, it says, in the same jarring curly writing:

Kate,

I thought about it. I'd like to try.

Tom x

Something inside me leaps. I read it again, and again, and then I find a smile is spreading across my face. There's a fizzing running through me that I don't recognize, a lightness, as if I could float upward.

Happiness, I realize. It's been a long time.

I reach for my phone to call Tom, to thank him for the beautiful flowers, but there's another buzz from the front door. Tom in person? But I know that's too hopeful; he wouldn't expect me to be home and in any case he would have called first. Severine is leaning against the door when I get there, blocking me from opening it. I gesture her out of the way, but she remains in place, her dark eyes fixed on me expressionlessly. The buzzer sounds again. I sigh and reluctantly swing the door open through Severine and have the disconcerting experience of seeing her face replaced by the dark wood and then by the face of the last person I expected to see on my doorstep.

Caro.

CHAPTER NINETEEN

Caro.

It *is* Caro, but for a moment I'm thrown, disorientated by the flash of Severine, then the door, then who? For a moment it could be . . . But no, it's Caro, encased in a smart dark coat and wearing a very trendy trilby that hides the dirty blond of her hair. She has unusually dark skin and eyebrows for a blonde; with her hair hidden one might easily mistake her for a brunette. Something jerks in the recesses of my mind. I find I'm staring at her.

"Well," says Caro, and the moment she speaks she *is* Caro; all suggestions of anything otherwise are swept away. I pull myself together. There is something in her eyes, some sly satisfaction that has me on guard—more on guard, that is. "Aren't you going to invite me in?"

"Actually, Caro, I'm really not feeling well." I've kept the door only a couple of feet ajar: enough not to be rude, but not wide enough to invite an entrance. "Didn't Julie call you?" But Julie must have called her, otherwise Caro would have expected me around this time at her offices . . .

"She did. I thought any combination of these might help." She holds up a bottle of wine, a packet of Lemsip and some handbag-sized tissues.

"Oh. Well, that's . . . Well, that's kind of you." Confronted with gifts, normal behavior demands I swing the door wide, and after all, I have resolved to follow normal behavior. "Come in."

She enters, and I take the gifts from her as she unbuttons her coat and removes the dark red trilby, looking around her with sharp, greedy glances, stripping away every detail to store in that carnivorous mind of hers. I glance around myself, trying to see things as she must see them. It's a nice flat in a Georgian block, small but welcoming, with some lovely old features such as the original bay windows, but it can't hold a candle to Caro's own apartment. *Or Tom's.* Just the thought of him is a delicious secret inside me, to be held tight and treasured. The florist's card is still in my hand; I shove it surreptitiously into my pocket.

"Lovely flowers," says Caro. "A secret admirer?" Her eyes scan me, eager and hot and hungry—and something else, too, something like anger, but why on earth should she be angry at me receiving flowers?

"Hardly." I give a careless laugh.

"No? Who then?" she presses insistently.

"They're from a very happy client. Anyway, come on through to the kitchen," I say quickly, self-conscious in my lie; anything to do with Tom is too new for me to be sure I can hide it. I lead her through the flat; it's hard to overstate just how uncomfortable I feel with her inside my home sanctuary. Severine isn't proving helpful, either: she's trailing Caro, never more than a foot away, more present and more insistent than I've ever seen her before. "Tea, coffee?" And then because Caro is looking expectantly at the bottle she gave me, which I've placed on the kitchen counter, I add reluctantly, "Wine?"

"Yes, please. Is it a flu bug?"

I find some wineglasses and pull a corkscrew out of a drawer as I answer her. "The beginnings of one, I think. I'm all achy and my head is pounding." That's all true, actually, or it was before the flowers arrived and boosted my endorphin count, but a flu bug has nothing to do with it. Before the flowers . . . suddenly I remember—"Fuck, the bath!"

I dash out of the kitchen, leaving Caro and her surprised expression behind. The bath hasn't flooded yet, but it has reached the level of the overflow, and the bathroom is misty with steam. I turn off the tap quickly, looking at the tub longingly. Perhaps I can get rid of Caro quickly enough that it will still be warm . . . but then I see Severine under the surface, clothed and completely still, her eyes closed and her hair fanning out lazily around her head. For all that I've become accustomed to having Severine around, it's an arresting image. Arresting and chilling. Then she sits up abruptly, her soaking wet hair slicked back tightly against her head, and opens her eyes, staring straight at me. I have to stifle a small scream.

But in that instant something unlocks in my brain, and suddenly I know exactly what happened, all those years ago in France. I stand there for a moment, staring at Severine, letting it all unfurl in my mind, like leaves touched by the first rays of the morning sun . . . *yes, that's how it must have been; yes, that, and that* . . . I see a plan of the farmhouse from above, laid out in miniature, like looking down on a doll's house: there's a tiny version of me asleep in the bedroom I shared with Seb, my tear-streaked face calm in unconscious oblivion; a mini-doll Lara dozes in Tom's bedroom, tangled in sheets redolent of sex; Seb's figurine is passed out in the barn, where a stray rake lies abandoned near the door, while a tiny Severine and tiny Tom are grouped by the pool. And only one question remains: where to place Caro and Theo? But I know the answer to that too now.

And then another question follows: what can I do about it? A cold, hard fear is growing inside me, too, but this is different from the fear I have been living with of late; that was paralyzing, diminishing, it made me less than I want to be, less than I am. This fear is steel cold and equally as hard, and it's forging me into the same. Or perhaps it's stripping me back to what was always there, underneath: the Kate I like best, who faces life head-on. Kate of the high-risk strategy.

Severine sits in the bath, water still streaming off the ends of her long hair, her soaked black shift plastered to those eternally perfect tiny breasts. She sits and looks at me whilst I puzzle and plan, and there is not a jot of expression in those black eyes.

I leave the bathroom abruptly, closing the door tight. In the living room I grab my handbag and find what I'm looking for buried at the bottom of it; I sweep it into my pocket to lie snugly against the florist's card: all my secrets in one dark, warm place.

Back in the kitchen, Caro has opened the wine and poured out two glasses; she looks up inquiringly as I reenter. "Sorry, I forgot I left the tap on; I was just running a bath when you arrived." I sound unnatural, but Caro doesn't seem to notice. Severine has joined us, too, thankfully no longer dripping wet. She prowls the kitchen, unusually active. Caro removes her suit jacket, turning to lay it carefully on the counter; as she does so I notice that she has a ladder in her stockings, running in an ever decreasing inverted V from the back of one of her patent heels to disappear under her skirt. She would hate it if she knew: *chinks in her armor*, I think, though without the rancorous glee that might once have called up within me. I've had a glimpse of what lies beneath Caro's surface, and I can't unsee it.

She starts off with small talk—business talk, around the candidates we're winning over to Haft & Weil, but it's small talk nonetheless. We sip our wine and verbally circle each other. Five minutes pass. Ten even. I can't quite understand why she's delaying. It's an effort to keep my hand from the dark, snug pocket of secrets.

"You must be wondering what's so urgent that I turned up on your doorstep unexpectedly," says Caro with a small laugh, settling herself onto one of my bar stools. *Now*, I think, and my hand slips unremarkably into my pocket and just as unremarkably out again whilst I remain standing, my back resting against the countertop.

"Yes."

"It's not so much to do with the partnership process—"

"No?"

"Well, it is, but . . . the thing is, in the office they've obviously heard about the investigation, what with all the rumors flying round about, well, you. Someone asked Gordon about it, and he let slip I was there, too . . ." A flash of irritation makes a dash across her face. "Anyway. There's beginning to be a perception that it might be too much, that if I'm distracted by that, it'll be hard for me to really shine through this crucial period." She rolls her eyes. "I mean, it's completely ridiculous; I'm totally focused on partnership, but it's hard to fight this kind of thing." Twin spots of color are burning faintly over her cheekbones. She blows out a breath, then admits grudgingly, without meeting my eye, "They're talking about pulling me off the slate. Holding me over to next year."

For a moment, I'm lost for words. On the worst interpretation of facts, this is deliciously—maliciously—ironic. If Caro is indeed the source of the rumors about me, then she is very much being hoisted on her own petard. Despite the cold steel within me, I realize how much I want to be *wrong*. I want the sum of the layers of Caro to be something better than the surface shell. I search for something neutral to say. "I see. And I suppose you were thinking, with the issues I hear Darren Lucas is facing, that you had rather a clear field—"

"Exactly," she rushes in. "This is my year. My *year*." She finally looks me directly in the eye, and I'm taken aback by the desperation

I see within her. It's as strong as the cold, hard fear that still fills my belly. "I can't be held over," she says with quiet ferocity. "This is my year."

Her words are solid, impermeable, immovable. I gaze at her helplessly for a moment, then try one more doomed attempt: "Caro, I know you don't want to hear this now, but there are other law firms—"

"No." It's a statement of finality: for Caro, it's Haft & Weil or bust, partnership or nothing. I've met many driven candidates over the years, all of whom display a similar single-mindedness, but nonetheless something about Caro seems particularly extreme. I realize I'm staring at her bent head as I sip my wine, trying to puzzle her out.

I shake my head and remind myself of my endgame. I have a plan, after all, and solving Caro's partnership woes is not part of it. After a moment, I say casually, "Do you still speak to Mark Jeffers?"

Her head whips up. "No," she says carefully, after the barest hesitation, but it's enough: I am not wrong about her. I sip my wine to hide the irrational disappointment that runs through me. "Why do you ask?" she adds, with just the right amount of mild curiosity.

"He's been shooting his mouth off round the market about the investigation; specifically, about how one Kate Channing is about to be arrested," I say evenly. "I've even had prospective clients asking me about it."

"Well, I know him quite well from days of old," she says smoothly. "He's a dreadful blabbermouth, but I could speak to him and try to get him to pipe down if you like."

"I rather think you've spoken to him already, haven't you?" She is gazing at me steadily, her eyes still burning over-brightly, as if she's the one with a fever, but her face is carefully blank. "He had my name, and that hasn't been in any of the papers."

"That's ridiculous," she exclaims. It's a very good performance of outrage, such that a part of me can't fail to be impressed. "What on earth would I have to gain from that?"

It's a valid question, and one I can't answer; I continue as if she hasn't spoken. "And now this Darren Lucas situation. He's a very formidable opponent, but he's already been stitched up, hasn't he? So now your own rumormongering has come home to roost, in the very year that everything is miraculously in your favor."

Now her eyes have narrowed and her lips are almost invisible, clamped in a tight line. "If you have something to say, perhaps you should come right out and say it," she says, in a tightly controlled voice.

"I thought I was." I take another sip of wine. It's a sauvignon blanc, absolutely not what I would have chosen, and there's an aftertaste that definitely isn't winning me round. "I think Darren Lucas was in your way and you found a way to remove him. And now you need a way to make sure you can capitalize on that, which means you need the investigation to disappear."

She picks up her glass and swirls it carefully before looking at me again, with those greedy, hot eyes. The desperation within her lies not quite hidden beneath. "You should be careful throwing around accusations you can't prove."

"You're right." I pull back my hand before it can sneak into my pocket—*later*—and take a drink myself. "I can't prove it. Anyway. Back to the point. You're here to ask me to blame Theo for all of this."

Her glass pauses halfway to her mouth, then smoothly resumes its trip. "You've been talking to Alina."

"Yes," I agree. Again, she's undeniably impressive, with her quick, devious intelligence. She barely missed a beat there.

"In that case, I might as well admit it. I *was* coming here to ask you to blame Theo." She shrugs. "After all, why wouldn't you? Your own business is struggling because of this—"

"My business is fine."

"Really?" She arches a brow. Something in her has changed. I knocked her off balance with my frontal assault, but I can see she has already regrouped. There's a tension within her, like a vibration: a quiver of anticipation. The eyes are only the tip of the iceberg. What have I missed? "How fine would it be if Haft & Weil dropped you? You'd lose Stockleys, too, I'd warrant . . ."

This is what I've missed. I wonder how long she has been planning for this. Perhaps she perennially sees life as a chess game: putting pieces in place to defend her position should certain events come to pass . . . Or perhaps there was never any plan, and she's just taking advantage of what lies before her. I stare at her, waiting to feel panic or despair, but there's nothing but the cold, hard fear inside me that wills me inexorably on. And, out of nowhere, tiredness. Bone-crushing tiredness; a wave of it is rolling over me. I pull out a bar stool and sink onto it. "There's a contract—"

"There's a clause that gives an out for reputational risk," she says flatly. "A debatable interpretation, but you'd run out of cash before you could face us in court over it."

She is right, but I won't give her the satisfaction of hearing me say it. So I say nothing, and she eyes me carefully, allowing herself a small smile. "So yes, that is what I was going to say. Blame Theo."

"No," I answer bluntly. Even before my epiphany in the bathroom, I would have said no. If Tom were here, he would be furious with me; he would urge me to row back, look out for myself, look after my business . . . but no. I want to be better than that; I *need* to be better than that. In Tom's eyes, at least, I need to be the Kate I like best. And I won't let Tom be a Tom that, over time, in the dark hours of the night, he becomes ashamed of. Not even for me. "No," I say again.

"No," she repeats thoughtfully. Then she shrugs, the skin moving over her bony breastplate revealed by the V-necked shirt. No fat there at all. Caro has no time for anything superfluous. "That's what I thought you would say. Though I don't really understand why.

After all, it really could have been Theo, couldn't it? I mean, who knows?"

"Who knows," I echo, in barely more than a whisper, fighting the urge to close my eyes. This is the moment to make my move; this is what I've been waiting for. But even as the thought crosses my mind, somehow I know it's too late: it suddenly seems incredibly difficult to funnel words into my mouth, let alone form them in a coherent argument. Something is wrong, something is badly wrong with me, but I have no energy to figure out what.

"Kate? Who sent you the flowers, Kate?" Her voice is overloud; it forces my eyelids open. Perhaps this isn't the first time she's asked the question.

"The flowers?" I repeat stupidly. My tongue feels thick. I look at Severine, but there's no help to be had from that quarter. I look at my glass of wine. It's nearly empty, but one glass is hardly enough to affect my speech. My head is so heavy that I feel I ought to lie it on the counter; instead, I prop my chin on my hands. I really must be getting ill: why else would I feel like this?

"Look at you," she says dispassionately. She puts her wineglass down decisively on the counter and pushes back her stool. "You always think you're so clever, don't you, Kate? You always have. Clever Kate, trying to show you're so much better than the rest of us because *you* went to a *state* school. No expensive upbringing for you, oh no. You've done it all on your own merit." She's suddenly very close to me, but I don't remember her bridging the gap. Did I close my eyes again? "Only now it doesn't matter how clever you are. Even the flowers don't really matter anymore. They're not from a client; a client would send them to your office." I shake my head, not understanding, but she's insistent. "They're from Seb, aren't they? Now he's back in London you're trying to pick back up where you left off."

"Seb?" Something is wrong. I'm drifting sideways—but no, I'm not, I'm sitting at the counter; it's the world that's moving, spinning

LEXIE ELLIOTT

as if I'm drunk. Severine is next to me, something insistent in her manner; I don't understand her expression, but then, I never did.

"Seb," Caro repeats impatiently. "He sent you the flowers, didn't he?" There's something else within her now; the rapier edge that has always lurked is now glitteringly, dangerously unleashed, stabbing with an urgency I haven't seen before. As if she has taken the cloak off the dagger. Why would she do that? What have I missed?

It's an effort, but I manage to turn my head to her. The rest of the room is blurry, but Caro is in pin-sharp focus. "No, Caro, he didn't. He loves his wife." *At least*, I think, *I hope he does.* He certainly ought to. Then: *dear God, why am I feeling like this?*

She snorts dismissively. "Rubbish. That won't last." She frowns. "But he really shouldn't be sending you flowers when we have an understanding."

I stare at her. "Understanding? Don't you know? Alina's . . ." My words peter out. There's too much to overcome for them to be born into the world, too much effort in creating them, moving my mouth and tongue, using my breath. This time I really do lay my head on the counter.

"Alina's what?" demands Caro, drawing disconcertingly near to me. She angles her head to match mine. I'm close enough to see that her irises are curiously devoid of flecks or variation, a flat, uniform, alien blue. "Alina's *what*?"

"Pregnant," I manage to say, then I close my eyes. *Must sleep*, I think. Then—*no, I mustn't sleep, I have a plan to execute, this is all wrong, what have I missed?* With a gargantuan effort I open my eyes. Caro's face is still right in front of me. "What have you done to me, Caro?" I whisper.

She ignores me. "Pregnant?" she hisses, disbelieving. "No. She can't be." For once I see everything she's thinking displayed on her face: her mind is racing down avenues, searching for alternative truths. "I don't believe it." Only she does believe it; I see the moment when that happens, and it's desperately sad to watch: the outer shell falls away to reveal her awful hurt and fury and grief, laid bare for all to see, the vulnerable thirteen-year-old cruelly wounded once again. But there's only Severine and me to witness.

"What have you done to me?" I whisper again. My eyelids are drifting closed.

"Pregnant." I hear her almost spit the word. Then, "Pregnant," I hear her say again, but thoughtfully this time. She's already re-grouping; the shell is already patched up and lacquered back into place. Once again, it's admirable, if psychotic.

I try to force my eyes open again. There's an important question I should be asking. Asking again. "Caro. What have you done to me?"

She's gazing into the distance, but on my words she glances back at me. "Flunitrazepam," she says succinctly. "About enough to fell an elephant. Also known as Rohypnol, or roofies. Mostly it hits the headlines as a date rape drug, but did you know that a study in Sweden found it was the most commonly used suicide drug? Lara would like to know that, I'm sure . . ." She frowns again, or maybe she doesn't. I'm losing my ability to focus. I don't understand what she is saying. A malicious smile crosses her face. "I know you, being such a *clever* Kate, must be thinking that no one will believe you committed suicide . . ."

Suicide?

Suicide. Caro is murdering me. Has been murdering me for a good while now, surely, for this drug to have taken effect to this extent. I should feel something about that, and I do, but it's a small feeling, a tiny glowing ball of panic, smothered deep within me beneath cotton-wool layers of exhaustion and apathy. I can see what's happening, I can see what's going to happen, but I seem incapable of being anything other than a detached observer. The cold, hard, fear-forged Kate is gone, blasted away by mere chemicals; she may as well never have existed.

But . . . murder. How long has Caro been thinking of murder? Whilst I've been wondering . . . I'm not sure if I've said that out loud; Caro's head turns to me, so perhaps I did speak. "I've been wondering . . . if we would have been friends . . . if I hadn't been with Seb. Whilst . . ."—it's almost funny; a gasp of a laugh escapes me—"you've been planning murder." I think she stops in what she's doing, I think her face is thrown into uncertainty for a moment, but my eyes are barely open. After a moment, they drift closed once more. I wonder what might have happened if I hadn't jumped off the wall into Seb's arms; if I'd turned to Tom instead. How would the spider's web have been spun then?

But Caro is talking now; I wrench my eyes open again. She is talking, though she is doing something with her glass at the same time. Washing it, I realize, and putting it away, all the while taking care not to touch it with her bare fingers. Now she is rubbing down the wine bottle with the dishcloth, still talking. ". . . But actually everyone will believe it. Even your secretary Julie was saying how you didn't seem yourself today, how you haven't for a while. You've been overcome with guilt at killing that girl, you see. It's what they'll say; your death will be the proof of it. There's no real evidence to point to any one of us over another; you and I both know Modan's case is weak, but suicide is as good as a confession, isn't it? Then this will all go away . . . And, yes, I know you must be thinking that nobody would believe you had access to drugs. But you've had a drug dealer's number stored in your phone for a good long while now. Ever since my party, actually." She gives a small self-congratulatory smile and reaches for my phone, which is lying on the counter. She scrolls adeptly through the contacts, then pushes it in front of my face, but it's just a blurred mess of color to me. "You really should put a security code on your iPhone, you know."

As she speaks I realize I have to do something, and I have to do it now before it's too late for me to do anything at all. I summon up all the strength I can to make a grab for her, but once again I've already missed the moment. The grab is more of a swipe really: she jumps back easily, out of my limited field of vision, and the follow-through overbalances me, tumbling me into an awkward heap on the floor. It feels good to lie down. My cheek is resting against the lovely coolness of my kitchen tiles.

I don't move. It's unclear to me whether I even could if I tried. I look at the tiles, at the contrast of their smooth sheen with the uneven texture of the rough black grout; I let my focus relax further, and it seems that I am buoyed up on a sea of pale ivory tiles stretching before me to the horizon.

But Caro is still talking. I'm only getting snatches of what she's saying, though, and only flashes of vision. It's simply too difficult to keep my eyes open, and I can't imagine why I should be trying to. There's something about Seb kissing her, but I don't know when that happened: recently, or in France, or years ago as teenagers? It doesn't matter anyway. Time is stretching out, each event like a pearl on a string, each leading inevitably to the next. Seb was Seb, is Seb, could only ever have been Seb, and in his careless affection for Caro—never enough but sometimes too much—he sparked something in Caro, who could only ever be Caro. And therefore here we are . . . but Caro is still talking, and it's all of it about Seb, about him sowing wild oats before settling down, how he said she was the only one who understood him, who was always there for him . . .

At one point I open my eyes again and find my iPhone a few inches from my nose. I don't think it was there before.

My eyes close again.

Something shakes me impatiently and insistently until eventually I open my eyes again. Caro's face is swimming right in front of me; she has pulled my head up by the hair.

Perhaps she says something—her lips move, but I can't make sense of it, and she recognizes that; she speaks again, almost defiantly, and this time I understand. "We wouldn't have. We wouldn't have been friends." I see her flat eyes, the intensity within them, and deep down I marvel at it: that insistence, that passion for what she wants. I think I had that once, but the drug has wrested it from me now.

Something bangs. It takes a good while to recognize it's my own head, lolling back on the floor after she drops it.

Time passes. Or perhaps it doesn't. I'm an unreliable witness to life now.

At some point I become aware of Severine folding her beautiful walnut limbs fluidly to sit cross-legged beside me on the cold tiles, her eyes fixed on mine, and I feel . . . something. It takes a while to identify it, but I do: it's gratitude. Gratitude for her continued presence. I feel it wash through me now I've named it. *Don't leave.* I don't say the words, but I can see she won't: for the first time I have penetrated her inscrutability and can read what those dark eyes hold. She won't leave me. She will never leave me. She will be here until there's no more here for me. And now I know at long last what the point of her is, why Severine has been here all along. For this. This is where the ribbon of time has been leading for me. There should be no emotion because this was all determined a long time ago. Because Seb is Seb, and Caro is Caro, and Kate is Kate, and Tom is . . .

Tom, I want to say, but the word cannot be formed. There is only thought, and the thought of him, the dream of *us* that had only just begun to take form, pierces the cotton wool within me a little. Severine is speaking, gesturing at me urgently. She hasn't done that before, but I can't hear the words and I can't understand what she wants. It's too late in any case. It seems that she's trying to pick up my phone, but she's a ghost, bound too tightly by the ribbon of time. Material things are for her no longer. But she isn't giving up. It's almost enough to make me smile, if I had the ability to form a smile, the urgency with which she is trying to rally me into . . . what? Something. I don't know.

Tom. I want another ribbon, a different one. I want *us.* I want to step sideways, into a time stream where Kate is Kate and Tom is Tom and neither of us are snubbed out by a pearl on the string of time. I want lazy Sunday mornings together and hectic dashes to work on the tube and holidays and home days and workdays and . . . days. I just want days. Days that start and end with Tom. *Tom.*

I'm slipping further away now. I can't fight it, and Severine has stopped trying to make me. I want to tell her that I know what happened, that I can see it all now; I want to say that I'm sorry I can't tell the world, but she knows it anyway and I don't think she cares. That was never why she was here. She remains watchfully cross-legged on the ivory sea beside me, not moving, not leaving; forever beautiful, forever unsmiling.

I would have liked to have seen her smile.

CHAPTER TWENTY

'm waking up.

This is . . . unexpected.

And painful. Oh my God, this is painful. My head, my throat, my stomach, my eyes, but most of all my head, my head, my head . . . It pounds as if the ebb and flow of the blood within it is a violent storm raging against the shore of my brain. Where is that cool, calm ivory sea to lay my hot, aching temple against?

Perhaps I make a movement as I try to open my eyes, because I hear a voice, a woman, but no one familiar: "Kate? Kate, are you with us?" And then light rushes in, swirling around until my brain gets control of it and forces it into blocks of colors and shades: I'm in a room. A pale room, nowhere I know, but it's instantly recognizable as a hospital.

A plump woman in dark blue scrubs is leaning over me, still saying my name, but I look past her, looking around for Severine, but she's not there; I can't see her anywhere, and now I really start to panic. She wouldn't leave me, I know she wouldn't leave me; what does it mean that she's not here?

"Kate? No, shhh, just lie still . . . It's all right, you're all right. You're in a hospital." She turns as someone enters the room, but I can't see who it is—is it Severine? But no, that can't be right, though I can't quite remember why that can't be right . . . "She's just come round," she says to them. She turns back to me. "Kate, do you know who this is?"

And then he's right beside me, reaching for my hand, and the panic dissolves. "*Tom*." My voice is more of a croak; nonetheless the relief on his face is staggering.

"You're back," he says simply, and lays a hand against my face. I want to move into it, but I'm unsure of my body, of what it can and can't do. As the nurse suggested, lying still seems safest.

"Was I away?" I croak out. He looks awful. He hasn't shaved in days, and it's possible he hasn't slept, either. I have the feeling I've been dropped onstage in the middle of a play without a script or any knowledge of the first act. How did I get here?

"Yes. You've been . . . away . . . for two days." He takes a shuddering breath and starts to say something, but the nurse cuts him off.

"Let's get you a drink of water and then I just need to check a few things, Kate." She brings the bed a little more upright, holds some water to my lips and starts to flash lights in my eyes, all the while asking me questions. What's my name? When was I born? What year is it? Do I know where I am? With each answer the words come easier, as if the route from my brain to my mouth is clearing.

"Did I hit my head then?" I ask suddenly, recognizing the questions as more than information gathering, and then I remember—or do I? The memories are inconstant, jumbled, the colors too strange. "I did, didn't I . . . I think . . ."

"Yes, you gave your head rather a thwack, I'm afraid. We've been quite worried about you." This is from someone new. I turn my head a little, gritting my teeth against the wave of pain that accompanies the movement, and find the source: a tall woman in her early forties, dark hair scraped back into an elegant bun, standing in the doorway with a faint smile in place. She's in scrubs, too, but she wears the cloak of her authority over them, further underlined by her enormous diamond studs: you wouldn't expect to see those on a low-paid nurse. "Welcome back. I'm Dr. Page." She steps into the room and picks up the chart, scanning it quickly. "And you, I rather think, are going to be fine, after a lot of rest. What do you remember?" she asks, but there's something in her face that doesn't quite match the casual tone. My eyes fall on the nurse. She's busying herself so completely with changing a drip that she must be listening intently. Even Tom has a little tension in his face. Again I have the feeling that I'm missing the script.

"I don't . . . I'm not sure . . . I was at my flat." I remember that, definitively. "I wasn't feeling well. I was running a bath." Severine was in the bath; once again I see the water sheeting off her hair as she sits up. "Caro—oh my God—"

Tom gives a start. "Caro? Caro was there?"

"Yes. She came round. She put something in my wine, I think—"

"Caro put something in your wine." It's more of a statement than a question. His voice is tightly controlled, but there's an anger lurking beneath that somehow puts me in mind of his impressive fury during the poolside debacle in France.

Caro. Caro and Seb. Seb and Alina—"Oh God, Alina; is Alina okay?"

"Rohypnol," says Dr. Page, ignoring my question. Her tone is crisp, but her face has relaxed. "Rather a large dose, I'm afraid." *Enough to fell an elephant.* Tom hasn't reacted to her words; it dawns on me that this is not news to him. "We had to pump your stomach, and also you had subcranial bleeding so we—"

I cut across her. "Yes, but Alina—is she okay?"

"Why wouldn't she be okay?" Tom asks, but he's simultaneously pulling his phone out of his pocket. The nurse starts to protest that mobile phones can't be used in the hospital, but Dr. Page cuts her off with a quick shake of her head.

"Because Caro is obsessed with Seb. Because that's what this was all about: Severine, everything. All about Seb—"

But Tom is speaking on the phone now. "Alina? Hi, it's Tom." I hear a voice replying, but I can't make out the words. "Yes, I'm in the hospital with her now. She's woken up, thank God. The doctor says she's going to be fine."

"Has Caro been to see her?" I ask him urgently.

He nods at me as he listens for a moment and then says, "No, it definitely wasn't that." Wasn't what? "We're just figuring out what really happened. Sorry to ask a slightly strange question, but has Caro been to see you?" He listens then shakes his head at me.

"Don't let her—" I start, but he is nodding at me already, one hand up.

"Look, I'm not sure quite what's going on right now, but sounds like you're being a smart girl," he says approvingly down the phone. "I'll give you a call when I know more. Let me know when you and Seb are back in town."

He disconnects and looks at me. "She was feeling pretty rubbish so she's taken a week off work and she and Seb drove to Cornwall yesterday to stay at her mum's place. Caro called her a couple of times the night before they left, but Alina thought she was being a bit, well, odd, so she said she didn't have time to meet before they left."

I do the maths on the timing; it's horribly hard work on my aching head, though it occurs to me the painkillers I must be on are probably not helping, either. Alina said Caro called the night before they left, and she also said they left yesterday. So, Caro called her two days ago. And I've been out of it for two days. Caro must have left mine and immediately started calling Alina. I wonder what it was that raised alarm bells for Alina, but whatever it was, she's a smart girl indeed for listening to them. I relax back onto the pillow. Then I remember my puzzlement at Tom's words. "Wasn't what?" I ask.

"What?"

"You said no, it wasn't that. What did you mean?" Once again I notice that Dr. Page and the nurse are thoroughly involved in other things and therefore are actually at full attention. Then it hits me. "Oh. You thought I'd attempted suicide." I can see on all the faces that I've got it right. Something flickers in my memory. "She said you would think that," I murmur.

"It's a reasonable assumption for that quantity of drug in your bloodstream," says Dr. Page with an unapologetic shrug. "I'm astonished you were able to call for help at all." I look at her, nonplussed. I called for help? Who did I call? But she's moving on: if I want to be able to hold a conversation on my own terms I had better increase my mental processing speed. "How did it get in your system?"

I'm not sure if she doesn't believe me or she's just being thorough. "Caro brought wine," I say evenly, though perhaps not as evenly as intended. My voice isn't quite working as normal, and my throat seems to close up even more when I think of what happened, or might have happened . . . What did happen? "I wasn't in the room when she opened it and poured me a glass. I didn't try to kill myself; I wouldn't do that. Ever. Plus I wouldn't even have a clue how to get hold of Rohypnol." A half memory triggers: *you really should put a security code on your iPhone.* That same iPhone on the floor, the colors on the screen swimming too vividly . . .

"That's a serious accusation," Dr. Page says carefully.

"It was a serious attempt to kill me," I reply, not nearly as evenly.

She nods, though more as if she's weighing things up than as a sign of agreement. "Look, I'm not trying to influence you in any way, but you should be aware that Rohypnol does rather scramble your memories." Tom is very still. I can't tell what he's thinking as he focuses on the good doctor. "To be frank, it makes you an unreliable witness in the eyes of the law. Are you sure you want to take this to the police?"

Do I? I look inside myself, for the cold, hard fear I remember, for the fury I want to be there, for the Kate I wanted to be, but I'm not sure where any of those are. A longing for Severine washes over me, to once again see my beautiful, inscrutable ghost. But she isn't here. Caro took her from me; twice, as it turns out, and on that realization I finally find a bright, shining edge of steel. Tom looks at my face. "If Caro was prepared to do this," he says quietly, almost in a growl, "is there something else she's done?" Bless him for his quick understanding: he's already joined the dots. I wonder if he'd half made the links already. But he's looking at me gravely, a stillness in his face as he awaits confirmation. I nod silently, and he breathes out slowly, the stillness eroded into bleak disappointment edged with anger.

"I want to take this to the police," I say, as emphatically as I'm currently capable of sounding.

"Okay," sighs Dr. Page. "We'll get everything in order from the medical side." She looks at Tom and me, and her eyes soften. "For the record, your man here never believed you tried to kill yourself," she says, a half smile on her face. "He told anyone who would listen that they were wrong. Same for your friend Lara." I look at Tom again, who has at some point taken my hand once more, though it doesn't quite feel like mine yet; I look at those eyes that are all his, above that wonderful nose, and I'm suddenly afraid I may burst into tears. "Now may I actually tell you about your medical condition?" asks the doctor wryly.

I smile and nod, and she launches into an explanation that involves some quite terrifyingly dramatic medical terms that I choose to mostly ignore because against all odds, the upshot seems to be that I'm actually here and I'm fine, or I'm going to be, and Tom is holding my hand, a hand that becomes a little more *mine* with every stroke of his thumb. Time is a ribbon, and there is more of that ribbon ahead for me. Despite the drugs Dr. Page has just explained I'm being pumped with, it's dawning on me slowly what almost happened to me, what was almost taken from me, and suddenly the tears that threatened begin to spill down my cheeks.

"Don't worry," says Dr. Page kindly. "This is not an unusual reaction to the drugs."

"I think," says Tom grimly, "it's more of a reaction to attempted murder," but his hand is gentle as he places it against my face again. This time I turn into it, and my head doesn't thump too hard at the movement.

"*Alors*, attempted murder?" a familiar voice drawls from the doorway. "I think that is something I should hear about, *non*?" Modan. He's not wearing a suit, but nonetheless he is still impeccably dressed, in casual jeans, a shirt and a pullover—the same sort of outfit that millions of men choose every day, but somehow his screams French sophistication. Or perhaps that comes from the way he positions his lanky frame against the doorway and raises one eyebrow.

"*Bonjour, monsieur*," I say wearily. I am in fact excessively exhausted all of a sudden. Surely he won't arrest me in my hospital bed? "You really find your way everywhere, don't you?"

"True, but today I thought I was just the bag carrier," Modan replies, raising one hand with a self-deprecating smile. I recognize Lara's tan handbag dangling from it; hostilities must have ceased. "Lara is just in the bathroom. Though maybe I need to change roles, *non*?"

"Maybe, but not yet," says Dr. Page firmly. "This patient needs some more sleep. As soon as your friend Lara has said hello it's time for a sedative."

"You are very lucky to be here," says Modan, advancing diffidently into the room. His voice is serious, and for once the mouth bracketed between those deep lines is sober. "In my career I have seen . . . *alors*, more than enough overdoses. It is . . . it is an unbelievable pleasure to see you with us again."

His simple, genuine words catch at my throat. All I can do is nod. When I find my voice again I ask, "How . . . how am I here? How did I get help?"

"You called me," says Tom simply. "On your iPhone. Voice activated, probably; I never thought I would have cause to say this, but thank the Lord for Siri. I thought you were calling about the flowers . . ." Flowers. A pocketful of dark secrets. Something tugs in my brain, then slides away. "You didn't really say anything except something that sounded maybe like . . . help." He's silent for a moment. There's a bleakness in his expression that frightens me to see. "It didn't sound much like you at all." There's something odd in his voice, a touch of puzzlement as he remembers. "I almost could have sworn it was . . ."

"Who?" I ask, though I know the answer; I believe I know who my savior was. But the moment has passed; Tom shakes his head.

"Anyway, I called Lara since I knew she had a key, and she called Modan." He nods appreciatively in the direction of the Frenchman; there seems to have been some manly bonding between the two that I have missed. "They both went straight over there and found you and called the ambulance. I got there about ten minutes after them, and the ambulance was only a few minutes after me—"

"Wait," I say suddenly. My jumbled brain has reminded me that I have something important to say. "Modan, Caro killed Severine. She was in the Jag, taking cocaine; she went to the bus depot to pretend to be Severine; with a scarf on her hair you wouldn't even know she's blond . . ." Modan is staring at me sharply, halfway through pulling a chair across to the bedside. "You have to believe me."

Modan nods seriously. "Then you will have to tell me everything."

"But not right now," interjects Dr. Page sharply. "As I said—"

"You're awake!" Lara has spilled into the room, and in an instant the mood has lifted, despite the tears that bracket her laughter, because she is once again the sunshine girl and she takes it with her wherever she goes. Lara is Lara, and Tom is Tom, and I've yet to learn what Modan is, but time is a ribbon, and there is more of that ribbon for me, so perhaps I will find out.

My head is not broken, but still there are cracks. Cracks in my memory, cracks in my understanding, cracks in my experience of time; fractures that allow things to bleed in, and others to slip out. At times a sly beast of exhaustion pads unnoticed through the openings to leap lightly onto my shoulders; then it digs in its claws and drags me to the floor. My next few days consist of infrequent periods of wakening that sink abruptly and dramatically into an oblivion that is so deep and complete that I'm both scared by it and powerless to resist.

Somewhere in those days the police talk to me. I'm not clear on how many times. Modan appears to be running point, despite overtly deferring to a local granite-hewn officer (do they mine all British policemen from the same quarry?) whose doubtful expression is, I have to hope, habitual rather than specific to this case. By this case, I mean Caro's poisoning of me—nobody is talking to me about Caro's murder of Severine, which I don't understand and can never quite seem to get a straight answer on. Modan and his British colleague come to talk with me, they go away, they come again; or perhaps it is me that leaves and returns.

Lara comes, too, bringing magazines I can't read because the words crawl around the page, but she also brings chocolate and grapes and flowers and herself. I hear the full story of my rescue; she paints a picture that has Modan glittering in the forefront, and I can't help thinking that my near-death is almost entirely responsible for the resurrection of their romance. "Honestly," she says in a half-awed tone, "he was brilliant. I was totally beside myself, but he knew exactly what to do. Really, you should have been there."

"Well," I say drolly, "I was, actually."

Her face sobers instantly. "God, I know. I know. You know what I meant."

"I'm sorry." I reach for her hand remorsefully, and we share a smile that's a little wobbly on her side. "And then? Modan?"

She blushes. "Well, once we knew you were out of immediate danger, he took me home. It must have been about six in the morning. He grabbed croissants from that bakery on the corner by my flat; you know the one? It opens really early . . . Anyway, we had croissants and then he tucked me up in bed and he was going to leave, but I didn't want to be alone so he stayed and he didn't try anything, he was just totally taking care of me, and well . . . it's gone from there really." The giddiness is in her eyes and her voice again; it creates a glow that lights up her very skin. "He's going to apply for a post with this international liaison department that's based in London—it's kind of like Interpol, I think. It's a move he was thinking about anyway, but there's an opening coming up. Anyway," she says with a meaningful look, "what about you and Tom?"

I find I'm blushing, too. Tom is here, somewhere; he has just nipped out to get coffee for Lara. Tom is here, Tom is almost always here, to the point where yesterday I asked him if he still had a job. He gently pointed out it was Sunday, but that makes today Monday (It does, doesn't it? Yes, it does), and he's still here, holding my hand, dropping kisses on my (unwashed) hair, yet we've never talked about what that means. I'm saved from having to answer Lara's question by the return of the man himself, armed with three coffees, though we all know I will fall asleep before I can drink mine.

Finally Modan and the British policeman come to see me with serious expressions that, head injury notwithstanding, I can interpret without them even having to open their mouths.

"You're not charging her," I say flatly, though they've yet to take a seat. I'm sitting up in bed in my private room (thank God I didn't scrimp on health cover when I set up my own company). Tom, who was idly flicking through the sports section of a newspaper on a chair beside me, rises to meet Modan with what I can only describe as a man-hug. I keep meaning to ask about that, but I haven't; another thing that has slipped through a crack.

"Well," says PC Stone, whose name isn't Stone, and who isn't a PC, either; he's probably a DI or something, but neither of those details will stick for me. "No, we're not." He spreads his hands wide, but the gesture is blunt and choppy; it lacks Modan's elegant sweep. Then he hitches his trouser legs to settle in a chair and leans forward, elbows on knees, his broad, thick head topped with short gingerish bristles jutting forward like a bull preparing to charge; it would take more than a sea of white tiles to put a dent into that skull. Modan remains standing, seemingly just to emphasize the differences between the two: the stocky Brit and the beanpole Frenchman, one direct and no-nonsense, the other deviously charming. It's actually a pretty effective mix. "The thing is, it's just a he said, she said." Surely a she said, she said? But he's still talking; I must concentrate or I will lose track. "There's no evidence she was even at your flat. No fingerprints on the wine bottle."

"Not even Kate's?" asks Tom meaningfully.

"Not even Kate's. Which, yes, is strange, but it doesn't prove a case against Miss Horridge. The date Kate's phone was updated with the dealer's number matches the date of her party, but that hardly proves anything." He scratches at his stubble, his frustrated dissatisfaction clear.

"You're not charging her," I repeat.

Modan, silent up till now, steps forward, his expression earnest. "What can we do? There's no evidence."

"There isn't any evidence on Severine's murder, but you still seemed to be trying hard to pin it on me," I say tartly.

Modan blows out a breath. "I'm afraid you are behind the times. The case has been closed."

I stare at him. "You've arrested Caro?" I wait for a wave of relief, but it doesn't come.

He shakes his head. "*Non*. There is not enough evidence on that also. But the investigation has been closed. It is . . . politically unpopular, shall we say, but that is how it is."

"Closed? Over?" Over . . . No more threat of arrest—but Lara's words come back to me. *It's never really over. Even if they consign it to the cold case pile, it could still come alive again.* Can it be truly over without a conviction? I find myself looking for Severine again, before I remember that she isn't here anymore.

Modan nods grimly. "Closed." I can see it irks him. "I know who was responsible, but there is nothing I can do without evidence." Evidence. He says it heavily, emphatically, in his French accent, whilst holding my gaze. Evidence. It feels like he is challenging me.

"I know who was responsible too, and it wasn't me."

"Ah, but you misunderstand me," he says, shaking his head. "I have never thought it was you." I stare at him. "Well, not for a long time, at least," he amends, and I find a bark of laughter escaping me. He grins back at me, sly humor in those clever eyes.

"Really? Why not?" asks Tom, with what sounds like academic interest.

"Because she drove, of course," he says to Tom, as if it was self-evident. "All the way back."

Tom and I exchange glances, not comprehending. "But no one else was insured," I say blankly.

"*Exactement*. You wouldn't bend the rules, not even for that. I could not . . . make it fit. I could not believe you killed her on purpose. And if you had killed her, by accident, you would have called *les gendarmes*, the police, the ambulance; it is not in your nature to deceive. *Et voilà*. It could not be you." Tom and I share another glance, slightly dazed. Even PC Stone seems a little taken aback by this remarkably unscientific explanation.

"I suppose instinct is part of your job," says Tom after a moment. It sounds like he is trying not to look a gift horse in the mouth.

"True," admits PC Stone, though he, too, still seems thrown.

"It is very much in Caro's nature to deceive," Tom presses. Caro. So this is how it will be. Caro will get what she wants. Perhaps not immediately, but she plays a long game. Sooner or later, Alina will be swept aside in some as-yet unknown way, and then Caro will have Seb, partnership at Haft & Weil and a field clear of rivals. I can just imagine her now, whispering to Seb about how poor, deranged Kate tried to kill herself and blame it on her. And not just whispering to Seb, come to think of it. *So desperately sad about Kate. She obviously had some kind of breakdown; she overdosed and blamed it on me, can you imagine? I mean, the police even investigated her claim, but of course there was no truth to it, so they had to drop it. Poor girl.* In that moment my stomach drops as I realize my business is over. There is no return from this. It doesn't matter that the police are dropping the Severine case; Caro will never cease in her rumormongering. I look at Tom, and by the bleakness in his expression I can see he's drawn the same conclusion.

Modan nods heavily. "We found cocaine in the auto, the Jag. Down in the, ah, the seams—seams, yes?—of the driver's seat. I think she was in love with Seb; I think she has always been in love with him. I think she was delighted when Kate and Seb had a fight; she thought it was her turn, *n'est-ce pas?*" Ordinarily a man of gestures, he is unusually still, allowing his words the space to have maximum impact. "It must have enraged her beyond reason to find him taking up with Severine. I expect it was just chance, that she happened to be in the Jag as Severine came by en route to her house, and in her fury Caro lost control . . ." I stare at Modan even as I see it unfold: Severine with her hand to her bloody temple, caught in the headlights of the approaching, accelerating Jag. "But she would have immediately realized that she couldn't allow the police to be called with the drugs in her system. Even if she wasn't charged for murder, it would be the end of her legal career. Other than Seb, that has always been the most important thing in her life." I continue to stare at him, slightly disturbed by his ability to casually condense a whole person to two main ambitions. But he's right: partnership at Haft & Weil and Seb are at the root of everything. "So she disposed of the body."

"By herself?" asks Tom softly.

Modan knows what he is asking. "I don't know for sure," he says, equally softly, "but I would think she must have had help."

Tom nods, looking at the floor. Modan's gaze rests on him for a moment, and then he continues. "The car has damage to the under-carriage, but it is impossible to tell how long that has been there. And we can't prove Miss Horridge was in the car, even with the cocaine. We can't even prove Severine died as a result of a . . . how you say . . . hit-and-run." He spreads his hands, his mouth twisted in regret. "We are too late to prove anything."

"But she went to the train station to mislead everyone. That's why she was late when I wanted to leave." All the while I was driving back, desperately unhappy behind the wheel of my little car, Caro was settled in the back, fresh from covering up a murder. How is it possible I couldn't tell? "Like I told you, with her hair up in a turban, like Severine wore it, it's quite hard to tell she's blond." I see Caro again with the red trilby, superimposed on Severine's image. "Can't your bone measurement thingy prove it was her?"

Modan is already nodding. "*Oui*. I have thought that for a while. A very smart thing to do, in fact. But again, no hard evidence. We can prove it *could* have been her at the depot, but we can't prove it definitely *was* her. There is no . . . stomach . . . for a high-profile loss on this. Perhaps, if it was less political . . ."

At last PC Stone speaks up. "I couldn't agree with you more about the character of Miss Horridge," he says heavily. His hand is working at his red-tinged stubble again. He is the sort of man who must have to shave twice a day if he has an evening out planned. "Given we can't get her on the French murder, we were really hoping to nail her on attempted murder of you. Is there really nothing else you can tell us? Nobody who might have seen her? Heard you talking? We've asked all your neighbors, but . . . nothing."

"You spoke to Ben? From across the hall?"

"Ken," says Modan. "Ken Moreland." There's no judgment in his tone, but I feel it all the same. My memory, or lack of it, is the elephant in the room, though aren't elephants supposed to never forget?

"I never really did catch his name," I mutter mutinously.

PC Stone clears his throat. "Yeah, well, anyway, we spoke to him. He said you appeared to be alone when he delivered the flowers, and then he went out for a bit. He got back as the ambulance was just leaving."

Flowers. I look at Tom and almost wail, "But your flowers will be dead."

He smiles. "No matter. I can buy you more, and with more romantic cards if you like."

But still, this mention of flowers is tugging at something, a tendril of a thought that curls up from a crack. The flowers, the card, all my secrets in one dark pocket—"My clothes!" I exclaim suddenly.

"Dr. Page won't let you up yet," says Tom, warningly.

"No, I mean the clothes I was wearing. Where are they?"

"They're in evidence," says PC Stone.

"There was something in my pocket."

Modan speaks up. "Perhaps you are a little tired. We should come back later, *non*?"

"No, no, this is actually relevant," I say testily. "There were two things in my pocket. The card from the flowers. And a Dictaphone. I don't know if it will have picked up much, but maybe . . ." Once again I feel my hand slipping quietly into my pocket and slipping back out again just as quietly.

Suddenly Modan and PC Stone look a lot more interested. "A Dictaphone? You're sure?" asks PC Stone. I nod. "But there's nothing in evidence," he objects.

"A Dictaphone, did you say? Looks a bit like a mini cassette player, yes? Oh, that's in your top drawer," says a breezy voice from across the room. It's the nurse; I didn't notice her coming in to check on the bathroom supplies. "It looks a bit bashed up, I'm afraid."

I turn toward the drawers, but Modan is faster, pulling a glove out of his pocket. He rummages in the drawer and comes out with the little black device in his gloved hand, turning it over carefully. One corner looks crushed, and a crack runs across the face of it. Both the Dictaphone and I bear the marks of the crash to the tiles. I'm working, mostly; is it?

"It was in my pocket," I say, horribly anxious. "I don't know how much that will have muffled the sound. And it's pretty old anyway; it's not even digital . . ." Tom takes my hand, and I realize I'm babbling, so I trail off. Modan is carefully rewinding the tape, which makes a whining sound I don't remember, and stutters and grates from time to time, causing me to hold my breath each time until it recovers. And then it stops abruptly. Modan's eyes catch mine and hold for a beat. Then he presses play.

I'm talking, but my mouth isn't moving: "Arrange to meet candidate in advance of the, uh, Stockleys recruitment drive becoming common knowledge; have Julie arrange on Monday—"

I shake my head at Modan, still linked to his eyes, and talk over myself, "No, this isn't it—" but the tape abruptly switches scene. Indistinct, muffled sounds can be heard, and then indistinct voices. There's almost certainly a woman, probably two; it certainly sounds like a not-quite-heard conversation. Modan raises his eyebrow, and I nod back imperceptibly, then he looks for a volume knob. It's already at maximum.

"I can't—" I start, but Modan holds up a hand to silence me. So we listen, the four of us, to a conversation played out too far beyond the veil of time and technology to be audible. Tantalizing words slip out: I hear *Darren Lucas*, I hear *accusations*, I hear *flowers*, but I have the benefit of having been at the first screening; Tom looks utterly in the dark. But still, even with my advantage it's plain to me the tape is not clear enough. It was all for nothing. We sit, as the gently rotating tape spools out into our silence, and I consider my future. I can't pick up and start again; the rumors will never die. What on earth will I do? The words mostly peter out after a while, dwindling to short snatches interspersed with indistinct movements; it's oddly soporific. But then the recording ends with an overloud scrunch, as if something bashed the microphone. I remember that crunch distinctly, the sea of white tiles rising up to meet me . . . Modan presses stop with a theatrical click.

"It's useless." Even to me, I sound hollow.

"Not at all," says Modan, seeming oddly pleased. I suddenly realize even PC Stone is almost smiling. "We hear two people, two women, speaking. If we can hear this much, the technicians will be able to do a great deal with this, *oui*?" PC Stone nods in agreement, then Modan turns back to me. "Bravo, Madame." *Madame.* It gives me a jolt. I am *madame* now, whereas Severine will always be the mademoiselle next door. It takes the edge off the swelling hope that perhaps all is not lost after all.

"Though, I have to say," interjects the British policeman, somewhat reluctantly, his face returning to its usual granite, "it's not strictly legal to record a conversation without permission."

"It was an accident," offers Tom, deadpan. "She often has the Dictaphone in her pocket, and it's quite easy to knock it on." I nod furiously, despite the fact that I only use the Dictaphone perhaps once or twice a month.

"Is that so?" says PC Stone dryly. He looks at Modan.

"An accident," says Modan, his eyes gleaming. He spreads his hands wide. "A happy accident. These things happen, *oui*?"

"I suppose they do," says his colleague reluctantly, though I can see a corner of his mouth twitching as he climbs to his feet. "Right, we'd better get that to the technicians. No promises, but I'm hopeful . . . if we can just at least prove she was there . . ." Tom and I watch them depart, looking even more like a comedy duo now that there is a lightness to their mood.

"It won't work, you know," says Tom gently. I turn to him with eyebrows raised. The bleakness hasn't left his eyes. "I don't want you to get your hopes up. They might arrest her, but they won't nail her for it."

"Why do you say that?"

He sighs. "Because she's Caro. She'll get the best legal representation money can buy; her dad will make sure of that. You'd need physical evidence and a sworn confession to convict her; nothing less will do. And they don't have the first, and I'm pretty sure, even after the police do their technical wizardry, that tape won't amount to a sworn confession. I could be wrong, but . . ."

I stare at him while I think it through. Did she actually confess? It's hard to pick through my fragmented memory. *Enough to fell an elephant.* So she did confess, but will the tape have caught it? Where was she standing when she said that? Where was I? I don't remember; it's slipped through a crack. "So that's it. You think she gets away with it." He nods unhappily. I try to fit the pieces together myself, to come up with a different answer, but I can't. The injustice hollows me out. I ought to want to rail at something, or someone, but who or what? "So she gets away with it and I get left with nothing," I say dully at last.

"Well," he says, taking my hand and staring at it intently. "Not exactly nothing, I hope." He looks up, and the intensity in his gaze steals my breath. "It tore me in pieces to see you in here. I can't imagine what the hell I've been playing at, waiting on the sidelines all these years. I don't intend to wait a single second more."

I stare at him. Tom, my Tom, the Tom I should have always known he was. "All these years?"

"*All* these years." There's a hint of a smile at the corners of his mouth.

"But you've slept with Lara!" I don't know why I'm throwing up obstacles given that I adore this man.

He rolls his eyes. "I was twenty-one and my cousin was sleeping with my dream girl. Sure, I was madly, unbelievably jealous, but that didn't make me a monk. And anyway, you've slept with my cousin, many times. That'll be much harder to explain round the family table at Christmas."

"*We* haven't even slept together yet," I muse thoughtfully.

He waggles his eyebrows suggestively. "I'd love to remedy that immediately, but the nursing staff might not be so keen on the idea. But our first kiss held definite promise . . ." He holds my gaze, and something moves between us, a current that thickens the air into something solid enough to lean into. "So," he whispers, in a low murmur that takes me right back to that dark, delicious corridor, "are you in?"

"I'm in," I whisper, and then he's kissing me, and I find I am feeling very much better indeed.

CHAPTER TWENTY-ONE

Time passes. I can't keep it or save it or mark it—the ribbon slips through my fingers regardless. And time shows that Tom is right, of course: the Dictaphone tape is cleaned up, but not all of it is audible. Crucially, not the part where Caro confessed to dumping roofies in my wine, if that confession truly happened at all, though it remains fixed in my memory. Despite the lack of confession, the police question Caro, and they even find her drug dealer (the unexpected casualty in all of this, as his is the only actual arrest); they leave no stone unturned. It is my repeated and most fervent wish that this investigation has completely annihilated any chances of Caro making partner this time round; surely, even more than the Severine investigation, it must be diverting her attention from that process? But in the face of the finest legal representation money can buy (Tom was right on that, too), the decision is made not to prosecute.

By that point, I am back at work—hollow cheeked but clear-eyed, with most of my cracks papered over. Paul did an admirable job of holding the Channing Associates fort in my absence by the remarkably sensible solution of promoting Julie to work alongside him and hiring a temporary secretary. Julie, it turns out, loves the role, and I can't bring myself to demote her, so now I am up a head count with zero prospect of raising any new contracts given the impending tidal wave of gossip that is no doubt beginning to circulate. We are diligently working out the contracts we do have, but every time I talk with Paul I find myself imagining scales behind his eyes, weighing up the best time to jump. Still, I'm actually relieved to have Julie in place; the first few weeks back at work are incredibly exhausting, and I barely pull my weight. Neither of them quite understand what happened, though I suspect Tom may have told Paul more than I realize; anyway, in communications to clients Paul wisely blamed my hospitalization on an accidental blow to the head and left the rest well alone.

The Haft & Weil contract hasn't been revoked, to my surprise. Paul picked it up in my absence, liaising with someone other than Caro due to the need for her to focus on the partnership selection process (official line only, I hope); I have made no move to regain control of it. Therefore it's a complete surprise to find Gordon Farrow waiting by my office front door when I step outside one lunchtime to get a sandwich; I grind to a halt halfway down the steps.

"Hello," he says diffidently when I make no sound. "I don't suppose you expected to see me."

"No," I reply warily. "I didn't."

"Can I buy you a coffee?" It's very much a question; he shows no expectation of a positive response. Perhaps that's why I nod.

"There's a café this way where we can get a sandwich, too, if you haven't eaten."

I glance at him as we walk along. He looks like he always does, a nondescript man in all respects. He must be appraising me, too, as he says, "I'm glad to see you looking so well. How do you feel?"

"Tired," I say, yawning messily on cue. "Head injuries can do that, apparently."

We find a table in the café and settle down, each of us hiding behind the menu. It's not the same café as the one where Lara and I experienced the bird incident, but I still find myself glancing at the window and almost exclaim aloud when I see Severine sauntering by in her black shift dress. She turns her head and eyes me coolly, then continues down the pavement outside, away from the café. What does it mean, that she is back? Is she staying, or is this her version of good-bye? "I'm so pleased you agreed to meet with me," Gordon says abruptly, putting down the menu. I drag my attention back to him, resisting the urge to crane my neck to see if she has really gone. "I wasn't sure you would. I should have known you wouldn't blame me for any . . . difficulties . . . between you and Caro—"

"Difficulties." I put down my own menu. "Difficulties, Gordon? Is that the right word? She tried to kill me. She put so much Rohypnol in my drink that she damn near succeeded. So forgive me if I find the word *difficulties* a little too weak."

"There is no evidence of that—" He tries to hold my gaze, but even his legendary steel is wavering.

"So I'm told. Doesn't mean it didn't happen. If you'd heard the tape—"

"I heard it." He looks away.

"Who—" I start, but the waitress comes to take our order; she is a plump brunette continually smiling even as she speaks. I can't imagine why she's quite this happy at work. It's jarring.

When she leaves I find Gordon appraising me again. "You're angry with me," he says mildly.

"Yes."

"Because I stand by her? She's my daughter; failing evidence to the contrary I have to believe her." He explains this like it's an intellectual discussion on the finer points of a legal draft.

"Do you have to?" I consider that. "Perhaps. I don't know. What would you do if there was evidence but she claimed it was all fabricated?"

He shrugs, with a slight smile I don't entirely understand.

"Anyway, that's not why I'm angry with you."

His control is superb. "Why, then?"

"Because I do blame you, for her behavior: you and your wife. You *are* partly responsible. How did she come to believe this kind of behavior is allowed? Where were the boundaries when she was growing up? You got divorced and then you felt guilty and you let her get away with murder and then, well, then getting away with murder wasn't a metaphor anymore." I stop and pick up my water glass, feeling oddly shaky after my savage words. I had no idea that was going to come out of my mouth. Is that how I really feel about it? Do I really blame him?

He looks at me sadly, saying nothing until the silence stretches out. I find myself holding my breath for a response. I shouldn't care at all what Gordon thinks of me, but it's clear I do. Finally he sighs. "I'm not sure I entirely agree with your position, but I do fully respect your right to say it. In truth there is very little you could say to make me feel any more wretched than I already do." In that moment I can see through to the anguish in his eyes.

"Well," I say, after a moment, "I'm sure it's not as simple as all that." He inclines his head, acknowledging my softening. The waitress has returned with our drinks, her smile in no way dimmed. Surely her cheeks must hurt?

"There is one thing I wanted to tell you before it becomes common knowledge," Gordon says as he stirs milk into his coffee.

"Yes?"

"Caro has been suspended from Haft & Weil."

My eyes fly to his face. He smiles a little ruefully at my shock. "Why?" I ask warily when he doesn't add anything further.

He sips his coffee. "As I already mentioned, the police played me the tape. A French detective, it was; very bright chap, I thought." I mentally cheer Modan as he shrugs. "Our firm can't afford to ignore allegations of impropriety around the partnership process. I would have done the same with any employee, and Caro cannot be treated any differently."

"You took it to the operating committee?" I must be round-eyed in shock.

"Yes. I was duty bound to." This is arguably true, but still . . . his own daughter. I'm trying to wrap my head around the fact that he reported allegations against his own daughter to the operating committee of the firm. The integrity of that action is staggering. "Therefore we have been further investigating Darren Lucas's case, and he has been entirely exonerated."

"And Caro?"

"The evidence seems to be stacking up against her. She's suspended pending the final results of the investigation." He pauses, then says delicately, "She claims the evidence is fabricated. So I suppose I will find out the answer to your question in time." I can't help it; I start to laugh. After a beat he joins in with a half-hearted chuckle or two. So my most fervent wish is to be granted: Caro will not now be a partner at Haft & Weil, or any other legal firm for that matter. I can't imagine how she will reconcile herself to that: for the first time in her life, there is a boundary she cannot bend or cross. And then it also occurs to me that a disgraced, struck-off lawyer is much less likely to be believed when attempting to spread scurrilous rumors . . . I try to imagine Caro in disgrace, stripped of her stellar career, robbed of her brittle artifice, and disturbingly find myself imagining a defenseless baby bird.

"It's not actually in the least bit funny," Gordon says sadly when the black humor has subsided.

"Yes," I say, soberly, both Severine and the baby bird image still stuck in my mind. "I know."

W e are lying, Tom and I, propped on our sides in the darkness of Tom's bedroom; he has blackout blinds, a concept he liked in Boston and brought back to London, and the darkness is a complete absence of light. It's a comfort to me now; I think of it like a physical place—a retreat we like to run to where we are safely cocooned and can just be. Tom's hand is idly running up and down the length of my arm from shoulder to elbow. The promise that always lurked in his hugs is borne out in the bedroom: he touches with just the *right* amount of pressure, firm and deliberate but never too much. He makes me giddy and he makes me safe.

I know I have to tell him; I can't think of a way to do it except to just do it.

"I see Severine," I blurt out. Tom's hand halts, a short hitch, then continues on its route, at a slower pace. "I mean, obviously I don't really *see* her; this isn't *The Sixth Sense* . . . But I see her. Ever since you told me they found her in the well. It used to be her bones sometimes, her skull . . . but now it's mostly her. She went away, for a bit, after I hit my head, but she's back again." Tom doesn't say anything. "Do you . . . do you think I'm crazy?"

"Kind of," he says, but I can hear the smile in his voice.

"I take it you don't see Theo then."

"No." He's quiet for a moment, his hand arrested in its trail; my skin misses it, the bones within miss it. "It's more like . . . sometimes I see his absence. Once I notice it, it's hard to get past it: a space where he should be." I can hear rather than see a wry smile on his face. "Maybe I don't have your imagination to fill the gap."

I think about that as we lie there, the darkness folding around us, holding us safe. Am I filling the gap? Though Severine was never a part of my world, or my friendships. It doesn't seem to quite fit, as an explanation, but perhaps there's something to it.

"Does she talk?" asks Tom suddenly.

"No." Except perhaps for one vital occasion. "Silently enigmatic."

He laughs softly. "I imagine she would have liked that description. Sounds like you've re-created her perfectly." His hand takes up its trail again. "It's strange, though. I mean, it's not like you two were friends or anything—"

"Hardly."

"—so it's strange your mind should fix on her, of all people."

"I'm sure a shrink would have a field day with it all." I say it with a small laugh, but I'm really waiting for his response. This, after all, is the crux of this conversation.

He hesitates, unusually awkward for Tom, feeling his way. "Do you *want* to speak to someone about it?"

I hadn't imagined that question. I consider it. "Not really. It's not normal, exactly, but it's not a problem, either. I've become . . . accustomed to it." I've become accustomed to her, I should say. I like to think she has become accustomed to me also.

Tom falls silent, thinking. The trail is moving up and down along my hip now, from just under my breast sweeping over the swell of my hip bone and along the line of my thigh. "Then I don't see a problem." I smile to myself. Bless him for his pragmatism. "Is she here now?"

"No," I say, though in truth it's too dark to tell.

"Good." He starts to follow his trailing hand with his lips. "I'd rather not have an audience . . ."

A nd so the lovely ribbon of time keeps slipping through my fingers.

We see Lara and Alain, we see Seb and Alina; as a group we don't talk of the week in France and we don't talk of Caro. For a while it's an awkward subject we're all avoiding, a stain across our memories that we slide our eyes away from—we were all guilty of suspecting one another; we are all tarred—but life moves on, and in time we have so much else to talk about; and after all, no one sees Caro. I see Severine, but I know I'm the only one. From time to time I notice that Tom doesn't see Theo.

Tom and I talk about France; we talk about Severine. We both dread the day someone across the Channel takes it in their mind to trawl through cold cases and decides to reopen this one. I know there will never be enough evidence to convict Caro, so all that can happen is months of distress and no satisfactory outcome. Not that this current outcome is satisfactory, though it *is* an outcome—ultimately Darren Lucas went to the police and Caro was prosecuted for fraud, though her sentence was suspended. It's hardly a murder conviction or even an attempted murder conviction, but she can never practice law again, she can never be a partner at her father's firm and Seb has cut her off completely. A messy, oblique sort of justice, if it's justice at all, though I think for her it's somehow fitting. I don't know what she is doing now, or where she is doing it. I don't think of the baby bird.

And then one day I do see Caro, in an airport lounge. I'm hunched over my phone in an armchair, trying to connect to the airport Wi-Fi, and she sits next to me. "Hello, Kate," she says; my head lifts, and there she is.

"Caro." I'm completely floored; her name slips out before I can stop myself from saying anything at all. She's dressed in casual clothes, jeans and a blazer, typically stylish. She looks older, of course, and just as thin. Her hair is a brighter color than I remember.

"I'm sure you don't want to talk to me—" she begins. High color is climbing her cheeks.

"I don't. Leave."

"I just—" But I've grabbed my bag and I'm out of the armchair before the rest of her sentence can reach me. I cannot allow myself to expend one iota more of mental energy on Caro. I don't even tell Tom I saw her; I refuse to waste the seconds it would take. I never see Caro again.

Severine, though, I do see. If I'd ever entertained the notion that once the case was "solved" she would depart—turn and walk happily (not happily, exactly, not Severine, but at least not reluctantly) into a bright light, perhaps, or evaporate slowly like an early-morning mist that fades with the rising of the sun—well, if I'd ever expected that, it's not to be. Severine still hovers.

Perhaps, one might say, not as much as before. It's instructive to note what piques her interest. On the whole, family life seems to bore her; she was nowhere to be seen for the birth of our children. She's much more likely to make an appearance in my workplace, or any kind of event I'm dreading: the parents' socials at the twins' school, for example. Tom reckons it's a reaction to stress, to which I reply with a certain vehemence that the twins' birth was about as stressful as anything I can imagine, and where the hell was she then? He just shakes his head, amused, and says, "Not that sort of stress."

Tom is often amused now. Gently and also to the point of genuine laughter. We both laugh more; I can't remember a point in my life up until now when I have laughed this often. It's the twins, especially at the age they are now. They are literal, no room for grays; they don't understand irony or cynicism. They strip that away from us and instead extract an exaggerated politeness and a readiness to laugh; they make us into the people we want them to see—they make us kinder. More tired, certainly, but kinder.

Channing Associates makes me tired, too. We are seven now, with larger offices, and champagne glasses hidden in the back of one cupboard in case we have new contracts to toast. Paul is smugly satisfied that he stayed, but no less bipolar. Gordon Farrow has become the firm's informal mentor, and I meet him at least monthly for lunch or dinner, and often more. We don't talk of Caro. Sometimes

I wonder if he is a father figure to me now, in which case am I a daughter figure? Though I should know by now not to assume symmetry in relationships.

And so the lovely ribbon of time keeps slipping through my fingers, and through it all, a walnut brown girl with impossibly slender limbs saunters by, her dark, unreflective eyes taking everything in but revealing nothing. I never do see her smile.

Acknowledgments

So . . . here's the thing.

It turns out writing *Acknowledgments* is hugely stressful. And difficult: you're trying to be grateful, sincere, funny and all-encompassing within two pages or less, which is no mean feat. Consequently, I've decided to set the bar a little lower and just tick the sincerity box. And if at the end of this you think I have missed anyone, please accept my very sincere apologies . . .

Firstly, I'm enormously indebted to my absolutely wonderful agent, Marcy Posner, who has provided unending encouragement, cajolement and invaluable editorial advice ever since we met. It has been, and continues to be, a pleasure working with you, Marcy; please accept an entire universe of thanks.

To Kerry Donovan and all of the team at Berkley, enormous thanks for getting behind *The French Girl*. As a debut author, I have only just begun to understand the hard work and dedication that is required to get a book on the shelves; I'm hugely appreciative and rather awestruck to have all that talent and commitment focused on my novel. Thanks all!

To my family—Matt and our gorgeous boys, Cameron and Zachary, and my wider family, Elliotts and Davisons all—and to all my lovely friends: I know you are my biggest fans, thank you so much for being so endlessly supportive. Of course, you also make it kind of hard to write, because there's always something else that's fun going on with you all . . . but I won't hold it against you.

To all who have provided enlightenment and advice on the process of writing over the years, including the various presenters at the Writers' Workshop Festival of Writing and the extremely helpful people at Cornerstones Literary Consultancy, many thanks for helping me find my own voice. To the staff of any and every café that I have sat in to write (and particularly the staff of the Roehampton Club café, which is my favorite place to write), many thanks for keeping me fed and watered.

And to Severine: thanks for showing up. I couldn't have written this without you.